PRAISE FOR RACHEL LACEY

Midnight in Manhattan Series

Don't Cry for Me

"A slow-burn romance that will tug at your heartstrings."
—The Lesbian Book Blog

"Love when they least expect it! With the first book in her new lesbian romance series Midnight in Manhattan, Rachel Lacey takes us on a delectable journey of healing with *Don't Cry for Me*. It was emotional and super satisfying!"
—Thoughts of a Blonde

It's in Her Kiss

"I would totally recommend it to anyone who wants an exceptional feel-good novel."
—Les Rêveur

"*It's in Her Kiss*, by Rachel Lacey, is a very sweet story, with just the right amount of angst."
—Jude in the Stars

"This tender love story is a wonderful romance!"
—The Lesbian Book Blog

"A page turner!"
—Rainbow Moose's Reviews

Come Away with Me

"Rachel Lacey has become a go-to author for heartwarming books."
—Jude in the Stars

"*Come Away with Me* is beautifully written."
—Rainbow Moose's Reviews

"Utterly delightful!"
—Thoughts of a Blonde

"Looking for a well-crafted, heartfelt lesfic romance? Rachel Lacey's *Come Away with Me* is a lovely one."
—The Lesbian Book Blog

Read Between the Lines

OTHER TITLES BY RACHEL LACEY

Women of Vino and Veritas Series

Hideaway

Midnight in Manhattan Series

Book 1: Don't Cry for Me
Book 2: It's in Her Kiss
Book 3: Come Away with Me

Almost Royal Series

Book 1: If the Shoe Fits
Book 2: Once Upon a Cowboy
Book 3: Let Your Hair Down

Stranded Series

Book 1: Crash and Burn
Book 2: Lost in Paradise

Rock Star Duet

Book 1: Unwritten
Book 2: Encore

Read Between the Lines

a novel

RACHEL LACEY

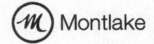

Published by Montlake, Seattle

www.apub.com

Amazon, the Amazon logo, and Montlake are trademarks of Amazon.com, Inc., or its affiliates.

ISBN-13: 9781542033541
ISBN-10: 1542033543

Cover design by Caroline Teagle Johnson

Printed in the United States of America

Read Between the Lines

CHAPTER ONE

"There aren't nearly enough women in this display." Rosie Taft braced one hand against the stepladder as she reached to place yet another book whose cover featured a dashingly handsome man into the display case in the front window of Between the Pages Bookstore. She was in the process of filling the window display with a colorful array of romance novels, her absolute favorite genre.

"Not to worry. There are plenty of ladies waiting," Lia said as she handed Rosie the next book on the stack, a sunny yellow paperback with a woman holding an adorable pup on the cover. Lia was Rosie's best friend and the manager of Between the Pages.

"This is more like it," Rosie said as she tapped a finger against the illustrated dog's nose. "I *loved* this one. Did you read it yet?"

"I haven't," Lia said in her crisp British accent. "Unlike you, I actually try to have a social life when I'm not in the store."

Rosie carefully added the book to the display before flipping off her friend. "I go out plenty, and between you, Nikki, and Paige, I never get a moment alone at home either."

"You go out with friends, which is not the same as a date, and you know it."

"What's the point of wasting my time with the wrong person?" Rosie wouldn't apologize for being picky about who she dated.

"Because sometimes you have to date Ms. Wrong to find Ms. Right," Lia said.

Rosie balanced on her toes as she placed the yellow book on the shelf. "I'd date Ms. Maybe to find out if she could be Ms. Right, but not if I already know she's wrong for me."

"Or maybe you're holding out for Ms. Perfect." Lia lifted her eyebrows as she handed Rosie the next book.

Rosie's cheeks warmed as she recognized the cover, which depicted a woman in a business suit wearing killer red pumps, with the Manhattan skyline visible outside the window behind her. It was the latest lesbian romance by Brie, a notoriously reclusive author who also happened to be Rosie's favorite.

She had stumbled across one of Brie's books about three years ago and immediately fell in love with her writing. There was something so evocative about Brie's words. Rosie could lose herself in one of her books and not come up for air until she'd finished. Brie wrote heroines Rosie related to and the kind of swoon-worthy romance she wanted for herself someday. Books like Brie's had shown her what she wanted in a real-life partner, and she wouldn't settle for anything less.

She and Lia booked authors into the store for monthly signings, so she'd immediately reached out to Brie's publisher and to Brie herself through the contact form on her website, inviting her for a signing, only to receive the same response from both: Brie didn't do in-person events.

Rosie supposed it went along with Brie's enigmatic persona. Her headshot was artfully styled so that her hair obscured most of her face, and her bio contained almost no personal information. A few months ago, Rosie had replied to one of her tweets, and from there, they'd struck up an online friendship on Twitter that only increased Rosie's fascination with her.

Brie was warm and funny, and she and Rosie never seemed to run out of things to talk about. It was more than that, though. Rosie had never been one for celebrity crushes or even online dating, but when she chatted with Brie, she felt . . . smitten. Sometimes their interactions seemed flirty, or maybe it was all in Rosie's head. She was a hopeless romantic, after all. And if she ever met Brie in real life, she definitely wouldn't say no to a date.

"Go on and put Brie's book right up front," Lia said with a knowing smile. "You know you want to."

Rosie placed it in the center of the display. "It's a great book with a stunning cover. It belongs up front."

"Mm-hmm," Lia said. "When are you going to tell her who you are? She might agree to come into the store now that you two are friends."

Rosie shrugged as she adjusted a regency historical so that it didn't block the FALL IN LOVE sign at the top of the display. Paper leaves in various shades of red, orange, and yellow decorated the shelves. "We're just online friends. I don't even know her real name."

"Online friends are perfectly valid," Lia said. "I've met lots of lovely people online."

"Okay, that's true," Rosie admitted. "But as you know, she doesn't do signings. Maybe she has a good reason for staying anonymous. Besides, she probably doesn't even live here in the city. Her author bio just says New York. It's a big state."

"And right now, you're having too much fun flirting with her on Twitter," Lia teased.

"It's chatting, not flirting," Rosie deflected, tired of trying to define her relationship with Brie. She extended a hand so Lia could pass her another book. "We talk about books and TV, not specific things about our lives. She's very private. I'm afraid if I told her now, she'd think I was only chatting with her to try to get her into my store."

"Well, aren't you?"

"No. I like her as a person, and I like talking to her." Rosie placed the last book on the shelf and then hopped down from the ladder to survey her work. The display featured a diverse array of romance novels that made her heart happy. When her mom first opened Between the

Pages over thirty years ago, she'd wanted to create a store that would welcome everyone and every genre, and now that she was gone, Rosie was doing her best to follow in her footsteps.

In today's ever-changing book market, she worked hard to keep Between the Pages relevant. She offered lots of in-store events and extras, including subscription boxes and gift baskets. Rosie's specialty was matching a person with their perfect book when they came into the store, and she had a loyal following who returned to be matched over and over again.

Books spoke to her on a soul-deep level. They had the power to change lives when someone saw themselves represented on the page for the first time, and nothing made her happier than helping a customer find that connection.

"You know, Brie may have already been in the store," Lia said, pushing her glasses up her nose. Today, she wore a blue-striped jumpsuit that would have looked ridiculous on Rosie but perfectly suited Lia's offbeat aesthetic.

"What do you mean?" Rosie asked as she led the way outside so they could see the display from the street. The September afternoon was cool and breezy, and the air was lightly scented with herbs and tomato sauce, courtesy of the Italian restaurant on the corner.

"Well, she lives somewhere in this state," Lia said. "And she obviously loves books. So, for all you know, she may have already visited us."

Rosie put her hands on her hips as she surveyed the window. The yellow book with the dog on the cover was slightly off center. "I don't think the chances are very high. Plus, she told me she mostly reads e-books."

"Maybe you should keep an eye on the women who come into the store, just in case," Lia said playfully. "You never know."

"I don't—Brinkley, no!" Rosie lunged for the door as her dog's little brown head appeared in the window display, knocking over several books. She rushed inside and scooped him up before he caused any more damage. "Of course you wake up the minute I step outside."

His tail swished happily as he wriggled in her arms, leaning to kiss her face.

"He's probably ready for a walk, and I could do with some fresh air myself. Want me to take him?" Lia offered as she knelt to straighten the books on the bottom shelf of the display.

"Sure, thank you." Rosie pressed her lips against the little flat spot between his eyes that just begged for kisses before setting him down.

Lia retrieved his leash from behind the counter and was clipping it to Brinkley's collar just as the bell tinkled over the front door, announcing that someone had entered the store. She mouthed, "Maybe that's her."

Rosie opened her mouth to give Lia a hard time for even putting that thought in her head, but it wasn't a woman who'd come through the door. It was the mail carrier, Brad. With a shrug, Lia slipped out the door behind him, taking Brinkley with her.

"Hi, Brad. Can I help you with something?" Rosie asked, because he usually just put her mail in the slot outside the door.

"Hey, Rosie. I've got a certified letter for you that requires a signature." He set the envelope on the counter and slid a small tablet toward her.

"Oh, okay." She signed her name on the screen and handed the device back to him.

"Have a nice day," he said.

"You too." She turned her attention to the envelope. It was from Breslin Property Development, the company that had bought this building a few months ago, and since the letter came certified, it almost certainly wasn't good news. This was probably a notice that her rent was about to double or even triple. Rosie's stomach swooped, leaving her feeling vaguely nauseous. She ripped the tab and removed a bundle of paper with a letter on top.

Breslin Property Development
132 W 21st Street
New York, NY 10001

Ms. Taft,

This letter is to inform you that the lease for 1450 Lexington Avenue, New York, NY 10128, will terminate on December 31st and will not renew. I have attached a copy of the lease agreement for your reference.

Thank you for being such a reliable tenant, and please don't hesitate to contact me if you have any questions.

Sincerely,
Jane Breslin
Property Manager

"No," Rosie whispered, blinking at the paper as if it might somehow change the words printed there. This couldn't be happening. Breslin Property Development couldn't just kick her out of the space Between the Pages had occupied since before Rosie was born. Well, of course they *could*. But why? As the letter said, she'd been a reliable tenant. She always paid her rent on time and kept her inspections up to date.

She couldn't lose the store. She'd spent her whole life here. Memories of her mother inhabited every inch. As she swept her gaze around the room, Rosie saw her mom adjusting books in the window display, sitting in the red chair in the corner reading to a group of eager children, standing beside Rosie here at the counter. Her chest constricted painfully around her heart.

There must be a way to stop this. Frantically, she began to read through the attached lease agreement, looking for something to fight.

She was deep in rental-termination clauses when the bell over the door chimed, and she looked up to see Lia and Brinkley reentering the shop.

"It's so nice outside today," Lia said as she unclipped Brinkley's leash. "I just love fall weather—reminds me of home. You should sneak out for a walk of your own."

Rosie stared at her as tears blurred her vision.

"Rosie? Are you okay?"

She held up the paper with shaking fingers. "Breslin Property Development just terminated our lease."

Jane Breslin walked down Lexington Avenue as her nine-year-old niece, Alyssa, skipped ahead of her, brown ponytail bouncing with each step. Jane had helped her sister out of a bind by picking Alyssa up from school today, but it meant she'd had to bring her niece with her to a meeting with the architect on her upcoming renovation project, which hadn't been much fun for either of them.

"Look!" Alyssa exclaimed, stopping on the sidewalk. "A bookstore. Can we go in, Auntie Jane?"

Jane shook her head. She owned every building on this block, or Breslin Property Development did, anyway. She'd mailed a lease-termination letter to Between the Pages Bookstore earlier in the week, and the last thing she wanted was to go into a store she had probably just put out of business. "We've got to meet your mom soon."

"Fine," Alyssa said with a sigh.

Something familiar snagged Jane's attention out of the corner of her eye, and she glanced at the bookstore's window display.

No freaking way.

Brie's latest release, *On the Flip Side*, was featured prominently at the center of the display. Jane gaped at the book for a moment in disbelief before standing a little taller in her stilettos because . . . wow. When she'd released her first book as Brie, she'd made the decision to stay anonymous. She could only imagine what her coworkers and clients would say if they found out she wrote sexy books, and her parents—well, okay, mostly her dad—had openly scoffed at the idea of her becoming an author, so it had seemed easier to keep her two lives separate.

After a while, she'd started to like it this way. She could be buttoned up and professional at work, helping to transform outdated buildings into something modern and beautiful. And at night, she let out her inner romantic, penning scorching-hot romance novels about women finding love, which was ironic, since she wasn't overly concerned with romance in her own life. She was incurably awkward when it came to relationships, preferring to live vicariously through her characters.

After her first book was released, she'd gone into a few local bookstores, trying to spot it on the shelves just for fun, but she'd never found it. In five years, she'd never seen her book on a shelf.

Until today.

There it was in the window of a building she was about to demolish. Clearly, the universe was having a laugh at her expense.

"Oh my gosh, there's a dog in the store," Alyssa said, cupping her hands against the glass and peering between them. "Can we *please* go in?"

"Just for a minute." Jane relented, because really, what kind of aunt—or author—would she be if she refused to let her niece go in a bookstore?

Alyssa grasped the door's handle and pulled it open. A bell chimed overhead as Jane followed her into the store, and sure enough, a little brown dog trotted over to greet them. Alyssa knelt to rub its head, and the dog's tail wagged happily.

"Welcome to Between the Pages Bookstore," the woman behind the counter said. "Let me know if there's anything I can help you with."

Jane gave her a quick smile before returning her attention to Alyssa. She didn't want to notice anything about this store, not the neatly arranged shelves of books, the cute dog currently charming her niece, or the attractive woman behind the counter with her bouncy blonde curls. She especially didn't want to notice the way the blonde's gaze slid appreciatively over Jane's suit.

"What's his name?" Alyssa asked, looking at the blonde.

"That's Brinkley," she told her.

"Is he yours?" Alyssa asked, still rubbing the dog, who was sitting in front of her now, tongue out and looking thrilled by the attention.

"He is," the woman behind the counter confirmed. "This is my store too. I'm Rosie. What's your name?"

"Alyssa." She giggled as Brinkley licked her hand.

Jane feigned interest in the nearest display of books, because *shit*, that must be Rosie Taft, and there was a good chance she'd already received a lease-termination notice with Jane's name on it. She slid her fingertips over a row of mystery titles, listening as Alyssa and Rosie talked about books.

"Do you know any stories about dogs that have a happy ending?" Alyssa asked. "Because I *hate* when the dog dies at the end of the book."

"Oh, me too," Rosie agreed, and when Jane darted a glance in her direction, she had a hand pressed dramatically against her heart. "But luckily, I know a lot of books where the dogs live happily ever after. Do you want to read something set in the real world or more of a fantasy setting?"

Alyssa twisted her lips to one side as she pondered the question. "A fantasy world."

"Okay. And do you want the dog to be the main character, or would you rather read about a girl or boy who has a pet dog?"

"The dog as the main character," Alyssa answered without hesitation.

Rosie beamed at her. "I know just the book for you."

Alyssa followed her to the opposite side of the store, with Brinkley at her side. Jane watched them go, noticing another employee on the other side of the store, stocking books. The woman glanced in Jane's direction with a polite smile.

While she waited for her niece to decide on a book, Jane browsed on her own. A case full of colorful paperbacks drew her attention to the romance section. Of course she would gravitate here. Her gaze tracked automatically to the beginning of the alphabet. There were several Brie titles on the shelf.

Jane inhaled sharply, the rush of seeing her books on a shelf for the first time tempered by an unfamiliar surge of guilt. Why did this have to be the one store that carried her books? Breslin Property Development was going to demolish the existing structures on this block to put in a new condominium complex. It wasn't personal. Just business. But that didn't make her feel any less terrible when she saw Rosie and Alyssa walking in her direction, laughing like old friends.

"Is it okay if I get three?" Alyssa asked somewhat sheepishly as she displayed an armful of books.

"Sorry about that," Rosie said. She had the cutest dimples in her cheeks when she smiled, and she seemed to smile a lot. She was also younger than Jane would have expected the owner of the shop to be, likely younger than Jane herself. "Sometimes I have too many book recommendations for my own good."

"But look at them," Alyssa said, showing Jane a book featuring a sparkly dog running toward a castle, another depicting a girl about Alyssa's age hugging a puppy, and one with a ballerina in a pink tutu twirling across the cover.

"Those do look perfect for you," Jane said, giving her niece's ponytail a playful tug. "And yes, you can get all three."

"Thank you," Alyssa said, hugging the books against her chest.

"You're welcome." Jane had mixed feelings about this particular store, but she always tried to encourage Alyssa's love of reading.

"Can I help you find anything for yourself?" Rosie asked Jane, gesturing to the shelf behind her. "If you like romance, I have plenty of suggestions."

Jane shook her head. "Not today, but thank you."

"No problem. I can ring you up if you're ready," Rosie said, leading the way toward the counter in back. Brinkley trotted behind her and curled up in a dog bed against the wall.

Alyssa placed her new books on the counter. "Is that you?" she asked, pointing to a photograph on the shelf behind the counter, showing a blonde girl about Alyssa's age with a woman who was probably her mother. It looked like it had been taken right here in the store.

"It sure is," Rosie said, glancing over her shoulder. "That's me and my mom. She owned this store before me."

Great, like Jane needed one more thing to feel guilty about. Her gaze landed on the envelope from Breslin Property Development beside the cash register, and she quickly looked away.

"Cool," Alyssa said, watching as Rosie rang up her purchases.

She scanned each of the bar codes and tucked the books into a blue paper bag with the store's logo on it. "That'll be thirty-four twelve."

Jane pulled her wallet out of her bag, but she couldn't bring herself to let Rosie see the name on her credit card, not after she'd been so sweet to Alyssa. Instead, she pulled out two twenties and handed them to her niece. "Would you like to pay for the books yourself?"

Alyssa nodded, passing the bills to Rosie.

"Thank you," Rosie said as she took them. "I don't think I've seen you in the shop before. Do you live around here?"

Jane shook her head. "I had a meeting nearby."

"And you went with your mom to her meeting?" Rosie asked Alyssa.

Alyssa grinned, shaking her head. "She's my aunt."

"I'm just helping her mom out of a childcare jam this afternoon," Jane said.

"My mom and my aunt work together," Alyssa told Rosie.

"Oh, that's fun," Rosie said as she handed Jane's change to her. "Well, I'm glad you got some new books out of the deal."

"And I got to meet Brinkley," Alyssa added, walking behind the counter to pet him. His tail thumped against the dog bed.

"Well, if you're ever in the neighborhood again, stop in," Rosie said. Then she looked down at the envelope from BPD, and the sparkle in her blue eyes dulled.

"I'll do that," Jane said. "Alyssa, we need to get going or we'll be late to meet your mom."

Alyssa hurried over and picked up the bag of books. "Bye, Rosie."

"Bye, Alyssa. It was nice meeting you." Rosie waved as they headed for the door.

"She was so nice," Alyssa said as they pushed through the door onto the street.

"She was," Jane agreed, darting one last glance at her book in the window. She really wanted to take a photo, but Rosie was just on the other side of the display, and Jane didn't want to draw attention to herself.

She and Alyssa walked two blocks to the Ninety-Sixth Street subway station and boarded the 6 train, headed downtown. Twenty minutes later, they exited at Grand Central Terminal, where Jane's sister, Amy, was waiting for them. Alyssa was still talking about her new books and the nice lady in the bookstore when Jane left them.

Yes, Rosie was nice. Pretty too. Maybe she'd reopen her store in a new location after she left her current space on Lexington Ave. Actually, Jane hoped she would. She boarded another train, headed for her apartment in Greenwich Village.

While she rode, she checked the messages on her phone, hoping she might have heard from @AureliaRose113. At first, it had been weird for Jane, messaging with one of her readers, especially since she wasn't very active on social media, but she and Aurelia seemed to have a lot in common, and before she knew it, they were chatting about everything from favorite books to dating woes. Jane opened a new message and began to type.

@BrieWrites: How was your day?

@AureliaRose113: Shitty. Tell me about yours instead.

@BrieWrites: Sorry to hear that. Mine wasn't great either. Actually, I'm pretty sure I ruined someone's day, in a roundabout way. 😖

@AureliaRose113: You?! I can't imagine that.

@BrieWrites: It's complicated. I was just doing my job, but I still feel bad about how the whole thing played out.

@AureliaRose113: Aww, I'm sure the person knew that.

@BrieWrites: Thanks. That makes me feel a little better about it.

@AureliaRose113: I'm glad.

@BrieWrites: Read anything new I should add to my wish list?

@AureliaRose113: If you're in the mood for a romance, I know just the thing.

@BrieWrites: I'm *always* in the mood for romance.

Aurelia told her about a new series set in London, and by the time Jane exited the subway, she'd already downloaded the first book and read a few pages. As promised, it was delightful. Aurelia had yet to steer her wrong with a book recommendation. Jane climbed the steps to the street, wishing she'd brought flats to change into, because her feet were killing her in these heels and she still had a four-block walk ahead of her.

As she walked, her thoughts drifted to Rosie Taft. For a moment when Jane had first walked into the store, she'd been sure Rosie was checking her out, although she certainly wouldn't have been interested if she'd known Jane's name. And wasn't that just the story of her life? She never seemed to have her timing right when it came to dating.

Luckily, she was a lot better at writing romance than experiencing it. On the page, she had control of all the variables and could guarantee a happy ending for her characters. She thought of Brie's book in the display window. Did Rosie read her books? Jane had a vague memory of a bookstore owner contacting her for a signing a few years ago. Had that been Rosie?

Finally, Jane let herself into her building, grateful for her first-floor apartment so she wouldn't have to take another set of stairs in these heels. She walked straight down the hall to her bedroom to change into a T-shirt and lounge pants and then backtracked to the kitchen to pour herself a glass of wine.

She was on a tight deadline with her latest book, which meant she'd be writing until she went to bed. But first, she picked up her phone and tapped out a quick message to Aurelia.

CHAPTER TWO

@BrieWrites: Sorry your day was shitty. If you want to talk about it, I'm here.

Rosie swiped the message from her screen with a smile. Brie was so sweet, and if Rosie hadn't been in the middle of a beer-and-bitch-fest with her roommates, she definitely would have taken her up on her offer. She took a swig of her Yuengling and held an arm out for Brinkley, who hopped into her lap to kiss her face.

"I'm certain we should fight this," Lia said, sounding even more British when she was worked up about something.

"Definitely," Nikki agreed. She was seated at one end of the couch with her feet in Paige's lap in adorable couple fashion.

"I'm not opposed to fighting," Rosie said, stroking her fingers through Brinkley's soft fur. "But I think it will be a losing battle."

"That's not a winning attitude," Paige admonished. "My brother's a lawyer, you know? Give him a call and see if he can help you out. Here, I'm texting you his number now."

On cue, Rosie's phone dinged with a new text. "Thanks. I'll call him, but as much as it sucks, I don't think there's anything illegal about not renewing our lease."

"Then maybe we need to try a different tactic," Lia said, tapping a finger against her beer bottle, something she did when she was lost in thought. "For instance, what if we give Breslin Property Development a reason to keep us, instead of trying to start a legal battle we can't afford to lose?"

"What kind of reason?" Rosie asked, looking at her friend as hope loosened the knot in her chest, because if anyone could find a way out of this, it was Lia.

"Our store has a separate entrance from the rest of the building. Since they're a property-development company, I assume they have some sort of renovation planned, which is why they're terminating leases, but maybe they'd let us stay after the project is complete if we make it worth their while, increasing our rent or whatnot."

"I love that idea. Do you think they really might let us stay?" Rosie scrunched her nose as Brinkley went in for another round of kisses on her cheeks. No doubt they were salty from the many tears she'd shed after she'd left the store tonight.

"It doesn't hurt to ask."

"You're right." Maybe her status as a long-term tenant could work in her favor, because she'd already proven herself to be dependable. Rosie's mom had first rented this space over thirty years ago, after all. Rosie had grown up in the store, reading quietly in back after school while her mom worked. When she was a teenager, Rosie's first job had been staffing the cash register. That was where she got her first taste of recommending books to customers, and she was hooked.

When her mom got sick right after Rosie graduated from college, she started working in the store full time. And when the unthinkable happened, Rosie took over Between the Pages herself. It had kept her going when the grief threatened to swallow her whole. She couldn't even comprehend losing it now. The store was her whole life, and it was all she had left of her mother.

Her eyes burned, and she buried her face in Brinkley's fur to hide her tears, but she must not have been successful, because Paige slid off the couch and came to wrap her arms around Rosie, holding her tight while she cried.

"Oh, sweetie, it's going to be okay," she murmured. "This sucks. It sucks so hard, but we'll be here for you every step of the way."

"All of us," Nikki added.

"I love you ladies," Rosie said as she dried her eyes, wishing she cried as delicately as the heroines of her favorite romance novels. Since she didn't, she excused herself and went down the hall to the bathroom to clean herself up. She splashed cold water on her face and blew her nose while Brinkley sat beside her, looking up at her with worried eyes. "Love you too, Brinks."

She rubbed his head before making her way back to the living room, thankful for the best roommates—and the best dog—to help her get through the shitstorm to come. Also, a really sweet internet friend named Brie. Rosie sat cross-legged on the floor and picked up her beer, taking a hearty gulp.

"Lia was just telling us about the hottie who came into the store this afternoon," Paige said.

Rosie toyed with her hair as her cheeks warmed. She tugged at a curl, pulling it straight, and it reached almost to her nose. She was overdue for a trim, and yeah, the gorgeous brunette in her sleek suit had been the highlight of Rosie's otherwise lousy afternoon. "She was pretty."

"And exactly Rosie's type," Lia chimed in. "You know, fancy suit and expensive perfume, with the added bonus of an adorable niece. Plus, she was definitely checking you out, Ro."

"What is it with you and a business suit?" Nikki asked with an exasperated smile.

"Give me ripped jeans and tattoos any day," Lia said, her expression gone dreamy.

"I don't suppose she slipped you her number?" Paige asked Rosie.

She shook her head. "No, but who knows, maybe she'll come into the store again sometime . . . I mean, if it's still there." Her shoulders slumped, but she really did hope the woman came back, because Lia was right. She ticked all Rosie's boxes. Not only was she impeccably dressed, but there was something so soft about the way she interacted with her niece.

Rosie generally trusted her first impression of people, and her gut said this woman was worth taking a chance on. And what could be more romantic than meeting the love of her life right in her own store?

"Fingers crossed, but in the meantime, we need to get you on a date," Nikki said.

"Hotties in suits aside, dating just fell down my list of priorities," Rosie said as she polished off her beer. "Unless Lia and I pull off some kind of miracle, we're going to be unemployed by the end of the year, and who's going to want to date us then?"

"Speak for yourself," Lia said, eyes round behind her glasses. She went on a lot of dates, and Rosie didn't imagine that would change, regardless of her employment status.

"We should have a Tinder night soon," Paige said. "Nikki and I can live vicariously through you two while you swipe left and right."

Rosie shook her head. "I hate Tinder. Hate. It."

"That's because you're waiting for something romantic to happen like you read about in your books, but that's not real life," Paige said. "Nikki and I met on Tinder. You've got to get out there and test the waters. Maybe you'll find the woman of your dreams."

"Tinder's not my favorite either," Lia chimed in, giving Rosie a sympathetic look. "It's a nightmare when you're bi. I swear, most of the people who contact me are men and women in relationships looking to have a threesome, and that's just not my scene."

"Are you serious?" Nikki asked, a scandalized look on her face.

"Dead serious," Lia told her with an expression to match.

"So no Tinder for either of us," Rosie said. "I want a real-life meet-cute like my romance novels, and Lia wants . . ." She waved a hand for Lia to fill in the blank.

"A dating app that has the option to exclude threesomes, I suppose," Lia said as she took a drink of her beer. "I'm so bloody tired of couples considering me a plus-one."

"Then let's find you a new dating app," Nikki said. "We'll schedule a 'find Lia a date' night."

"Yes," Paige exclaimed, clapping her hands together. "And a night out where we can introduce Rosie to all the pretty girls."

Rosie smiled in spite of herself. "Okay. But first . . . Lia and I save the store."

Paige sobered. "Yes. But once that's done—no matter which way it goes—you need some fun to balance it out."

Rosie nodded. "Yeah, okay."

And then, as Nikki started looking for dating app recommendations for Lia, Rosie picked up her phone to reply to Brie's last message.

@AureliaRose113: Thanks for the offer. My roommates cheered me up tonight, but the next few months are going to be hard, so I'll definitely take you up on it sooner or later.

@BrieWrites: Anytime. I'm not always good with advice, but I'm a good listener.

Rosie pressed her fingers against her lips to cover her smile.

"What are you all giddy about over there?" Nikki asked.

"I know that look," Lia said. "She's messaging Brie again."

"Oh my God, Rosie," Paige said. "You're hopeless! We need to find you a woman who lives here in the city . . . and who knows your full name."

Jane sank into the chair behind her desk and spun it to face the window. She liked to start her mornings this way, drinking her coffee while she watched Manhattan come alive on the other side of the glass. She had a long workday ahead, but today, her head wasn't in the game. She was only a few chapters away from finishing her current manuscript, and her mind was buzzing with plot points and dialogue. Her fingers were impatient to type.

She always got this way when she was close to finishing a book, but she was especially invested in this one. Some books just resonated with her more than others as she was writing them. She felt the characters' emotions as her own. Last night, she'd cried while she wrote a particularly gut-wrenching scene. She dreamed of a future where she wrote full time, but after publishing ten books, she still wasn't able to support herself on royalties alone. Maybe once she sold her next series . . .

And then there was the fact that her parents didn't know she was an author. That would be an interesting conversation. "By the way, I'm a published author, and yes, I write *those books* that you were so offended by when I told you I wanted to write them years ago." She didn't see it going well, so for now, she bided her time and oversaw building renovations for the family business, the career her father had envisioned for her.

"Daydreaming over your coffee as usual, I see," Amy said from behind her.

Jane turned her chair to face her sister. "Good morning to you too."

Amy grinned as she dropped into one of the guest chairs in front of Jane's desk. "Want to grab a drink after work? I owe you one for taking Alyssa for me yesterday afternoon."

"I'd love to, but it'll have to be quick. I'm on deadline this week."

Amy was the one person in the world—other than Jane's agent and her editor—who knew she was Brie. "Sure. We can stop in that martini place on the corner, if that works for you."

"Perfect," Jane told her.

"Okay. I'll let you get back to your daydreaming, then. Just stop by my office when you're finished today, and we'll walk over together." Amy stood to leave.

"It's called plotting, and will do. Around six?"

With a nod, Amy was out the door.

Jane smiled into her coffee. A drink with her sister was just what she needed tonight. She hadn't been out in weeks, between renovation projects and working on this book. If Amy didn't nudge her, Jane's inner introvert would prevail, and she'd go straight home every day to put on her pajamas and write.

She finished her coffee and picked up her laptop for a meeting with her father, who also happened to be the CEO of Breslin Property Development. She reviewed her current projects with him, receiving his approval on the final architectural plans for the new condominium complex on Lexington Avenue, before heading to the budget meeting that would take up the rest of her morning.

After lunch, she spent several hours at her desk, reviewing quotes from various contractors, before heading to a meeting with the lead architect on the project. It was just after six by the time she made it down the hall to knock on Amy's door.

"Come in," her sister called.

Jane pushed the door open to find Amy kicked back behind her desk, talking on the phone, so she sat quietly to wait for her to finish.

"It's in her closet," Amy said, making a face at Jane. She must have been talking to her husband, Garrett. "Yep, the blue one. And her hair needs to be in a bun. She can give you a hand with it, if you need help."

Jane smiled as she looked at her phone, picturing Garrett trying to get Alyssa ready for her ballet class without Amy's help. While she waited, Jane sent a quick message to Aurelia.

@BrieWrites: Thought of you today. There was a cheese plate in the break room, and I knew you would hate it. Who hates cheese?! Hope your day was better than yesterday.
@AureliaRose113: Ha! Curdled milk = yuck. You're just biased because you share your name with (a really gross kind of) cheese.
@AureliaRose113: Today was a little better. Thanks for thinking of me!
@BrieWrites: I'm not named after cheese, although brie is actually delicious.
@BrieWrites: And glad to hear it.

"Okay, I'm ready," Amy said as she put down her phone. "Garrett's taking Alyssa to ballet tonight, if you didn't already guess. Should be interesting."

"I want a picture of the bun," Jane told her. "Pretty please."

"You got it." Amy shoved a few things into her bag and stood. "Martinis, here we come. God, I need a drink."

"Long week?" Jane asked.

"Alyssa's in a weird phase where she's afraid of balloons," Amy said as she led the way out of her office. "And she went to a birthday party last weekend where there were naturally a ton of balloons, so she's woken up every night this week with nightmares. Kids, man."

"Hey, I went to college with a girl who was afraid of balloons. As far as I know, she still is. It's a real phobia."

Amy gave her an incredulous look. "Really? Well, I'm not up for another ten years of this, so I hope Alyssa grows out of it."

"Even if she doesn't, I doubt she'll wake every night forever scream-ing about balloons," Jane said. "But what do I know? My knowledge of kids is pretty much limited to Alyssa."

"Speaking of, she's already started reading one of the books you bought her yesterday. Thanks for that, by the way," Amy said as she pushed the button for the elevator.

"Oh, the books were my pleasure, but she dragged me into a book-store on the block we're about to demolish, which was super awkward. And one of my books was in the window display."

"Damn," Amy said. "That's unfortunate."

"Tell me about it," Jane said. "The owner is really sweet too. She's the one who helped Alyssa pick out those books."

"Did you say anything to her?" Amy asked.

"About my book or the fact that I work for Breslin Property Development?"

"Either," Amy said. "Both."

"I said nothing. Absolutely nothing."

"Coward," Amy teased as they stepped into the elevator together.

Jane pushed the button for the lobby. "Guilty, but what could I have possibly said that wouldn't have made things even more uncomfortable?"

Amy shrugged. "I would have just introduced myself, but you've always been a conflict avoider."

"Guess who I get that from?"

"Our dear mother," Amy said with a playful eye roll. "God forbid she should ever disagree with anyone about *anything*."

"She's a pleaser, that's for sure," Jane agreed. "And yet also a master of passive-aggressive guilt trips."

"She's a trip, all right. And you're more like her than you think."

"Excuse me?" Jane gave her sister a look.

"You're so busy trying to be what our parents want you to be that you won't tell them what *you* want to be. And now you've convinced yourself that the whole world will judge you for writing romance novels, so you just live out your dreams in secret."

"That's not why," Jane protested as they exited the elevator in the lobby and headed for the street. She was grateful for the gust of fresh air that met her as they stepped outside after a full day in the office, breathing recycled air pumped through the ventilation system. She tipped her face toward the sun, sucking in a deep breath.

"Then why?" Amy pressed.

"Okay, fine, but they *will* judge me, and it's kind of fun having a secret second career no one knows about. I know that probably sounds crazy, but I like keeping it separate."

"Even if it means you can't fully embrace your life as an author? Because I think it's pretty damn cool that my sister writes books, and I really wish I could tell people."

"Once I'm able to support myself full time as an author, I'll quit this job. Then I can tell people," Jane said as they walked toward the martini bar on the corner. As much as she wanted the things Amy talked about, they also terrified her. "I don't want to have to explain it at the office."

"Then I should probably send you straight home so you can finish your book and earn more money, but I'm selfishly going to keep you for a drink because *I* need a drink, and I need some sister time now that I've gotten myself off ballet duty for the night."

"I need some sister time too." Jane nudged her shoulder against Amy's. "Thanks for convincing me to come out tonight."

They stepped into the bar, which was shiny and modern with glass-topped tables and a blue neon glow beneath the shelves behind the counter. Jane and Amy took two available stools toward the back. Jane hung her bag on the hook under the counter and reached for a drink menu.

Almost immediately, a man in a business suit sauntered over to stand beside them, giving Amy an appreciative look. "Hey, ladies. How are you tonight? Can I buy your first round?"

"I'm married," Amy told him. "And she's gay. So . . . pass, but thanks for the offer."

Jane pursed her lips to hide her smile as Amy turned her back to her would-be suitor before waving to catch the bartender's attention. She ordered an appletini, and Jane chose the raspberry lime martini. When she risked a glance over her shoulder, the businessman was long gone.

"Any prospects on the dating front?" Amy asked as they waited for their drinks.

Jane shook her head. "No time."

"What about that woman you're always chatting with online?"

"Just friends," Jane told her, although if she was being completely honest with herself, she'd thought about it. She and Aurelia had a lot in common, and their online connection might help Jane overcome her insecurities if they ever met in person. "Not to mention, I don't have any idea where she lives . . . or what her full name is."

"Well, here's a thought. You could ask her name."

"I could," Jane agreed. "But then she'd ask mine."

"Oh my God," Amy said with a groan. "You really need to lighten up. So what? She already knows you're Brie. Why would she care who you are in real life?"

"It just feels weird to me, okay? And besides, she's going through something difficult right now."

"What?" Amy asked.

"I don't know exactly. See? We don't even know each other that well."

The bartender returned with their drinks, and Jane took hers gratefully, lifting it for a sip. It was the perfect mixture of sweet and sour, which balanced out the burn of the liquor.

"I don't understand you, Jane," Amy said as she sipped her appletini.

"That makes two of us, then." Jane swirled the plastic stirrer through her drink, mesmerized by its vivid pink color. "The thing is, I don't have many friends, and I don't want to do anything to mess this up."

"I really can't argue with that," Amy said.

Jane took another sip of her drink, already feeling the warmth of alcohol in her stomach. "Sometimes I feel more comfortable with myself behind a keyboard than in person."

"Oh, Jane. Why?" Amy rested a hand over Jane's.

"I don't know. I'm just . . . stiff and awkward in social settings, especially when I'm interested in someone. Surely you've noticed."

"I have," Amy admitted. "But I'd argue that you're shy, not awkward. You're also gorgeous, and you can be ridiculously charming when you want to be. You just need to get out of your own head."

Jane stared into the rosy depths of her martini. "That's easier said than done."

Rosie sat on the couch in her apartment with Lia on one side and Brinkley on the other, laptop balanced on her knees. The email she and Lia had spent the last half hour composing gleamed on the screen, waiting for her to hit send.

To: jbreslin@breslinpropertydev.com
From: rosie@betweenthepagesbooks.com
Subject: Meeting request to review terms of lease

Ms. Breslin,

I received your letter yesterday stating that the lease for my bookstore on Lexington Avenue won't be renewed when the current term is up at the end of the year. As I'm sure you can imagine, this is very upsetting news for me as a small business owner, especially since my family has leased this space for more than thirty years.

Would you be able to come into the store for a meeting this Sunday, October 3rd, at 2:00? I have some questions for you regarding the terms of the lease and options for the future of Between the Pages Bookstore. I would offer to come to your office, but there are a few things in the store that I would specifically like to show you, as they pertain to my concerns listed above.

Sincerely,
Rosie Taft
Owner, Between the Pages Bookstore

Rosie moved the cursor so that it hovered over the Send button. "Here goes nothing."

"Do it," Lia encouraged.

"Done." With a click, the email was on its way.

Every Sunday, Rosie and Lia hosted an afternoon tea service at Between the Pages. It was Lia's idea, in honor of her British roots. Rosie had initially balked at it, because tea and crumpets in a bookstore? It sounded messy. But now, it had become an unofficial weekly book club for the store's regulars. They gathered in the store's basement room, where signings and other events were held, drinking tea and talking about what they'd read that week. Inevitably, most guests bought a few new books to take home with them.

It was *also* Lia's idea that they should invite Jane Breslin to the store during this week's tea service. Rosie was certain Jane would balk at the idea of tea, so they hadn't mentioned that part yet. Once they had her in the store, they hoped to convince her to join them for tea before Rosie met with her privately to go over the plan she and Lia had put together for why Jane should let them stay in the building, including an offer to increase their rent.

"I hope she comes," Lia said.

Rosie sighed as she closed her laptop. "So do I, but honestly, if I were her, I would stay far away from our store."

"Think positively, Rosie. If you focus on a negative outcome, you might manifest it."

"I'm trying." Usually, Rosie was an optimist, but the prospect of losing the store had really shaken her. She loved that space as much as if it were an actual member of her family.

"As a businesswoman, she owes it to herself and her company to meet you and see what you have to offer," Lia said with a nod.

"I hope so. Okay, I'm trying it your way." Rosie waved her hands in front of her face, wiggling her fingers. "I'm sending up lots of positive energy to manifest a big *yes* from Jane."

"There's the spirit," Lia said. "It's fair to assume she's left the office for the day, so she probably won't see your email until the morning. That means you need something to distract yourself so you don't refresh your email ten thousand times before bed."

"Very funny," Rosie said, making a face at her friend. "Also very accurate. I'm going to walk Brinkley and then read for a while. No email checking, I promise."

"Perfect." Lia got up and went into the kitchen to make herself some jasmine tea. Honestly, the woman drank more tea than anyone Rosie had ever known.

Resisting the urge to refresh her email—just *once*—Rosie looked at Brinkley instead. "Walk?"

He leaped off the couch and twirled a happy dance on the rug before darting over to sit beneath his leash, which hung beside the door. Laughing, Rosie got up and clipped it to his collar, then grabbed her jacket. They went into the hall, and Brinkley hopped down the stairs in front of her. His fuzzy butt bounced on each step, while his tail stuck straight up in the air. Watching him go downstairs was one of her favorite things, because it was just so ridiculously adorable.

Outside, he dashed to his usual tree to relieve himself, then started down the block toward East Ninety-Seventh Street. Apparently, he'd decided they should walk to Central Park, and who was she to disagree? It was a gorgeous evening, and a little exercise might keep her from obsessing about what was going to happen to her shop.

Brinkley trotted in front of her, head up and ears pricked, stopping at each lamppost and trash can to sniff.

"Aw," a woman said as she passed by in the opposite direction, smiling at him.

Brinkley's tail wagged wildly, the way it always did when someone smiled at him, which happened a lot. He just had one of those faces that made everyone want to stop and pet him. As she walked, Rosie's mind drifted to the woman who'd come into the store yesterday, with her glossy brown hair and impeccably tailored suit. Her legs in that skirt . . .

Rosie wasn't even sure why she gravitated toward women in suits, because she didn't necessarily see herself falling for a corporate type. An image of the bookshelf in her bedroom passed through her mind, with the row of Brie's books all featuring women in suits on the cover. *Shit.* Was that where Rosie's suit infatuation came from? She really needed to get a grip where Brie was concerned.

She sighed, attempting to change the subject in her brain as she and Brinkley entered Central Park. He started for the trail that looped around the reservoir, and she followed. Apparently, he was more decisive than she was tonight, but she wasn't complaining. She enjoyed walking around the reservoir. It was a scenic walk and great for people-watching, although it was getting pretty dark now. Lamps illuminated the path ahead in yellowish patches.

Brie probably never wore business suits, which was all the more reason for Rosie to develop an affinity for . . . what did authors wear when they wrote? Leggings and sweatshirts, maybe. Brie had a day job, though. Just this afternoon she'd mentioned a cheese plate in the break room. So maybe she did wear suits.

Rosie's friends were right. She needed to go on a date. She needed a real woman to daydream about, because this was ridiculous. The problem was, Rosie didn't enjoy dating. She liked being with someone, but she hated first dates and all the awkward "getting to know you" stuff. And maybe her standards were too high, but so far, her dating life had been disappointing. She wanted to be romanced like the heroines in her favorite books, dammit.

So, more often than not, she curled up with a book and read about fictional characters falling in love instead of putting herself out there. But when she finished the book and put it back on her shelf, she was all alone in her bedroom. Well, she had Brinkley to warm her feet, but maybe she should be looking for more. She'd be thirty soon, after all. At any rate, dating was something to worry about after she had things sorted out with the store.

"What am I going to do if I lose it?" she asked Brinkley.

He looked over his shoulder at her, tongue out and panting, not a care in the world.

"You'll miss it too, you know," she told him. He went to the store with her every day. The customers loved him, and he loved them right back.

Her phone chimed, and she swiped it from her back pocket, hoping irrationally that Jane Breslin might have emailed, even though Rosie knew that logically she wouldn't be checking her work email from home on a Thursday night. But it wasn't an email. It was a message from Brie. She'd pasted in a quote from her favorite motivational author, something she did from time to time. This one read, "Never trust your fears. They don't know your strength."

Rosie sent back a couple of heart emojis. She was absolutely a sucker for inspirational quotes, and it made her a little mushy inside to know Brie was thinking of her. Even though Brie didn't know exactly what Rosie was dealing with right now, that quote was exactly what she needed to hear.

Brinkley yipped, tugging his leash as he lunged at a pigeon on the path. Rosie started to put her phone away when it chimed again, and this time Jane Breslin's name appeared on the screen. Rosie's stomach lurched, and she fumbled Brinkley's leash. He broke free, dashing after the pigeon.

"Brinkley!" she screeched, loud enough to make the couple on the path in front of her turn and look at her with startled expressions. Brinkley froze for a moment before continuing his mad dash after the pigeon, which flapped its wings and soared over the pond, leaving him staring after it with big eyes.

She grabbed his leash and wrapped it around her wrist so she could call up the email.

To: rosie@betweenthepagesbooks.com
From: jbreslin@breslinpropertydev.com
Subject: Re: Meeting request to review terms of lease

Ms. Taft,

I'll come to your store this Sunday as you requested, although Monday would be preferable if you're available.

Sincerely,
Jane Breslin
Property Manager
Breslin Property Development

Rosie fist-pumped the air. She felt a little guilty declining Jane's request to move the meeting to Monday, but the Sunday tea service was key to Rosie's plan. She'd built a community she was proud of, and it was something that made her store unique. Surely, once Jane had seen it, Rosie could convince her to let her stay in the building. She thought of the quote Brie had sent. It had to be a sign. Rosie was stronger than her fears. She was going to pull this off. She had to.

By the time Sunday rolled around, Rosie's stomach felt like she'd swallowed a flock of the pigeons Brinkley was so fond of chasing. She and Lia had cleaned and dusted and carefully straightened all the books on their shelves, as if that might somehow convince Jane Breslin to let them stay. They'd also put together a written proposal that would probably be more effective, or at least Rosie hoped so.

Customers started trickling in around one thirty, browsing the shelves while they waited for Rosie and Lia to open the door that led to the lower level. On Sundays, one of their part-time employees, a woman named Betty, managed the counter while Rosie and Lia oversaw the afternoon tea service. Betty had been working here three afternoons a week for as long as Rosie could remember, long before she'd taken over ownership of the store, and Rosie adored her.

"Chin up, my dear," Betty told her, resting a hand on Rosie's elbow. "You're going to get through this."

"I hope so," Rosie said. "Cross your fingers that our meeting with the property developer goes well, because if we can't convince her to let us stay . . . I just don't know what we'll do. I can't imagine leaving this space."

"I know it," Betty said, glancing over Rosie's shoulder in the direction of the photo of Rosie and her mother that resided on the shelf there. "I've always felt like Joy was here with us, watching over you, but I also know that if she were still alive, she'd be telling you it's only a building. You're the heart of Between the Pages—you and Lia—and you'll keep that heart beating whether it's here or in a new location."

Rosie swallowed past the lump in her throat. "That's exactly what she'd say."

"It's going to be all right, no matter what happens." Betty wrapped an arm around Rosie's shoulders and gave her a squeeze.

"Thanks, Betty."

Lia walked over to stand beside them. "Ready?"

Rosie nodded. "Yep."

"Okay. I'm going to open the door. Good luck with Jane when she gets here." Lia walked to the back of the room to unlock the door, and the store began to empty as people made their way downstairs for the tea service.

The bell chimed, and Rosie turned to see the woman who'd visited with her niece a few days ago approaching the counter. *She came back.* Rosie felt a little ping in her belly. The woman wasn't wearing a suit today, probably because it was Sunday. She had on fitted black jeans paired with a gray button-down top, but this look definitely worked for her too. Her hair was pulled back in a sleek ponytail that drew Rosie's attention to the graceful sweep of her neck, and okay, she definitely had the beginnings of a crush on this gorgeous stranger.

"Hi," Rosie said. "It's good to see you again."

The woman nodded, resting her palms on the counter. She glanced around the store before turning her espresso-brown eyes on Rosie. "I'm afraid I should have introduced myself on Wednesday, but at the time, I didn't think we'd meet again, at least not in person."

"What?" Rosie felt like she was missing something here.

The woman extended her hand. "I'm Jane Breslin."

CHAPTER THREE

For a moment, Rosie just stared. This woman, the one she'd daydreamed about for the past four days, was Jane Breslin? What kind of sick joke was the universe playing on her right now?

"I'm sorry for the confusion," Jane said, dropping her gaze to the counter.

"Oh my G-God," Rosie stammered as her cheeks flushed hot and indignation burned in her chest.

Jane had come into this store and bought books for her niece, knowing full well that she had just evicted Rosie from the building. The *nerve*. Rosie wanted to scream. She wanted to tell Jane exactly what she thought of her. But Jane was here now because Rosie had invited her. She had to convince Jane to let Between the Pages stay in its home, and that meant she had to play nice.

Jane cleared her throat. "You wanted to go over the terms of your lease?"

"Um, yeah." Rosie sucked in a cleansing breath, trying to re-collect her thoughts.

"Would you like some tea?" Betty asked Jane, giving Rosie's hand a squeeze as she nudged her back on topic.

"Tea?" Jane's brow wrinkled. "In a bookstore?"

"It's unusual, right?" Rosie said as her brain clicked up to speed, because this was her moment, her chance to impress Jane. "We host an afternoon tea service every Sunday. Lia, my manager, is from London, so it was her idea, but it's become really popular. We drink tea, eat crumpets—or pastries, really—and talk about books. And today, I was hoping you'd join us before I meet with you about the lease."

Jane blinked slowly, resting a hand on the counter as those rich brown eyes locked on Rosie's. "Tea and crumpets."

"And sharing our favorite books." Rosie could tell she was nodding too much, and she had a feeling she was smiling like a maniac. Her emotions were all over the place right now. "Do you like to read?"

"Ms. Taft—"

"Please call me Rosie. Ms. Taft was my mother."

"Rosie, then," Jane said, and her tone was all business today, none of the warmth that she'd displayed with her niece. "I'm just here to go over the details of your lease."

"Yes," Rosie said, clenching her fingers around the edge of the counter. "But will you join us for tea first? Please?"

Agreeing to meet with Rosie Taft on a Sunday afternoon had been a serious lapse of judgment. Jane didn't have time for tea and crumpets or talking about books, not when she had a book of her own to finish writing and certainly not when Rosie was staring at her like Jane had the power to let her keep her store if only she asked nicely enough.

She didn't. Even if she wanted to, Jane couldn't change the outcome. She wasn't even sure why she was here, except she seemed to be drawn to both Rosie and her store, which was unfortunate, considering. But after she'd misled Rosie the last time she was here, surely she owed her the courtesy of hearing her out now. "A quick cup of tea, but I really can't stay long."

Rosie beamed at her, looking unfairly adorable in her pink dress. Her smile seemed to brighten the whole room. "Okay. Have some tea, and then we'll sneak out to talk about business things."

Jane, by comparison, felt like a buzzkill. She couldn't smile at Rosie, not when she was probably going to have to say no to whatever Rosie asked of her. She shouldn't stay for tea, either, and yet here she was, following Rosie toward a door at the rear of the store. They descended a flight of stairs to a cozy room with copper-colored walls covered in poster-size prints of famous book covers.

A circle of chairs ringed the room, and most of the seats were already taken, occupied by a variety of women and even a few men, teacups in hand. The sound of their chatter filled the room. Jane paused, discomfort tightening her stomach. These people had gathered for an afternoon of tea and conversation, a roomful of booklovers. She should belong here, but she didn't.

She'd cut herself off from this community by choosing to keep her identity a secret. And she wasn't even here today as Brie. She was here as the woman poised to put this shop out of business.

The employee Jane had seen the last time she was in the store approached with a warm smile, waving Jane toward a row of teapots set up against the back wall, and she had never felt so shitty about her day job. She hated absolutely everything about this moment.

"Help yourself," the employee said in a British accent. "I recommend the Earl Grey. It's my favorite."

"Thank you," Jane told her. She stepped to the row of teapots behind a woman with short black hair, and since she didn't know much about tea, she took the employee's advice and poured herself a cup of Earl Grey. After stirring in some sugar, she bypassed the tray of pastries and looked for an available seat. She wasn't going to be here long enough to eat anything.

Her choice of seating was limited to the chair directly beside Rosie or one on the opposite side of the circle, so Jane took the one that put her as far from Rosie as possible. She didn't need the temptation of idle chitchat with her. Jane's seat put her between the woman with short black hair and an older man who seemed to be the husband of the woman on his other side. They were telling another couple about a new cookbook that they loved.

I shouldn't be here.

She sipped her tea and wished she could teleport herself back to her apartment. Since she couldn't, she did the next best thing, which was to quietly observe the people around her, letting them inspire the creative side of her brain. She'd nearly finished her current manuscript, but the next was never far behind, and she could always use inspiration for characters, quirks, or situations that she could apply to her writing.

"I'm Tracy," the woman beside her said.

"Jane," she replied, watching as Brinkley made his way around the room, tail wagging as people bent to pet him.

"Read anything good lately?" Tracy asked.

Jane felt an uncomfortable warmth creeping up her neck, because most of the books she read were lesbian romance or lesbian fiction of another variety, which didn't always go over well with people outside the community. And then there was the fact that she rarely discussed books with anyone but her sister . . . and Aurelia, of course. "I loved Maura Green's latest," she said, naming her favorite lesbian romance author.

"I haven't heard of her," Tracy said. "What does she write?"

"Romance," Jane told her, purposefully vague.

"Oh, I love romance," Tracy said enthusiastically. "I'll have to look her up."

Something bumped Jane's leg, and she looked down to see Brinkley sitting there, watching her with a hopeful expression. She reached out to rub him behind his ears, and his tail swept back and forth across the floor.

Apparently satisfied now that she'd petted him, he moved on to greet the man sitting beside her. Jane hadn't known what to expect from afternoon tea in a bookstore, but this was less structured than she would have imagined . . . more like friendly chaos.

She heard people discussing everything from comic books to thrillers. Most of the people here seemed to be regulars and had seated themselves accordingly, so they could chat with others who shared their reading interests. Periodically, people got up to refill their plates or cups. When Jane glanced across the circle at Rosie, she found Rosie watching her from across the room, looking unreasonably enthusiastic about this whole thing.

And that was the reminder Jane needed that she shouldn't be here, discussing romance novels with Tracy or anything else with anyone in this room. She finished her tea and rose to put the empty cup on the tray in the corner for that purpose. Then she ducked into the hall. To hell with this tea party. She was going home so she could change into the leggings and T-shirt she'd rather be wearing and get back to work on her book. She'd talk to Rosie tomorrow during business hours, preferably on the phone.

She was halfway down the hall when she heard her name.

"Jane, wait," Rosie called, the sound of her footsteps echoing on the tiles as she hurried after Jane.

She spun to face her. "Why am I here?"

"Because I wanted to show you what the store's really like." Rosie stopped a few steps away, twisting her hands in front of herself. Her blue eyes met Jane's, and her pulse kicked in response.

"You said you wanted to go over the terms of your lease, and instead you brought me down here to drink tea," Jane said, trying to keep the irritation out of her voice. "It's Sunday afternoon. Believe it or not, there are things I'd rather be doing."

"I'm sorry," Rosie said quietly. "Lia and I thought that if we showed you our Sunday tea service . . . the way it brings people together through a love of books . . . well, it's just one of the things we do here that makes Between the Pages more than your average bookstore. But I'm sorry for asking you to come out on a Sunday."

Brinkley joined them in the hallway, his toenails clicking over the laminate surface as he walked. He sniffed Jane's leg before looking up at her, tongue out and tail wagging.

She pushed her hands into the front pockets of her jeans so she wouldn't be tempted to pet him while Rosie was watching. "I can see that you have a nice store, Rosie. The decision not to renew your lease was never a judgment on you or your business."

Rosie wrapped her arms around herself. "Could we, um, could we talk in my office for a few minutes? Since you're already here?"

Jane sighed. "Fine."

Rosie gestured for Jane to follow her, leading the way to a room at the end of the hall. A large wooden desk took up most of the room, and the corkboard behind it was covered with photos of Rosie and Lia and their families. Jane took the guest chair while Rosie sat behind the desk. Brinkley trotted over to a dog bed in the corner and spun several times before curling up in a little brown ball.

"Between the Pages is more than just a store for me," Rosie said. "I grew up in this building, and I really want a chance to stay after Breslin Property Development has renovated it. I'm prepared for an increase in my rent and to negotiate whatever terms you'd like to include, but I'd like to stay here, in this neighborhood that I know and love and that loves me and my store. Surely if we work together, we can come up with a mutually beneficial arrangement."

Jane schooled her expression. She definitely should have handled this conversation over the telephone. "I'm afraid I can't do that."

"Between the Pages has a separate entrance from the rest of the building," Rosie persisted. "Surely you can find a way to let us stay."

"But I can't," Jane repeated, resting her palms on her knees. "Breslin Property Development is going to demolish this building and several others on the block to make way for a new set of high-rise condos."

"No!" Rosie exclaimed, lurching to her feet. "You can't."

Jane rubbed her brow. "My company owns this building, and we can and will do whatever we see fit with it. I can't renew your lease, so I'd advise you to start looking for a new storefront, if that's what you want."

Rosie's mouth dropped open, and Jane could swear that even the mop of blonde curls on her head drooped as she absorbed Jane's words.

"I'm sorry," Jane told her for the second time that day, and since there was nothing else to say, she stood and left Rosie's office.

Rosie didn't go back to the tea service. Instead, she closed the door to her office, sat behind the desk, and rested her head on her arms. There was an odd sort of emptiness inside her, like Jane had reached in and taken Rosie's heart with her when she walked out that door.

She'd been so sure she and Jane would be able to work something out so that Between the Pages could stay here in its home that she'd failed to prepare herself for the alternative. And she had *never* considered the possibility that her bookstore crush was Jane Breslin. Somehow, that just made everything worse.

Rosie had no idea how long she'd sat there before she heard the door open and Lia's footsteps as she entered the room.

"It didn't go well, I take it," Lia said.

"Nope." Rosie sat up, blinking. The overhead lights were blinding after she'd had her head buried on her arms for so long. "First of all, it turns out that the hottie in the suit who came into the store last week is actually Jane Breslin."

"I had a feeling when I saw you talking to her earlier," Lia said as she sat in the chair Jane had vacated. "That's bullshit, Rosie. I'm sorry."

"I know." Rosie sighed. "Anyway, that's not the worst of it. She says they're going to demolish this building—the whole block, actually—to put in a new high-rise condo building."

Lia gasped. "No."

"Yep."

"Oh my God." Lia slumped in her chair. "I guess it's time to move on to Plan B, then."

Rosie pushed a hand through her hair, nodding. "We'll have to look for a new storefront."

"This isn't the end of the world," Lia said. "There's plenty of available retail space in Manhattan. Maybe we'll find someplace even better than this."

"Do you think we can?"

"We'll have to be willing to pay more in rent, but we can look for ways to recoup the cost. You had talked about setting up an online store, a way for our customers to request books when they can't make it into the shop. That might help tide us over while we move as well."

"Yeah. That's a good idea."

"We'll be all right, Ro. You just need to have faith."

"I'm trying." She looked down at her hands as the tears she'd been waiting for since Jane's departure finally filled her eyes.

"You're the one always telling me that Between the Pages is more than a bookstore. Now is our chance to prove it."

Rosie swiped at her eyes. "You really think we can pull this off?"

"I know we can," Lia told her. "I don't know what it will look like, but this isn't the end for Between the Pages."

"I hope you're right."

"I'm always right." Lia came around the desk and pulled Rosie in for a hug. "Come on, then. Let's get to work."

Rosie followed her down the hall to the meeting room, which was empty now that the tea service had ended. Brinkley dashed ahead of them to lick crumbs off the floor. She pushed her feelings aside as she helped Lia clean up the room. Leftover pastries were bagged to go home with them. Between Rosie and her three roommates, nothing ever went to waste. She rinsed the teapots at the sink in the kitchenette and emptied the trash while Lia vacuumed.

And then, since Betty handled the counter on Sunday afternoons, Rosie clipped Brinkley's leash onto his collar, and she and Lia left the shop together to walk home. Their apartment was only four blocks away, which had been so amazingly convenient the last few years. So much was going to change, even if they did find a new space for the store.

"We should spend the afternoon browsing available storefronts," Lia said as she unlocked the door to their building.

"Yeah," Rosie agreed. They didn't have any time to waste if they were going to find a new home for Between the Pages before they had to close the doors of their current location.

Brinkley hopped up the steps beside her. He'd been unusually quiet this afternoon, no doubt having picked up on her mood. He was sensitive that way, but unfortunately, he didn't have a future as a therapy dog. Rather than trying to cheer her up when she was upset, he just got sad too.

Upstairs, they let themselves into the apartment, and Rosie was relieved to find it empty. She loved Nikki and Paige, but right now she didn't want to have to tell them the bad news. She didn't want to talk about it at all.

Lia opened her laptop and sat on the couch, and Rosie sat beside her, patting the cushion so that Brinkley jumped up to snuggle against her leg. "Let's find a new home for our bookstore," Lia said as she clicked onto a real estate website.

"We should look for a real estate agent too," Rosie said.

"Definitely," Lia agreed. "Let's browse on our own this afternoon to get a feel for what's out there, and then we'll start making calls."

"Okay." Rosie felt her spirits rebounding in the face of Lia's unflappable poise.

Two hours later, though, she was ready to cry all over again. It seemed unlikely that they would be able to find a new space for anything close to what she was currently paying in rent. Even at the top of her price range, the pickings were slim.

"A Realtor will be able to help," Lia said as she closed her laptop. "They may have access to listings we can't see."

"I sure hope so."

"Hey, are you going to be okay here on your own tonight? I have a date that I need to start getting ready for, but I could cancel and stay in if you like." Lia leaned over to rest her head on Rosie's shoulder. "Pop some popcorn and put on a silly movie?"

"That's sweet of you, but I'll be fine," Rosie told her. "Enjoy your date. I'm probably going to tune out the real world and read for a while."

"Are you sure?"

"Positive," Rosie said. "Where are you two going?"

"I'm meeting her at that new Mexican place on Third," Lia said. "And we might go to the planetarium at the Natural History Museum afterward, depending how dinner goes."

"Oh my God, this sounds like your dream date," Rosie said. "Who suggested the planetarium?"

"I did, but she was keen on the idea. Will you help me choose an outfit?"

"Of course." Rosie reached over to rub Brinkley's belly while she waited for Lia to get changed. This was a routine they shared, modeling outfits for each other before a date, but Lia had the best clothes. She really couldn't go wrong with anything from her closet.

She reappeared from her bedroom a few minutes later wearing wide-legged jeans and a floral-patterned bohemian top with a funky pink belt.

"This is a solid contender," Rosie said. "It's very you, and those jeans make your ass look great. But show me what else you've got."

"It's also comfortable," Lia said. "And I may be doing some walking tonight, so bear that in mind."

"Cute and comfortable," Rosie said. "Noted."

Lia went back into her room, and when she returned, she was wearing a red-patterned skirt that flowed to her ankles with a white off-the-shoulder top and black boots.

"Take your hair down and put on that gold-link bracelet that I love, and this is the winner," Rosie said. "You look amazing."

"Ooh, yes, that bracelet would be perfect. Okay." Lia tugged the elastic from her hair, which tumbled over her shoulders in honey-colored waves. She readjusted her glasses.

"You're going to knock her socks off," Rosie said, reaching over to give Brinkley another rub.

"I hope so." Lia went into the bathroom to do her makeup while Rosie chatted with her from the couch. When she came back out, she was wearing the bracelet and some seriously smoky eye shadow.

"Have fun tonight."

"Thank you. Sure you're going to be okay?"

"Yep," Rosie told her.

Lia picked up her purse and headed for the door. With a wave, she was gone.

Rosie sat there on her couch, facing an evening home alone with her dog, and suddenly that felt lonely instead of enticing. She imagined herself heading out for a date like Lia was or, better yet, settling in for a romantic evening with her girlfriend. If only . . .

The prospect of losing her store, her income, and the only life she'd ever known had left her feeling lost and adrift tonight. She had a sudden urge to go to the store. It was closed for the night now, but she could wander through the deserted aisles. She'd always enjoyed doing that.

When she was a little girl, she and her mom would roam the store in the evenings, rearranging books and setting up new displays. Her mom would patiently answer Rosie's endless questions about genres and authors and why some books came in hardcover and others were paperback. Then Mom would sit in the red chair in the corner with Rosie in her lap and read her favorite children's books.

If Rosie went there tonight, she'd surely sit in that chair and cry. Instead, she picked up her phone, searching for a distraction. There was a message waiting from Brie.

@BrieWrites: This book is trying to kill me.

She'd followed the message with a variety of dramatic emojis. Rosie touched her fingers against her lips, surprised to feel the smile there. She loved when Brie shared bits of her writing process with her. It made her a little starry eyed.

@AureliaRose113: Still hoping to finish today?
@BrieWrites: Hoping to, but I have 4 more scenes to write.
@AureliaRose113: You've got this! You should reward yourself when you finish.
@BrieWrites: Did I mention I'm tired?
@AureliaRose113: It was implied. ☺
@BrieWrites: Wine? I need more wine. Lots of wine. 🍷
@AureliaRose113: Definitely! And you should go out to drink it.
@BrieWrites: We'll see about that part. My pajamas are very comfortable.
@AureliaRose113: I hear that! I was about to change into my pajamas too. My roommates are all out for the evening, and I have an important date with a book.
@BrieWrites: How many roommates do you have?
@AureliaRose113: 3
@BrieWrites: That's a lot of roommates!
@AureliaRose113: It's the only way I can afford to live in the city lol.
@BrieWrites: What city do you live in?
@AureliaRose113: New York.
@BrieWrites: Small world. So do I.

Rosie sucked in a breath. There it was. She and Brie lived in the same city. She'd always wondered, but now she knew for sure . . . and so did Brie. This had to be a sign, didn't it? She could invite Brie to meet for coffee and talk about books. It didn't have to be a date. In fact, it was naive of Rosie to assume Brie would even think she was inviting her on a date. They were just friends.

@AureliaRose113: What are the chances?!
@BrieWrites: I know, right?
@BrieWrites: Well, I'd better get back to work.
@AureliaRose113: Good luck! Let me know when you finish so I can cheer for you!
@BrieWrites: Will do.

Rosie put her phone down, losing her nerve. This week had already been awful. She couldn't take it if Brie rejected her the same day she found out she was going to have to close her store. She pictured Jane Breslin with her perfect clothes and her gorgeous face—the face that still made Rosie's pulse race, no matter how much she disliked Jane herself. Unfortunately, her hormones had a mind of their own.

She went into her bedroom to retrieve the book she'd been reading, a women's fiction novel that had already made her cry more than once. She curled up on the couch, wrapping an arm around Brinkley as she settled in to read. Two hours later, she set the book down, tears streaming over her cheeks. *Wow.* That one had really ripped her heart out. Maybe she should have picked something more uplifting to read tonight, but this author would be signing at Between the Pages in a few weeks, and Rosie wanted to make sure she'd read her latest to discuss it with her at the event.

Since her roommates weren't home yet, Rosie washed her face and took Brinkley for a walk, stopping at the deli down the street for a sandwich to bring home. That nagging sense of loneliness wouldn't leave her alone tonight, or maybe it was just melancholy over the future of the store. She ate her sandwich and selected the fluffiest romance on her shelf, hoping it would cheer her up.

She had just made it to the point where the characters were about to kiss for the first time when her phone chimed. Rosie's heart was racing as she turned the page, and then she sighed when the couple was interrupted before they managed to kiss. And speaking of interruptions . . .

She picked up her phone to find a new message from Brie.

@BrieWrites: Finished! ☺
@AureliaRose113: Yay!!! Time to break out the wine.
@BrieWrites: Unfortunately, I got distracted this week and never bought any. But I'll celebrate tomorrow. Right now, I think it's time to collapse into bed and sleep.
@AureliaRose113: Yes! Sleep! And if you want someone to celebrate with, let me know.

Rosie's heart lurched in her chest as she hit send. *Holy shit.* She'd really done it. Hopefully she wasn't going to regret this.

@BrieWrites: What?

Not exactly the response Rosie was hoping for, but there was no going back now. She held her breath as she composed her reply.

@AureliaRose113: Well, since we both live here in the city, maybe we should meet?

CHAPTER FOUR

Jane stared at the message on her phone as an uncomfortable tightness spread through her chest and down into her stomach. Aurelia wanted to meet. A small part of Jane wanted to leap at the chance. The rapport she shared with Aurelia was special, especially for someone like Jane who had few friends and struggled to form connections with people in person. Maybe she'd be less reserved with someone she was already comfortable with in another format.

But the reality was that she'd probably still be awkward, and then she risked ruining their online friendship. All she knew for sure right now was that she was 100 percent brain fried after writing the last two chapters of her book. This was definitely not the time to commit to meeting Aurelia in person. Although, with a freshly written "happily ever after" still circling her mind, she was feeling a bit more romantic than usual, and there *did* seem to be a flirtatious vibe between her and Aurelia lately.

@BrieWrites: Maybe!
@BrieWrites: Ask me again tomorrow after I've slept ☻

Jane put her phone down, but despite what she'd told Aurelia, she wasn't ready to sleep. Yes, she was exhausted, but her brain was wired. So she grabbed her Kindle and curled up to read the London-set romance

Aurelia had recommended last week. She read for about an hour before her eyelids started to get heavy. As she climbed into bed, her last thought was of Rosie Taft and the devastation on her face when Jane had told her the building would be demolished. A career low point, for sure.

She slept deep and dreamless that night, the way she always did after finishing a book, as her brain recharged itself. Even so, she headed to work the next morning feeling vaguely hungover, although she hadn't had any alcohol. She sat at her desk with her coffee, staring out at the Manhattan skyline, her mind already spinning ahead to new plots and characters.

Once she'd edited and handed in the book she'd just completed, she would be out of contract with her publisher. It was time to pitch something new, which was always an exciting and terrifying time. Assuming she was able to sell another series, could she pitch something marketable enough to earn an advance that would allow her to quit her day job?

It was definitely a long shot, but she was inching closer to her goal, and with every step she took in that direction, she felt more disconnected from Breslin Property Development. Her heart just wasn't in it anymore. Maybe it never had been.

Her phone dinged with an incoming message.

@AureliaRose113: So what do you say, drinks one night this week to celebrate finishing your new book?
@AureliaRose113: Coffee if that's more your style!

Wow, she was really persistent about meeting in person, but in the light of day, Jane could see that this was a terrible idea. She was being romantic and silly last night to even consider meeting Aurelia in person, but how could she back out of it now without hurting her feelings? Jane frowned at her phone as she reached for her coffee and took another sip.

"Morning," Amy said from behind her. "How was your weekend?"

"Finished the book," Jane told her, spinning her chair to face her sister. "Crushed a bookstore owner's spirit. And found out Aurelia lives here in Manhattan."

Amy's eyebrows went up. "Sounds like an eventful weekend. Congratulations on the first, condolences on the second, and holy shit on the third!"

"She wants to meet in person," Jane said.

Amy sat in the chair on the other side of the desk, making herself comfortable as she sipped her own coffee. "You didn't turn her down, did you?"

"Not yet," Jane told her.

Amy lifted a hand. "Okay, hear me out, because you should definitely do this, even though I know your natural inclination is to say no."

Jane's lips quirked. "I'm listening."

Amy leaned forward, setting her coffee on the desk. "You like this girl, right? She's more than just an online friend to you. She's someone you've romanticized in your mind. You've flirted with her. You've fantasized about her, even though you don't really know that much about her. She could be married or sixty years old for all you know."

"I'm pretty sure she's neither of those things, but that's the crux of the problem, yes," Jane agreed. Aurelia's profile picture was a stack of books, which gave her nothing to go on. "I've got an idea of her in my head that probably doesn't match the real-life person, and I think it's better if I don't find out."

"Oh, but it's better if you *do*," Amy said with a delighted smile. "What have you got to lose? You know you two have lots in common, so you don't have to worry about that. It's entirely possible that you won't be attracted to her when you meet her in person, and that's fine. She can still be your friend. You need friends, Jane, friends you go out with, even if you're just talking about books. And if you two *do* have a spark in person? Well, then . . ."

"What if it somehow ruins our online friendship?" Jane couldn't help asking.

"Why would that happen?" Amy countered. "Worst case, your online friend becomes a real-life friend, and best case, she also becomes your girlfriend."

"Well, when you put it like that . . ." Jane looked at her phone. Amy's argument made sense, but she was still inexplicably terrified by the idea of meeting Aurelia in person.

"Say yes, Jane."

"Fine," she said. "Okay."

"Do it now." Amy tapped her index finger against the desk. "Text her back before you change your mind. Go on."

Jane sighed, annoyed by how well her sister knew her. If she left Jane's office without her sending the message, Jane would talk herself out of it, and maybe she *should* talk herself out of it. Or maybe she was being neurotic about absolutely nothing. She could always back out of their meeting later if she changed her mind.

@BrieWrites: When and where? I'm free most evenings after 6.

And then, under Amy's watchful stare, she sent the message. "There. Happy?"

Amy grinned as she stood. "Oh, I'm very happy about this, and you should be too. Call me after and tell me all about your date?"

"It's not a date," Jane called, but Amy was already gone.

Rosie yelped as the message appeared on her phone, and a ping of excitement raced through her system. She'd been so scared Brie would say no, almost certain of it by this morning, and she'd really had enough disappointment this week.

"What are you carrying on about?" Lia asked, adjusting her glasses. She'd just come from the back room, where she was assembling this month's reader subscription boxes.

"Brie agreed to meet me," Rosie told her.

Lia's eyebrows shot up her forehead. "Wow. This is a big deal."

"I know, right?" Rosie tapped her fingers anxiously against the counter. "Where should we go? She suggested meeting after work, which probably means real drinks and not coffee."

"Definitely invite her for a real drink," Lia said. "If she wanted coffee, she'd have suggested you meet earlier in the day, and alcohol will help you get over any nerves."

"Okay," Rosie said. "Know any great bars? You go on way more dates than I do . . . not that this is a date, but you know what I mean."

"It might be a date," Lia said, tapping her lips thoughtfully. "What about the Red Room on Twenty-Fifth? It's upscale and funky but quiet enough to have a conversation. They have tables, and you can order food, should the mood strike."

"Okay, I'll suggest that," Rosie said. "Thank you."

@AureliaRose113: How about the Red Room on 25th. Wednesday at 6?
@BrieWrites: Sounds good. See you there!
@BrieWrites: Wait, how will I know you?
@AureliaRose113: I have short blonde hair, and I'll wear my book earrings.
@BrieWrites: Ha! Perfect.

"Oh my God." Rosie stared at her phone and then at Lia. "This is really happening. We're meeting on Wednesday."

And it was Lia's turn to squeal with excitement. "I can't wait to hear about it. In fact, we're going to need a girls' night on Thursday so you can tell us everything."

Rosie laughed. "Okay."

"And don't worry, I'll help you with date prep too."

"Oh, I was counting on it," Rosie told her.

"Of course," Lia said. "All right, I have just a few more boxes to finish before we leave for our appointment with the Realtor."

Rosie nodded, her excitement dissolving at the reminder of what was happening to her store. Thank goodness for her meeting with Brie, because she desperately needed something to look forward to right now. Lia went back downstairs to finish packaging the subscription boxes, and Rosie made her way around the store, chatting with customers as she helped them with their purchases.

She spotted a middle-aged man standing in the romance section with a pensive look on his face and walked over to him. "Is there something I can help you find?"

He turned toward her with a grateful smile. "I'm shopping for my wife. It's her birthday this weekend."

"What kind of books does she like?" Rosie asked.

"She'll read most anything, but these love stories are her favorite," he said, and the fondness in his voice warmed Rosie's heart. Nothing was more romantic in her opinion than someone shopping for books for their spouse.

"They're my favorite too," she told him.

"Hey, are you Rosie?" he asked.

"I am," she confirmed.

"I'm Fred Schwartz, Dolores's husband. She's mentioned your name."

"Dolores," Rosie exclaimed. "Yes. She's in here all the time, and I happen to know we just got in a new book by one of her favorite romance authors."

She helped Fred pick out several books she was confident Dolores would love, plus a bookmark and a "Coffee. Books. Repeat." tote bag. He left with a satisfied smile, and Rosie felt it in her soul. This was what she loved most, and she couldn't lose it. She couldn't lose this store.

While she was with him, Betty had clocked in and made herself at home behind the counter, cheerfully ringing up customers. Rosie went over to say hi, and she and Betty spent a few minutes catching up.

"Mia took her first steps," Betty told her proudly, holding out her phone to show Rosie a video of her granddaughter toddling across the living room.

"Well, that's the cutest thing I ever saw," Rosie said. "I just love how babies walk like little drunk zombies." As they watched, Mia plopped onto her butt, turned to face the camera, and clapped her hands. "You should bring her in soon. I can't believe how big she's gotten."

"She sure has," Betty agreed. "I'll see if Rebecca can stop by with her later this week."

"Awesome," Rosie said. "Lia and I are heading out soon to meet our new Realtor."

"Oh, that's right," Betty said. "I hope everything goes well."

"Thanks. Me too."

On cue, Lia came through the back door, purse in hand. "Ready?"

"Give me just a minute." Rosie dashed downstairs to use the bathroom and grab her jacket, and then—after saying goodbye to Betty—she and Lia were on their way to meet with Marcia Guzman, a Realtor who had been recommended to them.

Outside, the air was crisp and cool, and the ornamental trees lining the sidewalk had started to change color, yellow and orange leaves mixed in with the green. They stopped by the apartment first to drop off Brinkley, who gave Rosie a disapproving look when he realized she was leaving him behind.

"We'll be back soon," she told him, and then she and Lia set out for the subway. Rosie's stomach felt vaguely queasy at the enormity of finding a new home for her store. Suddenly, it all felt a lot more real. Her phone dinged as they walked down East Ninety-Sixth Street.

@BrieWrites: Opinion—for my next series, I'm thinking about departing from my usual workplace romance in favor of a celebrity series. I've got a concept that's been nagging at me for a few years, but do you think it's too big of a leap from my usual corporate setting?

Rosie almost walked straight into a lamppost while she was reading Brie's message, saved at the last moment by Lia, who hooked an arm through Rosie's and yanked her out of the way.

"Earth to Rosie," she said. "Let me guess. A message from Brie?"

Rosie nodded breathlessly. "She wants my opinion on her new series."

"Well, well," Lia said. "Isn't that fancy?"

"It is." Rosie was practically drooling at the chance. She and Lia crossed the street and entered the subway station. Once she was seated on the train, she opened Twitter to reply to Brie.

@AureliaRose113: I personally *love* celebrity romance. I think you could totally branch out. Plenty of authors do it! Is there a reason you're worried about the change?
@BrieWrites: Well, I'll be pitching a new series to my publisher. My sales have plateaued with my last few books, and I'm ready to shake things up a bit, hoping to get to the point where I can make this my full-time job.
@AureliaRose113: Gotcha. Well, from what I know of the industry, celebrity romance always sells, so I think you should go for it!

Rosie was halfway tempted to tell Brie she owned a bookstore right then and there, but they were going to meet the day after tomorrow, so at this point, it seemed like a conversation to have in person. Her heart was racing at the thought.

@BrieWrites: Thank you! I think I will (go for it, that is).
@BrieWrites: And now you've got me curious about your industry knowledge—care to share?
@AureliaRose113: I'll tell you over drinks on Wednesday!
@BrieWrites: 🍸🍸

"Earth to Rosie . . . again," Lia said, drawing Rosie's attention from her phone. "I hope you can put your phone away long enough for our meeting." She said it in a mock-serious voice, but her eyes twinkled playfully.

Rosie elbowed her. "You know nothing's more important to me than finding a new home for the store, but in the meantime, you're probably going to have to sedate me so I don't hyperventilate between now and Wednesday evening."

CHAPTER FIVE

Jane stepped through the door of the Red Room, her eyes sweeping the bar for a woman with short blonde hair and bookish earrings. Jane's stomach was in knots, and her palms were slick. She was absolutely awful at blind dates, or whatever this was. Despite everything, she was excited to meet Aurelia, and she desperately wanted tonight to go well. She had neglected her social life for too long, and tonight was a first step toward changing that.

The bar was funky and modern with red velvet booths along the wall to her left and a handful of people on barstools on the right. Jane's gaze caught on a woman with short blonde hair seated about halfway down the bar, and surely that was Aurelia. Jane pressed a hand against her chest as a dizzying mix of anxiety and anticipation built beneath her fingers. Aurelia's back was to Jane. She wore a purple patterned dress, and the recessed lighting beneath the bar made her almost seem to glow.

Jane's pulse jumped and her stomach flip-flopped, flooding her with adrenaline and . . . could it possibly be attraction, when she hadn't even seen Aurelia's face yet? She sucked in a shaky breath and crossed the room, stopping behind her. "Excuse me."

The woman turned, and Jane found herself staring into the wide eyes of Rosie Taft. For a moment, they just stared at each other while Jane's frantic brain screeched to a halt.

Rosie's mouth opened and closed, and then her eyes narrowed. "What do *you* want?"

"Rosie?" she stammered, her fingers clenching around one of the buttons on her jacket, suddenly too clumsy to unfasten it. What was happening right now?

Rosie glared at her. "Yeah?"

"I'm sorry. I thought you were someone else." Jane stepped back as heat crept up her neck. Her heart raced as she fumbled with the buttons on her jacket. How was she ever going to relax and enjoy a drink with Aurelia while Rosie was sitting here at the same bar?

"Obviously," Rosie snapped. "Well, I'm waiting for someone, so if you don't mind . . ." She turned away, and that's when Jane saw the little books dangling from her ears.

"Oh fuck," she mumbled. A prickly sensation spread over her skin, and her stomach pitched like she'd just missed a step and gone into freefall.

Rosie shot her a nasty look before returning her attention to her drink.

Jane sucked in a breath as all the puzzle pieces snapped into place: Aurelia's comment about her knowledge of the business, Brie's books in Rosie's store . . . *oh God*. Aurelia Rose was Rosie. Tears pricked at Jane's eyes, and panic tugged at her feet, urging her toward the door.

She wanted to run as far and as fast from this bar as she could manage, but that would've been an asshole thing to do. As much as it would hurt to lose one of her only friends, Rosie deserved the truth. Jane swallowed, and her throat seemed to stick to itself it was so dry. She coughed, eyes watering, which only added to her humiliation.

"What'll you have?" a male voice asked.

She turned to see the bartender standing in front of her. "A glass of riesling, please, and also some water." Because she couldn't seem to stop coughing, and now she was sweating, a combination of embarrassment and the temperature in the bar. She finally managed to unbutton her jacket and slipped out of it.

Rosie was typing furiously on her phone. She set it down, and Jane's phone dinged inside her purse. *Fuck me.* This was a disaster. She silenced her phone and reached for the glass of water the bartender had placed in front of her. She took several grateful sips until the tacky feeling in her throat dissipated.

"Rosie . . . ," she started, and her whole body flushed again when Rosie looked at her.

"I think it's best if we just *don't*, Jane." Her voice lacked its usual bubbly effervescence. There was nothing warm or friendly about the way she looked at Jane tonight. She didn't smile, keeping those dimples hidden.

And Jane felt herself blinking back tears, because this was her fault. She'd kicked Rosie's bookstore out of its home and lost any potential for friendship in the process. She nodded, gripping her water glass and watching the way the overhead light glinted off the ice to keep from looking at Rosie.

The bartender brought her wine, and she thanked him. She sipped, darting a glance in Rosie's direction to find her draining the contents of her glass. Jane's gaze drifted to her throat as she swallowed, and Jesus, she was in trouble. She'd been drawn to Rosie since the first time they'd met, but the knowledge that Rosie was Aurelia had sent her hormones into chaos.

Jane had harbored an online crush on Aurelia for months, had hoped—however naively—that it might translate into a real relationship. Well, the attraction was real, all right, at least for Jane. As Rosie set her empty glass on the counter, the glare she gave Jane hit like a barb, making her chest ache with regret.

Silence spread between them, thick and uncomfortable. Jane had never told anyone but her sister that she was Brie, and she just couldn't do it for the first time in such a hostile situation. Maybe she could message Rosie after she left and tell her what happened. Surely that would be a less embarrassing outcome for both of them. Jane gulped her wine, eager to finish her drink and get the hell out of here.

Rosie signaled the bartender and ordered a new drink. "I can't believe you're here," she said to Jane. "*Why* are you here?"

"I just . . . stopped in for a drink after work," Jane said with a stiff shrug.

"Evict anyone new today?" Rosie asked bitterly. "Level another building? I'd probably need a drink, too, if that was my job."

Jane lifted her wineglass and took another sip. "It's just business, Rosie. It's not personal."

"It's personal to me," Rosie whispered, and Jane wished she could melt through the floor and disappear.

"I'm sorry," she said quietly.

Rosie looked at her out of sad eyes. "You should be."

Rosie was halfway through her second Long Island iced tea before she realized her night might be about to get even worse, because it was starting to look like Brie was going to stand her up. And the only thing worse than being stood up by the woman she'd been fantasizing about for months was to be stood up in front of Jane freaking Breslin.

Rosie took another gulp of her drink and glared at Jane. At first, she'd been annoyed by the idea of having Jane nearby while she met Brie in person for the first time, and now . . . well, now everything sucked. "You could at least sit somewhere else," she said grumpily in Jane's direction.

Jane gave her a sharp look, eyebrows raised. "Excuse me?"

"I'm having a shitty night, okay? And you're kind of making it worse."

Jane gaped at her, looking unfairly gorgeous in her black dress that highlighted every perfect curve on her body. The dress wasn't overtly sexy. It was probably what she'd worn to the office today, but it played right into Rosie's corporate fantasy, and right now, she was having a hard time keeping her eyes off it.

She wished Jane hadn't brought her niece into the store. That's what it came down to. Rosie's first impression of her had been so wildly wrong, and now she was attracted to someone she shouldn't be, which was annoying and inconvenient—not that it was any excuse for the way she'd acted tonight.

Rosie looked at the glass in her hands, embarrassed by her behavior. She could hardly believe the words coming out of her mouth. She was never rude. She was usually a happy, silly drunk, but Jane made her feel way too many conflicting, confusing things, and Rosie just really, *really* wished she wasn't here right now.

"I think it's possible you're confusing me with my employer," Jane said.

"I don't think so," Rosie said, lifting her drink for another swallow. "Your name is the same."

"Jesus Christ," Jane muttered, sipping her wine.

Rosie looked at her then, really looked at her for the first time since she'd come into the bar. Jane's posture was tense, and she looked vaguely upset. Why had she come to a bar by herself for a drink after work? Possibly she'd had a shitty day, too, and now Rosie was biting her head off when she was just trying to enjoy her wine in peace.

Rosie wanted to leave. She wanted to go home, lock herself in her bedroom, and cry, but it was only 7:20 p.m. She'd gotten here early, and now she was half-drunk on Long Island iced tea, stuck in this awful limbo. She finished her drink and signaled the bartender for another. If Brie hadn't shown up by the time she finished this one, she'd go. It wasn't wise to drink this much so quickly, but she couldn't seem to help herself, not with Jane sitting two stools down, looking so obnoxiously beautiful.

Where was Brie? Rosie had sent her several messages, but Brie hadn't replied or even viewed them. Had she gotten held up at work? Had something happened? Or had she just decided she didn't want to do this? Rosie feared the latter, and the rejection hurt.

The bartender placed a fresh glass in front of her, and Rosie lifted it for a sip as she checked her phone again, hoping against hope that Brie would have messaged. Beside her, Jane finished her wine and pushed her credit card toward the bartender to settle her tab.

Rosie was struck again by the feeling that Jane looked . . . sad. "I'm sorry," she blurted. "For being rude to you tonight. It's not like me."

Jane gave her a half-hearted smile. "I know it's not. No hard feelings."

Rosie nodded, although she wasn't sure she could reciprocate the sentiment. There would always be hard feelings where she was concerned. Jane had taken the thing Rosie loved most in the world from her, and despite what she said, it *was* personal.

Jane signed the receipt the bartender had given her and stood, smoothing her hands over the front of her dress as she turned toward Rosie. "Will you be okay to get home by yourself?"

Oh geez, did she look *that* drunk? "Yep. I'm not driving."

"Right." Jane shrugged into her jacket and picked up her purse, then paused, still looking at Rosie. "Was it a date? The person you were meeting tonight?"

Rosie bristled at the intrusiveness of Jane's question. Was it a date? That was the question, wasn't it? She shrugged. "Guess I'll never know now, will I?"

Jane bowed her head, perhaps ashamed for prying. "I'm sorry. Goodbye, Rosie."

"Bye." Rosie watched her go, giving herself a moment to admire Jane's ass in that dress. If only . . .

No. Rosie would probably never see her again, and that was fine. Just because Jane had been nice to her tonight—even in the face of Rosie's rudeness—didn't make up for the fact that she had evicted Between the Pages from its home of thirty years. Rosie blinked back tears as she took another gulp of her drink.

She checked her phone again, but Brie still hadn't viewed her messages. Hopefully that meant she'd gotten held up somewhere and not that she was ignoring Rosie. She finished her drink. It was 7:30. Brie wasn't coming, and Rosie had had enough of this bar. She signaled the bartender for her check.

"Your friend took care of it," he told her, resting his hands on the counter.

"My friend?" Rosie asked stupidly. Her brain was sluggish from alcohol, but surely he didn't mean . . .

"The woman in black?" He gestured to the stool Jane had vacated.

"Oh," Rosie said. *Oh.* Why had Jane paid her tab? Rosie had ordered three pricey drinks. She was trying really hard to stay angry with her, but Jane sure hadn't made it easy tonight.

At any rate, she was too drunk to make sense out of *anything* that had happened, and she needed to go home. She put on her jacket and walked outside, grateful for the blast of cold air that met her, because it helped to clear her head, at least a little bit. She shoved her hands into her pockets and headed for the subway.

Thirty minutes later, she climbed the steps to her apartment, hoping she wouldn't burst into tears in front of her roommates the minute she stepped inside. She unlocked the door and let herself in.

"Hey," Lia called from the couch, a book in her hand and an expectant look on her face. "You're home earlier than I expected. Everything okay?"

Rosie shook her head, bottom lip trembling. "Sh-she stood me up."

"Oh no," Lia said, patting the couch beside her. "Did she say why?"

"No." Rosie dropped her jacket and purse on the table and sat next to Lia. "She was a no-show."

"Well, fuck," Lia said. "That's really disappointing. I'm so sorry, Ro."

"Yeah, me too." Rosie leaned back and closed her eyes. She'd been so excited when she left the apartment earlier, giddy over meeting Brie, and now . . . now she felt like the universe was trying to kick her while she was already down. "I drank too much to compensate, and now I feel kind of sick."

"Have you eaten?" Lia asked.

"No. I was going to order food when Brie got there."

"You've got leftover Thai in the fridge," Lia offered. "Want me to warm it up for you?"

"Yes, please," Rosie said, not opening her eyes. "Thanks."

"Of course."

She felt the warm press of Lia's hand on her knee, and then the cushion shifted beneath her as her friend stood. The refrigerator opened and closed, and then she heard the hum of the microwave. Soon, the savory scent of drunken noodles filled the room. "I feel like a drunken noodle," Rosie muttered, slumping on the couch as the room spun around her. She was starting to regret that third Long Island iced tea. A cold wet nose met her hand as Brinkley crawled up beside her, and she reached out to rub him.

"Come here, my darling drunken noodle," Lia called from the direction of the kitchen. "Food will make you feel better."

Rosie stood, swaying on her feet. She blinked, resting a hand against the arm of the couch as she regained her equilibrium before making her way to the kitchen table, where Lia had set a plate of noodles and a tall glass of water. "Thank you."

"You're welcome." Lia sat across from her. "Do you want to talk about it?"

"Jane Breslin was there," she said as she twirled noodles around her fork.

"What? Why?"

Rosie shrugged. "Just a coincidence, but why does she keep popping up in my life lately? I never want to see her again."

"This city has a strange habit of throwing people in our way when we'd rather avoid them, doesn't it?" Lia commented.

"Did it happen to you too?" Rosie asked before taking a bite, and mm, this was definitely a good idea. Suddenly she was starving, and she couldn't imagine anything better than greasy noodles.

"I bumped into Shawn on the subway a few weeks ago," Lia said.

"Oh geez, why didn't you tell me?" Rosie asked after she'd swallowed her noodles. Shawn was Lia's ex, a man she'd spent many tearful nights missing after their breakup last year.

Lia waved a hand dismissively. "Slipped my mind, to be honest. Guess that means I'm finally over him, doesn't it?"

"I guess it does," Rosie agreed. "Good for you."

"Thanks. I'm really sorry Brie stood you up. Hopefully she'll come through with a good reason for why."

"But let's face it, she probably won't," Rosie said as she set down her fork. She gulped from the glass of water Lia had given her, already feeling better now that she'd put something other than alcohol in her stomach. "Usually when someone stands you up, it means exactly what you think it does."

"Unfortunately, yes," Lia agreed. "But in this case, why would Brie have agreed to meet you if she didn't intend to follow through?"

"I don't know," Rosie said. "Because people suck, I guess."

She finished her dinner and gave Lia a hug in thanks. Then she took Brinkley for a quick walk and changed into her pajamas to hide in her room and read for a while. She'd sobered up significantly after eating her ironically named noodles, and now she was just tired. As she curled up in bed, she picked up her phone, realizing she hadn't checked it since she left the bar.

@BrieWrites: I'm really sorry about tonight.

Rosie's heart lurched in her chest. The message was vague and not at all reassuring. Brie hadn't given any reason for not showing up, which could only mean that it had been intentional. Rosie blinked back tears as she closed Twitter without replying, reaching for her book instead.

CHAPTER SIX

Jane picked up her phone and put it back down for at least the fifth time that morning. Aurelia—*Rosie*—had read her message but hadn't replied. She was upset. Jane knew that all too well, having gotten a front-row seat to Rosie's disappointment last night. Jane had tried to tell her the truth, but Rosie had been so *angry*. Her rudeness had been unexpected and, to be honest, hurtful.

Jane knew Rosie was upset about losing her storefront, and she wasn't unsympathetic to her pain. It sucked, but this project had been greenlighted by her father months ago. There was nothing Jane could do to stop it, even if she wanted to. And it was just business . . . wasn't it? Rosie's building was old and outdated. Several of the apartments on the upper floors weren't up to code. It was for the best to bring it down and build something modern and energy efficient in its place, with all the bells and whistles that today's renters were looking for.

She'd intended to message Rosie after she left the bar and tell her everything, but as Rosie continued to lash out at her, Jane lost her nerve. Maybe it was better if Rosie thought Brie had stood her up than to know that Brie was Jane. Because Rosie sure as hell didn't like Jane.

For a moment, she'd dared to hope they could go back to the way they'd been on Twitter—online friends and nothing more. But no, that ship had sailed. And Jane had nothing to show for it but hurt feelings and an inconvenient crush on a woman who hated her.

To elicit such a strong reaction from a woman as sweet as Rosie? Well, Jane had shed a few tears about it once she got home last night. And now, she had to move on. Already, she missed her conversations with Aurelia. Her phone was too quiet, and it made her unbearably sad.

There was a knock at the door to her office, and before she could react, Amy stepped inside, smiling brightly. "Well? How did it go?"

"It was a disaster."

Amy's smile withered. "Oh no. Was she awful?"

"No." Jane rubbed a hand over her brow. "Well, in a way, yes. It's a whole complicated mess."

"Lunch?" Amy asked. "I was just on my way out to grab a sandwich, and now I need to hear all the sordid details so I can cheer you up."

"Fine," Jane agreed, not really in the mood to talk, but maybe she'd feel better after confiding in her sister. They went to the deli around the corner and chose a quiet table in back so Jane could share her sad tale with a modicum of privacy.

"Tell me everything," Amy said as she bit into her sandwich. "Was she weird? Rude? What?"

Jane picked at her chicken club. "She was . . . . Rosie Taft."

Amy gave her a blank look. "Who?"

"The bookstore owner I evicted last week, the one who invited me for the awkward tea on Sunday?"

Amy's eyes widened. "Oh shit."

"Right." Jane took a half-hearted bite of her sandwich.

"Was she super pissed?" Amy asked.

Jane chewed and swallowed, then reached for her water. "That's putting it mildly."

"Oh, Jane." Amy set down her sandwich and reached across the table, touching Jane's hand. "I'm so sorry. She really can't get past your job, even after all you two have shared online?"

"She . . . well, she was so angry with me for even being there that I never actually told her I'm Brie."

"You didn't tell her?" Amy's voice rose.

"I tried, but she was so upset, and she said some really hurtful things. I've never told anyone before that I'm Brie, and I just couldn't do it while she was so angry. I know that makes me a coward, but I can't help it."

"You aren't a coward, but you do have a tendency to back away from difficult conversations. So, she thought you happened to randomly be at the same bar where she was meeting Brie?"

Jane nodded. "And she very much wanted me to leave."

"This girl sounds like a piece of work," Amy said as she picked up her sandwich. "Maybe it's for the best that you cut ties with her."

Jane heaved a sigh. "She's not, though. She's the nicest person."

"She doesn't sound very nice."

"She inherited the bookstore from her mother, and they've been in that location for thirty years. Maybe I *am* an asshole for kicking her out." The thought had been tugging uncomfortably at Jane ever since she left the bar last night.

"Except it was never about her," Amy said. "We don't know the personal history of the renters in the buildings we purchase. How could we?"

"Well, maybe we should, because now a perfectly nice woman hates me for doing my job, and I feel like shit about it." She pushed her sandwich away. She'd picked at it until the bread fell apart, and now she didn't even want it.

"Oh wow," Amy said, going serious. "You really like her."

Jane sipped her water. "I do like her, and she was sweet to Alyssa. Remember?"

"Oh, *that* bookstore owner," Amy said. "I had forgotten she was the one who helped Alyssa pick out those books. So wait, the woman who had both you and Lyss swooning that day is also your online crush, and now she hates your guts?"

"Essentially, yes."

"Well, shit. What are you going to do?"

"What can I do? I sent her a message to apologize for standing her up last night, and she didn't reply. Now she hates both Jane *and* Brie, I guess."

"Jane, you have to tell her."

Jane grimaced. Last night had been traumatic enough. The idea of disappointing Rosie again made her sick to her stomach. "It's probably easier to just leave it be."

"That might be easier, but Jane, you *like* her, and it's been a long damn time since you've been interested in a woman. Rosie gets you riled up in a way I haven't seen in ages. Don't you owe it to yourself to see if it could be more? And don't you owe it to Rosie to tell her the truth?"

"Even if it means hurting her all over again?" Jane countered. "Because I'm afraid if she knew I was Brie, I might take her favorite author from her in addition to her store."

"Or maybe, if she knew you were Brie, she'd see a side of you she didn't know was there," Amy said. "Maybe it would help her get past your day job and see the real Jane, because you *are* Brie, my dear. We just need Rosie to see that. Plus, I want you to be happy . . . and to not have pretty bookstore owners hating you."

But Jane was already shaking her head. She couldn't bear Rosie's anger on Twitter too. "I can't do it. I just can't."

Later that evening, Jane was at home in her pajamas, attempting to plot her new series, the celebrity series she'd asked Aurelia for her advice on only a few days ago. In the first book, two up-and-coming pop stars realized they were more than friends after collaborating together on a song. Jane needed something high concept, something that would get her the kind of contract that might let her quit her day job. She'd had a call with her agent about it earlier today. But right now, Jane just wanted to hide under the covers and throw herself a pity party for one.

She couldn't stop thinking about Rosie's answer to her question about whether she'd been waiting for a date. *"Guess I'll never know now, will I?"* Rosie had wanted it to be a date, and Jane could hardly stand knowing it, not when she wanted a date with Rosie more than anything.

Her phone had been silent all evening, and she hated it. She was starting to think her sister was right, because surely this was as painful as whatever Rosie might say if Jane told her the truth. Right now, Rosie thought Brie had stood her up, and Jane hated that too.

She sighed, flopping backward in bed. If she were the selfie-taking type, maybe she would just send Rosie a picture and be done with it. She could let Rosie sleuth it out on her own. But Jane had never taken a selfie in her life. She'd feel ridiculous even trying. And a photo would be just another cop-out, really. She either needed to suck it up and tell Rosie the truth to her face, or she needed to put it all behind her and move on with her life.

And right now, she couldn't fathom moving on.

Her stomach clenched as she pulled up Between the Pages' website on her phone, checking the store's hours. It closed at nine, which meant if she left now, she might get there before Rosie left for the night. Was she seriously considering this? Apparently she was, because she slid off the bed and stripped out of her pajamas almost against her will, like her body had rebelled against the commonsense part of her brain.

She pulled on jeans and her favorite hoodie. In the bathroom, she brushed her hair but decided to forgo makeup. If Rosie wanted to meet Brie, she'd show her the real deal. This was the woman who sat at home writing romance novels, not the corporate bitch who'd evicted her from her building. Not to mention that if Jane paused long enough to dress herself up, she might lose her nerve entirely.

As it was, she was physically shaking as she left her apartment. Restless energy propelled her toward the subway station at the end of the block, and she walked so quickly she was out of breath by the time she'd descended to the platform. She boarded a train and sat with her hands twisting anxiously in her lap as she headed uptown toward Between the Pages.

This was a terrible idea. She was going to kill Amy tomorrow for even putting the thought in her head. As she approached the Ninety-Sixth Street station, she checked her phone one last time, almost hoping Rosie would have messaged, that she'd have told Brie off for standing her up, something so harsh that Jane would come to her senses, turn around, and go home.

But there weren't any new messages.

If Jane didn't walk into the store tonight and explain herself, she'd never hear from Rosie again. There was a good chance tonight wouldn't go any better than last night had, but at least Jane would be able to say she'd tried.

Jesus, she felt like a character from one of her books right now. In a romance, this was the part where the protagonists would quit fighting their feelings and have wild sex against a bookshelf, but Jane knew better than to expect any such outcome tonight. Rosie would probably throw her out of the store, wishing she'd never heard of Jane *or* Brie. She liked it a lot better when she was in control of the story. Real life was messy . . . and terrifying.

She shook her head as she exited the train, nerves swarming in her stomach until her whole body was crawling with them. She was practically twitching by the time she made it to Between the Pages' front door, already reaching for the handle before she realized the lights were off. The store was closed. She was too late.

She deflated on the spot, shoulders slumping. Of course, she could come back tomorrow, but deep down, she knew she'd never work up the courage to do this twice. She checked her phone to find that it was ten minutes past nine. Maybe Rosie hadn't left yet. Did she even work on Thursday nights? She had other employees, after all. Jane really hadn't thought this through.

She lifted her hand and knocked on the glass panel on the door. What was the worst that could happen? She'd already come this far. Her knock was louder than she'd expected, and she flinched at the noise. There was no response from inside the store. Rosie was probably long gone, if she'd even worked tonight. Just to be sure, Jane knocked again.

A light flicked on in back. Jane thought it was the stairwell leading to the basement room where she'd attended afternoon tea last weekend. A shadow crossed the doorway, and then Rosie stepped into the store, wearing a blue jacket and a confused expression as she squinted in Jane's direction.

A tingly sensation crept over Jane's skin, because there was no going back now. Rosie's eyes locked on hers, and then she was walking straight toward her as the hesitant smile on her face faded away. She unlocked the door and opened it, brow scrunched.

"Jane? What are you doing here?"

Well, this was a friendlier reception than she'd received last night, and it was probably the best opening she was going to get. Jane tried to ignore the way her pulse raced just from standing this close to her. "Can I come in, just for a minute?"

Rosie hesitated. "What's this about?"

Jane pushed a strand of hair behind her ear, regretting the decision to come here in her jeans and sweatshirt, because right now, she needed her corporate armor to face Rosie. She felt exposed and vulnerable this way. Also, she was freezing without her coat. "There's something I need to tell you."

"It's late for business, isn't it?" Rosie asked, still not inviting her in. Her dog—Brinkley, if Jane remembered correctly—had come up behind her and now stood watching their exchange with bright eyes.

"This has nothing to do with the store or your lease," Jane told her.

Rosie stepped back, motioning her inside. "I suppose I owe you an apology for last night, at the very least."

"It's fine," Jane told her.

"No, it's not," Rosie said, shaking her head so that her blonde curls bounced, looking almost silver in the darkened store. With Brinkley at her heels, she turned and walked toward the counter in back, where she turned on a lamp. "I was rude to you last night, and I'm sorry about that. I got stood up, and I took it out on you, and that wasn't fair."

Jane exhaled. "Thank you. I appreciate that."

"So what did you need to talk to me about?" Rosie asked, fingers tapping against the counter.

Jane gulped, completely lost for words. Instead, she pulled out her phone. *Show, don't tell.* That's what she'd learned in her writing classes, and maybe it could work for her tonight. She pulled up the conversation between Brie and Aurelia and set her phone on the counter, sliding it toward Rosie.

Rosie looked at the phone, and then she recoiled as if it had stung her. "What in the . . . ? These messages are private! How did you get these?"

And Jane had apparently screwed up yet again, because Rosie had misinterpreted what she was trying to say. She pushed out a breath, shaking her head. "These are *my* private messages. You didn't get stood up last night. I . . . I'm Brie."

CHAPTER SEVEN

"What are you talking about?" Rosie spluttered, pressing a palm against her forehead as her mind whirled. There was no way the woman standing in front of her was Brie, the super-sweet author who'd become so important to her. Jane Breslin was the anti-Brie, cold and corporate.

"I'm Brie," Jane repeated quietly, lowering her gaze to the phone still illuminated on the counter between them, displaying their online conversation.

And as Rosie blinked at her in confusion, she realized that the version of Jane standing in front of her right now wasn't cold or corporate. This Jane wore a pink hoodie and no makeup. Her hair was windswept, and her demeanor was hesitant, almost shy. This woman . . . well, she actually looked like what Rosie had imagined Brie might be like. "Shit," she whispered.

"I know." Jane tapped her phone, and the screen went black.

"How . . . how did this happen?"

"Just coincidence, I guess," Jane said with a stiff shrug.

"And you didn't know?"

Jane shook her head. "Not until I walked up to you in the bar last night."

"Why didn't you just tell me then?" Rosie's cheeks were warm, and her heart was pounding. The idea of her online crush and her real-life nemesis being the same person . . .

"I tried," Jane said, still not meeting Rosie's eyes. "You were so angry, and I . . . well, it sounds stupid, but I've never told anyone my pen name before."

"Oh my God." She lifted a hand and dropped it, pressing her palm against the counter to ground herself. She felt . . . disappointed, slightly sick at the thought of Jane being Brie, but at the same time, her pulse sped through her veins as they stood so close to each other in the semi-dark store. Jane licked her lips, and Rosie felt an unmistakable tug of attraction low in her belly. She gave her head a slight shake to clear it. "I don't know what to do with this information."

"That makes two of us," Jane said. "I'm sorry for misleading you last night. I was blindsided, and I panicked."

"I get that," Rosie said, and it was true. She wasn't thinking very clearly right now herself.

Jane watched her quietly, seeming to give Rosie the lead over where the conversation would go from here, and she was struck again by how different Jane looked tonight, younger and more innocent without her expensive suits. She almost wished Jane had worn one tonight just to make it easier for Rosie to remember who she was up against.

"I just . . . I don't know what to say," she mumbled.

Jane nodded. "I'll go."

"No," Rosie blurted. "Wait."

Jane looked up, and her expression was unexpectedly hopeful.

Meanwhile, Rosie had no idea what to say or why she'd even asked her to stay. "I'm sorry. This is a lot to process. I have so many questions, but . . ."

"You could message me?" Jane suggested with a tight smile, and Rosie realized how difficult it must have been for her to come here tonight after the way Rosie had treated her yesterday. Surely, she at least owed her the courtesy of hearing her out.

"No, I think we need to have this conversation face to face," Rosie told her. "Maybe, I don't know . . . do you want to come downstairs and have a cup of tea while we figure things out?"

"Tea at this hour?" Jane asked, her lips quirking.

"The noncaffeinated kind," Rosie said. "Lia stocks every variety imaginable."

"Okay, then," Jane said. "Tea would be nice, thank you."

Rosie shut off the lamp and led the way downstairs. Brinkley followed, toenails clattering on the steps. Jane brought up the rear, silent in her sneakers.

Sneakers.

Rosie still wasn't used to this version of her, and she was completely boggled by the idea that Jane was Brie. It didn't make sense, and maybe that was why she'd asked Jane to stay for tea. She needed to understand, because right now, she had no idea which end was up. "You can sit in my office if you want," she told Jane. "I'll be back with tea in a minute."

"Okay." Jane entered her office, and Brinkley followed, the little traitor.

Rosie ducked into the kitchenette and made a pot of chamomile tea. It was supposed to be calming, right? Well, right now she needed to calm the hell down. She couldn't seem to stand still, bouncing restlessly from foot to foot as she waited for the water to boil. And she was hot. She took off her jacket and clutched it against herself, debating whether to text Lia for emergency guidance, but she didn't really have time for that.

She poured two cups of tea and brought them down the hall to her office. Jane sat in the guest chair, the same chair she'd sat in while telling Rosie she was going to demolish this building, but tonight she was bent forward in her seat, rubbing Brinkley behind his ears while he gazed at her adoringly, and *dammit*, Rosie really did have a soft spot for anyone who was soft for her dog. She set both mugs on the desk and edged around to her chair.

"Thanks." Jane took the mug nearer to her, wrapping her fingers around it as if to warm them. She was probably cold, if she'd come all the way here in nothing but that hoodie. Why had she done that? Why had she done any of the things she'd done?

Rosie sipped her tea, burning her tongue in her impatience. She set down the mug and looked at Jane. "Did you see your books here when you brought your niece in that day?"

Jane nodded. "Yes."

"And you still decided to level the building?" That came out more harshly than Rosie had meant for it to, and Jane flinched.

"The decision had already been made," she said. "The entire project was greenlighted months ago. I didn't know your store was here then, Rosie, but even if I had . . . I probably couldn't have stopped it from happening."

"I wrote to you," Rosie told her. "Years ago. I invited you to the store for a signing."

"I don't remember," Jane said, staring into her tea.

How could you forget? But Rosie held her tongue because she was tired of antagonizing Jane. It wasn't like her, and the woman sitting across from her looked contrite and humble, not like a bulldozing corporate asshole.

"I mean, I remember the email, but I didn't remember your name," Jane said, darting a glance at Rosie. "BPD only bought this building a few months ago, so I never made the connection."

Rosie gripped her mug. "Oh."

"Your email meant a lot to me, because no one else ever invited me to sign," Jane said. "I had never even seen one of my books on a shelf until I came into your store last week."

"Then why didn't you come when I invited you to sign?"

Jane shrugged. "I probably should have, but I was committed to keeping my identity private, especially here in the city where I live."

Why? Rosie wanted to ask, but that felt too personal. Jane wrote lesbian romance, after all, and Rosie presumed she was queer herself, but maybe she wasn't out. Maybe she had to hide her identity to protect herself, and maybe Rosie was the asshole in this situation. She sat back in her chair, sipping her tea and trying to organize the chaos in her brain.

She wanted to like the woman sitting across from her. She'd been attracted to Jane from the moment they met, and now that she knew Jane was Brie . . .

"Oh my God," she blurted as it all came together in her mind. Jane's power suits, and Brie's sexy corporate heroines that had inspired Rosie's suit obsession in the first place.

"What?" Jane asked, looking adorably cozy in her pink hoodie.

"It's just still sinking in," Rosie said, giving her head a shake. "Your heroines are all corporate badasses, and you . . ."

"Are a corporate bitch?" Jane supplied with a wry smile.

"Sometimes," Rosie admitted.

"I never thought of myself that way until I met you." Jane blew on her tea before lifting it for a hesitant sip.

"But you kick people out of their homes for a living. No offense, but how can you feel okay with that?"

Jane pressed her lips together. "Believe it or not, that's not how I define my job."

"How do you define it, then?"

"Well, Breslin Property Development buys land or existing buildings and improves on them, whether by renovating or building new. Here in the city, we often take tired, outdated buildings and turn them into something modern and profitable."

"That's a convenient way of looking at it," Rosie said, "if you're focused on money. I see the people who live in those 'tired' old buildings, people who love their homes. I think old buildings are beautiful. I think *this* space is special and irreplaceable."

"Your space is beautiful," Jane told her. "I'm sorry it had to be this way."

"You could change your mind."

Jane shook her head. "You overestimate my importance in the company."

"Your name is on it, Jane. How am I overestimating the importance of that?"

"That's my father's name on the letterhead," Jane said. "The company is his. The vision is his. My sister and I work there because it was expected of us. One of us will take over for him when he retires, but it won't be me."

"Oh," Rosie said, deflating. "Is that why you write in secret?"

"My family frowns on it," Jane said, again staring into her tea. "They basically think I write porn. It embarrasses them, so I decided to keep it to myself when I was published."

"I'm sorry," Rosie said. "That really sucks. I get so tired of people looking down on romance."

Jane sighed. "I'll tell them eventually."

"So, no one knows you're Brie? No one but me?" That felt unsettlingly intimate.

"You, my sister, my agent, and my editor," Jane said.

"How does your sister feel about it?"

Jane smiled, maybe the first genuine smile Rosie had ever seen from her. "She wants me to quit my day job and shout my pen name from the rooftops."

"I like her already," Rosie said.

"You two would hit it off, I'm sure."

"Is that what you want too?" Rosie asked. "To quit your day job?"

"As soon as I can support myself full time as an author."

"Dammit," Rosie whispered.

"What?"

"You're making it really hard to not like you right now," she admitted.

Jane scoffed, taking another sip of her tea. "Believe it or not, most people don't hate me."

"I don't *hate* you," Rosie said. "I wanted to, but I don't."

"And how do you feel about our online friendship?" Jane asked, again with that hopeful expression that crumbled Rosie's resolve and caused a warm flutter in the pit of her stomach.

"I don't know yet," she admitted. "I think I probably need to sleep on it and see how I feel tomorrow."

"Fair enough," Jane said with a nod.

"For the record, I'm still your biggest fan—and not in a Kathy Bates kind of way. I adore your books, Jane, despite what I think about your day job."

Jane's cheeks turned an adorable shade of pink, and she fidgeted with the mug in her hands. "Thank you."

"You really aren't used to talking about your books, are you?" Rosie had never met an author quite like her, and she'd met a lot of authors.

"No," Jane said, still looking flustered. "If I didn't spend all my spare time at home in my pajamas writing books, I might actually forget I'm Brie."

"I hope you're able to fully embrace your author career," Rosie told her. "It must be hard keeping everything separate."

"It's the only thing I've ever known. Telling people I'm Brie almost feels like coming out all over again," Jane said, answering Rosie's earlier unasked question. "It's intimidating, so I'm not in any hurry."

Rosie nodded. She'd finished her tea, and so had Jane. It was late, and she was tired and confused and becoming increasingly smitten with Jane the longer she sat here.

"I should go," Jane said, echoing what was probably written all over Rosie's face.

"We both should," she said, standing. "It's late."

"It is," Jane agreed. She picked up her bag and slung it over her shoulder.

"I'll let us out the back," Rosie told her as she put on her jacket and gathered her things. Brinkley stood, too, tail wagging as he walked over to stand beside her. She clipped on his leash and led the way out of her office. They went up the stairs and out the back door into the alley behind the shop.

Jane was quiet as Rosie led the way onto East Ninety-Fifth Street, and then she hooked a thumb over her shoulder in the direction of the subway. "I'm that way."

Rosie could easily walk that way too. Her apartment was only a few blocks away, but it seemed easier to part ways now, so she took a step backward, indicating that she was walking in the opposite direction.

"Thanks for the tea," Jane said as she turned away. "Good night, Rosie."

Rosie's mind flashed to Jane leaving the bar last night and the unusual question she'd asked on her way out the door. "Jane . . ."

She turned back. "Yes?"

"Why did you ask me if I was waiting for a date last night?" Suddenly, that felt enormously important. She remembered Jane's slinky black dress . . . the dress she'd worn to meet Rosie.

Jane's eyes widened, and when she exhaled, her breath crystalized in the air between them. "I . . ."

"Did *you* want it to be a date?" Rosie pushed, because she had suggested coffee, and Jane was the one who'd suggested drinks, and now Rosie could hardly breathe.

"I don't know," Jane said, but she had a terrible poker face. She dropped her gaze to the sidewalk, biting her lower lip.

Rosie couldn't seem to stop staring at Jane's mouth. She stepped forward almost involuntarily, tripping over Brinkley's leash in the process. Jane's hand shot out to steady her, landing on her shoulder. It was the first time they'd touched, and *oh* how Rosie wished she could feel

Jane's fingers through her coat. They were standing way too close now, and Rosie's pulse raced until her head felt fuzzy with anticipation. She swayed forward, and her lips met Jane's. She felt Jane's inhale and her hand tightening on Rosie's shoulder, drawing her closer.

Jane made a little sound, almost a moan. Her lips were as cool as the night air around them, and yet they filled Rosie with an immediate rush of warmth. Jane pressed forward, and Rosie settled her hands on her hips, discovering that the hoodie was as soft as it looked.

Jane's lips were also impossibly soft . . . and sexy as hell as they moved against Rosie's. Before she knew it, Jane was nipping at her lower lip, much the way she'd done to herself a minute ago, and Rosie went weak at the knees. Arousal licked through her, the kind of chemistry she hadn't felt in so long, and now it was burning her up with an almost overpowering intensity.

She pulled back, somewhat relieved to see that Jane was breathing just as hard, looking just as dazed, her lips wet and glistening as she blinked at Rosie.

"Whoa," Rosie said.

"Yeah," Jane agreed, shoving her hands into her pockets. She had to be freezing out here in that hoodie. Why hadn't she put on a real jacket tonight?

Rosie didn't want to look too hard at the answer. "I'll message you tomorrow, okay?"

Jane nodded. She reached out to give Rosie's hand a squeeze, and then she turned and walked away, her stride as brisk and purposeful as if she wore one of her power suits.

Jesus. This Jane really was *that* Jane.

The leash in Rosie's hand jerked as Brinkley attempted to follow Jane down the sidewalk, breaking Rosie from her trance. She touched her lips as she began to walk in the opposite direction. That kiss . . . holy shit. Her online crush, her real-life crush, and the woman who'd crushed her dreams were all the same person, and her mind was still struggling to snap all the pieces into place.

She walked home in a daze, allowing Brinkley to guide her from one edge of the sidewalk to the other as he found things he wanted to sniff. Jane Breslin was Brie, and Rosie had kissed her, both of which were plot twists she'd never seen coming and had no idea how to handle now that they'd happened.

By the time she let herself into her apartment, she was starting to freak out. Lia, Nikki, and Paige were in the living room watching *Love It or List It*, a home-renovation show, which felt a bit ironic at the moment. Lia glanced at Rosie. "You're late tonight."

"Yeah, I got . . . held up." And she was bursting to talk about it, but suddenly she was unsure if she should. Jane had entrusted her with her identity tonight, and maybe Rosie needed to keep that to herself to keep Jane's confidence.

"You okay?" Lia asked, giving her another look as Rosie bent to unclip Brinkley's leash. He headed for his dog bed in the living room, spun twice, and curled into a little ball.

"No," Rosie admitted. "I just kissed someone, and I really need to tell you about it, but I think I need to protect her identity."

Lia's eyes rounded behind her glasses. "Whoa. Hold up. You just kissed someone?"

"I did," Rosie said, fingers shaking as she unbuttoned her jacket and slipped out of it.

"Holy shit." Nikki paused the TV. "This is completely unexpected."

"Was it someone you wanted to kiss?" Lia asked. "Because you look kind of upset."

"I'm upset, but not about the kiss." Rosie dropped into the empty chair beside the couch. "It's complicated."

"Then let us uncomplicate it," Paige said, leaning forward to hug her knees. "Who is she?"

How should she answer that? "Um . . . Brie."

"What?" Lia exclaimed. "Back up . . . you met Brie?"

"I did. She came to the store as I was closing up to explain what happened last night, and we talked, and as we were saying good night . . . I kissed her, or she kissed me. Kind of a mutual effort, I guess."

"Whoa, whoa," Lia said. "This is huge. What's she like? I need to know everything."

"Well, that's where it gets complicated, because apparently the only other people who know her identity are her sister, her agent, and her editor, which means . . . I don't think I can tell you who she is, although I didn't think to ask her about that specifically."

"Damn, Rosie, this feels like something out of one of your books," Paige said with a giddy smile. "You met your favorite author—who you've had an online crush on for months now—and minutes later, you two are kissing?"

"I know." She swallowed. "It's a lot to process."

Lia was still staring at her, eyes narrowed. "I feel like I'm missing something, because you should be *giddy* about meeting and kissing Brie, and you're not."

"You are missing something," Rosie told her. "And I *so* wish I could tell you what it is, believe me."

"Well, give me a hint," Lia pressed.

She opened her mouth and closed it, needing a moment to think through what she could and couldn't say. "I have an issue with her day job."

"Can't be that much of an issue if you kissed her," Nikki said.

"It's a pretty major issue," Rosie said. "I don't know how to get past it, honestly."

Lia sat up straight on the couch. "Bloody hell. Does this have anything to do with the person you ran into at the bar last night?"

Oh shit. Well, there was no point denying it. If the look on Lia's face was any indication, she already knew. "Yes."

"Oh my *God*," Lia blurted. "Oh, that's very complicated indeed."

"Well, this isn't fair," Nikki said with a pout.

Rosie pressed her lips together, staring at her lap. This was a mess. She already felt like she was betraying Jane, and now she was acting like an ass to her friends too. "I'm sorry. I think I need to figure this out on my own, or at least have another conversation with her first."

Lia stood, shaking her head. "I need to talk to you for a minute in your room."

CHAPTER EIGHT

Rosie shut her bedroom door and turned to face Lia.

"Please tell me you didn't kiss Jane Breslin tonight," Lia said, hands on her hips.

"Shh," Rosie whispered. "Keep your voice down. I'm as surprised as you are, honestly. I am *reeling*."

"How did this happen?" Lia asked. "How did you find out she's Brie?"

"She came to the store as I was closing, and she told me."

"I can't believe . . ." Lia gave her head a quick shake. "I cannot believe that woman is a romance author, for one thing. Did she know who you were all along?"

"No. She had no idea until she saw me at the bar last night."

"Why didn't she just tell you then?" Lia asked.

"Because she's very private about her identity, and I was busy biting her head off." Rosie paced from one end of the room to the other, ridiculously relieved to be able to unpack this with Lia after all.

"And what changed her mind?"

"Her conscience, ironically enough," Rosie said. "She felt bad about lying to me last night."

"And how does she feel about terminating your lease?" Lia asked. "Because the last time I checked, you hated her for that."

Rosie plopped onto her bed. "I know. I did. I *do*. I don't know how I feel anymore."

Lia sat beside her, squeezing her hand the way Jane had done before she walked away. "Talk to me."

"She says she's only working at Breslin Property Development because it's what her family expected of her. They sound kind of shitty, honestly, except maybe her sister. She wants to quit and write full time, but she can't afford it."

"Interesting. And how did you feel when you talked to her tonight, knowing she's Brie?" Lia asked.

"Confused, mostly," Rosie admitted. "She was so different tonight, Lia. She was reserved and sincere and almost . . . sweet."

"Well, just to play devil's advocate here, but she's always struck me as a decent person. You saw her as the enemy—and rightfully so—because she sent your lease-termination letter, but she was just doing her job, and it seems that maybe she's more passionate about writing romance than kicking people out of their places of business, so I don't think this is an impossible situation."

"I don't know how to feel about any of it," Rosie admitted, leaning to the side to rest her head on Lia's shoulder.

Lia brushed a hand through her hair, giving her a reassuring pat on the back. "You were attracted to her from the first moment you laid eyes on her."

"I was," Rosie confirmed.

"And you had your online crush on Brie."

"Yep."

"You're always telling me about the sweet and thoughtful things Brie says to you," Lia said. "If I recall correctly, she even tried to cheer you up after you found out you were losing the store."

"She did." Rosie had forgotten about that, at least since she'd found out that the woman sending those supportive messages was the same one who'd evicted her.

"Obviously this is just my opinion, and you have to decide what to do on your own, but I think you owe it to yourself to see her again, to talk when you're less emotional and have had a chance to process all of this."

"I need to think first," Rosie said. "And sleep. I'm too tired to figure this out tonight."

"Good plan." Lia gave her another pat on the back. "And maybe tomorrow you'll send her a message. Just say hi, and then take it from there."

Jane did an extremely uncharacteristic thing the following morning and took a personal day. She was out of sorts after her encounter with Rosie last night, both emotionally and in her feelings about her day job. Today, she wanted to be Brie. She needed to funnel the turmoil inside her onto the page. She didn't have the first book in her new series fully plotted yet, but as she sat cross-legged in her pajamas in the middle of her bed, the words just came pouring out.

She wrote two angsty scenes and then sat back to stretch her cramped muscles. Someday, this would be her life. She could ditch her suit collection and become a hermit. Actually, that was her biggest worry about becoming a full-time author. She feared she'd never leave home. Her inner introvert would finally prevail.

There was one person she would happily leave her apartment for, though. Rosie had been a constant presence in Jane's mind since their kiss last night. Her pulse jumped every time she remembered the warm press of Rosie's lips against hers, and she'd thought about it a *lot*. In fact, she couldn't seem to stop thinking about it, or about Rosie in general. Jane wanted to kiss her again, although she wasn't sure she'd get the chance. She wanted a real date with her. She just wanted Rosie, plain and simple, even though nothing between them was simple.

Jane climbed out of bed and changed into jogging shorts and a sports bra to spend some time on her stationary bike, peddling through her frustration, and then she hopped in the shower. Afterward, her empty stomach led her to get dressed and head out in search of lunch. She packed up her laptop and brought it with her, deciding to work while she ate.

In the back of her mind, she wondered whether she should message Rosie, but she felt like she'd left the ball in Rosie's court last night. Rosie was the one who needed to decide if she could put professional differences aside or if she even wanted to see Jane again. For now, she would sit back and wait for Rosie to make the next move.

Jane bought a sandwich at the bodega down the street and brought it with her to East River Park, in the mood for some fresh air. Why didn't she take personal days more often? She sat on a bench facing the river, closing her eyes to soak in the crisp fall air and the sounds of conversation as people passed her by. She was stuck on the next scene in her book, and hopefully this would help.

After a few minutes, she unwrapped her sandwich and began to eat, taking the opportunity to do some people-watching. A family walked past, kids in brightly colored coats chasing each other down the sidewalk. Here and there, tourists leaned against the railing, snapping photos of the choppy water with the Williamsburg Bridge as a backdrop. She saw businessmen and women out for a lunchtime walk and couples sneaking a midday rendezvous.

And her mind started to spin with ideas of her pop-star heroine sitting on a bench like this one as she wrote new music, using the passersby for inspiration much the way Jane currently was. She pulled out her laptop and began to type. Skye—her heroine—had just realized the song she was writing was actually about her fellow pop star, Lucy, when Jane's phone began to ring, displaying Amy's name on the screen.

Jane closed her laptop and answered with a smile. "Miss me already?"

"Why aren't you at work today?" her sister asked. "I was worried, especially after your disastrous date the other night."

"I took a personal day," Jane told her. "I'm fine. I just didn't want to have to talk to people today . . . other than you, of course."

"Well, as long as *I'm* not on your shit list."

"Never," Jane said.

"I'm jealous you gave yourself a three-day weekend, as long as you're using it for fun things and not moping about what happened with Rosie."

"No moping involved," Jane said. "Actually, I went to her shop last night and told her the truth."

"Oh my God!" Amy exclaimed. "You told her you're Brie?"

"Keep your voice down," Jane said. "Unless your office door is shut. And yes, I did."

"Wow, Jane, this is huge. What happened?"

"She was upset and confused—about how I felt when I found out, I guess. But we talked, and I think it went well overall. She served me tea." Jane paused, touching her lips involuntarily. "And then she kissed me."

"Holy shit!"

"Right. So . . . stay tuned."

"How did you leave things last night?" Amy asked.

"She said she'd message me today. Hopefully she does."

"And if she doesn't?"

Jane watched as a group of teenagers cruised by on skateboards. "I don't know yet. I feel like she should make the next move. I laid out all my cards for her. She's the one who has to decide if she can get past my day job."

"Okay, that's fair, but if she doesn't follow up today, maybe you could send her something innocuous, one of those quote memes you like or something," Amy suggested.

"Maybe," Jane said. "I'm playing it by ear for now and hoping she follows up on her own."

"I hope so too. These are *very* exciting developments. This is a big deal for you, not only on the dating front but also sharing your author persona with someone. I've been waiting for you to open up to someone for years, and I'm thrilled for you."

"Thanks," Jane told her, cheeks warming.

"Keep me posted," Amy said. "I mean it. I'm going to need regular and extremely detailed updates."

"Geez," Jane said with a laugh. "Nosy much?"

"You bet your ass I am," Amy said. "I've got to run to a meeting, but seriously, message me. And come over for dinner this weekend? Alyssa wants to see you."

"Sure," Jane said. "Text me and let me know when."

She finished the call and set her phone on the bench beside her. Then she opened her laptop and spent the next twenty minutes working on her outline before she got any further into drafting. She'd only write herself into a corner if she didn't take the time to figure out where she was going first.

Then, outline complete, she replied to an email from her agent, Pilar, asking how the new book was coming. Pilar was eager to get her a new contract—and so was Jane, for that matter.

She packed up and stood, needing to stretch her legs before she did any more work. She shouldered her laptop bag and began to walk. A small passenger boat chugged by on the river, its wake spreading a V of waves that eventually lapped against the seawall beside her. Her phone chimed with a notification, and she lunged to grab it from her bag, hoping for a message from Rosie.

@AureliaRose113: Hi. It's really weird to know who I'm messaging.
@BrieWrites: It is weird! How's your Friday going?

@AureliaRose113: Spent the morning with my Realtor, looking at new storefronts.

@BrieWrites: Anything promising?

@AureliaRose113: Not even a little bit.

@BrieWrites: I'm sorry.

@AureliaRose113: Thanks. And how's your Friday?

@BrieWrites: I did a very un-me thing and took the day off.

@AureliaRose113: Interesting! So what are you doing with your free time?

@BrieWrites: Writing and people watching.

@AureliaRose113: Want to grab a coffee with me? I think I'm ready to be more civil than I was last night.

@BrieWrites: You were perfectly civil and understandably upset.

@BrieWrites: And yes to coffee. Just let me know where to meet you.

@AureliaRose113: Where are you now?

@BrieWrites: East River Park.

@AureliaRose113: I'm not that far from you, actually. Know a good place nearby?

Jane sent her the name and address of her favorite local coffee shop and then stood by the railing, staring out at the water while she got her breathing under control. Her heart was pounding as if she'd just finished a session on her stationary bike, and there was a tingly feeling in her stomach.

She and Rosie were going to have coffee. This would be their first encounter where there weren't any surprises or revelations to be made, just two women enjoying a drink together and hopefully re-creating the rapport they shared on Twitter in a real-life situation.

Jane wished she had a compact in her bag to check her appearance. Certainly, her hair was windblown, but at least she'd put on makeup before she left her apartment. She set off in the direction of the coffee shop, hoping the walk would help settle her nerves.

She got there before Rosie, so she messaged her to ask for her coffee order, then used the kiosk by the door to order her cappuccino and Rosie's flat white. Ten minutes later, she had just sat down at a little table near the window with their drinks when she saw Rosie coming through the door.

Rosie's cheeks were pink from the cool air, and her blonde curls were tousled from the wind, and Jane's pulse spiked at the sight. She lifted her hand to wave, and Rosie turned toward her with the sort of easy smile that Jane imagined she gave most people in her life. Jane had received it herself that first day in Between the Pages, when she was with Alyssa.

"Hi," Rosie said as she stopped at their table. "Thanks for the coffee."

"No problem," Jane said.

Rosie sat across from her and began unbuttoning her coat. "You buy me too many drinks."

"Well, you've made me a lot of tea," Jane countered, not sure how to take Rosie's comment.

They shared a beat of uncomfortable silence, both of them becoming unnaturally interested in their drinks. Jane wanted to ask more about Rosie's real estate search, but she didn't want to bring up a contentious topic. Actually, as she sipped her cappuccino, she couldn't think of a single safe subject.

"I don't want things to be awkward," Rosie said finally.

"I don't either," Jane said with a sigh. "I don't want to bring up things that are uncomfortable for you."

"What if we act like two people who just met?" Rosie suggested. "Because in a way, we are. Let's just forget about the bookstore for a little while."

"Yes," Jane said, relieved. "That's a good idea."

"Do you live near here?" Rosie asked, watching Jane as she sipped her coffee.

"I do, just a few blocks over," Jane said. "I love the Village."

"I don't spend much time down this way," Rosie said. "Do you live by yourself?"

Jane nodded. "I have a one bedroom on Seventh."

"Fancy," Rosie commented, and Jane remembered that she lived with three roommates.

"It was a necessary splurge," Jane told her. "I'm a bit of a hermit when I'm not at the office, and making conversation with roommates can be exhausting."

"You're an introvert," Rosie observed.

"Yes."

"And I'm an extrovert with a capital *E*." She smiled, and Jane felt herself starting to relax.

"I noticed that about you," she told Rosie. "What do you like to do for fun, besides reading?"

"I love to wander the city and find random amazing spots that only the locals know about. I have a whole gallery on my phone of my favorites."

"Will you show me sometime?" Jane asked, curious to see all the places Rosie had discovered. She was more of an observer by nature.

"Sure," Rosie said.

"What else do you do for fun?"

"I hang out with my friends, take my dog to the park, and, well . . . I read a *lot*."

Jane smiled into her coffee. "I could spend an entire afternoon talking to you about books."

"I could spend an entire afternoon talking about *your* books," Rosie countered.

Jane's cheeks warmed. "I'd rather not."

"Okay, so no talk about books or bookstores," Rosie said, lips twisting slightly to one side, and Jane had the uncomfortable feeling she'd misstepped . . . again. "Do you have any pets?" Rosie asked.

"No," Jane told her. "Unless houseplants count."

"That depends," Rosie said slyly. "Do they have names?"

Jane laughed, shaking her head. "No."

"Then no," Rosie said. "I'm actually surprised that a self-professed homebody like yourself doesn't have a pet."

Jane sipped her cappuccino. "I didn't have pets growing up, so I guess I never thought about it."

"You're good with Brinkley," Rosie told her.

"He's hard not to like."

"Very true," Rosie agreed. "I could see you with a cat, though."

"I don't know a thing about cats," Jane said. "And to be honest, they freak me out a little bit."

Rosie lifted her cup. "How so?"

"They don't blink when they stare at you."

"That's true," Rosie said. "What about friends? Do you have many of those?"

"I keep in touch with a few people from college," Jane said, "but mostly on social media. And I go out for drinks with my coworkers sometimes."

Rosie's smile looked forced. This wasn't working, and Jane didn't know how to make it better. She liked Rosie so much, but the harder she tried, the more stilted their conversation seemed to become.

"I guess we need to address the elephant in the room after all," Rosie said finally. She leaned back in her chair and crossed her arms over her chest.

"Which one?" Jane asked, because there were so many minefields for them to avoid. Jane's day job. Last night's kiss. The fact that she had trouble talking about Brie.

Rosie's lips quirked. "I meant our impasse over the store."

Jane looked down at her hands. "I don't know what to say to make it any less awkward."

"It's not so much awkward as it is painful, at least for me," Rosie said, and the hurt in her voice was palpable.

"I'm—"

"I don't want you to apologize again." Rosie waved a hand in front of her face. "I just . . . I don't know where to go from here. I like chatting with you. I think that under other circumstances, we could have been friends, maybe even more than friends, but the reality is that there are so many topics that are off limits to us, I don't see how it could work."

"Oh." Jane fiddled with her empty coffee cup as her heart sank. Here she'd been hoping this would be a fresh start for them, and Rosie had been on the other side of the table deciding she was done.

"It's all too raw for me right now. Maybe in a few months, once I've found a new storefront and gotten Between the Pages back up and running, we can try again."

Jane nodded, gripping her empty cup.

"We can still chat on Twitter," Rosie offered.

"Sure," Jane said as tears pressed behind her eyes and her throat clenched painfully. "Well, you know how to reach me."

"I do," Rosie said with a nod.

Jane stood and slipped into her jacket. She reached for her laptop bag and swung it over her shoulder, but somehow she managed to snag it in her hair, and there she was, standing in the middle of one of her favorite coffee shops, head cocked awkwardly to the side as she tried to free her hair from the strap of her laptop bag, and those tears were still threatening to break free. "Dammit," she muttered, squeezing her eyes shut as she tried to get control.

"Hold still. I've got it." Rosie's fingers brushed against Jane's, and her warm scent reached Jane's nose, something sweet like honey. Rosie carefully freed her hair, smoothed out the strap against her back, and stepped out of Jane's space.

Jane turned to face her. "Thank you, and good luck with the store. I really do hope everything works out for you." And then she turned and left before she did something really embarrassing, like cry over a lost relationship that had never been real in the first place.

CHAPTER NINE

Rosie watched Jane go, feeling a tug of regret. Jane looked genuinely upset, and Rosie hadn't expected that. She'd thought Jane would agree that it didn't make sense to start a relationship right now when things were so fraught between them because of the store. Jane had seemed to be the more practical of the two of them, the least emotional.

And now Rosie had the uncomfortable feeling that she'd hurt her. She didn't like to hurt people. But as they drank coffee and skirted around all the realities of their lives that didn't mesh, Rosie had felt like she was postponing the inevitable. She liked Brie. She even liked Jane. But she didn't like Jane Breslin, and in the end, they were all the same person.

Rosie couldn't date or even be friends with the woman who had kicked her out of her store. At least, not right now. She meant what she'd said. In a few months, if she was up and running in a new location, maybe she could put all this behind her and look ahead to a future that included Jane.

With a sigh, Rosie put on her jacket and headed for the door. After a fruitless morning of real estate showings, she needed the comfort of her store . . . and her best friend. Lia had stayed behind to run the shop, and Rosie's morning hadn't been nearly as fun without her.

Rosie boarded the subway and headed uptown. While she rode, she pulled a book out of her bag and began to read. It was a corporate lesbian romance by a new-to-her author that sounded similar to Brie's books, but this one lacked the emotional punch Rosie had come to expect from Brie. She wanted to feel it when the characters on the page were hurting, when they were happy, and when they were madly in love.

This book left her cold. She wanted to message Brie and tell her about it, but she couldn't now that the real-life Jane had run out of a coffee shop not thirty minutes ago, visibly upset. What a mess.

Instead, Rosie powered on with her current read. The book wasn't terrible, but she probably wasn't going to revisit this author in the future. When the train pulled into her station, she put the book away and joined the stream of passengers headed for the street overhead. A few minutes later, she stepped inside Between the Pages, immediately calmed by the familiar space.

This store felt more like home than any apartment she'd ever lived in. It was embedded in her soul and her memories of her mother. And she'd find a new storefront to keep Between the Pages alive if it was the last thing she did, even if it meant sacrificing a potential relationship with Jane.

"How did it go?" Lia asked from behind the counter. She had her laptop open there and was typing away, probably updating one of the many spreadsheets that kept the store running like a well-oiled machine.

"Total bust," Rosie told her. "One space we looked at had roaches all over the floor. I barely made it through the front door."

"It's okay," Lia said. "We're just getting started. I've saved a whole list of places I think we should reconsider, spaces we discounted the first time for whatever reason but that might be worth a second look."

"Okay, and I think we might need to increase the amount of rent we're willing to pay, but I'm not sure how to increase our profits to compensate."

"It will come to you," Lia said. "I'll run the numbers to figure out exactly how far we can afford to go, but you're the one who's good at figuring out the value-added ideas to help increase our revenue."

"I've been thinking about that," Rosie said as she took off her jacket and stepped behind the counter with Lia. Brinkley popped out of his bed and trotted over to greet her. "And I have a few ideas, like expanding our selection of subscription boxes. I wondered if we could offer a more expensive box that includes an autographed book and higher-end swag."

"Autographed books, hmm?" Lia said, tapping her lips thoughtfully. "I love that idea, but do you think it's practical?"

"My experience with the authors we've worked with so far has been that they're mostly eager to participate in promotional ideas if it leads to more exposure and sales for them."

"And I know which author you'll ask first," Lia said with a smirk.

Rosie grimaced. "I could ask Jane, but . . . it just feels like every time I interact with her, things get even more awkward. And I'm pretty sure I hurt her feelings just now."

"How? Did you see her while you were out?" Lia asked.

"We had coffee, and it was . . . I don't know. It was weird. She didn't want to talk about her books, and I didn't want to talk about my store, and that only left trivial stuff. It's like . . . I want to like her. I *do* like her. But I just don't see a way around our roadblocks."

"Generally, the best way to tackle difficult things is to go through, not around," Lia commented. "There's a spark between you two. I've seen it, and obviously it keeps pulling you back together, despite the circumstances."

Rosie sighed as she scooped Brinkley into her arms for a kiss. She couldn't deny the spark. Her head and her libido were in definite disagreement there. "Right now I've got to focus on saving the store, and that feels harder to do with the woman who signed my lease-termination letter sitting across from me. So I told her that we shouldn't see each other again until after I've gotten things settled with the store."

"Wow," Lia said, blinking behind her glasses. "That's a strong stance."

"It felt like the right thing at the time," Rosie said, feeling a pinch in her chest as she remembered the way Jane had left the coffee shop, flustered and rushed, the opposite of her usual cool demeanor. "I didn't think she'd care, and I thought I'd be saving myself from the future heartbreak of trying to date her, knowing what she did."

"But she did care," Lia said. "Because she *does* care, Ro. This store is your whole life, but I think you sometimes forget that for most people, a job is just a job. She's more than the woman who signed your lease-termination letter."

"She's so much more than that," Rosie agreed, remembering the warmth of Jane's kiss and the sincerity in her eyes as she apologized for the letter. "I just . . . I tried, and I don't think I can do this with her right now. I have to focus on the store first."

"Fair enough," Lia said. "Let's find you a new storefront, then."

Jane buried herself in work for the next week, determined to put her ill-timed infatuation with Rosie behind her. She went through the motions at the office, attending meetings and overseeing the architectural plans for the Lexington Avenue project while she scouted new properties for BPD to acquire.

But every time she viewed a property, she found herself looking at the existing tenants. No matter how old or out of date a building was, it was their home. She couldn't seem to unsee the reality Rosie had shown her.

And to that end, Jane spent every free moment at home working on her new book. As her characters pined for each other on the page, all she had to do was look inside her own heart for inspiration, because she was pining right now, big time.

Yesterday, she'd sent a few sample chapters to her agent for feedback. She hoped this series could land her a bigger contract and let her get serious about making Brie her full-time career, no matter how terrifying that felt.

If her time with Rosie had taught her anything, it was that she needed to quit her day job. She'd always wanted to be a full-time author, and now she was more motivated than ever to make it happen.

Jane checked her phone, hoping against hope she might have heard from Rosie, but the screen—as usual these days—was blank. They'd exchanged a few scattered messages over the last week, but they'd been brief and impersonal. Rosie had moved Jane to the back burner while she found a new home for her store, and Jane respected that.

It still hurt, though. Jane had finally made a connection with someone, and now she'd gone and fucked it up, because . . . of course she had. Thank God she was better at writing romance than finding it in real life. On impulse, she sent Rosie a meme that said, "Fueled by sunshine and rainbows," because it made her smile and the woman in the graphic had bouncy blonde curls. How did she miss someone so much whom she'd only met in person a handful of times?

"Hello, Jane."

She looked up in surprise at the sound of her father's voice. He didn't come by her office very often. Usually, she had to seek him out on her own if she wanted to see him. "Hi, Dad."

He stood in her doorway in his usual gray suit. Jane was convinced he must have an entire closetful of identical suits, like uniforms. "Your mother asked me to confirm that you've made your travel plans for Thanksgiving."

Jane blinked, realizing she hadn't replied to her mother's email on the subject, nor had she booked her flight. It was a tradition her parents had initiated a few years back, traveling somewhere new as a family each Thanksgiving as a way of celebrating the things they had to be thankful for that year, namely the success of the business. This year, they'd be roasting a turkey in their rental cabin in Breckenridge, Colorado. "I haven't, but I'll do it this weekend, I promise."

"Please do, so your mother will stop nagging us both," he said wryly.

A smile tugged at her lips. "Sorry. I've had a lot on my mind the last few weeks, but I've got Mom's email starred in my inbox with all the details. Look, I'm setting a reminder on my phone right now." She picked it up and tapped in the reminder as he watched, hoping he wouldn't notice the way her breath caught as she saw the new message from Rosie on the screen.

"I appreciate it. All right, I'll let you get back to work. See you tomorrow." With a wave, he headed toward the elevator. After decades of long hours, he'd been making an effort to leave on time lately, and Jane knew this was spearheaded by her mother, who had pushed him to delegate, to slow down, to enjoy life outside the office as he approached his retirement years.

She knew he felt comfortable doing that with Amy and Jane managing most of the daily operations these days. He'd be so disappointed in her when she quit. So would her mother. And their disappointment would only grow when they learned she'd quit to pursue a career writing sexy books.

Jane sighed, rubbing at the tension headache brewing behind her eyebrows. Then she picked up her phone to see what Rosie had written.

@AureliaRose113: Add a book to that meme, and it's me!

@AureliaRose113: A woman came into the store looking for a book about two women falling in love, with a happy ending. She said she'd never read a story like that before. I recommended On the Flip Side.

@BrieWrites: You're putting a lot of pressure on me for her first lesrom! I hope she likes it, and thank you for the rec.

@AureliaRose113: I wanted to start her off with the best.

@BrieWrites: I'm blushing (seriously).

@AureliaRose113: Speaking of your books, I'm putting together a new series of subscription boxes that contain an autographed book and a letter from the author along with some themed goodies and swag. Would you be interested in participating?

@BrieWrites: Of course. You've got most of my contact info already, but feel free to call if you want to go over any details. 212-555-5935

@AureliaRose113: Thank you. I appreciate it.

Jane spun her chair to face the window, where Manhattan gleamed in an endless maze of interconnected buildings. Her heart thumped in her chest, and her tongue—should she try to speak out loud—was hopelessly twisted. She was flustered by Rosie's praise and ridiculously excited about the prospect of the subscription boxes. Not only would she get to see Rosie again, but it would also be a great opportunity for her as an author, and as she worked to grow her career, this would be a solid step forward.

Her phone started to ring, and Jane almost vaulted out of her chair in some kind of nervous overreaction, because she'd just given Rosie her number, but her agent's name flashed on the screen. Pilar had said she would call after she read Jane's sample chapters, and now she was anxious for an entirely different reason.

"Hello?" Jane said as she connected the call.

"Jane, it's Pilar," her agent said. "Do you have a minute to chat?"

"I do," Jane told her as she stood and crossed her office to shut the door.

"Perfect," Pilar said. "I just read the material you sent me, and I have a few thoughts."

"Okay," Jane said.

"I think you're off to a great start. I love Skye and Lucy, and the world you've created for them is exciting and a fresh new direction for you. But you told me that you'd like this to be your breakout series, so I think we should look at a few ideas that could really elevate your concept."

"Okay," Jane said as she sat, tapping her fingers idly against the desk. "Is there something specific you'd like me to focus on?"

"Tropes, to start," Pilar said. "You need as many big-ticket words as you can get in there to hook publishers and, later, readers. This is a celebrity romance, so what if you play up a rivalry between your heroines? Readers love an enemies-to-lovers or even rivals-to-lovers story."

"Yes," Jane said, grabbing a notepad to jot down notes. "I love that idea."

"Maybe they're in competition for the same award," Pilar suggested. "And let's see if we can come up with a few other ideas to pump up the appeal."

She and Jane spent several more minutes on the phone together. Pilar was full of good advice, but when Jane hung up the phone, she felt deflated. She'd hoped her concept would be solid on its own, and now she had to go back to the drawing board. This was why she had an agent, though, and Pilar's instincts were usually dead on.

With a sigh, she packed up to head home. As she waited for the elevator, she remembered her last interaction with Rosie. Would she call?

The stack of books hit the floor with a horrific thud, glossy hardcovers and paperbacks sliding past each other onto the carpet, and for a moment, Rosie just stared in horror. Then she dropped to her knees, hoping she hadn't bent or scratched any of their covers.

"Did you decide to demolish the building by yourself, or what?" Lia asked as she poked her head out from the hallway in back.

"Just dropped this week's shipment of new releases all over the floor," Rosie grumbled as she carefully stacked books back onto the rolling cart she'd used to bring them to the shelves.

"Need a hand?" Without waiting for an answer, Lia crouched beside her and began picking up books.

"Thanks," Rosie said.

"You're distracted," Lia observed.

"No kidding." She laughed without humor. "It feels like time's flying all of a sudden. October's halfway over. I'll be closing these doors before I know it, and I haven't found a new space yet."

"You will," Lia said. "The perfect space is out there. I just know it."

"I'm scared it's not," Rosie admitted, groaning as she discovered a book with a bent cover from her careless slip. She'd have to discount this one.

"Have patience," Lia said. "It's not time to worry yet."

But that time was coming, and soon. In the meantime, Rosie was doing her best to focus on comforting routines like shelving new releases while her future crumbled before her. Next weekend, a popular women's fiction author she adored—Darcy Fine—would have a signing here in the store, and that was something to look forward to, at least. She needed more of those.

"I think we should have a party," Rosie said.

"Darling, I've been begging you for weeks to plan something for your birthday. Let's do it."

"Not a birthday party," Rosie clarified. "A farewell party here at the store, where hopefully I'll be telling people where to find us after we move. It can double as a Christmas party. I just think we should do something special here before we leave, you know? Invite authors and readers, have a big bash."

"I am one hundred and ten percent on board with your holiday slash farewell party," Lia said with a nod. "But first, we need to make plans for your birthday. You're turning thirty, Ro. It's a big deal. Let's do something fun."

"I'm just not in the mood," she said as she placed the last fallen book on the cart and stood. She was distraught over having to find a new home for the store. Truly, she hadn't felt this helpless since the days when she'd sat beside her mother's hospital bed, watching her fade away.

And as much as she hated to admit it, she missed Jane. She'd come to count on their daily interactions more than she'd realized, not to mention the way her whole body buzzed with awareness every time they were in a room together.

"Just so you know, I'm not letting you work that day," Lia said, dragging Rosie from her thoughts.

She pushed her hair out of her face. "Try and stop me. I'd rather be here than anywhere else on my birthday, especially with so few days left."

"Nope," Lia told her. "I'm insisting that you take the day off. At the very least, curl up with Brinkley and read, but once Nikki, Paige, and I are home from work, we're taking you out."

"Okay," Rosie acquiesced. "Where should we go?"

"Anywhere you like," Lia said. "We can have a nice dinner or go dancing, bowling, a movie. Oh, what about one of those escape rooms? Or a museum."

"Now you're thinking about your own birthday wish list," Rosie teased, grateful to her friend for lifting her spirits. "But dinner sounds perfect, and maybe we can go out to a bar afterward or something, have some outrageous drinks."

"As if you'd drink anything outrageous." Lia rolled her eyes playfully.

"Truth," Rosie said. Her tastes were pretty limited when it came to food and drink, a fact her friends liked to tease her about. "So maybe a place that serves great beer."

"I'll get right on it," Lia said, and Rosie knew she meant it.

"Thanks, Lia."

"Anytime." She rested a hand on Rosie's shoulder. "Thirty will be a good one for you. I have a good feeling about it."

Rosie swept her gaze around the store she was about to lose. "I can't see how."

CHAPTER TEN

There was a nagging feeling at the back of Jane's consciousness, like she'd forgotten something. Since she had no idea *what* she'd forgotten, she focused on her inbox instead, responding to several emails before the date caught her eye. November 3. She exhaled. That was it. Rosie's Twitter handle ended in 113. Were those numbers random, or was it her birthday? And if it was her birthday, was it January 13 or November 3?

Jane reached for her cell phone and opened Twitter. When she clicked on Rosie's profile, balloons began to float over her screen. Well, that answered her question, but what should she do with the information? They'd barely spoken since their disastrous coffee date almost a month ago. Rosie hadn't even followed up with Jane about the subscription boxes.

Jane respected her boundaries, but . . . dammit, she really wanted to acknowledge Rosie's birthday, and a tweet felt inadequate. Rosie had said she still loved Jane's books, and there was a box of advanced copies of her next release in her bedroom closet. Would she be overstepping if she gave her one?

Jane glanced at her calendar. She had a meeting in ten minutes, but after that, her afternoon was relatively clear. Was she actually considering leaving in the middle of the workday? Apparently, she was. The chance to see Rosie—even just for a moment—was too tempting to pass up. Jane updated her calendar to say she'd be working from home after lunch. She'd drop off a book to Rosie at her store and then go home and write.

"Hello, Jane."

She looked up to find Daniel Tran, the architect on the Lexington Avenue project, standing in the doorway to her office. He was a few minutes early for their meeting, but that suited her just fine. "Good morning, Daniel. Come on in and have a seat."

"Did you receive the final mockups I sent over?" he asked as he settled in her guest chair.

"I did. They look amazing." She opened the file on her computer and spun the monitor so they could both see the renderings he'd prepared, showing the high-rise apartment building that would replace the one where Between the Pages currently resided. The new building was sleek and modern, with large windows and clean lines.

She listened while Daniel went over all the details with her, walking her through each level of the building with mockups of the various units that would be available for purchase once construction was complete. The condos were top of the line and visually inviting. They should sell quickly.

She went over a few final tweaks with Daniel and arranged for him to send her the final plans for approval before they went to the construction company, which was set to begin demolition after the first of the year, once all the current tenants had moved out.

"I'll have those in your inbox by Friday," Daniel told her as he stood from the chair.

"Perfect. Thanks so much." She shook his hand and said goodbye, and as soon as he had left her office, she slid her briefcase out from beneath her desk and began to pack up for the day, hoping to sneak out without running into her sister. On the very real chance her birthday gesture was ill received, she'd rather not have to rehash it later with Amy.

Luck was on her side as Jane made it into the elevator without having to talk to anyone at all. She buttoned her wool peacoat as she stepped outside, where the brisk November air was an instant shock to her system. She hurried to the subway station, and thirty minutes later, she entered her apartment, dropping her briefcase by the door.

She walked straight to her bedroom closet, where boxes of books were stacked neatly behind her suits, one for each of her ten releases, plus a box of advanced copies of her eleventh book, *Yours for the Taking*. Jane opened it and pulled out a book, smiling to herself as she imagined Rosie's reaction to the cover model's tailored suit and mile-high stilettos.

Jane backtracked to the living room for a pen. And then she sat on the couch, tapping it restlessly against her thigh as she tried to figure out what to write. Finally, she opened the book and composed a short note to Rosie, signing it as Brie. On an impulse, she grabbed her phone and pulled up the Twitter account she'd found one afternoon last week when Rosie was on her mind. She jotted it down on a piece of notepaper, folded it, and stuck it inside the book.

Now to hope she had some sort of appropriate wrapping paper lying around. The chances weren't high, considering that most of the gifts she wrapped these days were for a nine-year-old girl, but she found a roll of hot-pink paper that would do. She wrapped the book, and then, not giving herself even a moment to second-guess this, she stuck the package in her bag and headed for the door.

She rode the subway to Ninety-Sixth Street, pressing a hand against her stomach as she exited the train, nerves swarming beneath her fingers. *Here goes nothing.*

But her nervous excitement turned to disappointment as she pulled open the door to Between the Pages a few minutes later and spotted Rosie's coworker behind the counter. Of course she'd taken her birthday off. Well, it was probably better for Jane to drop off her gift and go, anyway, no matter how much she'd been hoping to see Rosie.

She approached the counter, where the woman's eyes rounded comically as she caught sight of Jane, and this was off to a *fantastic* start. It was all she could do not to turn around and walk right back out, but she forced herself to smile instead.

"Hi, Jane," the woman said, and at least her tone was friendly. "I don't think we've been officially introduced. I'm Lia Harris." She extended a hand. "I'm the manager here."

"Nice to officially meet you, Lia," Jane said as she shook her hand.

Lia's grip was warm and firm. "Is there something I can help you with?"

"I was actually looking for Rosie. Is she in today?"

Lia shook her head. "I insisted she take the day off." She gave Jane a conspiratorial smile. "It's her birthday."

Jane's stomach gave a little swoop to know that at least she'd gotten this part right. "Could I leave something with you to give her?"

"Oh sure," Lia said. "Are you dropping off some paperwork?"

"No," Jane said simply as she pulled the pink-wrapped package out of her bag. Heat spread over her skin, because who did she think she was, bringing Rosie a gift? Oh God, this was a stupid idea.

Lia looked at the package and gulped. "Is that . . . is that a birthday present?"

"Sort of," Jane said. "Can you give it to her for me?"

"Oh, you should give it to her yourself," Lia said, pushing the gift toward Jane. "She's at home, probably reading in bed with Brinkley. It's just a few blocks from here."

Jane shook her head. "I don't want to intrude."

"I wouldn't send you to our apartment if I thought she'd be upset to see you," Lia said. "I'm her best friend, and I'd never ruin her birthday."

"Really?" Jane asked, surprised to realize she had an ally in Lia. She'd assumed she was a persona non grata with all of Rosie's friends after everything that had happened.

Lia nudged the package toward Jane's hand. "It's possible she's stepped out, but if you catch her at home, I think it will be a happy surprise."

"I should just leave this with you," Jane said, taking a step backward. Dropping off a gift at the store was one thing, but going to Rosie's apartment was something else entirely.

"Trust me," Lia said. "299 East Ninety-Fifth, apartment three. Just ring the buzzer when you get there."

Jane regarded her for a moment, but Lia seemed sincere. Surely, as she'd said, she wouldn't upset her best friend on her birthday. "Are you going to let her know I'm coming?"

"No," Lia said with a delighted smile. "I'm going to leave you with the element of surprise."

"Are you sure that's a good idea?" Jane couldn't help asking, her stomach already in knots.

"Well . . ." Lia pressed a finger against her lips, and Jane took another step backward, leaving the gift on the counter. Lia picked it up and held it toward her. "I'm just messing with you, Jane. Take this and go."

Rosie was not having a great birthday. This ought to have been perfect, curled up in bed in her pajamas with Brinkley snuggled against her leg and a paperback in hand, but she couldn't get into the book, and she was restless. She'd rather be at the store.

At least she was going out with her friends later, and she'd spent an hour on the phone with her friend Grace earlier that morning. She and Grace had been best friends in high school. Grace had even lived with Rosie and her mom their senior year after losing her parents in a car crash, but Rosie didn't get to see her very often these days since Grace had moved to Spain to be closer to her grandma.

Rosie reached over to rub Brinkley, and he rolled belly up, back leg kicking gleefully as she found that perfect spot. She sat up, making the snap decision not to spend any more of her birthday moping in bed.

This wasn't like her. Maybe she should get dressed and go to the store after all. She didn't want to be alone today.

The buzzer on the door rang, and she frowned. She wasn't expecting anyone, but it was possible someone had sent her something for her birthday. She slid out of bed, padding barefoot through the living room to press the button on the intercom. "Who is it?"

"It's Jane," came the response, and Rosie blinked at the panel in confusion. What in the world was Jane doing here? How did she even know where Rosie lived? A tingle spread through her belly, something annoyingly warm and welcome. She didn't *want* to want to see Jane, especially not here at her apartment on her birthday, but who was she kidding? She'd been trying to work up the courage to call Jane for weeks now. The truth was, she missed her a lot.

"Um, okay," Rosie said, pressing the button to buzz her in. She heard the door downstairs open and then Jane's footsteps on the stairs. Was she wearing heels? Rosie's body temperature skyrocketed. A few moments later, there was a knock, and she pulled the door open to reveal Jane on her doorstep.

"Sorry to show up unannounced," Jane said, her expression hesitant. "Lia told me you wouldn't mind."

"Lia?" Rosie motioned for Jane to come in, utterly confused.

Jane stepped into her living room, wearing a wine-colored sheath dress, a black wool peacoat, and *oh yes*, the sexiest black stilettos. Rosie felt weak in the knees at the sight. God, Jane was gorgeous, especially dressed like that. She'd been in casual clothes the last few times Rosie had seen her, but corporate Jane was absolutely, 100 percent Rosie's catnip. "I stopped by the store to leave something for you, and Lia insisted that I bring it over."

"Oh," Rosie said, the heat inside her cooling, because corporate Jane would have come straight from the office, and the last thing Rosie wanted on her birthday was any sort of notice or paperwork about the building demolition.

Jane's gaze dipped to Rosie's breasts, and oh *God*, she'd completely forgotten she was in her pajamas. This damn apartment was always too warm, even in the winter. Consequently, she was wearing a white tank top and cotton lounge pants, no bra, and she was probably giving Jane quite a show. She crossed her arms self-consciously over her chest.

Jane's tongue darted out to wet her lips as she reached into the oversize leather bag slung over her shoulder. She pulled out a pink-wrapped package and held it toward Rosie. "Happy birthday."

The sight of Jane handing her a present was so unexpected that Rosie just stared. Jane's hand lowered slightly, regret written all over her face. This was the shy, insecure woman who'd kissed Rosie in a pink hoodie, not the flawless corporate executive Rosie had first met.

"Um, thank you," she said as she took the gift. Their fingers brushed, and Jane's were cold from the air outside. "How did you know it was my birthday?"

"Your Twitter handle," Jane said, clasping her hands in front of herself as she looked down, avoiding Rosie's gaze. Brinkley took the opportunity to snag her attention, moving in for pats, which Jane readily obliged.

"Good sleuthing," Rosie said. "Do you want to sit? And, um, I can take your coat." Because it really was hot in here, and not just because Rosie's hormones were firing out of control.

Jane slipped out of her coat, and Rosie struggled not to gawk at her curves in that dress. Oh, she had it bad for this woman. She put Jane's coat in the closet and grabbed one of Paige's flannels to cover her tank top before leading the way to the couch. The package in her hand was rectangular and heavy, obviously a book, and the implication had Rosie already swooning.

She sat at one end of the couch, and Jane sat at the other end, too far away. Brinkley hopped up between them, tail beating enthusiastically against the upholstery. Rosie slipped her finger under the paper and ripped it open, revealing a copy of Brie's not-yet-released *Yours for the Taking.* Instinctively, she opened the book to its title page, where Jane had signed it to her.

To the woman who inspired me to look outside the pages - Brie

Rosie's vision went hazy with tears. "Jane, this is really freaking sweet. Thank you."

"You're welcome," Jane said. "I really didn't mean to barge in on you on your day off."

"I'm glad you did," Rosie told her, and Jane's smile was like the sun coming out from behind the clouds. There were so many layers hidden beneath those expensive clothes, and Rosie's barriers were crumbling. She liked Jane, and she wanted to get to know her better, day job be damned. As she closed the book, a little piece of paper fell out. "What's this?"

"Just a little something I thought you might appreciate," Jane said, eyes downcast in the most adorably shy way.

Heart fluttering against her ribs, Rosie unfolded the paper. *For your next adventure* was written in Jane's swirly writing, followed by a heart and a Twitter handle. Intrigued, Rosie picked up her phone and typed it in, bringing up an account that shared hidden spots to explore around New York City.

"Wow, Jane, I . . ."

"It's silly, I know."

"No, it's not. It's perfect." Rosie felt something shift inside her as she looked at Jane. This was unexpectedly thoughtful. Jane had listened to what Rosie said she liked, and she'd figured out all on her own that today was her birthday and brought over a really sweet and personal gift just . . . because. That was something one of Brie's heroines might do, and now Rosie was *really* swooning. "I really appreciate this."

"Well, I'm glad. I didn't want to overstep."

"You aren't," Rosie told her. "In fact, I overreacted last month at the coffee shop, and I've really missed you, which is probably why Lia sent you here."

"I've missed you too," Jane said, again with that shy little smile. It was weird having her in Rosie's living room, especially dressed like she'd just walked out of a boardroom while Rosie was in her pajamas, but she didn't want her to leave.

"Do you want to find one of the places on this blog with me?" she asked.

"I'd love to," Jane said. "But I don't want to interrupt your pajama party with Brinkley, if that's what you wanted for your birthday."

"It's not. I'm only here because Lia kicked me out of the store, and I didn't know what else to do with myself today, but it's my thirtieth, so I should be out doing something, right? It's a milestone."

"It is," Jane agreed. "I spent mine at the beach with my girlfriend."

"Girlfriend, huh?" Rosie asked, raising an eyebrow.

"Ancient history," Jane said. "Both my thirtieth birthday and my ex-girlfriend."

"Can't be that long," Rosie said. "How old are you?"

"Thirty-five," Jane told her.

"Not ancient," Rosie said. "And I need to get dressed before we head out."

"Okay," Jane said. With her dark hair and tanned skin, that wine-colored dress was *really* working for her. Her black pumps might be a problem, though.

"Those don't look very comfortable," Rosie said, gesturing to her shoes. "If we're going to walk around the city."

"I'll live," Jane said with a shrug.

"What size are you?"

"Six."

"Goodness," Rosie said. "I'm a seven, and I thought *I* had small feet. You're welcome to poke through my closet if you want to look for something more comfortable to wear."

"I might take you up on that," Jane said, reaching over to give Brinkley a rub. His tail swished happily over the cushion.

"Okay, you can find some walking shoes while I make myself presentable." Rosie retrieved jeans and a sweater from her room, gesturing for Jane to come in while Rosie went into the bathroom to get dressed. "Help yourself to whatever you find," she told Jane.

But once she was in the bathroom, her mind started wandering. She'd just given Jane free rein over her bedroom. Was there anything embarrassing in there? Rosie was generally a tidy person, so she wasn't too worried, but she probably should have at least checked to make sure there wasn't any dirty underwear visible in her laundry basket.

Rosie gave her head a little shake as she stared at herself in the mirror. Jane was here. This was so weird, and also weirdly wonderful. She was tired of fighting her attraction to Jane. On the surface, it didn't make any sense, but maybe it didn't have to. Obviously, Jane felt the same pull, and maybe the strength of that connection could get them through whatever bumps lay ahead, because it would definitely be bumpy to try to date Jane while she moved her store.

When Rosie came out of the bathroom, Jane was in the living room rubbing Brinkley, wearing a pair of Rosie's chunky black ankle boots, and the image was so foreign that it almost made her laugh. "Ready?" she asked.

"Do you mind if I freshen up first?" Jane gestured toward the bathroom.

"Of course not." While she waited, Rosie scrolled through the Twitter feed Jane had sent her, looking for something fun that wasn't terribly far away, because she needed to be back in a few hours for her birthday celebration with her friends. She'd been looking for a distraction this afternoon, but she'd never imagined it coming in the form of Jane Breslin.

Behind her, a key turned in the lock, and the apartment door swung open. Rosie turned as Paige stepped into the living room. "Hey, Ro."

"Oh hey," Rosie said, mildly embarrassed over the introduction that was about to occur.

"I got off early in case you wanted to hang out," Paige said, wrapping an arm around Rosie's shoulders. "We could watch one of your favorite rom-coms? Or go for a walk in Central Park? Whatever you want."

"Actually, I was just heading out," Rosie told her apologetically.

On cue, the bathroom door opened, and Jane came down the hall, stopping short as she caught sight of Paige.

Paige's eyes widened, and then she broke into a delighted smile, extending a hand. "Hi. I'm Rosie's roommate Paige."

"Jane," she said as she shook Paige's hand. "Nice to meet you."

"Oh shit, you're Jane," Paige said, smile fading. "Like, *the* Jane? Obviously you are, because you look exactly how Rosie described you. What . . . what are you doing here?"

"Paige, it's okay," Rosie said, resting a hand on her friend's shoulder. Paige was the mama bear of their group, and Rosie appreciated the hell out of it, just not at this exact moment, when she and Jane were on such newly mended ground.

"I don't understand," Paige said, glancing between them.

"Things have changed, okay?" Rosie told her.

"I should go," Jane said.

"No, you shouldn't." Rosie reached out and took her hand, giving Paige a pointed look.

"Oh my God," Paige said. "Clearly, I've missed something."

"It's complicated," Rosie told her. "But I'm happy Jane's here, okay?"

"If you're happy, I'm happy," Paige said, giving Jane an apologetic smile. "Are you coming out with us later?"

Jane glanced at Rosie. "Oh, I . . ."

"Paige is going to mind her own business for now, isn't she?" Rosie said, giving her roommate a playful nudge. "Jane and I were just heading out."

Paige mimed zipping her lips. "Totally minding my own business, and your dog if you want to leave him with me."

Rosie looked down at Brinkley, who was watching her with a hopeful expression. He'd love to explore the city with her and Jane, but if she brought him, they'd be limited by how far they could walk, since he couldn't come on the subway. "Yeah, if you don't mind, I'll leave him here with you."

"Brinkley and I are going to catch up on *Real Housewives* together," Paige said. "Have fun, you two."

"Thanks," Rosie said as she grabbed her purse and coat and led the way out of the apartment. "Sorry about that," she said as Jane pulled the door shut behind them.

"I thought she was going to throw me out for a minute there." Jane buttoned her coat, drawing Rosie's attention to her plum-painted fingernails.

"I'll get an earful from her later, but I have a feeling this will be worth it," Rosie said. "Now let's go have a birthday adventure."

The gentle splash of water was soothing, washing away the last of Jane's hesitation over her impulsive afternoon. She and Rosie had started with a trip to the Lolly Pop, because sweets seemed like a birthday necessity and Rosie had never been there before. The store was colorful and chaotic, one of Jane's favorite places to take Alyssa when she wanted to spoil her silly.

Now Rosie had a tin of her favorite candy tucked in her bag, and they'd both eaten way too much sugar. Since Jane had forgotten lunch in her earlier haste, she was currently on an M&M-induced high. After they left the candy store, they'd discovered a mural-laden courtyard decorated by a local artist, where Rosie had taken lots of pictures to add to her collection.

And now they were strolling through the atrium of the Ford Foundation Building on East Forty-Third Street, which contained a tropical garden that was open to the public during business hours. Jane was always glad for a chance to experience greenery here in the city, and this had an added bonus of climate control, although she didn't have any trouble keeping warm every time she glanced at Rosie, no matter how cold it was outside.

"This is so nice," Rosie said as they stopped in front of the reflecting pool at the center of the atrium.

"It is." Jane stared into the water, seeing the reflection of their faces rippling across the surface, and she couldn't hold back her smile as Rosie's hand slid into hers.

"Not at all how I thought my afternoon was going to go," Rosie said.

"Or mine." Jane looked at the woman beside her. Rosie was bundled in her blue jacket now, but the image of her in that white tank top, nipples jutting against the thin fabric, was forever etched into Jane's brain.

"Still can't quite believe you showed up at my apartment bearing gifts on my birthday," Rosie said, and since she was currently holding Jane's hand in the midst of an impromptu afternoon spent together, she hoped that meant it had been a happy surprise.

The hum of awareness that buzzed inside her whenever she was near Rosie was stronger today, sending a warm tingle through her system every time their eyes locked. "I can't believe I did either."

"I think we made a mistake trying to avoid the awkward topics before," Rosie said. "If we're going to have any sort of relationship—even as friends—we need to just talk through the uncomfortable things, don't you think?"

"Well, I'm a person who generally avoids difficult conversations," Jane told her. "But I suspect you're right, and I *do* want to know how your real estate search is going."

"Yeah, and that's really my whole focus right now, so it feels weird not to talk about it."

"And I want to hear about it, so let's start there," Jane said.

"Okay. Let's keep walking, though. It's warm in here in our coats."

"Agreed." Jane released her fingers, and they walked outside, heading in the direction of the East River without any specific destination in mind.

"The short answer is, it's not going well," Rosie told her. "I'm going to have to be willing to pay a lot more in rent to find a space even remotely comparable to what I'm leaving."

"I'm really sorry," Jane told her, hoping Rosie could hear her sincerity. She hated her role in Rosie's current predicament.

"Thanks," Rosie said. "I'm still looking, and I'm trying to be flexible with my wish list, so . . . fingers crossed."

"I look at a lot of real estate at work," Jane told her. "I can keep an eye out for you."

"I'd appreciate that," Rosie said, and Jane didn't detect any bitterness in her tone. "In the meantime, I'm ramping up my online offerings to tide me over while we move. That's where the expanded selection of subscription boxes will come in."

"We need to talk about that too," Jane said. "Actually, I need to put you in touch with my publisher so you can order the copies you need, and then we can figure out the logistics for me to sign them."

"I've already got their contact information, and yes, I was dragging my feet on that because I've been distracted," Rosie said. "But I'll get it done this week, because I'd like yours to be the first autographed subscription box, if that's okay with you."

"More than okay," Jane said, warmth blooming in her chest. "Sometimes I don't feel like a real author, you know? I've distanced myself from a lot of things that come with it, because . . . I don't know, imposter syndrome, I guess. I've never done a signing or even chatted with other authors."

"It doesn't make you any less of an author, Jane," Rosie told her.

"Well, I feel like a fraud most of the time," she admitted. "I didn't realize how much until I was at your afternoon tea. Everyone was talking about books, and I just . . . I didn't belong."

"That's not how it looked from where I was sitting," Rosie said, and her fingers brushed Jane's as they walked. "I didn't even know you were an author that day, but you looked like you belonged. Anyone can talk about books."

"I'm trying to get better at it," Jane said.

Rosie reached into her bag, pulling out the candy tin with a sly smile. She snagged a gummy bear and held it toward Jane, and while she was already half-sick on sugar, she took a gummy too. "I'm kind of fascinated by your weird relationship with authordom," Rosie admitted as she pushed the tin back into her bag.

Jane scrunched her nose as she chewed the gummy bear. "I don't even understand myself half the time."

"The community is so welcoming, though," Rosie said. "And plenty of authors use pen names, so there's no pressure to reveal anything about yourself that you don't want to. If you want to get more involved, I think you'll find that other authors and readers would love to get to know you. You already use Twitter. Just interact with people and see what happens."

"I don't really *use* Twitter, other than to chat with you and post book news," Jane said. "But you're right. That could be a good place for me to start."

"Only if you want to," Rosie said.

"I do," Jane said. "I'd really like to make some personal connections. I'm just terrible at it, if you hadn't noticed."

Rosie grinned at her. "You have your moments. I found you very charming that first afternoon in the store with Alyssa."

"Good to know," Jane said as butterflies flapped inside her. She and Rosie had wandered into the gardens behind the United Nations Visitor Centre and were now strolling along the path beside the river.

"See?" Rosie said, turning her head to smile at Jane. "It's better now that we're talking instead of trying to tiptoe around the awkward stuff."

"Tiptoeing obviously didn't work," Jane agreed, and she really wanted to kiss Rosie. She wanted more than this tenuous friendship. She wanted to know anything and everything about her, to let Rosie guide her toward embracing her life as an author, to lose herself in the warmth of Rosie's touch. Right now, she just wanted Rosie, any way she could have her.

"I'm not much of a tiptoer in general," Rosie said, curls whipping in the breeze as she turned to face Jane.

Jane took a hesitant step closer. "Well, I am, so I'll let you take the lead here."

"Like this?" Rosie took both Jane's hands in hers as she leaned in.

Jane seemed to have lost the ability to speak, so she nodded, pulse jumping as she dropped her gaze to Rosie's lips. Rosie pressed those perfect pink lips against Jane's, and she closed her eyes, immersing herself in Rosie's kiss, the softness of her mouth and the sugary taste of her as she teased Jane with her tongue.

Jane loved her candy-sweet taste, courtesy of the gummy bears, but she suspected Rosie was always sweet. She dropped Rosie's hands in favor of tangling her fingers in her wind-tossed curls. Jane's head was spinning, a combination of her sugar rush and the adrenaline from this kiss. Her heart raced, and that tingling feeling spread through her belly, settling into a warm ache in her core.

God, it had been a long time since she'd wanted anyone this badly. Rosie pressed closer, hands sliding inside Jane's unbuttoned jacket to rest on her waist, and she gasped at the feel of Rosie's warm fingers through the fabric of her dress. Their first kiss outside the bookstore had been hesitant, over almost before it had started, but this one . . . Jane couldn't have written anything more perfect than this kiss.

"I have to get back," Rosie murmured against her lips. "I'm going out for dinner and drinks with my friends."

"Oh," Jane said, disappointed even though she had no right to be, because this had been the most amazing afternoon.

Rosie pulled back to look at her, lips glistening and eyes sparkling against the sunset. "Will you come with me?"

"Oh, I don't know," Jane deflected. They barely knew each other, and she definitely didn't belong at Rosie's birthday celebration.

"Please?" Rosie asked. "Come out with us tonight."

How could she possibly say no to that? Jane felt herself nodding before she even realized she'd made up her mind. "Yes."

CHAPTER ELEVEN

"Oh no, you didn't," Rosie said as she saw the cake topped with sparklers heading toward their table. In response, her friends burst out laughing, whoops and whistles erupting around their table as a group of employees gathered behind Rosie to sing. Beside her, Jane was mostly quiet, but her eyes twinkled happily.

The waitstaff sang a silly, upbeat birthday song that involved a lot of clapping, and then they placed the cake on the table with a stack of serving plates and utensils.

"Make a wish," Lia said.

Thankfully, there were only three candles, but they sparked like the trick kind. Rosie closed her eyes and wished for a new home for Between the Pages, a storefront she would love as much as her current location. Then she blew out her candles, grinning as she successfully snuffed them all on the first try. No matter what other hurdles she faced, at least she hadn't jinxed herself with her birthday wish, because yes, she was superstitious about these things.

"Happy thirtieth, Rosie," Nikki called, quickly echoed by the rest of the table.

"Thanks, ladies," Rosie said, getting a bit choked up as she looked around the table. Lia, Nikki, and Paige were all here, plus her friends Ashley and Shanice, and Rosie's former roommate Hallie, who had driven all the way from Boston to be here tonight. And of course Jane, who despite her reserved nature seemed to be enjoying herself.

They were at a restaurant called Jason's, which was one of Rosie's favorite places. She and her mom used to come here all the time, and she'd celebrated many birthdays in this dining room. Jason's served a variety of standard fare, so everyone could get what they wanted while Rosie got her all-time favorite meal, a burger with french fries.

"I've got this," Paige announced as she slid the cake toward herself and began slicing. She'd spent years working in a bakery before she started working at Nikki's catering business. Rosie had feared it might be disastrous for them, working together while dating, but so far they seemed to be balancing work and homelife well.

Paige handed out plates of cake, and while Rosie had already eaten a *lot* of sweets today, she couldn't turn down cake, especially not when it was for her.

She turned to look at Jane and found her watching Rosie quietly. Rosie squeezed her hand under the table, receiving a reassuring squeeze in return. It had been impulsive to invite Jane along tonight, but she seemed relaxed. Rosie's friends had welcomed her into the group, although she knew she'd get hell from them later as they pestered her for every detail leading to Jane's being here.

Rosie leaned toward her. "Having fun?"

Jane nodded. "I'm glad I came."

"Want to tag along for drinks after?" Rosie already felt like she'd hijacked Jane's day, but she didn't want to break the spell by saying goodbye, especially not after that kiss by the river.

"Yeah," Jane said, and her smile made Rosie's pulse race.

After they'd finished their cake, they left the restaurant in a group and walked to a nearby bar that Nikki raved about. It was cold outside, but Rosie barely felt it through her happy haze, which might have had a little bit to do with the beer she'd had with dinner, but mostly it was because of the people surrounding her. Her birthday had started out kind of shitty, and she was so glad it was ending well.

The bar was more crowded than she would have preferred, but it seemed to be her style, with plenty of good beer on tap and a pop tune she recognized playing over the sound system. She and her friends clustered near the door while they waited for a few stools to free up.

Jane still wore that burgundy dress, which had been slowly driving Rosie wild all evening. She'd touched enough of it to know the material was smooth, almost slippery to the touch, and she was intrigued by its seamless lines. Rosie didn't wear many formfitting clothes, so she didn't know all the tricks for hiding panty lines and bra straps. It looked like Jane wore nothing at all beneath it, and yet Rosie could see that she had on black tights, so what else was she hiding under that dress?

Jane stepped closer, her shoulder touching Rosie's. "Do they know who I am?"

"Which one of your many identities do you mean?" Rosie asked playfully, because they seemed to be past the awkwardness now.

"Brie," Jane said simply, but her voice dropped as she said it. She was so oddly shy about her pen name.

"Lia does," Rosie told her. "And I'm sorry about that. I didn't tell her directly, but she figured it out on her own."

"It's okay," Jane said. "I don't mind if you tell your roommates."

"Really?" Rosie asked.

"Yeah, although maybe just ask them to keep it to themselves for now."

"Definitely," Rosie said, eyeing her friends as she thought it through. "Actually, now that I'm thinking about it, Paige and Nikki might have already figured it out too."

"How so?" Jane asked.

"Because when I went home that night, I told them I'd kissed Brie, that I'd found out who you were, but I had a hang-up about Brie's day job."

"And now you're here with me," Jane said.

"Right, and they all know about my hang-up with *your* day job, so it's entirely possible they've already put two and two together, especially Paige."

"Well, you can fill in the holes for them after you get home tonight."

"Okay," Rosie said, thrilled to have Jane's blessing to dish everything with her roommates.

Jane held up her phone, and Rosie didn't mean to snoop, but she saw several missed calls and a text from someone named Amy asking where Jane was. It was unsettling to realize how little she actually knew about Jane's personal life. She hardly seemed the type to kiss Rosie if she had a girlfriend at home, but then again, she'd kept other things about herself secret, hadn't she?

"My sister," Jane said, obviously having noticed Rosie's not-so-subtle snooping. "She's probably just being nosy about why I'm not home on a Wednesday night, but I'd better check in, just in case."

And Rosie's concern melted into adoration, because Jane seemed to be close with her sister, which was so sweet. "It sounds like I'm not the only one who'll be gossiping about our day later."

Jane's smile was the kind that made Rosie swoon, one of those real smiles that seemed to light her up from the inside. "Amy will want all the details. For what it's worth, she's solidly on the side of us pursuing . . . whatever this is."

Rosie touched Jane's hand, hoping she wasn't going to wake up tomorrow and regret this. "I'm leaning in that direction too."

Jane's consciousness was slightly blurred at the edges by the time she finished her third martini. Ordinarily she wouldn't drink this much, but she wasn't driving, and the alcohol was helping to keep her relaxed in such a social setting. She was determined to have fun tonight and not be awkward around Rosie's friends.

"See, I told you Rosie would be glad to see you," Lia said, sliding in next to Jane at the bar with a cocky smile.

"I was skeptical, but you were right," Jane said.

"Well, even I didn't know I would be *this* right," Lia said.

"Hi, ladies." A woman with light-brown hair came to stand beside them. Rosie had introduced her earlier as Hallie, but Jane couldn't remember how she fit into their group of friends. "I'm glad I got to meet you tonight, Jane."

"Me too," Jane told her.

Paige joined them, wrapping her arms around Hallie with a warm smile. "There you are. I've missed you so much, Hall. You have no idea."

"Same," Hallie said, leaning her head against Paige's.

"Hallie used to be our fourth roommate," Paige told Jane. "And she's my best friend forever, even though she abandoned me to move to Boston."

"Job transfer," Hallie said with an apologetic shrug.

"What do you do for work?" Jane asked.

"I'm a manager with Belmont Hotels," Hallie told her.

"Ah," Jane said.

"Rosie seems happy tonight," Paige commented, turning to look at Rosie, who was deep in conversation with another friend Jane had been introduced to tonight, a Black woman named Shanice. Paige released Hallie, stepping closer to Jane. "I'm still not quite sure how you two got to this point, but just . . . don't hurt her, okay?"

Jane straightened on her stool, not sure how to respond to that.

"Geez, Paige," Hallie said, looking vaguely embarrassed.

Paige shrugged. "Sorry, but I'm protective of her, you know? She's been through a lot."

"I know," Jane said. "I want her to be happy, too, and I'm glad she has you looking out for her."

"I think I like you," Paige said, relaxing into a smile. "Don't prove me wrong."

"I'll do my best," Jane said.

"Not talking about me, are you?" Rosie gave Paige a pointed look as she slid in next to Jane.

"Never," Paige deadpanned.

"I came to steal her," Rosie said, hooking her elbow through Jane's. She seemed pretty tipsy, too, at least as drunk as she had been the night Jane realized she was Aurelia. "People are dancing," she told Jane as she led her toward an open area at the rear of the bar where a few people were indeed swaying to the music, but Jane would hardly call it a dance floor, and she wasn't nearly drunk enough to dance in a bar.

"I'm not one of those people," she told Rosie, who giggled as she laid her head on Jane's shoulder.

"You're no fun," she said.

"I never claimed to be," Jane countered, hoping they were still joking with each other. This was the part where she tended to mess things up. She was terrible at reading people and still rattled from her conversation with Paige.

"There's also a photo booth," Rosie said. "And I want to take lots of pictures to celebrate my birthday."

"That I can do," Jane said, wrapping her arm around Rosie's waist. Rosie leaned against her, and Jane stumbled, barely managing to keep them upright. They staggered together, laughing as they made their way toward the photo booth.

"It's empty," Rosie said cheerily as she peeked inside.

Jane held the curtain back while Rosie sat and then followed her in. They took a minute to get themselves situated, and since Rosie had left her bag with her friends at the bar, Jane paid for two strips of photos—because she wanted to remember this night too.

"Ready?" Rosie asked.

"Ready as a deer in headlights," Jane said, only halfway joking.

"Be silly," Rosie instructed as a timer on the screen in front of them began to count down from five. The flash went off, blinding Jane, and she blinked like . . . well, like a deer in headlights as Rosie giggled beside her. "Be *silly*, Jane. Come on. I know you have it in you."

And maybe she owed it to the copious amounts of liquor she'd consumed tonight, but she felt herself making a face as the camera flashed again. Rosie leaned in to kiss her cheek, and Jane turned her head, meeting Rosie's lips as the photo booth strobed with light. They alternately kissed and made faces at the camera, growing progressively ridiculous until an automated voice told them their time was up.

Rosie smiled at her in the darkened photo booth before leaning in for a real kiss, her tongue tracing the seam of Jane's lips. The noise of the bar seemed muffled in here, although only a flimsy curtain separated them from the rest of the room. Rosie's mouth was hot and hungry as it met Jane's, kissing her with an intensity that sent Jane's pulse racing.

Rosie rested a hand on Jane's thigh just beneath the hem of her dress, and even through her tights, Jane was exquisitely aware of Rosie's fingers on her skin. She leaned closer to do a little exploring of her own. She slid her hand beneath Rosie's sweater, resting it against the smooth, warm skin just above her waist, and Rosie gasped, arching into her touch.

"Could kiss you like this all night," Rosie murmured, and her hand slipped into the space between Jane's thighs.

Goose bumps rose on Jane's skin, and the ache in her core was almost overwhelming. As badly as she wanted Rosie's hand to keep going, to touch Jane where she throbbed for her, she didn't want that in this photo booth, no matter how drunk or horny she was.

"Knock it off, you two," Lia called from somewhere nearby, followed by a tapping on the side of the photo booth.

Rosie pulled back, grinning at Jane, lips glistening in the dim light. "No idea what you're talking about," she called to her friends.

"I hope you're decent," someone else said. Paige, Jane thought. "Because we're coming in. We want group photos."

"Come on in," Rosie said, scooting sideways on the bench to make room for her friends.

Jane hoped she looked more composed than she felt as Rosie's friends began piling into the photo booth. It wasn't meant for nearly this many people, and Jane wound up with Shanice on her lap and Nikki crouched at her feet.

There was much elbowing and good-natured cursing as everyone crammed in. Lia maneuvered herself to insert her credit card, and then they laughed and flailed as they attempted to get eight faces into a frame meant for half that many. Jane smiled gamely, but she was hot and starting to feel claustrophobic with so many bodies pressed around her. She was glad when the session ended and everyone started climbing out of the booth.

Jane took Rosie's hand as they slid off the wooden bench and stepped through the curtain. The lights and sounds of the bar felt overwhelmingly bright and loud after the relative isolation of the booth, and Jane drew several deep breaths as she readjusted. Her head swam, alcohol chasing adrenaline through her veins, and it took her a moment to register the women laughing and whooping behind her.

She turned to see them huddled around the photo strips that had been printed. Lia handed one of the strips to Jane with a knowing smile, and Jane looked down to see herself goofing around and kissing Rosie. A thrill rolled through her to see them looking so comfortable together, to see herself looking so happy. She was glad to have these photos to remember the moment, although she wasn't wild about sharing something so intimate with all of Rosie's friends. She pushed the strip hastily into her bag.

Meanwhile, Rosie was at the center of the group, beaming as she looked at the photos, including her copy of that first set. Jane envied her seeming inability to get flustered, even while her friends ribbed her for kissing Jane in the photo booth. After a few minutes, they migrated to the bar for a final round of drinks before they called it a night.

Jane suspected she probably shouldn't have another, but she'd already sobered up to the point where she was starting to feel self-conscious around Rosie's friends, so then again, maybe she should. They ordered flutes of champagne in honor of Rosie's birthday, and everyone lifted their glasses overhead to sing happy birthday before they shared a group toast.

Jane caught Rosie's eye as she tapped their glasses together, and Rosie grinned at her. Jane sipped her drink, which fizzed all the way to her stomach, re-creating the way it felt when Rosie kissed her. They shared champagne and laughter, and then they bundled up in their coats and headed out into the night.

"How's everyone getting home?" Paige asked. "Hallie's crashing with us tonight, and the five of us can walk, but does anyone need me to call a Lyft? We've all had a lot to drink."

"I'm headed for the subway," Shanice said, and Ashley said she'd walk to the station with her.

Jane held up her phone. "I'll call myself a Lyft."

Rosie took her hand and led her away from the group before pulling her in for a quick kiss. "I'm really glad you came tonight."

"Me too," Jane told her.

"We should do something soon, a real date with just the two of us," Rosie suggested.

"I'd like that." She liked it more than she could properly express at the moment.

"Okay." Rosie beamed at her. "I'll message you tomorrow."

"Perfect. Happy birthday, Rosie."

"Thank you." Rosie pressed her lips against Jane's again, and then they rejoined her friends. Shanice and Ashley had already started walking to the subway, but Rosie and her roommates insisted on waiting with Jane until her Lyft arrived, which was unexpected and sweet. They seemed like a great bunch, and Rosie was lucky to have them.

A few minutes later, a black sedan pulled to the curb, and after checking the license plate against the information in her app, Jane said goodbye and got in the car. Luckily, her driver was the quiet type, because she was all out of conversation. She had far surpassed her usual social limits tonight and had drunk too much on top of it.

But it had been *amazing*.

Forty minutes later, she stumbled into her apartment, head spinning. She toed out of her ankle boots, staring at them for a moment in confusion. Where had those come from? It took her several long seconds to remember swapping shoes at Rosie's apartment earlier that afternoon. Thank goodness she hadn't had to navigate the city in stilettos all day, though.

She went straight to the kitchen for a glass of water and a couple of ibuprofen, because she could feel a headache already starting to creep around her temples. She drank the whole glass and then went into the bathroom for a hot shower to help sober her up before bed.

What time was it, anyway? She had lost all concept of time, and she could barely focus her eyes on the clock. It was a little past midnight. *Jesus.* She had to work tomorrow. She'd left the office at lunchtime to run an impulsive errand to Rosie's store.

Twelve hours later . . .

She stepped under the shower's hot spray, which felt amazing. She scrubbed away her makeup and let the water course over her body for who knew how long, until the hot water ran cold, and then she hopped out and wrapped herself in a towel. She brushed her teeth and walked to the kitchen for more water.

When she closed her eyes, the room spun, so she didn't dare lie down yet. The last thing she wanted was to end this amazing day by puking. Instead, she put on her pajamas and sat in bed to check the notifications on her phone, which was silly since almost no one ever contacted her outside of work.

If she'd been subconsciously hoping to have heard from Rosie already, she would be disappointed. But she had three texts from Amy, and Jane felt a stab of guilt when she couldn't remember if she'd ever actually texted Amy back earlier or just thought about it. But when she scrolled up in the chat box, she saw that she'd told her sister she was with Rosie, and based on the string of replies she'd received, she was *never* going to hear the end of it tomorrow.

Cautiously, she lay down and closed her eyes. The room swirled slowly around her, but not enough to make her sick, so she rolled onto her side and drifted to sleep. She woke sometime later, disoriented to find herself on top of the covers with the overhead light still on. She got up to use the bathroom and climbed back into bed, shutting off the light as she did so.

The next time she woke, her alarm was blaring. Her whole body ached, and her brain was sluggish and sore. She squinted, rolling toward the nightstand to silence her phone as her stomach churned uncomfortably.

"It was worth it," she mumbled as she climbed out of bed and went into the bathroom. She really shouldn't have showered and passed out with wet hair, though. It was a wavy, rumpled mess, and she didn't have the time or energy to tame it. She freshened up and went into the kitchen for coffee and oatmeal, hoping it would help her feel slightly more human.

An hour later, hair slicked back in a bun and gelled half to death, she stepped into her office, only to find Amy already waiting in the guest chair with a giddy grin on her face.

"Shut the door," she said, gesturing to the two mugs of steaming coffee on the desk in front of her. "I need to hear *everything*."

"Because you brought caffeine, I might actually let you stay," Jane said as she shut the door and dropped into her chair.

"You look like you had a rough night." Amy gave her an assessing look, eyes widening. "Holy shit. Did you spend the night with Rosie?"

Jane shook her head, reaching for the coffee to cover for the blush she could feel burning on her cheeks, because after last night, she definitely hoped their relationship was heading in that direction, and *wow*, that was such a huge turnaround from where they'd been twenty-four hours ago, she could hardly wrap her mind around it. "No, but I did drink too much."

"Oh, Jane," Amy chastised. "You got drunk on your first date in . . . what, two years?"

"Have you ever known me to be a 'get drunk on a first date' kind of woman?"

"I'm not sure I've ever actually seen you drunk," Amy said. "Spill."

"We went out with a bunch of her friends to celebrate her birthday. Everyone was drinking a lot, so I did too. It helped to keep me from overthinking things, you know?"

Amy looked like Alyssa on Christmas morning when she'd just gotten her biggest, most exciting gift. "You, my socially awkward and eternally single little sister, went out for drinks with Rosie *and her friends*, and you got drunk, and dare I say . . . you had fun? Please tell me you had fun, Jane."

Jane's lips quirked as she sipped her coffee. "I had fun. I had a lot of fun."

CHAPTER TWELVE

"I think this one has real potential." Marcia Guzman, Rosie's Realtor, led the way into what felt like the zillionth storefront she'd seen in the last month. "As you can see, it's currently being used by an accounting firm, but they'll be fully moved out by mid-December."

"It doesn't feel very homey," Rosie commented, looking around the room. There were no employees here today, just empty desks and scattered boxes. The space was cramped and dingy, with gray cinder block walls and marble-patterned linoleum floors underfoot.

"Think of it as a blank slate," Marcia said. "Once the office furniture is gone, you can paint the walls and install bookshelves, turn it into a cozy shop."

Rosie walked the room from end to end, imagining it filled with shelves of books. This space didn't have any character, but she was coming to terms with the fact that she would have to settle on a few items on her wish list in order to get an affordable space in a desirable retail area. "You're right. It could work. Does it have any meeting space?"

"There's a small office in back, but no, there's nothing comparable to the basement room you have now," Marcia told her.

Well, that was disappointing. Rosie would hate to give up Sunday tea. Not only did it give the store a sense of community, but it was also a big source of revenue. She was really trying to keep her mind open, though, because she was running out of time. Her phone vibrated with an incoming text message, and she felt a similar buzz in her stomach when she saw Jane's name on the screen.

In the cold—and sober—light of day, she could hardly believe they'd spent most of yesterday together. Rosie had been completely captivated by her, lost in that magical connection that seemed to exist whenever they were together. But as she stood here in yet another sub-par storefront, she wondered if she could really make a relationship with Jane work. Would she always resent her for kicking Rosie out of her original space?

This was the first time Jane had texted instead of messaging her through Twitter as Brie, and it seemed to signal a shift in their relationship. They were transitioning from the anonymity of the internet into real life. Maybe it would help Rosie transition her feelings about Jane too.

Jane Breslin:

Good morning! Here's an address for you to consider.

A link to a real estate listing followed, which was less personal than Rosie had been hoping for, but it was sweet that Jane was trying to help her find a new space. Or was it weird? Rosie's gut reaction said sweet, so she was going with that.

She clicked the link and followed it to a listing for an available space in SoHo, and *wow*, it was adorable. "Have we looked at this one, Marcia?" she asked as she walked toward her, holding out her phone.

Marcia took it and looked at the screen, swiping through photos. "No, it looks like this space is privately listed. How did you find it?"

"A friend sent it to me. What's a private listing?"

"It usually means the listing agent is well connected and only wants to work with a few agents they've preapproved. Obviously, they get fewer showings that way, but it works if your space is desirable enough and you don't want the hassle of dealing with the general public."

"Oh," Rosie said, frowning.

"If your friend has an in with the listing agent, I could probably set up a showing for you. Is your friend a Realtor?"

"No, um, she's a property developer, so she works with Realtors, I guess." Rosie clicked through photos of the space, feeling a spark of hope. This space would be perfect for Between the Pages, although it was far from home and slightly out of budget. She opened Jane's text and composed a reply.

Rosie Taft:

This looks amazing, but my Realtor says it's a private listing?

Jane Breslin:

Just give them my name, and you should be able to get on the list.

Rosie Taft:

Thank you! I appreciate this.

Jane Breslin:

My pleasure.

"You know Jane Breslin?" Marcia said, surprise evident in her tone.

"Yeah. Why, do you know her?"

"I know *of* her," Marcia said. "Anyone with a connection to real estate in the city knows Breslin Property Development."

"Is that a good or a bad thing?" Rosie asked.

"Neither, really. They build some of the most sought-after properties in the city, although I hear they can be a bit cutthroat in their business practices. But Manhattan real estate is pretty cutthroat in general."

"Hmm," Rosie said, not exactly reassured by Marcia's words. "Well, she says you can use her name to get us on the list for a showing."

"I'll call right now if you like," Marcia offered. "I've got time to fit it in this morning if you do."

"I can make time," Rosie told her. "Lia's covering for me at the store."

"All right. Let me just grab that number and the listing agent's name." Marcia squinted at Rosie's screen as she tapped the information into her phone, and then she walked off to place the call.

While she waited, Rosie wandered through the accounting office, trying to convince herself it could work. This space was affordable, and it was in a good location for foot traffic. It wasn't the end of the world to give up the quaint character of her current space or the downstairs meeting room. She'd find a way to keep Sunday tea alive, even if it meant crowding into the store itself. But as she glanced around the space, it just didn't feel like home.

She snapped a few photos to show Lia, hoping she'd have some wisdom to help Rosie make her decision.

"Well, Jane Breslin keeps her promises," Marcia said as she zigzagged between empty cubicles to reach Rosie. "We've got an appointment at the property on Spring Street in half an hour. We can head right over, if you're ready to leave."

"I'm ready," Rosie told her.

Marcia led the way outside, already summoning an Uber for them. Rosie sent photos of the accounting firm to Lia while she waited for the car to arrive, and then she and Marcia were on their way to SoHo. When their car pulled to the curb thirty minutes later, Rosie felt her spirits lift.

The building with the available rental space was about ten stories tall, brick fronted with decorative trees planted along the sidewalk in front. For the first time since she'd started hunting, Rosie felt like she could see herself here. SoHo was a long way from the Upper East Side, so she'd lose some of her current customers, and she'd either have to move or deal with a long commute on top of long hours at the store, but she was getting ahead of herself. She hadn't even seen the space yet.

Marcia opened the lockbox and let them in through the front door, and Rosie pressed a hand against her chest as she stepped inside. The storefront was gorgeous, with exposed brick along one wall and high ceilings. The paint was a soft blue that brightened the space and would complement Between the Pages' logo perfectly. Big windows along the front let in plenty of natural light.

"Dare I ask if there's meeting space?"

"There's a basement listed. Let's check it out," Marcia said.

They went through a door in back and descended a creaky set of stairs into the basement. Marcia located the switch to turn on the light, and . . . well, it was a room. That was about all Rosie could say about it.

"It's big," she said, but it was drab, mostly unfinished, and unsettlingly dark, even with the bulb overhead throwing off some light.

"It *is* big," Marcia agreed. "And it could be a fantastic space with a little work."

Rosie walked the length of the room and took a few pictures, and then they went back upstairs. She didn't have any trouble picturing the bookshelves in here. It was slightly smaller than her current space, but the extra room downstairs might make up for it once it was finished.

"Because this is a private listing, the owner isn't anticipating any trouble renting it out," Marcia said. "So you'll need to move quickly if you want it."

"Ah." Rosie pressed a hand against her forehead. She was terrible at making quick decisions. She had definitely hoped to stay closer to home. She'd lived on the Upper East Side her whole life, knew it like the back of her hand and loved every inch. Plus, her customers were there. But she was going to have to be willing to bend somewhere to find a new space before the end of the year. "Let me call Lia."

"Sure thing," Marcia said, walking to the front window to make a call of her own.

Rosie dialed, tapping her foot against the hardwood floors while she waited for Lia to answer. "Hey," she blurted the moment she heard the call connect.

"Good news?" Lia asked.

"I may have found a space," Rosie told her, "but I need to talk through it with you."

"Lay it on me," Lia said, all business now.

"I'm down in SoHo, so it's a haul from the apartment, but this space, Lia . . . it's nice." She described it for her in as much detail as she could—including the creepy basement—and then sent over some photos and a link to the listing. "It's far from home, and it's almost three hundred dollars a month over budget, but I kind of love it. What do you think?"

"Rent is going to be an issue anywhere we go," Lia said. "I think the bigger problem here is the location."

"Right," Rosie said, her excitement dimming.

"Approximately sixty percent of our regular customers live on the Upper East Side. It would be a significant disadvantage for us to lose their business."

"And I don't want to lose them," Rosie said quietly. Some of her regulars felt almost like family.

"Let me run some more data," Lia said, "because no space is perfect, and this one has a lot going for it. We'll talk it over once you're back at the store."

"Okay," Rosie said, immensely glad for her friend's business sense.

"Oh, and just a heads-up," Lia said. "Paige has called a girls' night to discuss the Jane situation, so be prepared for gossip and probably pizza later."

Rosie rolled her eyes, even though she'd expected this after bringing Jane to her birthday celebration last night. "Okay. I'll see you at the store in a little while."

"See you here."

Rosie ended the call and crossed the room to update Marcia on her conversation with Lia. "We'll try to have an answer for you by end of business today."

Marcia nodded. "I'd love to say, 'Take your time,' but this one will move fast, so if you want it, don't delay. Do you need a ride uptown?"

"No," Rosie told her. "I'm going to walk around the neighborhood for a few minutes, and then I'll hop on the subway."

Marcia let them out the front door and locked up behind them, and with a wave, she was on her way to the Uber waiting at the curb.

Rosie walked down the street, peeking into every storefront to get a feel for the neighborhood, and she liked what she saw. She went into the coffee shop on the corner, where she ordered a coffee and chatted with one of the baristas. This could be her new local shop. Would enough of her regulars follow her to SoHo to make it worthwhile?

She boarded the subway feeling hopeful for the first time in weeks. This space was her first real contender, and Jane had helped her find it. Just the thought of Jane sent warmth through her body. She sent her a quick text to thank her for the lead.

Rosie rode uptown and entered Between the Pages, where her mood was further bolstered to find a group of college students browsing the shelves, talking excitedly as they lifted various books to read the back cover. Lia and Betty were at the counter together, both of them watching Rosie expectantly as she approached.

"Those pictures you sent are charming," Lia said. "Now I'm falling for this space too."

"Despite the location?" Rosie asked.

"It's a concern," Lia said. "I've run some more numbers for us to look at."

"Okay." Rosie's phone rang with a call from Marcia. "Hold that thought," she told Lia as she headed for the back hall to answer it. "Hi, Marcia."

"Hi. Unfortunately, I have some bad news," Marcia said. "It seems that while we were touring the space in SoHo, someone else was signing the lease."

"What?" Rosie stopped in her tracks.

"These things happen, especially with a desirable space like that one."

"Shit," Rosie mumbled, irrationally disappointed considering she hadn't even been sure she wanted this one.

"The good news is that we've found one great space, and we'll find another. I'll go over the new listings in the morning and call you with anything I think might work," Marcia said.

"Okay," Rosie said with a sigh.

"And if your friend Ms. Breslin has any more leads, she seems to know your taste pretty well."

"Yeah, I guess she does," Rosie said. It was significant that Jane had sent along the first lead Rosie wanted to pursue, even if it hadn't worked out.

"I'll let you go, but keep the faith, and I'll check in with you tomorrow."

Rosie felt heavy on her feet as she made her way back to the counter where Lia and Betty were waiting for her. "Never mind. Someone else just leased that space."

"That fast?" Lia said. "Bummer."

"That's too bad," Betty said.

"Well, according to my numbers, we should try to stay closer to home anyway," Lia offered.

"I would hate to leave the Upper East Side," Rosie said with a sigh.

"And with someone else leasing the space, you're saved having to make a difficult decision," Betty said, wise as ever.

Rosie nodded. "Maybe this is a sign that I should try harder to stay in this neighborhood."

Rosie wasn't really in the mood for a girls' night by the time she and Lia made it home from the store that evening, still disappointed about this latest setback in her real estate search. But Nikki and Paige were already waiting with two large pizzas, a grilled-chicken salad for Rosie since she didn't like pizza, and several bottles of soda. Brinkley dashed across the living room to greet them while Rosie and Lia took off their coats.

They fixed plates and gathered in the living room to discuss the topic Rosie knew they were all dying to hear about, and while she was grumpy about real estate, she was bursting to talk about Jane, especially now that she had her blessing to share the whole story.

"So," Paige said with a sly smile. "I'm just going out on a limb here, but you told us that Brie's day job was a problem, and then Jane came over and presumably brought you that . . ." She gestured to the signed copy of Brie's book on the shelf. "Am I connecting the right dots?"

"You are," Rosie said. "So you see why the day job was a big issue for me."

"I do," Paige agreed. "And I wasn't exactly thrilled to see her yesterday."

"But you hid that so well," Lia deadpanned, causing them all to burst out laughing.

Paige held up a finger. "But I'd like to amend my initial opinion, because once I got to know her, she seems really nice, and you two are adorable together. I get a good vibe there."

Rosie smiled as she picked at her salad. "Yesterday was magical. It was the first time we really synced in person without getting bogged down in day job awkwardness, you know? I can't stop thinking about her, but I also can't help worrying that having to find a new home for the store will always make things hard for us, or at least until it's resolved."

"I think that if you want to date her, you have to let go of your feelings about her job," Nikki said. "You'll poison your relationship if you go in resenting her for a letter she wrote before you met."

"That's exactly what I'm afraid of," Rosie admitted.

"Nikki's right," Lia said. "And I also feel the need to point out that it was romance-novel-level swoon worthy when she showed up with a birthday present for you yesterday."

"It was," Rosie agreed, going all warm and soft inside as she remembered Jane's gesture.

"You're always telling me you want a romance straight out of one of your books," Lia said. "And I'd argue that maybe you've found it with Jane."

"It felt that way when she walked into my store the first time, before I knew who she was, but I never wanted a storybook romance with the woman who evicted me," Rosie said. "What if I can't get past it?"

"Don't you think you should at least try?" Lia asked. "After all, think how many romance novels start out with the protagonists hating each other."

"Enemies to lovers," Rosie said. "I love that trope."

"Worst case, you have a hot fling to get you through this tough spot with the store," Nikki offered. "Because the sparks between you two last night were definitely hot."

"This isn't like me," Rosie said as she scrubbed her hands over her face. "I'm not usually indecisive about things, especially relationships."

"No, you usually go with your gut," Lia said. "And your gut wanted both Jane *and* Brie before you knew what she did for a living, which is why I think you should go for it."

Rosie's gut still wanted Jane, and so did her heart, despite the alarm bells going off in her head that said the risks were just too big. "I think I have to try," she admitted. "I'll drive myself crazy with regret if I don't."

As she got ready for bed later that night, her gaze caught on the black pumps in her closet. Those stilettos she'd lusted after were now a tangible reminder of her day with Jane, like Cinderella's slippers left behind after the ball.

CHAPTER THIRTEEN

Rosie Taft:

Hey Cinderella, you left your slippers in my closet.

Want to grab dinner so I can give them back to you?

Jane Breslin:

Yes, I'd like that.

Rosie Taft:

Are you free tonight? Lia offered to cover for me at the store.

Jane Breslin:

I am, and I'd love to see you.

Rosie Taft:

Yay! I'm looking forward to it.

I feel like you know nicer places than I do, so I'll let you choose, but remember I'm a picky eater.

Jane Breslin:

So not the fondue restaurant?

Rosie Taft:

I can't tell if you're joking.

Jane Breslin:

😊

Rosie Taft:

Okay, Jane's got a sense of humor. Filing that away.

Jane Breslin:

How about Pearl on 55th?

Rosie Taft:

Hang on, let me Google.

Looks good to me!

Jane Breslin:

Tonight at seven?

Rosie Taft:

It's a date.

Jane set her phone down and sat there for a moment, staring at it. A date. She was glad Rosie had used that word, because she wanted to make sure she wasn't misreading the context. And now Jane was sitting in her office, smiling like a fool, because she had a date with Rosie tonight.

She reached into her bag and pulled out the strip of photos she'd shoved in there on Wednesday night. She'd looked at them a few times since, because she hardly recognized herself in them. She looked so happy and carefree. Rosie brought that out in her, and she liked it. She liked it a hell of a lot. She liked *Rosie* a hell of a lot.

Putting the photos away, she turned to her computer to get back to work. She was distracted, though, both by anticipation for her date with Rosie and by the plot of her new book, which had been buzzing around in the back of her mind all afternoon. She'd had an idea for how to take things up a notch like Pilar had asked for, but she wanted to run it past Rosie before she officially wrote it into the plot.

She worked for another hour before she packed up to leave for the night. As she headed for the elevator, she had a mental image of Rosie wearing those heels Jane had left in her closet for their date tonight.

Cinderella, indeed.

Later that evening, Jane rummaged through her own closet, trying to decide what to wear. Mostly, her wardrobe consisted of business suits and lounge clothes that she wore when writing. She had very few outfits appropriate to wear on a date, which was sadly indicative of how often she actually went on dates.

Eventually, she settled on a black cocktail dress, because you could never go wrong with a little black dress. It was simple and understated but plunged in the back, which meant she'd have to forgo a bra. When she wore it to corporate events, she'd wear pasties, but they were so uncomfortable, and for a date she thought she could pull this off. She dressed and spent entirely too long in the bathroom, flat ironing her hair and touching up her makeup.

Her mind drifted to Rosie, getting ready in her own apartment as her roommates offered opinions on her outfits. They seemed close and supportive, a kind of friendship Jane had never really experienced. In school, she'd been quiet and studious, mostly keeping to herself, and while she'd gone out pretty regularly in her twenties, lately she'd neglected her social life in favor of her writing career. As her gaze drifted around the sparse landscape of her bedroom, she wondered how different this evening might be if she had roommates here helping her get ready.

Then again, Jane was thirty-five years old, and she felt significantly past the age of roommates. She liked having her own space. In fact, sharing her home had never held any appeal, which was probably part of the reason she was still single. But Rosie brought out funny things in her, like the desire to have someone to talk to about her date. She'd probably end up calling Amy after she got home tonight.

Shaking her head at herself, she buttoned her coat, picked up her bag, and walked outside to call a Lyft, not having patience for the subway tonight. The restaurant she'd chosen was about halfway between her apartment and Rosie's and also close to a cute little dessert bar that she thought they might try afterward if they were having a good time.

And Jane *really* hoped they would have a good time. More than anything, she wanted to keep the rapport she and Rosie had established on her birthday. It wasn't just alcohol that had brought them together, because they'd been perfectly sober during their afternoon adventure. Jane wanted more of that. And more kissing. God, so much more kissing.

She sat quietly in the back seat of the Lyft, ridiculously nervous as the streets rolled by outside the window. Her legs bounced, and her stomach felt like she'd swallowed a swarm of butterflies. She hadn't been this nervous since the night she'd gone to meet Aurelia, or maybe her impulsive visit to Between the Pages to confess her identity. Apparently, Rosie had this effect on her.

The car pulled up outside the restaurant, and Jane thanked her driver and stepped out. The cool November air whipped at her face and ruffled her hair as she walked to the front door. She could see Rosie inside, looking at her phone as she stood by the hostess desk, and the butterflies in Jane's stomach began to flutter.

She entered the restaurant and smiled at Rosie. "Hi."

The smile Rosie gave her in return was luminous. "Hi."

"I made a reservation," Jane told her, and it was a good thing she had, because the restaurant was loud and crowded, louder than she'd anticipated. She checked in with the hostess, and they were shown to a small table along the wall, sandwiched between two other tables. It wasn't the most romantic location, but it would be fine. They hung their coats on a hook nearby, and Rosie visibly gulped when she caught sight of Jane's dress.

"Oh, wow," she said as her gaze traveled to Jane's knees and back up. "You look amazing."

"Thank you," Jane said, taking in Rosie's plaid dress, which was belted at the waist and full of vibrant fall colors. "So do you."

They sat and studied the drink menu as the restaurant bustled around them, the clink of silverware mixed with the din of conversation. It was a lot of noise, but when she looked at Rosie, it seemed to fade into the background.

"Did the property in SoHo pan out for you?" she asked to get the conversation started.

"Almost," Rosie said. "Someone else signed the lease before I'd made up my mind."

"Oh damn, I'm sorry," Jane said.

"It's okay. It was pretty far away from where I want to be, but it's a great space," Rosie said. "I think my Realtor is impressed with your connections. And thank you for that, by the way . . . for sending it to me, even though it didn't work out."

"You're welcome," Jane said, picking up her drink menu.

"Okay, I feel like I should get a fancy drink tonight, but I really only know beer. Any recommendations? You seem like a woman who knows her way around a drink menu."

"I think you're mistaken about the extent of my social life," Jane told her with a small smile.

Rosie studied her. "Yeah, I can't quite figure you out. You look like the epitome of cool, like the kind of woman who dresses up and goes to fancy restaurants and always knows just what to order. And then, you act all shy and tell me you basically stay home in your pajamas and write every night, but I can't quite picture it."

"It's true, though," Jane said with a shrug. "I do attend cocktail parties and things for work, but I don't go out very often for fun, and the truth is that I'd always rather be home in my pajamas, writing."

"Still can't picture it," Rosie said, her expression teasing.

"We'll have to work on that, then," Jane said. "But I do prefer cocktails to beer, so I can guide you through the drink menu if you tell me what you like."

"I like simple," Rosie said. "And not too strong. I don't think we need a repeat of my performance with the Long Island iced tea at the Red Room."

"Yeah, those are deceptively strong," Jane said. "Are you in the mood for a mixed drink?"

"Maybe just wine," Rosie said. "Liquor tends to go straight to my head. Something light and sweet."

"I think you'd like riesling," Jane said. "It's one of my favorites. Want to share a bottle?"

"Yeah, I'd like that," Rosie said with a smile.

"Perfect. So have you had any luck with other properties?"

Rosie shook her head. "I've got one 'maybe' on my list, but I don't love it, mostly because there's no meeting space, so we'd probably have to give up our afternoon tea and book signings, and events are kind of my favorite, in case you didn't notice."

"I noticed."

"So do you think I should hold out for a rental with meeting space, or am I being too picky?"

Jane looked at Rosie, so pretty in the restaurant's warm lighting with those glossy curls and blue eyes as bright as her ambition. "I think you should hold out for the space you need. Lots of buildings in the city have basements, so it's not an unreasonable requirement."

"I just don't want to get stuck without a space at the end of the year," Rosie said. "And I already feel like that's where I'm heading. I've only got two months left, and that feels . . . well, terrifying."

"Is it feasible for you to carry out online orders for a month or so while you get set up in a new location if your search takes longer than expected?" Jane asked, hating her part in this, but at least it seemed like they could talk about it now.

"I don't know." Rosie rubbed at her brow. "We'd have to lease warehouse space to store all the books, and it might cost more than I'd earn in online orders."

"Then we'd better find you a space before the end of the year," Jane said, suddenly determined to do everything in her power to help Rosie save her business. She wanted to write a happy ending for this story, and maybe she could use her real estate connections to help make it happen, because at this point, she was pretty invested in both Rosie and her store.

"We?" Rosie asked.

"I want to help," Jane told her, hoping she sounded as sincere as she felt.

"This isn't your problem," Rosie said, looking down at the table.

"But I do have connections in the industry," Jane said. "And in a way, it *is* my problem. I brought this on you, and I'm sorry."

The waiter interrupted them to introduce himself and go over the daily specials, and then Jane ordered their bottle of wine. When he left, Rosie reached across the table to place her hand on Jane's.

"I think we both have to let go of the idea that any of this is your fault," she said. "You were just doing your job, and I have to get that through my thick skull if I'm going to hang out with you like this."

Jane wouldn't necessarily call this hanging out. She hoped it was more than that. "I'll try, if you'll accept my apology."

"Apology accepted," Rosie said. "And we're making a fresh start as of this moment. So tell me more about author things. Have you made much progress on your new book about the rival pop stars?"

"Actually, I had a question for you about that," Jane said. "My agent wants me to give it a little something extra, and I was thinking about adding in a subplot where they're online friends but don't know they're rivals in real life, but I wouldn't write that without getting your blessing first."

Rosie blinked at Jane for a moment in surprise. A subplot in her new book that mirrored their own relationship? "Um, yes, *please* write that."

Jane's whole face lit up. "Really?"

"Yes, definitely. It sounds like a great plot twist and a book I would totally want to read, and . . . not to be a fangirl, but knowing the hidden meaning behind it would be too cool."

"Okay, then," Jane said, and she seemed to settle in her chair, like the hard part of the evening was finally over, and Rosie hoped so too. She meant what she'd told Jane. She was going to try her best to put her hurt feelings aside, because they'd addressed them, and holding on to those feelings would only doom any chance they had at a romantic relationship.

And Rosie really wanted to try for that romance.

Their wine arrived, and the waiter poured two glasses. Rosie didn't drink much white wine, but this was good—crisp and fruity.

"Okay, I think I can add 'wine recommendations' to your list of talents," she told Jane. "I really like this."

"I'm glad," Jane said, giving Rosie one of those sweet smiles that was always her undoing. The more she got to know Jane, the more she realized her initial impression had been way off, and she liked the real Jane a lot, especially when she was dressed like that . . .

"So why Brie?" she asked. "How did you choose your pen name?"

Jane's lips quirked. "It's not the most exciting story, but I had a huge crush on Brie Larson at the time, and it's also a partial anagram of my last name."

"Brie Larson, huh?" Rosie said, fascinated by this new peek into Jane's psyche. "You like superheroes?"

"This was long before *Captain Marvel*—although I do like her in that, too—but she first caught my eye in *Trainwreck*. Cute and blonde. Maybe I have a type?" Jane lifted an eyebrow.

"Oh." Rosie sipped her wine, warmed by Jane's compliment.

"And you? What's the meaning behind your screen name?"

"I'm so original that I went with my name and birthday," Rosie told her.

"Really?" Jane asked. "Aurelia Rose is your name?"

She nodded. "My mom was Aurelia Joy and went by Joy, and she named me Aurelia Rose and called me Rosie."

"And why the stack of books for your profile picture instead of a photo of yourself?" Jane asked.

"I wanted to keep my personal account separate from the store, so I'd have a place to just be silly with my friends and fangirl over my favorite authors," she said. "But if you looked through my feed, you'd see plenty of selfies."

"Interesting," Jane said. "So, you're saying that if I'd done my homework properly, I could have solved this mystery months ago."

Rosie grinned. "Essentially, yes."

"What was your mom like?" Jane asked. "If you don't mind talking about her."

Rosie reached for her wine. "Well, I don't think it would surprise you to know she's the one who inspired my love of books."

Jane smiled. "No, it doesn't."

"We had so much fun outside the store, too, though. She picked me up from school every day, and if she didn't have to get right back to the store, sometimes we'd spend the afternoon at the park or visiting museums." Rosie closed her eyes for a moment, remembering her mom's laugh and the warm grip of her hand as they explored the city together.

"It sounds like you were close," Jane said.

"So close. We had weekly mother-daughter date nights, all the way through high school. We'd go out to dinner together, almost always at Jason's—where I had my birthday dinner. It was our favorite place."

"I love that," Jane said. "I don't spend much one-on-one time with my mom. Maybe I should."

"Yes," Rosie agreed. "It's the best."

They chatted through their meal, and then Jane suggested a dessert bar around the corner that Rosie was 100 percent in favor of. They put on their coats and headed out into the night, walking close together on the sidewalk. Jane had on a different pair of black stilettos tonight, reminding Rosie of the shoes in her bag.

The dessert bar had small tables scattered through the main space with a bar along the back wall. The lighting was low, and the whole space smelled vaguely sugary. Rosie and Jane took a table for two near the back, and when Jane turned to hang up her coat, Rosie got her first good look at the back of her dress.

And her throat went dry. The dress scooped low, almost to her waist, revealing endless smooth skin. It fastened at her neck with a silver clasp, and really, how was Rosie supposed to sit here and eat dessert with her dressed like that? Was she wearing a bra? Rosie tried not to stare at her breasts. Jane had left her hair down tonight, and it fell over her shoulders, straight and shiny. The overall effect made Rosie warm in all the right places.

A waitress brought them menus, which consisted entirely of cocktails, coffee, and dessert.

"Cake and Bubbles?" Jane said, looking at her menu. "I'm sold."

Rosie looked down to see that the daily special was a cupcake served with a flute of champagne, called Cake and Bubbles. "Me too. I'm in a celebratory mood tonight."

Jane ordered the carrot cake cupcake, and Rosie went with vanilla. When their dessert arrived, Jane lifted her champagne flute. "To new beginnings."

"I'll drink to that," Rosie said as she tapped her glass against Jane's. Then she sipped. The champagne was cold and tart, and the bubbles tickled her tongue.

"Plans this weekend?" Jane asked as she sipped her own champagne.

"The usual. Work, reading, hanging out with Brinkley and my roommates."

"What are you reading?" Jane asked.

"Guess," Rosie said, setting down her glass.

Jane's eyes narrowed, and a smile flitted around her lips. "Is it signed?"

"It is," Rosie said, "and furthermore, it's amazing. The only way I would have agreed to come out tonight without having finished it is to have dinner with the author herself."

Jane dropped her gaze to the table, adorably flustered by Rosie's praise. "You're one of the first to read it."

"And that makes it even more special," Rosie told her. "My favorite birthday present."

Jane swiped her fork through the frosting on her cupcake and brought it to her mouth. "Now you're just flattering me."

"A little, but it's also true. I'm sad to see the series end, although I'm pretty excited about the new one you're working on too."

"A new series means a new contract, and maybe my first opportunity to go full time."

"Really?" Rosie said. "This next contract could do it for you?"

"'Could' is the operative word," Jane said. "My sales are good but not great, which is why I'm trying to shake things up, but it's still kind of a long shot."

"Well, I'm crossing my fingers for you."

"Thanks," Jane said, taking a bite of her cupcake, and Rosie found herself captivated by her lips and the fleck of frosting lingering there. "It's a catch-22, because if I could quit my day job, I could write faster and increase my income that way, but I can't afford to quit yet."

"I've heard that from other authors too," Rosie said. "Sucks."

"It does, but we've got to pay the bills, right?" Jane looked up and smiled.

"Yep." A fact Rosie was highly aware of as she looked at the future of the store.

"Tell me what other books you've enjoyed lately," Jane said. "I've been so busy I haven't had time to do much reading."

Well, this was a topic Rosie could talk about forever, and since she'd noticed Jane's interests leaned toward lesbian fiction—a genre that was also near and dear to Rosie's heart—she happily chatted about her favorites as they finished their cupcakes and champagne.

The alcohol was definitely going to her head as she put her coat on to head outside with Jane. "I have to admit," she said. "I wondered if there was a hidden meaning in that book you brought me."

"A hidden meaning?" Jane asked as she buttoned her coat.

"Well, it's called *Yours for the Taking*."

"Oh." Jane met her eyes, and the air seemed to shimmer with the strength of the pull between them. "Well, my primary intention was to give you an advance copy of my next book, but I'd be lying if I said I didn't also notice the double meaning in the title."

"And?" Rosie asked breathlessly.

Jane rounded the table and stepped up to Rosie, placing one hand on the back of her head as she drew her in for a kiss. "I'd also be lying if I said it wasn't true."

Rosie gripped Jane's coat, pulling her closer as a delicious hunger awoke inside her, one that had nothing to do with food and everything to do with the beautiful woman in front of her. "I'd invite you back to my place for a drink, but I don't think I need any more alcohol tonight, and my roommates will be in the living room watching reality TV, which isn't exactly romantic."

Jane pushed one of Rosie's curls behind her ear. "I think this is one of those moments when it's advantageous not to have roommates."

"Yeah, they definitely complicate my dating life sometimes."

"Well, I live alone," Jane said, and her brown eyes seemed to gleam beneath the lamp overhead. "Would you like to come over for some hot cider and privacy?"

"Yeah," Rosie said, giddy at the possibility. "I'd love to."

CHAPTER FOURTEEN

Jane switched on the light in the living room as she led the way into her apartment, glad she was generally neat, because she definitely hadn't let herself entertain the idea of bringing Rosie home with her when she was getting ready earlier. She took Rosie's coat and hung it with hers on the rack beside the door.

"The place where the magic happens," Rosie said, looking around the living room.

"Magic?" Jane asked, watching her.

"Where you become Brie."

"That's true," Jane said. "I rarely let her out of this apartment."

"It feels very *you*," Rosie said, wandering through the room.

"How so?" Jane didn't bring many people here. She preferred to keep her space to herself, so she was curious what aspects of her Rosie saw in Jane's decor.

"Well, it's very modern and minimalistic, and sometimes modern spaces can feel almost untouchable, you know? So much metal and glass," Rosie said. "But your living room feels comfortable and inviting. You've got throw blankets on the couch like you cuddle up there with a book, and that plant in the corner livens things up."

"I love my plants," Jane said.

"And it looks like you take good care of them." Rosie crossed the room to stand in front of Jane's dragon tree, touching one of the leaves reverently.

"I do."

"No bookshelves," Rosie observed.

"No. I read mostly on my Kindle."

Rosie turned to face her. "And where do you keep *your* books?"

"Um, they're in boxes in my closet," she admitted.

Rosie pressed a hand against her chest. "For shame, Jane. You should at least have them somewhere you can see them, so you can take pride in them here in your own home."

"I'm working on it," Jane said. "Would you like that hot cider I promised?"

"Sure," Rosie said with a look that said she wanted more than the cider, but neither of them seemed to be very forward when it came to romance, so they were going to have to take this one step at a time.

Jane went into the kitchen and set the kettle to boil while she put cider mix into two mugs. When she glanced into the living room, Rosie was sitting on the couch, texting on her phone. Maybe she was letting Lia know where she was. She and her roommates seemed to check in with each other that way, which was sweet. Plus, Rosie had a dog to think about. She might need to ask someone to walk him for her.

Those roommates might come in handy if Jane got her nerve up to ask Rosie to stay, because surely one of them could watch Brinkley for the night. Jane stared at the mugs in front of her, thinking about her current heroine, Skye. She wouldn't hesitate to walk into the living room and seduce the woman she wanted. If only Jane were as bold in real life.

The kettle began to whistle, and she lifted it, pouring hot water into both mugs. She stirred the mixture, and the air filled with the rich, spicy scent of cider.

"Smells good," Rosie said from the living room.

"I love the smell of cider." Jane lifted the mugs and carried them to the couch, where she handed one to Rosie.

"Thank you." Rosie gave her a sweet smile, and Jane felt warmth in the pit of her stomach before she'd even taken a sip of her hot drink.

"So how did you meet your roommates?" she asked, taking a cautious sip and nevertheless managing to scorch her tongue.

"College," Rosie told her. "Well, I met Lia, Paige, and Hallie in college. We got an apartment together after we graduated so that we could pursue jobs here in the city, and we get along so well together we just stuck. Except for Hallie, whose job transferred her to Boston."

"And Nikki?" Jane asked.

"Nikki is Paige's girlfriend, so she moved in last year when things started to get serious between them. They share a room, and Lia and I have our own rooms."

"Helps with rent," Jane commented.

"It sure does."

"How did you and Lia decide to go into business together?"

"My mom got sick around the time we graduated college," Rosie said, gaze falling to the mug in her hands. "Pancreatic cancer. Lia had only come to the States for college, but she stayed after graduation to help me out because she's the most amazing friend ever, and since we're both major book nerds, when I took over the store, I asked if she'd like to be my manager. Sometimes I feel a little guilty for keeping her here in New York, when her family is in the UK, but she's happy here. I think she has one of those families where it's better to have some distance, you know?"

"I think I might *like* to know," Jane said.

"Is your family close?" Rosie asked. "I mean, outside of working together?"

"That's the thing," Jane said. "I've never had the space to know. Our lives have always revolved around the company, but it's not my passion, and it's starting to take a toll. I think I might get along with my parents better if my dad wasn't also my boss."

"I can understand that," Rosie said with sympathetic eyes. "You and your sister are close, though?"

"Very close," Jane said. "I love working with Amy, but she's ready for me to quit and be an author too. She says she wants to brag about me to everyone she knows."

"Aww, that's so sweet," Rosie said. "I think I'd like her."

"I know you would," Jane said, smiling as she pictured them together.

Rosie sipped her cider, and an easy comradery seemed to wrap around them. Jane felt herself fully relaxing, no longer worried about off-limits topics or even whether she'd work up the nerve to try to take their relationship to the next level. This was only a first date, after all, and she was going to enjoy it, wherever the evening led them.

"Do you have other family in the area?" she asked Rosie.

She shook her head, but Jane didn't see anything painful there. "It was just me and my mom. My dad took off before I was born, so I've never even met him. My grandparents used to live upstate, but we weren't super close, and they've both passed away now."

"I'm sorry," Jane said. "Have you ever tried to get in touch with your dad?"

Rosie shook her head. "I know his name. My mom gave me his information in case I ever needed him for medical reasons or anything. He's a truck driver, or he was back then. He chose not to be a part of my life, and now I choose to keep it that way."

Jane squeezed her hand, unsure what to say.

"It's okay," Rosie told her. "I've got great friends who're like family to me, and I had the most amazing mom for twenty-three years. I miss her like crazy, but I also feel lucky to have gotten those years with her, you know?"

"It sounds like you have a good outlook."

"I try," Rosie said. "I'm generally a positive person. This business with the store has been really hard, but I think I've moved from shock and outrage into determination to find a new storefront. Failure is not an option."

"And I'll do whatever I can to help." Jane rested a hand on Rosie's thigh, immediately aware of the warmth of Rosie's skin through the flannel fabric of her dress.

"I'll take all the help I can get," Rosie said, looking at Jane's hand before meeting her gaze, and Jane could swear the temperature in her apartment had skyrocketed.

She sipped her cider, holding Rosie's gaze as her pulse quickened and arousal stirred in her belly. "I'm really glad you're here tonight."

"Me too," Rosie said. "It's been a while since I've been out on a Friday night, sharing a drink with a beautiful woman."

"Same," Jane said. "Or any other night of the week."

Rosie shifted closer to her on the couch. "You seemed so cool and glamorous that first afternoon you came into the store with Alyssa. I imagined you could have anyone you wanted."

"Well, now you know the truth," Jane told her lightly. "I'm a hopelessly introverted author."

"I have a thing for hopelessly introverted authors," Rosie said, leaning in for a quick kiss. She tasted like cider, apple sweet and cinnamon spiced. "Actually, I have a confession that might make me sound even more hopeless."

Jane licked her lips. "Oh?"

"Part of the reason you caught my eye that day was your suit, because I'm a sucker for impeccably dressed women, and then I realized my suit fetish came from your books."

"Oh," Jane said as the heat inside her grew. "Really?"

Rosie nodded. "It all circles back to you, no matter how I spin it."

"That might be the sexiest thing anyone's ever said to me." She leaned in, capturing Rosie's lips again, lingering a bit longer this time, and her hand slid down to rest on Rosie's thigh, with only the leggings she wore beneath her dress between Jane's fingers and Rosie's skin, much the way Rosie had touched her in the photo booth.

Rosie finished her cider and set the empty mug on the coffee table, and Jane rushed to do the same, gulping the last few swallows, grateful it had cooled enough that she didn't burn herself this time. Rosie turned toward her, bringing their lips together for a different kind of kiss, the kind that didn't have to stop unless they wanted to, and right now, Jane wanted to kiss her forever.

One of Rosie's hands brushed across Jane's bare back, and she shivered.

"Cold?" Rosie murmured against her lips.

She nipped at Rosie's bottom lip. "Nope."

"Didn't think so." Rosie's fingers were warm against Jane's back, and it was a surprisingly intimate sensation while they were still fully clothed.

"Stay a while?" she asked Rosie.

"Mm-hmm," Rosie responded, sliding closer. "Been thinking about this pretty much since the moment I met you."

"Except for a little while there in the middle?" Jane teased, placing gentle kisses over Rosie's cheeks, and she felt the elusive dimple she loved so much beneath her lips as Rosie smiled.

"I kind of wanted to kiss you even then," Rosie said. "It was so annoying."

"Sorry about that," Jane murmured as she kissed her way down Rosie's neck to the dip of her collarbone. Goose bumps rose beneath her tongue, and Jane kissed them away one by one.

Rosie's hand slid down Jane's bare back to her waist. "Not your fault you're so sexy," she whispered. Her breath hitched as Jane's lips reached the top of her cleavage where it peeked from her dress.

"Likewise," Jane said, pressing a kiss between Rosie's breasts.

In response, Rosie slid into Jane's lap, straddling her thighs. Her skirt rode up to accommodate her, but her leggings kept her covered, much as Jane might have liked to see what was under that dress. She liked the feel of Rosie in her lap, though, the warmth of Rosie over her hips and a more convenient angle to kiss her.

Rosie dipped her head, pressing Jane into the cushion. Her tongue slid against Jane's, and she was dying in the very best way, heart pounding as desire built hot and tight in her core. Rosie's hips rocked subtly against Jane's as they kissed, and while their position had Jane's thighs pressed together so she couldn't feel Rosie where she ached for her, the overall effect was so erotic she could hardly stand it.

Rosie's mouth was hot and all consuming, and Jane closed her eyes, wondering if she'd ever been kissed like this before, every cell in her body humming with pleasure before they'd even begun to explore each other's bodies.

"You're really good at that," she murmured as Rosie slid a hand into the depths of her hair, giving a gentle tug that made Jane gasp with pleasure.

"Not a compliment I'm used to," Rosie said, sitting back to grin at her, cheeks flushed and eyes bright with desire. "Maybe we're just combustible together."

"We definitely are, but you're also a good kisser." Jane drew her back in, already missing the feel of her lips. Rosie sighed as she settled into the kiss, and Jane was lost, absolutely drowning in pleasure. They kissed until she was on fire, desperate for more. Her hips shifted beneath Rosie, attempting fruitlessly to bring their bodies into better alignment, but it wasn't going to happen in this dress. "Care to move this into the bedroom?"

"Yes," Rosie said, sliding out of Jane's lap. She stood and extended a hand to tug Jane to her feet, and she felt wobbly in her heels, but not from alcohol. Arousal burned so brightly inside her that she almost shook from the strength of it, centered in the ache between her thighs.

She led the way into her bedroom, then turned on the small lamp beside the bed so they wouldn't be fumbling in the dark. Rosie swept a quick glance around the room before locking her gaze on Jane's.

"I like it," she said as she stepped into Jane's arms. "A lot of gray, but it feels homey nonetheless. I can picture you sitting in the middle of the bed with your laptop, making magic as Brie."

"I spend a lot of time there," Jane agreed, reaching for the belt on Rosie's dress. She gave it a gentle tug. "Are you sure about this?"

"So sure," Rosie affirmed as she palmed Jane's breasts over her dress. "I've been wondering about your bra situation all night."

Jane arched into her touch. "There isn't one."

"Exactly what I was hoping," Rosie murmured, thumbs circling Jane's nipples over the fabric until they'd tightened, achingly sensitive beneath Rosie's touch.

Jane unfastened Rosie's belt and pulled it through the loops with a soft whir of fabric. She tossed it into the chair in the corner, the one she'd bought to sit in and write but used more often to hold her clothes while she sat in bed. The dress flowed loosely over Rosie's body now, the flannel warm and soft beneath Jane's fingers. Combined with the leggings she wore beneath, Jane imagined Rosie's outfit tonight had been much more comfortable than her own, but the way Rosie looked at her in this dress more than made up for it.

Jane slid her fingertips up and down Rosie's sides, familiarizing herself with her curves, before Rosie reached down to grab the hem of her dress, lifting it over her head. Now she stood before Jane in leggings and a black satin bra, and Jane couldn't take her eyes off her . . . or her hands. She palmed Rosie over her bra, taking the weight of her breasts in her hands.

She was so preoccupied she barely noticed that Rosie was fiddling with the clasp at Jane's neck, the one that held her dress in place. She bent her head to kiss Rosie's shoulder, presenting the clasp to her more easily.

"Got it," Rosie whispered.

Jane felt the dress come loose a moment before it slid to her waist.

"Oh, now I like this dress even more," Rosie said appreciatively as she took in the sight of Jane's bare breasts. "Easy access."

Jane slid it past her hips, catching it as it puddled to the floor and then tossing it onto the chair with Rosie's. And while she sometimes felt self-conscious undressing in front of a woman for the first time, tonight she felt nothing but heat and anticipation as Rosie looked at her.

"You're so beautiful," Rosie said breathlessly, running her hands over Jane's exposed skin. Her fingers felt like heaven, warm and soft, spreading heat everywhere they touched.

Rosie stepped back and stripped out of her leggings before pushing Jane onto the bed and crawling on top of her. But this time, her thigh slid between Jane's, and she couldn't help her whimper as Rosie's thigh pressed against her center. "Please," she whispered, not even caring how needy she sounded.

In response, Rosie hooked her fingers beneath the band of Jane's underwear. She tugged them down, and Jane kicked free of them. She could hardly catch her breath, and Rosie hadn't even touched her yet. Rosie smiled, revealing her dimples as she brought her fingers against Jane's center, and it was simultaneously sweet and erotic, a combination that might be Jane's new favorite—but then again, everything with Rosie seemed to be her favorite.

Rosie straddled her thigh, and Jane could feel her wetness through her underwear. She knew she was just as wet. She could feel it as Rosie stroked her, fingers ghosting over Jane's aching clit. "Rosie," she gasped, moving herself against Rosie's hand, desperate for more.

"Okay?" Rosie asked.

"So fucking great," Jane confirmed. "Please don't stop."

Rosie's grin widened as she pushed a finger inside Jane. "Wasn't planning to."

"God," Jane whimpered, grasping Rosie's hips for something to hold on to. Her eyes slid shut as she surrendered to the pleasure of Rosie's touch. Rosie's mouth closed over one of her nipples, and Jane cried out at the unexpected sensation.

Rosie flicked the hardened bud with her tongue, and Jane felt it in her clit, a surge of arousal so strong it almost took her over the edge. When Rosie repeated the gesture on her other breast, Jane was reduced to gasps and moans, writhing against the duvet as Rosie brought her to the brink of orgasm and then sent her flying.

She came hard and fast, everything in her tensing and then going loose as release rolled through her, leaving her warm and tingly.

"Wow," Rosie said quietly.

When Jane opened her eyes, she found Rosie staring down at her with an expression of wonder. "Definitely wow," she agreed, reaching up to touch Rosie's face.

Rosie grinned, snuggling in beside her, and Jane lay wrapped in her arms while she caught her breath. Then she turned toward Rosie, reaching for the clasp of her bra. "Time for me to try to wow you in return."

"That won't be hard," Rosie managed, already halfway gone as Jane pushed at her underwear. Her warm skin was all over Rosie's body, moving and sliding as she undressed her, and Rosie was so turned on that all she could do was hold on and lose herself in the sensation.

Jane kissed Rosie's bare chest, and her *tongue*. Jesus Christ. Rosie had never experienced anything quite like the pleasure of Jane's mouth, the way she kissed her way over every inch of Rosie's skin. It might've been the most arousing thing she'd ever felt.

Jane reached Rosie's stomach, placing hot openmouthed kisses there, and Rosie hadn't thought her stomach to be especially sensitive, but she was writhing beneath Jane, absolutely overwhelmed with pleasure. Jane's tongue swirled over a spot just above her hip bone, and Rosie arched her back, letting out a needy whimper.

Jane settled between her thighs, and Rosie thought she might come from the anticipation of what was about to happen. Jane pressed a kiss against Rosie's inner thigh, and then she looked up at her. "Is this okay?"

"Yes," Rosie gasped. "Really, *really* okay."

Jane smiled, and she was so gorgeous, cheeks flushed and dark hair hanging messily over her shoulders, that Rosie wanted to remember it forever. And when she brought that deliciously talented mouth against Rosie's most sensitive parts, she wanted to remember this forever too. Her body was on fire as Jane worked her magic, and almost before she was ready, Rosie felt her orgasm cresting.

Everything inside her sizzled as release pulsed through her core. When she came back to her senses, her fists were clenched in Jane's bedspread. She gasped for breath, eyes squeezed tightly shut as Jane peppered her thighs and stomach with kisses.

"Okay, you definitely delivered on the wow," Rosie said as she opened her eyes.

Jane wore a satisfied smile as she wiped her mouth. She slid up to join Rosie, looking impossibly happy and relaxed, maybe the most relaxed Rosie had ever seen her. "Yeah?"

"Big time." Rosie wrapped an arm around her.

"I'm so glad you're here," Jane whispered, nuzzling her face against Rosie's neck.

Those words settled in her chest, somewhere near her heart, because Jane sounded so sincere, so open, almost to the point of vulnerability. She shivered in Rosie's arms, and this time, it wasn't from pleasure. Her apartment was chilly, and they were naked and sweaty. Jane tugged at the blankets, and they crawled underneath, creating a warm cocoon together.

Her walls were painted a cool gray, but she'd added a touch of color to the room with lavender curtains and several landscape paintings on the walls. There were a handful of framed photos on her dresser that Rosie was curious to see up close, but not right now. Nothing was going to get her out of Jane's bed at the moment. There was a stationary bike against the wall, and Rosie pictured Jane in spandex shorts and a sports bra, sweating it out on the bike, an image she liked a whole lot.

Jane's fingers traced lazy circles over her back, and her hair tickled Rosie's chest. The sheets smelled vaguely like lavender, and somehow, that just seemed so Jane. You could learn a lot about a person from their bedroom, and Rosie liked everything she was learning in this one.

"Do you need to go?" Jane whispered against Rosie's neck, and she wasn't sure how to take the question. Was Jane trying to get rid of her? The arm wrapped firmly around Rosie's waist suggested otherwise.

"Not yet," she answered. "Unless I'm keeping you from something."

Jane shook her head before pressing a kiss on the tip of Rosie's nose. "I'd be perfectly happy to keep you here all night."

"Then do," Rosie told her.

Jane's next kiss seared Rosie's lips with a promise of things to come. "I think I will."

CHAPTER FIFTEEN

Rosie woke in Jane's bedroom, swathed in soft colors from the sunlight filtering through the curtains. It was a lot quieter than she was used to—no clatter of Brinkley's toenails or murmur of conversation from her roommates in the living room. There was only the whisper of Jane's breath as she slept beside her and the muffled honk and rumble of traffic outside.

On the one hand, she wanted to stay here forever in the warmth of Jane's bed. Jane lay facing her, eyes closed and peaceful in sleep, and Rosie didn't think she'd ever get tired of looking at her. But on the other hand, she had to pee, and she really shouldn't be *too* late to work after Lia had already covered for her last night.

With that thought in mind, she slipped out of bed and went into the bathroom to freshen up. When she came back out, Jane smiled at her with sleepy eyes.

"Morning," Rosie said. "Hope I didn't wake you."

"It's okay, probably time to be up." She pushed up on her elbows, squinting at the clock. "Almost nine. You have to work today, right?"

Rosie nodded as she sat on the bed beside Jane. "The store opens at ten."

"No time to waste, then." Jane sat up, blinking the sleep from her eyes.

"Trust me when I say Lia will be more than happy to open for me," Rosie told her. "But I don't want to take advantage since she worked until closing last night, so I do need to start getting ready. But I don't have to rush right out the door."

"I can live with those terms," Jane said. "Do you have time to stop at the café on the corner for a quick breakfast after we get dressed? Or I can fix you some oatmeal here, but that's about all I have."

"The café sounds perfect," Rosie said, eager to sneak in a few more minutes with Jane before she had to return to the real world.

"Will Brinkley be missing you?" Jane asked as she got out of bed.

"Oh, for sure," Rosie said. "But my roommates spoil him on my behalf on the rare occasion I actually go somewhere he can't come."

Jane kissed her cheek. "Well, I hope you'll have a reason to go out more often now, although he's welcome here any time."

"Really?" Rosie asked, ridiculously pleased with everything Jane had just said. "Are dogs allowed in your building?"

Jane hesitated before she answered. "BPD owns the building, so regardless of what's written in my lease, it's fine."

"Oh," Rosie said, determined not to let that tidbit of information bother her. This apartment was awfully nice for a single woman to afford on her own in the city. Did Jane even pay rent, or did she live here for free? Then again, she was older than Rosie and worked a corporate job that probably came with a hefty paycheck.

"I pay the same rent as everyone else in the building," Jane clarified, as if Rosie had asked her question out loud. "But let's just say, my landlord has a little more trust in me than most and isn't going to hassle me over a cute pup sleeping over."

"Fair enough," Rosie said.

She and Jane took a quick shower together before they got dressed. Rosie borrowed an oversize red sweater to wear with her leggings so she wouldn't need to stop at home before she went to the store, and she gave

Jane the shoes that were still in her bag. After some borrowed mascara and lipstick, they were on their way to the café for breakfast.

"Feel free to say no," Rosie said as they were finishing their meal. "But I'd love if you came to afternoon tea tomorrow."

Jane narrowed her eyes. "Do you really think that's a good idea?"

"Why not?" Rosie said with a shrug. "You don't have to come as Brie. Come as Jane, have a cup of tea, and chat about books. Or listen to everyone else chat about books if you don't want to join in. Plus, you get to see me."

Jane's expression softened. "That's a definite perk. You don't think it would be awkward?"

"Jane . . ." She reached across the table to rest her hand on Jane's. "I know *you* think you didn't fit in last time, but you looked perfectly at ease to me. In fact, I was a little annoyed at the time by how well you seemed to fit."

Jane stared into her coffee. "Well, I was on edge."

"And you sat as far from me as you possibly could," Rosie teased. "Don't think I didn't notice that part."

Jane smiled. "Oh, that was deliberate."

"I thought so. Anyway, you said you wanted to start integrating yourself into the book world, so I thought this might be a good first step. Plus, I want to see you again, but I'm working all weekend."

"I'll come," she said. "But as Jane, not Brie . . . at least for now."

"Totally fine," Rosie said. "And on that note, I've got to run. See you tomorrow?"

"Yes." Jane stood to give her a quick kiss.

"Last night was amazing," Rosie murmured against her lips.

"It was," Jane agreed.

"Bye." Rosie lingered for another minute in that kiss, and then she put on her coat and headed out. Not to quote a cheesy song lyric, but she felt like she was walking on sunshine. If she were an emoji, she'd be the one with hearts for eyes. She'd had the most amazing night, and for the moment at least, she felt like she could take on the world.

She boarded the subway and headed uptown, arriving at the store about forty-five minutes after it opened. There were several groups of people browsing the aisles, a good sign for a Saturday morning. Rosie greeted them as she walked past, finding Lia behind the counter.

Brinkley came bursting out from behind it, bounding around her feet like he hadn't seen her in a month rather than just one night. All the same, she was pretty excited to see him too. She knelt to scoop him into her arms, giggling as he licked her face.

"Nice of you to come to work this morning," Lia said with a mock-serious raise of her eyebrows.

"I owe you big time," Rosie told her. "Take tonight off, or tomorrow . . . anytime you want."

Lia waved her off as a smile tugged at her lips. "Good night?"

"So good," Rosie said as she put Brinkley down. He ran a lap around the counter and then headed for the back hall, probably to get a drink of water. "Like, oh my God, Lia, I don't know where to start."

"I'll take the highlights for now, but you're going to need to tell me everything after we get home."

Rosie took off her coat and joined Lia behind the counter, fairly bursting to talk to her best friend, but she forced a polite smile onto her face as a family who had been browsing the children's section approached. Each little girl held two books, which they placed on the counter in front of her with eager faces.

"Oh, Elephant and Piggie, I love these books," Rosie said as she slid the books toward the register to ring them up.

"Me too," the girl told her. "They're my favorite."

Rosie chatted with her while she rang up the family's purchases, feeling a slight pang in her chest as she sent them on their way. She felt like she had a ticking clock above her head, reminding her how little time remained before she had to close these doors.

"Okay, now spill," Lia said as soon as they had the counter to themselves. "And by the way, are you wearing her clothes?"

"Just the sweater," Rosie said, glancing down at herself. "So I didn't have to go home and change before I came to work."

"Interesting," Lia said. "Go on."

"It was so great, Lia." She could tell she was grinning like an idiot, but she couldn't seem to help it or bring herself to care. "She's surprisingly shy and just so sweet, and I could talk about books with her for hours. And she's also really, *really* great in bed."

"That's a lot of really's," Lia said, nudging Rosie with her elbow. "And I am *really* happy for you. I've seen her shyness too. In fact, I think that's probably why she came off as cold when she came here to talk business, because she felt uncomfortable about it. My little sister is painfully shy, and people often think she's rude, when the truth is that she just doesn't know what to say."

"Yeah, I think you're right about Jane," Rosie said. "But hopefully we're past the awkwardness now, and this time, we really talked through it instead of just shoving it under the rug because it was hard."

"That's good," Lia said. "I was kind of ambivalent about her until your birthday, but after she came out with us that night, I was sold. I like her, and more than that, I like seeing you with her. You seem happy together."

"I'll take all the happy I can get right now," Rosie said. "And speaking of happy things, we need to start planning our holiday party. I don't want to call it a going-out-of-business party, because hopefully by then we'll be celebrating a move to a new storefront, but we need to do something. I want to celebrate in this space one last time."

Jane hesitated in front of Between the Pages, working up the courage to go inside. The display in the window was different from the first time she'd visited, when she'd seen her book there. Now it featured a collection of hardcover thrillers with the heading "Thrills and Chills." A piece of paper to the right of the door caught Jane's eye. It was a flyer advertising a holiday party here in the store.

"Come celebrate with us here on Lexington Avenue one last time before we move on to new things," the flyer advertised, and Jane felt that all-too-familiar pang of guilt. She didn't belong here. Or did she? Had she redeemed herself? Rosie had invited her, and unlike last time, she knew full well who Jane was now.

A woman entered the store ahead of her, and Jane followed her in. Like the other time she'd come on a Sunday, the store was filled with people waiting to go downstairs for the tea service. Jane lingered near the door, taking a moment to convince herself that she should stay.

"Boo," Rosie whispered in her ear.

Jane whirled to face her, surprise making her heart race, and then it was just the sight of Rosie's smiling face that had her blood speeding through her veins. "Didn't see you there."

"I know," Rosie said, nudging Jane deeper into the store. "Come on in and say hi to some friendly booklovers. We don't bite, I promise."

"I'm working on it," Jane said, giving Rosie's hand a squeeze.

Rosie kept her hand in Jane's as she walked toward the counter in back, towing Jane along with her. "Did you get lots of writing done since I saw you last?"

"A good amount, yeah," Jane told her. "I made that change we talked about, and it really spiced things up, I think."

"That's great," Rosie said. "Will you spend tonight writing, too, or do you ever take a night off?"

"Actually, I'm heading to Brooklyn after I leave here to have dinner with Amy and her family, so yes, I'm taking tonight off. I took Friday night off, too, as you might remember," Jane said, feeling herself relax in Rosie's presence.

"Oh, I do remember," Rosie said with a sly look. "So you'll see Alyssa tonight? Because I got a new book in this week that I think she'd love."

"I will, and I'd love to buy her a new book. Just point me in the right direction before I leave."

"My treat," Rosie said. "Perks of sleeping with the owner and having an adorable niece."

"If you're sure," Jane said. "Thank you."

"My pleasure. Look, Lia's about to open the door. Go on downstairs and get a seat, and I'll be down in a few minutes, okay?"

"Okay." Jane gave Rosie's hand another squeeze before she headed for the stairs, joining the rest of the guests. Downstairs, the room quickly filled with people already talking about books as they got refreshments. Jane spotted Lia by the row of teapots and walked over to say hello.

"Hi, Jane," Lia said warmly. "Glad you could join us."

"Me too," she said, surprised to realize she meant it. Remembering Lia's advice last time, she poured herself a cup of Earl Grey, and since she wasn't planning to make a hasty exit today, she took a mini chocolate-filled croissant too.

"Oh, hi. Jane, right?"

She turned to see the woman with short black hair she'd sat beside last time. "Yes, hi. It's nice to see you again."

"Tracy," she said with a friendly smile, saving Jane.

"Right. Sorry, I'm terrible with names." Actually, she wasn't usually, but she'd been so distracted that afternoon.

"No worries," Tracy said. "Hey, I bought one of Maura Green's books after you recommended her to me. I'd never read a romance between two women before, but I enjoyed it a lot. I'll definitely read more."

"Oh, really? That's great. I'm so glad you enjoyed it." Jane's chest loosened, and the smile on her lips was one she hadn't even planned on.

"I'd love to hear more recommendations if you have some," Tracy said.

"Sure," Jane told her. They found seats together, and Jane shared a few of her favorite lesbian romance novels while Tracy looked them up on her phone and saved them to her wish list.

"Hi, ladies," Rosie said as she slid into the seat on Jane's other side, a cup of tea in one hand and a plate of pastries in the other.

"Jane was just sharing some book recommendations with me," Tracy told her. "I had read gay romance with two men, but I hadn't read one between two women until Jane recommended an author the last time she was here."

"Is that so?" Rosie looked delighted, and Jane felt a funny tingle in her stomach, even though she trusted Rosie not to expose her identity. "I have another recommendation for you."

"Please," Tracy said with a smile.

"The author's name is Brie," Rosie said. "She writes really sexy corporate heroines, and her books are set right here in the city. Start with *On the Flip Side*—which we have in stock upstairs—but you won't go wrong with any of her books."

"Perfect," Tracy said. "I'll grab a copy before I leave today."

Rosie nudged her knee subtly against Jane's, a silent cheer. "Awesome."

Jane picked at her croissant, somehow feeling even more awkward about pretending not to know Brie than if she'd just admitted to being her. Thankfully, the conversation shifted to less personal topics, and Jane settled into her chair, content to talk about books with a roomful of booklovers. Rosie was right. She did belong, at least as a reader. And maybe sometime soon, she'd be ready to introduce herself as Brie.

Once the tea service wrapped up, Jane headed upstairs, where Rosie rushed to the children's section to get the book for Alyssa.

"It's a graphic novel about a girl and her dog who save the world," Rosie told her.

"She'll love it," Jane said. "But please let me pay you for this."

"Nope," Rosie insisted. "It's my gift to Alyssa."

"Thank you," Jane said. "I really appreciate it, and I'll bring her in sometime soon to pick out a few books that I'll pay you for."

Rosie rolled her eyes playfully. "I'm glad Alyssa has an aunt to feed her love of books. That's so important."

"Well, it's not like Amy doesn't buy her books. It's just my special thing with Alyssa."

"And I love that. Tell her hi for me."

"Will do." No one seemed to be looking in their direction, so Jane leaned in for a quick kiss, immediately flooded with the warmth that filled her every time Rosie's lips touched hers. "Bye."

"Bye," Rosie said, giving Jane a slightly dazed smile.

Jane left the store and walked down Lexington Avenue to the subway station. Once she'd boarded her train, she settled into an empty seat and pulled up a book on her phone, the second in the London-based series Rosie had recommended to her the day they met.

Forty-five minutes later, she exited the train to begin the fifteen-minute walk to Amy's house. The air was cool and crisp, and the trees along the sidewalk had mostly lost their leaves now, branches bare as they awaited the arrival of winter. The row houses she walked past were decked out with pumpkins and pots of red, orange, and purple mums on their porches.

Jane loved fall. It was probably her favorite season, although she was pretty fond of spring too. But right now, she was completely enchanted by the decor around her, and for the first time, she found herself looking forward to Thanksgiving. She'd never been to Colorado, but she'd googled photos of Breckenridge, and it looked like an adorable mountain town. Maybe they'd even get to do some early-season skiing.

She climbed Amy and Garrett's front steps and knocked, grinning as Alyssa pulled the door open, wearing a green shirt with little Santas all over it. "Jumping the season a little bit, aren't you?" she asked.

Alyssa shrugged. "Christmas is my favorite holiday, and one month just isn't long enough for me to do all my celebrating. Mom said I could wear it."

Jane stepped inside and closed the door behind her, smelling the savory scent of meatloaf. "Well, if you put it that way, who am I to tell you not to start celebrating a little early?"

Alyssa giggled as she led the way into the living room, where Garrett sat on the couch, watching football.

"Hey, Jane," he called.

"Hi," she said, turning to Alyssa. "I have something for you."

"An early Christmas present?" Alyssa asked hopefully.

"Sure," Jane said with a laugh. "Let's call it that. It's from Rosie. Remember the nice lady at the bookstore we went into that day?"

"The one with the cute dog?" Alyssa asked.

"Yes," Jane said.

"Brinkley," Alyssa said dreamily. She'd been campaigning unsuccessfully for years to get a dog of her own, but Amy argued that they weren't home enough to give a dog the attention it needed, given her and Garrett's often long workdays.

Jane had to admit she had a point. In the meantime, she could shower her niece with books about dogs. She reached into her bag and pulled out the one Rosie had given her, then handed it to Alyssa.

"Cool," Alyssa said as she saw the cover, her face lighting up. "Thank you." She turned toward the kitchen. "Mom, Auntie Jane brought me a new book. I'm going out to my fort to read until dinner, okay?"

"Okay, sweetie," Amy called. "Auntie Jane, you'd better get in here to help me with dinner."

"Coming," Jane said as her niece dashed out the back door, book in hand, headed for the tent in the backyard she'd claimed as her fort. "I hope she's got blankets or something in there this time of year."

"A whole pile of them," Amy confirmed as Jane walked into the kitchen. "And I don't really need your help—although you can slice some tomatoes for the salad if you want—but I need to hear *all* about your date on Friday and whether or not that book you just gave Alyssa is from Rosie."

Jane knelt to pull a cutting board out of the drawer under the stove. "It is, and our date went really well."

"This is the kind of news I like to hear," Amy said as she began to whip the mashed potatoes. "Did you have sex with her?"

Jane pulled a knife from the block on the counter. "Yes."

The blender lurched in Amy's hands, and she turned to face Jane with wide eyes. "No shit, really?"

"Really," Jane confirmed as she grabbed a tomato and started chopping. "And you can stop looking so shocked any minute now."

"It's just, it's been a while for you," Amy said. "This is amazing, and I need more details."

"She spent the night at my place, and that's about as much detail as you're going to get," Jane said with a decisive chop to the tomato.

"That's huge," Amy said. "She brings out a side of you I haven't seen in a while. You're going out and having fun for a change, and it's what you deserve."

"I do have a tendency to get caught up in my own head sometimes," Jane admitted. "And in my books."

"Always with your books," Amy teased. "Which is why it's also awesome that Rosie knows these things about you. You've never dated anyone before who knew you were an author, and you two are both book nerds. I'm just calling it now, but you seem perfect for each other."

"Way too early," Jane told her. "But fun is good, and so is dating someone who knows all my secrets. I think the conflict with her store and my day job will always be there until she finds a new home or I quit at BPD, but either of those things are possible. Who knows what the new year will bring?"

"Maybe you'll bring her with you the next time you come for dinner," Amy suggested.

"Really?" Jane asked. "We've only just started dating. Shouldn't I wait longer to introduce her to Alyssa?"

"On the contrary, I think it's good for Alyssa to know you have a life," Amy said. "You're a responsible, mature adult, Jane. You don't have to marry someone before you introduce her to my daughter."

"Well, okay," Jane said.

"Bring her next time. I for one can't wait to meet this woman."

CHAPTER SIXTEEN

"Our turkey will be ready to pick up at four," Lia said.

Rosie looked up from her phone, where she'd been scrolling through real estate listings while she waited for one of the customers in the store to bring their purchases to the counter. It was two days before Thanksgiving, and the store bustled with happy shoppers picking out books to bring with them on their holiday travels. "Do you want to run out and pick it up, or should I?"

"I'll go," Lia offered.

"Jane's coming over after work to sign the books for our subscription box, so I can manage the store until closing if you want to take off early," Rosie told her.

"In that case, I'm going to run some errands and then pick up our turkey. See you later at home?"

"Yep. Have fun." Rosie waved her off with a smile. Every year, she and Lia cooked a turkey together at their apartment and invited any of their friends who didn't have Thanksgiving plans to join them. It was a tradition Rosie had come to cherish since her mom died.

Lia bundled up and headed out, and Rosie spent the rest of the afternoon busy with customers, which was pretty much her favorite way to pass her time at the store. At least, it was until she saw Jane coming through the front door, because any time spent with Jane was quickly becoming Rosie's absolute favorite. It had been two weeks since their first official date, when Rosie spent the night at Jane's place. They'd gone out a handful of times since, and Rosie had enjoyed every moment.

Spotting Jane, Brinkley hopped off his dog bed and trotted toward the front door, tail wagging. Jane crouched to pet him, talking sweetly to him with words Rosie couldn't hear as he gazed up at her adoringly. Jane stood and walked to the counter with Brinkley at her heels.

"Hey," she said.

"Hey yourself." Rosie's eyes fell helplessly to Jane's suit as she unbuttoned her coat. It was navy blue with a champagne-colored blouse beneath the jacket. A diamond pendant dangled just above her cleavage.

"Like it?" Jane asked, amusement in her voice.

"Love it," Rosie responded. "But I have yet to see you in anything I don't like."

"It's possible you're biased," Jane said.

"No, I think you just look good in clothes . . . and out of them." That came out louder than she'd intended. She slapped a hand over her mouth, glancing around to make sure no one had overheard her. Not that she cared who knew Jane was her girlfriend, but she didn't exactly want to shout about getting Jane naked in front of her customers.

Jane watched her with raised eyebrows, a smile tugging at her lips.

"Anyway, let's take advantage of this lull at the counter for me to run downstairs and get you set up. I'll check on you when I can, and please feel free to come up and hang out with me, but the store's been busy today, and I gave Lia the rest of the day off."

"Sure," Jane said.

Rosie led the way downstairs and flipped on the light in the meeting room, where she'd set up a long folding table stacked with books. "If you can't finish today, don't worry about it. I'm not mailing them out until next week."

"That's a lot of books," Jane said, eyes wide.

"Two hundred. I think it's a good amount for our first autographed subscription box," Rosie told her. "I've set out Sharpies for you and some of those little stickers that say the book is autographed by the author. Help yourself to anything in the kitchenette, and come up and visit me when your hand gets tired."

"Got it," Jane said.

"Really wish I could hang out down here with you, but I've got to get upstairs before the customers go wild without me," Rosie said.

"Go on." Jane waved her off. "As much as I love your company, I'll sign faster on my own."

"Okay. Have fun." Rosie gave her a quick kiss and jogged back upstairs. She took a quick lap around the store to see if she could help anyone with their selections. A college-age woman wanted a murder mystery to read on the train ride home to her family tomorrow, and a woman about Rosie's age was looking for picture books about trucks to give her nephews.

As much as she was dying to watch Jane in action, Rosie spent the next hour helping a steady stream of customers. The next thing she knew, the door to the basement opened, and Jane came up behind her, resting a hand discreetly on Rosie's waist beneath the counter.

"Have you eaten?" she asked.

Rosie shook her head. "I forgot to plan for dinner before I sent Lia off for the day."

"Want me to pick up something for us?" Jane asked.

"That would be great, actually. I'm starving."

"What's good near here?" Jane asked.

"There's a sub shop down the street and an Italian place on the corner," Rosie said.

"Italian sounds messy in these clothes and near books. Subs okay with you?"

"Perfect," Rosie told her. "I like the chicken-club hoagie."

"Chips?"

"Just the plain ones."

Jane grinned. "I could have guessed that."

"I'm boringly predictable like that," Rosie said, giving her a nudge.

"Nothing boring about you," Jane said, pressing a quick kiss against Rosie's cheek. "Okay, I'll be back in a bit."

Rosie touched her cheek, watching her go. Brinkley let out a little whine from his dog bed, and when Rosie looked down, he was watching Jane leave too. "I know the feeling, buddy."

A man approached the counter with a stack of historical fiction books, and Rosie refocused her attention to ring up his purchases. It didn't slow down from there, and she was still going when Jane came back in with their dinner. If Rosie had realized it was going to be this busy tonight, she might not have sent Lia home, but her friend had picked up so much slack for Rosie lately that she wasn't going to interrupt her evening now.

"The store is hopping tonight," Jane commented as she stopped behind the counter. "How do you want to do this? Should I just leave your food up here?"

Rosie shook her head. "I don't eat in the store. Why don't you put mine in the fridge downstairs for now, and I'll come grab it when I get a free moment?"

"Better yet, why don't I watch the counter for a few minutes while you eat?" Jane offered.

"Do you even know how to use a cash register?" Rosie asked.

"Well, no, but you can either give me a crash course or I can just text you if someone's ready to check out before you get back. I can at least watch over the store for you."

"Actually, I might take you up on that." Her feet hurt, and she had to pee. She hadn't had a break since before Lia left that afternoon. She gave Jane a quick overview on how to use the register, and after thanking her profusely, Rosie headed downstairs to her office. She set the bag of sandwiches on her desk and then poked her head into the meeting room on her way to the bathroom to see how much progress Jane had made.

There were several stacks of signed books, golden stickers neatly placed on the covers. Rosie lifted the cover flap on the top book to peek inside, finding Jane's swirly handwriting on the title page. This table full of books made her indescribably happy, both as a bookstore owner and as a booklover. And these subscription boxes were going to help keep her afloat while she transitioned to a new space.

Jane leaned her elbows on the counter and watched the customers browsing the store. Part of her hoped none of them were ready to check out before Rosie got back, but another part of her wanted the chance to interact with them, and to be helpful to Rosie. She'd never worked retail before, but she did deal with clients on a regular basis. She liked it here in Rosie's store. It was a warm and welcoming place, and despite initially feeling like an outsider, she felt relaxed and welcome here now.

Brinkley watched her from the dog bed in the corner, head between his front paws.

"Are you new here?" a middle-aged woman asked with a friendly smile as she placed two books on the counter in front of Jane.

"No, I'm actually just covering for Rosie while she eats dinner," Jane told her.

"Oh, that's nice. Are you a friend of hers?"

Jane nodded as she slid the books toward the register the way she'd seen Rosie do. Since the woman seemed friendly and was likely a regular, Jane decided to be honest with her. "It's my first time, so bear with me while I ring you up. If I have any trouble, I'll just call Rosie, but I'm hoping not to interrupt her dinner."

"I don't want to interrupt her dinner either," the woman said, then gave Jane a conspiratorial smile. "I'm sure we can figure it out between the two of us."

Jane returned her smile as she scanned the first book. The title and price showed up on the screen, just the way it had when Rosie demonstrated earlier, and the second book was just as easy. Jane swiped the woman's card and put her books in a bag, feeling irrationally proud of herself.

"Look at you," the woman said. "Like a pro."

Jane wiped her brow dramatically. "Phew. I'm relieved to have the first one under my belt. Thanks for being patient with me."

"It was my pleasure," the woman said. "Tell Rosie that Dolores says hi and that I'm happy she has friends looking out for her and making sure she takes her dinner break. I know she loves this store, but she works too hard sometimes."

"She does, and I'll tell her," Jane said.

"Such a shame she's going to have to close, isn't it?" Dolores said, shaking her head sadly. "I can't believe they're going to demolish this gorgeous building to put in another high-rise."

Jane's smile withered, but she nodded gamely. "I'm sure she'll find a new space to reopen."

"I sure hope so," Dolores said. "And hopefully not too far from here. This place is right on my way home from work, and it's hard to walk past without popping in for a new book."

"Fingers crossed," Jane said.

"Lovely to meet you," Dolores said, waving at Jane before she headed for the door.

Jane didn't have time to process her feelings about that little exchange before another person stepped up to the register, this time a man about her age who was clearly in a hurry. Naturally, the machine beeped with an error when Jane scanned his book. He grumbled impatiently as she tried again. Jane felt herself getting flustered, and she drew a slow breath, doing her best to ignore him as she fumbled with the scanner, finally succeeding on her third try. He paid and left without so much as a thank-you. *Asshole.*

Luckily, the rest of Rosie's customers were much friendlier, and all of them seemed to know her by name. After ringing up three more people, Jane had settled into a nice rhythm when Rosie stepped in beside her.

"You look like a natural," she said.

"I don't feel like one," Jane told her. "But I think I did okay. Oh, and Dolores says hi."

"Aw, you met Dolores," Rosie said with a grin. "She stops in here once a week or so on her way home from work."

"Yeah, she mentioned something like that." Jane rested a hand on Rosie's shoulder. "You know, I think I understand now why this place is so important to you, in a way I didn't before. You've built a real community here."

Rosie blinked, and her eyes went glossy. "That's what I was trying to tell you that first day in my office. But it doesn't matter now. You didn't have the power to stop it that day, and you certainly don't now. I'll find a new space."

"And I'll help, but in the meantime, I'm going to eat dinner and sign more books."

Rosie nodded. "We close in about an hour, so I'll come down and join you then, if you haven't finished."

"Okay." Jane headed for the stairs, surprised when she heard Brinkley clattering behind her. "Is it all right if he comes down with me?"

"He is *such* a traitor," Rosie said fondly. "Sure, that's fine, but he's probably going to beg you for dinner once he gets downstairs."

"My dinner or his?" Jane asked.

"Either, but don't give him yours," Rosie said. "His is in the cabinet under the sink. Just fill the cup in the bag and pour it in his bowl."

"Got it," Jane said.

"Now you're really going to be his favorite."

"I couldn't possibly be, not when you're around," Jane said.

"Oh, please. He adores you." Rosie grinned before she turned around to serve the customer who'd just stepped up to the counter.

"Rosie, I just saw the sign on the door, and I can't believe it," the woman said. "You're closing?"

"Moving," Rosie told her with what was probably forced cheer. "At least I hope so. I'm looking for a new space, so cross your fingers for me."

Jane went through into the stairwell and pulled the door shut behind her. Her face felt hot. She'd done this to Rosie, and now she had to do everything in her power to make it right. Surely if she got creative and pulled some strings, she could find a new home for Between the Pages.

Brinkley bounced down the stairs ahead of her. As predicted, when they reached the basement, he led the way into the kitchenette and stared up at her with expectant eyes.

"Hungry?" she asked. "Me too. Let's see what I can do about that."

She opened a few cabinets until she located the bag of dog food, and then she filled the scoop inside and dumped it into the silver bowl on the floor. Brinkley dived in, and the room filled with the rattling sound of him pushing kibble around the metal bowl as he ate.

Jane poured herself a glass of water, and since there wasn't a table in here, she hopped up on the counter to eat her sandwich. This way, she could keep an eye on Brinkley, but also, she didn't want to eat anywhere near the books in the other room.

By the time she'd finished eating, Brinkley lay on the floor beneath her, watching closely in case she dropped anything. She threw out her trash and then visited the bathroom in the hallway to freshen up.

When she came back out, Brinkley was in the hall, still watching her.

"Bet you might like to go outside, huh?" she asked. He hadn't been out since before she got there around five, and maybe that was fine, but she didn't want him to pee on the floor. Rosie was so busy today that she might have forgotten.

Jane went into Rosie's office and found a leash, which she clipped to his collar. "You don't mind if I walk you, do you?"

Brinkley tugged her toward the steps with an eager look on his face. Whether or not he needed to pee, he definitely wanted to go outside. She went out the back door with him, and they walked down the alley together. She'd forgotten to put her coat on, and it was pretty cold out, but she was okay for a few minutes in her suit jacket while Brinkley took care of business. Actually, as they rounded the corner onto East Ninety-Fifth, she decided she liked walking a dog.

Brinkley was entertaining to watch. He found joy in things she never would have noticed, like a pigeon on the sidewalk and a flower someone had dropped. Everyone who passed them seemed to smile at him, and Jane found herself smiling back. Usually, she walked with purpose from one destination to another. She couldn't remember the last time she'd wandered like this, and she let Brinkley set the pace and the direction of their exploration.

She window-shopped as they walked, noting a cute bakery and a bar that looked like someplace she might like to stop in with Rosie one day. Before she realized it, Brinkley was leading her toward the gate to Central Park.

"Oh geez," she said on a laugh. "You're a sneaky one, aren't you?"

As much as she'd love to walk him through the park, she was starting to shiver without her coat. Not to mention these heels were not made for walking, at least not this far. It seemed cruel to turn him around the minute they arrived, though, so she let him walk a short way inside. He led her across a grassy area and then squatted.

"Oh shit," she muttered. She was supposed to pick that up, wasn't she? But with what? As she glanced around frantically for some sort of dog station, she noticed the plastic canister dangling from the leash in her hand. Well, that was convenient. She did a quick cleanup and dropped the bag in a trash can, then turned Brinkley around toward the exit.

Luckily, he didn't seem to mind his short trip to the park and led the way happily back to the store. Since she didn't have a key to the back of the building, Jane looped onto Lexington Avenue and went in through the front. Rosie was deep in conversation with a customer, so Jane went straight through to the steps leading to the basement, bringing Brinkley with her.

Downstairs, she washed her hands and sat down to sign the rest of the books. Brinkley went into the kitchenette for a drink and then curled up nearby, watching her.

"You're good company, you know that?" she told him.

His tail gave an enthusiastic wag as if he understood what she'd said.

She uncapped her Sharpie and got back to work. Her hand had been starting to cramp when she'd quit before dinner, making her handwriting sloppy, but she was refreshed now. It was exciting, signing all these books. She'd never done this before. Sure, she'd signed a few books here and there for giveaways, but she'd never done anything like *this*.

As she surveyed the stacks of books in front of her, it was overwhelming in the best possible way. She felt a kind of pride she wasn't used to when it came to her career as an author. She knew she was good at her job as a property developer, but somehow she'd never felt that pride as an author.

She loved writing books. It fulfilled her in a way her day job didn't, but she'd never given herself the chance to embrace it. Without attending signings or events, she'd started to feel like a fraud, like a shell of an author, but maybe she was ready to change that. Or, at least, she was tiptoeing her way toward being ready.

She could do things like this—sign books for Rosie's subscription boxes—while she worked toward doing an in-person signing. Her pen swirled over the paper, and it was satisfying. She kept signing, making her way through the stacks of books with occasional breaks to stretch out the kinks in her hand . . . and to pet Brinkley.

Soon she heard Rosie's shoes on the stairs. Brinkley leaped to his feet and scrambled to greet her, bouncing and wagging his tail excitedly as Rosie joined them in the meeting room. She bent to scoop him into her arms before leaning in to kiss Jane as Brinkley wriggled between him, lunging to kiss Rosie's face and then Jane's.

Rosie set him down with a laugh. "Your hand must be tired."

"Oh my God, so tired," Jane said, rubbing it for good measure. "I never write anything by hand anymore."

"And you're a leftie," Rosie commented.

"I am."

"Lefties are supposed to be more creative, so that fits."

"I guess so," Jane said. "Alyssa's a leftie too. Maybe she'll follow in my footsteps."

"That would be amazing. Does she know you're an author?"

Jane nodded. "Amy brags about me all the time, I'm afraid."

"As she should," Rosie said. "That's what sisters are supposed to do, right?"

"True." Jane stood and pulled her in for another kiss, lingering this time since there wasn't a dog in the way. "Is the store closed?"

"Yep," Rosie said. "I'm all yours until you finish."

"I like the sound of that." Jane wound her arms around Rosie and held her close. "And I only have one stack of books left."

"Which I will be thrilled to sit here and watch you sign," Rosie said, before placing a playful kiss on Jane's cheek.

"Want to come over tonight?" Jane asked. "I'm flying to Colorado tomorrow, and I won't be back until Sunday."

"If you don't mind Brinkley tagging along, I'd love to," Rosie said.

"Oh, he and I are good friends now," Jane said, tossing him an affectionate look. "He's always welcome to sleep over."

"In that case, yes, definitely." Rosie crossed the room and brought a folding chair from the stack against the wall so she could sit beside Jane while she finished signing. "It's wild that you're spending Thanksgiving in Breckenridge. Is that a family tradition, or what?"

"Colorado isn't, but traveling for Thanksgiving is," Jane told her. "We go somewhere new every year. My dad is self-made. He never got to travel as a kid, and he's too busy with work most of the time now, but we carve out this week every year."

"Wow," Rosie said. "That's a really cool tradition. I love it."

"Thanks. I do, too, although I was dreading it a little bit this year, because I'm just so frustrated with everything at work right now. But it'll be good to get away, see someplace new, and spend some time with my family."

"I'm glad."

"What about you?" Jane asked. "Will it just be you and Lia this year?"

"And Shanice," Rosie said. "She has to work on Black Friday, so she's staying here in the city."

"Oh shit, yeah," Jane said. "You have to work, too, don't you?"

"Big time," Rosie said with a laugh. "Lia and I will be prepping inventory tomorrow for our Black Friday sales. I'm running a few extra deals this year to help clear out as many books as possible. From here on out, I'm only going to order the bare minimum stock so I have less to pack up in a few weeks."

"About that," Jane said. "After I worked upstairs earlier, it got me thinking about how beneficial it would be for you to stay in the same neighborhood, right?"

"That would be ideal," Rosie said with a nod. "A good percentage of my customers are regulars, and most of them live or work around here, so they come in because the shop is convenient. If I move somewhere else—like that space in SoHo—I'd have to work that much harder to find new patrons instead of just inviting all my regulars into the new space."

"Gotcha," Jane said.

"Why?" Rosie asked.

"I'm just mulling over your options, that's all," Jane told her. "Trying to think outside the box, if it might help find you a space we hadn't considered yet."

"Like what?"

Jane shrugged. "I don't know yet, exactly, but I'm thinking."

"Well, you're pretty when you think," Rosie said playfully as she leaned in for another kiss. "And I appreciate your help."

"The least I can do," Jane said. She fell quiet while she signed the last few books, since she couldn't seem to talk and sign at the same time. A few minutes later, she capped her Sharpie and moved the last book to the signed stack. "Done."

"Sweet," Rosie said, surveying the table. "Could I take a picture of you with them? I won't share it with anyone unless you give me permission to, but maybe we both want to remember this, and maybe someday you'll want to share it."

Jane bit back the "No!" that had automatically risen on her tongue, because everything Rosie had said made sense, and as she remembered the pride she'd felt earlier while she was signing, she thought Rosie might be right. She *did* want to remember this. "Yeah. Let's do it."

So she posed by the table while Rosie snapped several photos on her phone, and then they posed for a selfie together with the stacks of books visible on the table behind them. It might've been the first selfie Jane had ever taken.

"Aww, they're so cute," Rosie said as she tabbed through the photos on her phone.

"Will you text those to me?" Jane asked.

"Of course."

Jane's phone dinged several times as Rosie sent over the photos. She wrapped herself up in her coat while Rosie grabbed her own and put on Brinkley's leash. "Let's get out of here."

Rosie hooked her arm in Jane's. "Brinkley's first sleepover at Jane's."

CHAPTER SEVENTEEN

"Mm, that was good," Rosie said as she leaned back in her chair. She was comfortably full of turkey, mashed potatoes, and stuffing, the perfect trio of Thanksgiving food. Across from her, Lia and Shanice looked similarly stuffed.

"So good," Shanice agreed. "Thanks again for having me."

"I'm so glad you could come," Rosie told her. "It would have been a quiet meal with just Lia and me."

"I don't know about quiet," Lia commented as she buttered a roll.

"True. You're loud." Rosie stuck out her tongue playfully at her friend.

"I was talking about *you*," Lia shot back.

Shanice shook her head as she laughed. "You two are too much."

"We usually have a bigger group," Rosie commented. "In fact, Grace was supposed to join us this year, all the way from Spain."

"Your imaginary friend," Lia teased.

Shanice toyed with one of her braids. "She's not imaginary. Paige met her that one time."

"And yet, after all these years, I still haven't met her," Lia said.

"She doesn't make it back to the States very often," Rosie said. Still, she had to admit it was unusual that her best friend from high school and her best friend from college still hadn't met. She'd have to plan something the next time Grace visited. "Anyway, I love Friendsgiving. It feels good to make new traditions."

And having her friends around helped her not to miss her mom as much on holidays like this one. She'd been missing her more than usual lately, maybe because of losing her lease. Last night, she'd dreamed that she and her mom were touring new spaces together, and there'd been a hollow ache inside her ever since.

"Bonus for no family drama," Shanice said as she lifted her glass of cider. "This is so low key compared to what I'm used to. I think I could get used to it."

"Well, you're always welcome to join us," Rosie told her. "Although I think your family might object."

"Oh yeah, I can't get in the habit of skipping family holidays, nor would I want to," Shanice said. "But if I ever have to work on Black Friday again, I know where I'm coming for Thanksgiving." She and Rosie tapped their cider glasses together.

The three of them chatted happily as they cleaned up their meal and settled in the living room to watch a movie before dessert. Lia insisted on *Elf*, proclaiming that it was officially Christmas season now that they'd eaten their turkey. They drank more cider and giggled their way through the movie as Shanice hopped off the couch to reenact her favorite parts and Lia sang along with the Christmas carols.

Rosie snapped photos on her phone to commemorate the silly afternoon, and then she took a selfie with the movie visible on the TV behind her and texted it to Jane. A few minutes later, she received a photo of Jane, Alyssa, and a woman she assumed was Amy hiking along a snow-covered trail with mountain peaks visible behind them.

Rosie Taft:

Okay, your Thanksgiving looks more adventurous than mine!

Jane Breslin:

Yours looks warmer, though.

Tell Lia and Shanice hi for me.

Rosie Taft:

Will do! Miss you!

Jane Breslin:

Same 😘

On the TV, Buddy was throwing snowballs at warp speed, and Rosie doubled over in laughter as Shanice began balling up tissues and whipping them across the living room. Within minutes, they were engaged in an all-out tissue fight, bits of white paper fluttering through the air like snowflakes.

After the movie finished, they cleaned up—with a lot more laughter—and went into the kitchen to pull out dessert. Rosie and Lia had baked an apple pie last night, and Shanice had brought pumpkin.

"Two pies and three women," Lia said as she began slicing. "I like our odds here."

"So do I," Rosie agreed.

Lia passed her a slice of apple pie, knowing without asking that Rosie didn't like pumpkin. Once everyone had plates full of pie, they sat around the table together.

"Colin's getting married," Lia said. "He texted me this morning."

"Really?" Rosie had only met Lia's older brother once, but he seemed like a good guy, if a bit serious. "Who's he marrying? Do you like her?"

"Her name's Olivia. They've been together about a year." Lia shrugged before taking a bite of pumpkin pie. She chewed and swallowed. "I like her. They seem happy together."

Shanice sighed as she cut a piece of pie with her fork. "Seems like everyone's getting married lately, doesn't it?"

"Oh, don't even get me started," Lia said. "I'm never going to hear the end of it now that Colin's engaged. It was bad enough that Audrey was the first to get married, being the youngest. Now my mother can obsess about the fact that I'm the only one still single."

"Then we'll have to find you someone before Colin's wedding," Rosie said.

"I'm fully on board with that," Lia said, and the three of them clinked their glasses together. "Even better if I find someone before Christmas so I can head them off when I fly home for the holiday."

"Same," Shanice added.

Rosie raised her glass. "Holiday dates for everyone."

And they toasted again.

Jane spent Friday morning in her bedroom at their rental cottage, writing. She could hear the murmur of conversation as her family went about their day and an occasional shriek of laughter from Alyssa. Yesterday morning, they'd gone for a short hike before Thanksgiving dinner, and today was their relaxation day before they went skiing tomorrow.

Someone knocked on her door. "Jane? Are you planning to join us for lunch?" It was her mother.

"Yep. I'll be right there," she called. She typed a few more sentences to finish her thought, and then she closed her laptop and went down the hall to the living room. Their cabin was decorated in a rustic style with lots of exposed wood and earth tones, and the artwork on the walls showcased the Rocky Mountains in all their rugged glory.

"About time you joined us," her mom said with a slight rebuke in her voice.

"Sorry, Mom. Just had to finish some work."

"Work?" her dad asked, looking up from his phone.

This was where it got sticky for her, trying to hide her second career when her dad was her boss at her day job. "Not BPD stuff, just some personal things I'm working on."

"Like what?" Mom asked.

"Mind if we get going?" Amy interrupted. "Alyssa's starving."

"I am," the girl chimed in, already putting on her coat.

It had been easier for Jane to keep her two lives separate when she first started. She was only publishing one book a year then, and she'd done all her writing at home in her spare time. But she'd stepped up her schedule over the last two years in her attempt to become a full-time writer, which meant it was getting harder to avoid the questions from her family.

And as she followed them outside to the rental car, she wondered if it was time to just tell them. She thought of the photos on her phone, the ones Rosie had taken after Jane signed all the books for her subscription box. Something in her had changed since that day, like she felt validated as an author in a way she hadn't before.

They drove into downtown Breckenridge and had lunch at a quaint little farm-to-table restaurant. Afterward, they split up to do some shopping along the downtown strip. At Alyssa's insistence, Amy, Alyssa, and Garrett headed for the ice cream shop down the street, and Jane's dad went to buy himself some ski goggles for tomorrow, leaving Jane and her mom to browse the tourist shops alone.

Jane wasn't looking to buy much, especially since she'd have to carry it home on the airplane, but she did want to find a Christmas ornament. She collected them from all the places she'd visited, to put on the little tree in her apartment.

"How are you, Jane?" her mother asked as they both browsed a selection of ornaments. "You've been quieter than usual lately."

"I've been busy," Jane told her. "Actually, I'm seeing someone."

"Oh?" Her mom lifted a golden ball with snowflakes etched into it. "A woman?"

Jane let that one slide. Her parents were generally very accepting of her sexuality, but occasionally she wondered if they were holding out hope that she'd surprise them and date a man. "Yes. Her name is Rosie."

"Well, that's wonderful. Why haven't you mentioned her before now?"

"Because it's still really new," Jane told her as she picked up a carved wooden ornament that said "Breckenridge." "And we had kind of a complicated start."

"How so?" her mom asked.

"She owns a bookstore in one of the buildings we're demolishing."

"Oh dear, that does sound complicated. So you evicted her from her store?" Her mom picked up a glass ornament that Jane would never dare try to carry halfway across the country for fear of breaking it.

"I did," Jane confirmed. "And now I'm trying to help her find a new space."

"Well, I'm glad you were able to sort things out. That would make a great story to tell your grandchildren someday, you know." Her mom gave her a sly smile.

Jane laughed under her breath. "It would." She wasn't anywhere near ready to think that far into the future with Rosie, but she was relieved to have this kind of banter with her mom. It was the same way she'd teased Amy until she'd settled down and gotten married.

"You should bring her by for dinner. I'd love to meet her," her mom said.

"We've only been together a few weeks," Jane hedged. "Let's get through the holidays first and then see where we are."

"Or you could bring her to our New Year's party," she suggested.

"Maybe," Jane said. Her parents threw a huge party every year for all their employees and friends in the ballroom of the Belvedere Hotel, which was one of BPD's hallmark properties. It was an event that Jane sometimes looked forward to and sometimes dreaded, depending on her mood and what was going on in her life. But it might be fun with Rosie at her side, all the pieces of her life coming together in one place.

"A bookstore owner, hmm?" Her mom turned to browse a selection of scarves on the other side of the aisle.

"She's a total book nerd," Jane said with a smile. "It's what drew me to her in the first place."

"Yes, you two have that in common, don't you?"

"We do," Jane confirmed, feeling another urge to come clean with her mother about her own books. Maybe Amy was right, and Jane had let this thing get too big. Surely she ought to break the news to her parents before she quit her job, or even before she introduced them to Rosie. But not in the middle of a store. This was a conversation to have at home, and with both of her parents at the same time.

She and her mom spent the next hour browsing up and down the main street, sharing the kind of easy conversation that didn't always come naturally to them, and Jane was so glad it had today. The truth was that she and her mom didn't have much in common and sometimes struggled to find common ground. As she thought of Rosie, who'd lost her mom so young, Jane felt a rush of gratitude for her own family, imperfect as they might be.

"Jane, honey, look at this," her mother said as they entered yet another shop. She held up a glass ornament shaped like a colorful stack of books. Their pages shimmered with glitter. "I thought you might like to get something for Rosie."

"Yeah," Jane said, incredibly touched by the gesture. "Actually, she would love that. Do you think I could get it home in one piece?"

"They'll wrap it for you at the register," her mom said. "And you can put it in your carry-on if you're worried."

"Okay." Jane took the ornament from her mom, holding it up to admire the way it sparkled in the light. She also found a glittery little pair of skis that said "Breckenridge" for her own tree. She paid for her purchases, and the cashier indeed wrapped them well to travel.

As she followed her mom out of the store, Jane's thoughts drifted to the book she was writing. She'd been completely obsessed with it the last few days. In fact, she hadn't thought about Breslin Property Development since she'd gotten to Colorado. She felt separated from it here on vacation, where her family could just be family. Maybe this was the perfect place to tell her parents she was an author. It was time. Past time.

Jane spun her wineglass, staring into the fire that her dad had started earlier that evening. He sat in the armchair with a copy of *Newsweek* while her mom read quietly in another chair. Jane was alone on the couch, itching to get back to writing, but she also wanted to seize this opportunity with her parents before she lost her nerve. Amy and Garrett were in Alyssa's bedroom, getting her ready for bed.

Her mom set her book on the coffee table and reached for her wine, glancing at Jane. "Have you told your father about Rosie yet?"

Her dad looked up from his magazine. "What?"

"Jane has a new girlfriend," her mom said with a smile. "She might bring her on New Year's."

"Emphasis on *might*," Jane said. "We've only just started seeing each other, so it's still early to make plans for New Year's."

"Well, that's great, Jane," her dad said. "I look forward to meeting her."

"Rosie owns a bookstore," her mom supplied.

"Ah, a businesswoman," her dad said. "And a booklover. She sounds perfect for you."

"I hope so." Jane took another sip of her wine, noticing the way the glass shook as she set it back on the table. She was terrified of her parents' reaction to what she was about to say, but maybe they would surprise her. Either way, she was ready for them to know. "Remember when I told you after college that I wanted to write books?"

"I remember," her dad said. "And I'm so glad you came to join us at BPD instead. A much better career investment. You know what happened to Barry Hagan."

"I know." Jane had heard this story a hundred times. Her father's friend Barry had spent years toiling over a book he had felt sure was a literary masterpiece, and he'd received a modest publishing contract for it, but he'd never sold another book. Her father brought up Barry every time she mentioned writing. "But it's still my dream to be an author."

"Oh, Jane," he said, frowning. Her mother had grown very quiet in the other chair.

"In fact, I never stopped writing books."

"Really?" Her mom looked at her in surprise. "As a hobby?"

"It was a hobby for a long time, yeah," Jane told her. "I love to write, and I guess I don't know what to do with myself when I'm not writing, because I can't seem to stop."

"Well, it's good to have hobbies," her mom said, looking relieved.

Jane exhaled, fighting the sinking feeling in her gut, because there was no going back now, but it didn't look like they were going to surprise her after all. "It's more than a hobby for me, though. In fact, I've published ten books."

The room went so quiet Jane could hear herself breathing and the crackle of the fire. A gasp drew her attention to the doorway, where

Amy stood with a delighted smile on her face. She crossed quickly to the couch and sat beside Jane, reaching over to take her hand.

"Ten books?" her mother said, shaking her head. "I don't understand."

"Why haven't you told us about this before, Jane?" her dad asked, and she couldn't tell whether he sounded angry or disappointed. Probably a mixture of the two.

"Because I knew you disapproved, and I'm not naive. I knew it was unlikely I'd have any kind of success as an author, so I wanted to keep it to myself to start."

"What kind of books do you write?" he asked, and Amy's fingers tightened around Jane's.

"She writes beautiful love stories," Amy said proudly. "She's so talented, Dad. You should be proud of what she's accomplished, all while working full time at BPD."

"You knew about this?" her mom asked.

"Sisters share things," Amy said. "Jane needed someone to confide in. She didn't want you two to judge her if she failed, but she hasn't failed. She's become one of the top authors in her genre."

"I don't know what to say," her dad said. "Of course I'm happy for you, Jane, although I wish you hadn't kept this from us. And have you taken precautions to protect your identity and the reputation of BPD?"

"Our reputation?" Amy asked in outrage. "You act like she's doing something wrong."

"Well, I assume by love stories you mean . . ." He gestured with his hand as if for Amy to fill in the blank, and their mom became suddenly fascinated by her wine.

"I write romance," Jane said. "Lesbian romance, in fact. And yes, I write under a pseudonym. No one at BPD needs to know, and I don't intend to tell them."

Both of her parents seemed to have been rendered mute at the mention of lesbian romance, and she couldn't entirely blame them. It had to be awkward to know your daughter wrote about sex, but at the same time, she needed them to know she wasn't ashamed of her books.

"I . . . well . . ." He drifted off, and she wasn't sure she'd ever seen her unflappable father at such a loss for words.

"Remember all those romantic movies with Meg Ryan and Tom Hanks in the nineties?" she asked. "My books are like that, except with two women."

"Oh," her mom said. "Well, that's nice."

"It *is* nice," Amy said. "And you should be very proud of her."

Her dad cleared his throat awkwardly. "Of course I am."

"Thank you," Jane told him.

"Just don't make the same mistake as Barry and quit your day job."

CHAPTER EIGHTEEN

Jane Breslin:

Are you at work?

Rosie Taft:

Yep, I'm here until we close at 6.

Are you back from Colorado?

Jane Breslin:

Just got back, would love to swing by and say hi if that's okay.

Rosie Taft:

YES PLEASE 😊

Rosie put her phone down, excitement sparking at the possibility of seeing Jane later. The last few days had been crazy busy, between Black Friday and Small Business Saturday. She and Lia had coordinated with Betty and their other part-time employee, Emma, to cover the shop tomorrow so they could take Monday off together. Rosie planned to sleep in and catch up on her reading. It might be her last chance this year, because the weeks leading up to Christmas were always busy, and this year she'd be packing up to move on top of it.

All was quiet inside Between the Pages today, though. A lone couple browsed the shelves, and as much as Rosie loved a bustling store, right now she was glad for a lull to catch her breath. The door to the basement opened behind her, and Lia came through it.

"All finished," she told Rosie.

"Oh wow. I didn't think you'd actually finish today. That's amazing."

"They look beautiful too," Lia said. "I took photos of the finished product for our social media." She'd spent the afternoon packing all the subscription boxes, each of which contained a signed copy of *On the Flip Side* and an unsigned copy of one of Brie's older books, along with a letter from the author and a variety of themed trinkets, including a glittery stiletto-shaped ornament, a small print of the Manhattan skyline, and a rainbow sticker.

Lia scrolled through photos on her phone, showing Rosie a completed box with all the items packed in Between the Pages' signature periwinkle-blue tissue paper.

"Lia, they look amazing. How many extras do we have?"

"About twenty," Lia told her. "I'll schedule these to go out tomorrow. Once they've been delivered, I'll list the extras on our website, but we don't want to ruin the surprise for those who've paid for the subscription."

"Perfect."

"And speaking of our website, the online store went live today," Lia said.

"Oh my God, I'd forgotten about that," Rosie said. "How's it going so far?"

"I haven't made an official announcement yet, but we've already had a handful of orders, and so far, so good. Once I'm confident everything is running smoothly, I'll promote it to our customer list and on our social media." She opened her laptop to show Rosie how everything worked.

She had no idea how long they'd been at it when the bell over the door chimed. She looked up to see Jane entering the store in a burgundy coat, cheeks rosy from the cool air, and Rosie's heart lurched against her ribs.

Jane walked up to the counter, looking so ridiculously pretty Rosie could hardly think of anything except kissing her. "Hey."

"Hi." She could feel herself grinning. "Lia, can you cover for me for a few minutes?"

"Of course," Lia said, waving them off. "And, Jane, have a look at the subscription boxes while you're downstairs."

"I will, thanks," Jane told her.

Rosie took her hand and tugged her into the stairwell. She'd just started to close the door behind them when Brinkley wiggled through, yipping his excitement to see Jane. "It's a toss-up which of us is more smitten with you at this point," Rosie said as she leaned in for a kiss.

"The feeling is mutual," Jane said, pulling her close as she returned the kiss, "although I do have a clear preference between the two of you."

"Should my feelings be hurt?" Rosie asked playfully.

"Nope. I'm pretty fond of Brinkley, but there was only one person I spent my entire Thanksgiving trip missing, and it wasn't him."

"Careful. You're going to make me blush." Rosie led the way downstairs to her office.

"I told my parents," Jane blurted as Rosie flipped on the light.

She turned to her in surprise. "About us?"

Jane shook her head, and now that Rosie was really looking at her, she seemed worked up about something, although Rosie wasn't sure yet whether it was a good or a bad thing. "I mean, yes, I did tell them about us, but what I meant is that I told them about my books."

"Oh," Rosie said. She hadn't expected that. "You told them you're Brie?"

Jane unbuttoned her coat, still looking jumpy. "Actually, I don't think I told them my pen name, and maybe that's good for now, but I told them I've published ten books."

"Wow. Jane, this is huge," Rosie said. "How did they react?"

Jane rocked back on her heels. "About how I expected, I guess? They weren't thrilled. My dad always circles back to this friend of his who crashed and burned as an author, and they're both still embarrassed about me writing sexy books, but I think it's good that I started the conversation, you know?"

"Definitely," Rosie said, helping Jane as she slipped out of her coat. She was thrilled for her, even while her chest burned with indignation on Jane's behalf over her parents' reaction. She couldn't stand it when people got snooty about books, particularly romance. "Do you feel good about it overall?"

"I'm starting to." Jane tugged at one of her sleeves that had ridden up when she took off her coat. She wore an emerald-green sweater and jeans, and the color definitely suited her. "I was pretty disappointed at the time, which is probably why I didn't text you right away to tell you, but my mom took me aside this morning to say she supported me, so that helped."

"I'm so glad," Rosie said.

"Part of me wants to send her the picture that you took when I signed the books for the subscription boxes, and the rest of me wants to never mention it again unless she brings it up."

"Totally your call," Rosie told her.

"What do you think I should do?" Jane asked, uncertainty plainly visible in her eyes.

"I think your author life is becoming increasingly important to you, and you've opened the conversation with your parents, so it might be a good thing to keep going if you can. That photo could be a great place to start. I can't imagine that your mom wouldn't be thrilled to see it."

"You really think?" There was something fragile in her tone that tugged at Rosie's heart.

"Totally," Rosie said, hoping it was true. "Maybe she needs to see a picture of your success for it to sink in. Make it real for her. I have a picture of our window display from October that I could send you too."

"Oh," Jane said. "I'd actually love to have that. I wanted to take one myself, because I'd never seen my book in a display before, but you kind of hated me at the time, so I didn't want to hang around."

Rosie pressed her lips against Jane's cheek. "Lucky for you I took plenty of pictures."

Jane turned her face, bringing their lips into alignment. "Thanks."

"Send your mom a picture before you lose your nerve."

"Right now?" Jane's breath hitched, and Rosie wasn't sure whether it was because she'd just slid her hands around Jane's waist or from the thought of sending her mom a photo.

"Yes," Rosie murmured, letting her fingers slip under the hem of Jane's sweater to settle against the warm skin just below her rib cage.

Jane arched into her touch. "Distracting."

"Then do it quickly."

Jane leaned past Rosie and fished her cell phone out of her bag. She typed quickly with her left hand, her right resting possessively on Rosie's hip, and she was as impressed with Jane's one-handed texting skills as she was turned on by her touch.

The phone made a click to indicate the text had been sent, and then Jane slid it into her back pocket. She pressed herself more firmly into Rosie's arms, resting her forehead against hers. "I can't believe I just did that."

"I'm proud of you," Rosie told her. "And I bet your mom's feeling pretty proud right now too. That table of books is impressive as fuck."

"I have butterflies," Jane whispered, exhaling slowly.

"Sounds like you need another distraction." Rosie dipped her head to nibble her way over Jane's jaw.

"Yes, please," Jane said.

Rosie had butterflies of her own, but they had more to do with Jane's skin beneath her lips and the way she gasped when Rosie's fingers traced the waistband of her jeans. She slid her hands north, cupping Jane over her bra, which was satiny and warm against her fingertips. "How am I doing?" she murmured.

"Really well," Jane responded, pressing her breasts more firmly into Rosie's hands.

"Good," Rosie said. "Got plans tonight?"

"Hoping to spend it with you."

"Sounds perfect," Rosie agreed. "I'm off in about an hour."

"I can hang around and leave with you if you like."

"Oh, I like." She ran her hands up and down Jane's sides against her bare skin, rewarded by another gasp and the warm press of Jane's hands on her ass, dragging her closer.

Jane's phone dinged in her pocket, and she froze, eyes wide as they met Rosie's.

"Go on and see what she said," Rosie encouraged.

"Why am I so nervous about this?" Jane slid the phone out of her pocket, and Rosie saw her hand tremble.

"Because you care what your mom thinks of you."

Jane exhaled slowly, meeting Rosie's eyes as she seemed to gather her courage. "Okay, here goes." She clicked on the text.

Mom:

> I got tears in my eyes looking at this photo. Will you come to dinner one night this week and tell me more about your books?

Rosie looked up and saw the tears glistening in Jane's eyes a moment before they spilled over her cheeks. She leaned in and kissed them away as Jane wrapped her arms around her, holding her tight. Rosie had always had her mom's unconditional support, and it hurt to see Jane fighting so hard for her parents' approval. How did they not see how amazing she was? How could they not be thrilled for her success?

"Thank you," Jane whispered. "For encouraging me to do that. I probably wouldn't have done it on my own."

"You're welcome," Rosie told her.

The next thing she knew, Jane's lips were on hers, and this kiss was nothing like the teasing kisses they'd entertained for the last ten minutes or so. This one was hot and urgent. Jane nipped at Rosie's bottom lip before soothing the spot with her tongue, lighting Rosie on fire. She reached out, groping somewhat blindly for the door, and shut it with a solid click.

"Good idea," Jane murmured, hands tracing the contours of Rosie's body. She pushed one of her thighs between Rosie's, and Rosie automatically pressed herself more firmly against Jane, moaning at the friction against her clit. She could hardly believe they were fooling around like this in her office. She'd certainly never done this before, but right now, it felt like the best idea she'd ever had.

Jane moved against her, both of them finding the pressure they needed as their kiss grew more heated. Jane's tongue was in her mouth, dancing wickedly against Rosie's, and she was struggling to think of a reason not to get Jane naked and take her right here against the desk.

And then Rosie's phone chimed with the musical note she'd assigned to Lia. "Shit," she mumbled. She was supposed to be working right now. "I totally ditched Lia at the register."

Jane laughed quietly. She was breathing hard, and there was a glint of arousal in her eyes that echoed the fire Rosie felt burning inside her. "It's okay. We'll finish this later."

Rosie slid her phone out of her back pocket, already preparing her apology.

Lia Harris:

I can close up. You and Jane get out of here!

"Oh." Rosie held her phone up for Jane to see.

"Care to take her up on that?" Jane asked, sliding her hand into Rosie's pocket, fingers wiggling suggestively.

"Yes." She leaned in for another kiss, bringing the heat between them back to life.

"Good," Jane said. "Because I'm a little impatient at the moment. Is he coming with us?" She gestured toward Brinkley, who was watching them from the dog bed.

"Sure," Rosie said. He'd behaved the last time he'd joined her at Jane's, and truth be told, she was feeling pretty impatient too. "Let's go."

Jane kicked the door shut behind them, her mouth already on Rosie's as they stumbled into her apartment. Vaguely, she was aware of Brinkley jumping onto the couch, and she was glad he could entertain himself for a little while, because she needed Rosie naked *now*. She undid the button on Rosie's pants as she stepped her backward toward the bedroom.

"In a hurry?" Rosie asked breathlessly.

"Yes." Jane pushed down Rosie's zipper, and Rosie kicked her way out of her pants, then dashed the rest of the way into Jane's bedroom, beckoning to her over her shoulder.

In response, Jane took off her coat and scrambled out of her sweater and jeans in record time, so that when Rosie turned to face her, she was only wearing her underwear.

"Challenge accepted." Rosie unbuttoned her blouse and tossed it onto the chair.

Jane grinned at her, and for a moment they just stared at each other. Then Rosie reached behind her back to pop the clasp on her bra, lingering so that it came loose slowly, sliding gracefully over her shoulders. Jane groaned as Rosie's breasts came into view, her nipples already hardened from the cold air outside. As Jane watched, she shimmied out of her panties, swaying her hips in a way that definitely wasn't accidental.

Jane crossed to her, drawing her in for another kiss, ridiculously aroused by this little impromptu striptease. Their breasts met, and Jane's nipples tightened at the contact, shooting a bolt of need straight to her core. "Rosie . . ."

"Still in a hurry?" she teased, rubbing her hips against Jane's.

"I think you know the answer to that question."

Rosie slid her fingers between Jane's thighs, teasing her over her panties and sending the ache there into overdrive. "Well, now I definitely do."

"Killing me," Jane murmured, smiling because despite her complaints, she was loving every moment of this.

"Better take care of you, then." Rosie hooked a thumb under the waistband of Jane's panties and tugged them down. Jane kicked them away and took off her bra, and they climbed into bed together, finally blissfully naked.

Rosie's fingers circled Jane's clit, and she shuddered with pleasure, stroking Rosie with all the urgency building inside her. They gasped and moaned, moving against each other as they tumbled toward release. Jane pressed her face against Rosie's shoulder, kissing every part of her that her lips could reach as her fingers swirled and plunged inside Rosie's body.

Rosie's fingers were performing some magic of their own, and Jane moved her hips, increasing the pressure of her touch. Fire ignited in her belly, and then she was coming, release rushing through her in a scorching wave. She clutched Rosie, fingers still stroking her, mouth pressed against her skin, until Rosie had joined her.

Afterward, they lay together, breathless and sweaty. Rosie brushed a hand through Jane's hair, and she turned her head to kiss Rosie's cheek. Jane felt sappy and romantic, wrapped in Rosie's arms. She hadn't always believed her own words when she wrote about her characters melting for each other like this. She'd *wanted* to believe something this intense, this wonderful was possible, but now she knew it was true.

"That was quite a welcome home," she whispered. "Exactly what I needed."

"Happy I could help," Rosie said with a giggle.

"I have no idea what time it is," Jane told her. "My body's still on mountain time."

"I think it's about six," Rosie told her. "I don't want to move just yet, but then what do you say we order some dinner, because I'm pretty hungry. I didn't have much lunch."

"And my lunch was two time zones ago," Jane said. "What about Brinkley?"

"Oh shit," Rosie said. "I forgot to feed him before we left the store. Well, he'll be fine for a while. I just can't sleep over."

Jane nuzzled her cheek against Rosie's. "But I like sleeping with you, both literally and in other ways."

"Same," Rosie said. "If we get takeout, is there a grocery store nearby where we could buy some dog food?"

"Yes." Jane closed her eyes, surprised to realize how comfortable she felt with Rosie and how much she loved having her in her bed. She'd never encouraged a woman to stay the night. In fact, she usually preferred to sleep alone.

"So you had a good time in Colorado?" Rosie asked, one hand trailing up and down Jane's back.

"Yeah, it was nice. Lots of family time that had nothing to do with business. We went skiing yesterday, although I'm paying for it today with sore muscles. How was your Thanksgiving with Lia and Shanice?"

"Fun," Rosie said. "Lots of good food and laughs."

"Sounds perfect," Jane said.

They lay together for a few more minutes, kissing and cuddling as they caught up after five days apart. Then they rinsed off in a quick shower and got redressed to go out for dinner.

"Oh, before I forget, I brought you something from Colorado," Jane said.

Rosie beamed at her. "You did?"

Jane nodded, reaching into her nightstand for the ornament she'd wrapped as soon as she got home. She handed it to Rosie.

"You're always giving me gifts, Jane," she said, cheeks as pink as her name. "Careful, or you'll spoil me."

"It's just a little thing. Actually, my mom picked it out for you."

"Well, now I'm even more intrigued." Rosie ripped through the paper with her usual exuberance, and her eyes glittered as brightly as the ornament as she held it up in front of her face. "Oh, it's beautiful. It'll be perfect on the tree at the store. Thank you."

"You're welcome," Jane said, and she was pretty sure her cheeks were pink too.

Rosie carefully rewrapped the ornament in tissue paper. They put on their coats and went outside in search of dinner, with Brinkley trotting between them. The evening was cold and clear, and the sky was dark overhead. A few strands of Christmas lights already gleamed as some of Jane's neighbors got an early start on the season.

"Hey, do you have plans for New Year's?" She ducked her head as she walked, hoping she hadn't been too forward, but right now, she couldn't imagine not being with Rosie as she rang in the new year.

"Not really," Rosie said. "Usually, we have a few people over for fun snacks and drinks to watch the ball drop at our apartment. I don't have any desire to be out in those crowds."

"I don't either," Jane said.

"That's shocking information," Rosie teased, nudging her elbow against Jane.

"Right? Because I'm usually such a party animal." Jane squeezed her hand. "I wasn't going to ask you quite yet—so tell me if it's too soon—but my parents throw a big party at the Belvedere Hotel every year. I usually try to find an excuse to stay home, but this year, I was wondering . . . would you like to go with me? No crowds, plenty of free food and drinks, and a fancy hotel room just for us. What do you say?"

"Your parents' party?" Rosie asked, her expression hard to read.

"Yes, but they invite pretty much everyone they know, and they're always hassling me to bring a date, so it's not a huge relationship state-ment, if you're worried about that."

"Actually, I was wondering if it would be weird because of my store," Rosie admitted.

"Oh." Jane flinched. Somehow, she hadn't even thought of that.

"But it's only weird if we let it be, right? And I'd love to spend New Year's with you, so . . . yes."

CHAPTER NINETEEN

It was almost noon on Monday by the time Rosie got home. Jane hadn't had any meetings this morning, so they'd slept in and then made pancakes together, and it had been glorious. And now Rosie hoped to spend the rest of the day with Lia. Maybe they could go to one of the museums Lia loved so much. It was rare for them to have the same day off from the store, and she wanted to make the most of it.

"Someone's enjoying her day off," Lia said playfully as Rosie and Brinkley came in through the door.

"My girlfriend makes amazing pancakes—what can I say?"

"Your girlfriend, hmm? When's the last time you used that term?"

"It's been a while," Rosie admitted. "But she invited me to her parents' New Year's Eve party, so that feels like girlfriend territory, doesn't it?" Rosie asked as she unclipped Brinkley's leash and plopped onto the couch beside Lia. Brinkley crawled up between them, tail thumping against the upholstery.

"Wow, yeah," Lia said. "That's great, Ro."

"I'm pretty happy about how things are going for us, and maybe it's helping to keep my spirits up while I save the store, so I don't know . . . I'm not being stupid, am I?"

"Not in the slightest," Lia said. "But we do need to talk about the store. I've been running the numbers, and it's time to make some decisions."

"Oh geez," Rosie said, scrubbing her hands over her face. "What kind of decisions?"

"Well, the abbreviated version is that it's time for us to accept that we're not going to find a new storefront before we have to leave our current space. Even if you signed a new lease tomorrow, it likely wouldn't start until mid-January or later."

Rosie sighed. She'd known this deep down but hadn't acknowledged it yet. "So where does that leave us?"

"I see two options," Lia said. "But I don't think it's much of a choice. The first is that we close our doors permanently at the end of the year and move on to new ventures."

Rosie let out an agonized breath, resting a hand over her eyes.

"The other option is that we find a cheap storage unit to house our inventory for a few months while we keep looking for a new home. We'd still run our subscription boxes and online store."

"It would cost a fortune," Rosie said quietly. "More than we'd make from online stuff."

"Which is why we need to look at my spreadsheet and decide ahead of time how many months we're able to run things virtually, because I assume closing up without at least giving this a try is not an option, am I right?" Lia gave her an assessing look.

"You're right," Rosie said.

Lia nodded. "Okay, then. We'll look at the numbers together, because if we don't set some hard deadlines and thresholds for ourselves ahead of time, you'll go broke selling books out of a warehouse while you hold out for a miracle."

Rosie pressed her hands over her face and exhaled. "You've given this a lot of thought."

"I'm doing my job as your manager," Lia said. "I think you're a little bit in denial right now, floating along in your happy bubble with Jane and hoping a perfect new home for Between the Pages magically appears in time for us to move right in."

"Have I been in a bubble?" Rosie frowned as she rubbed Brinkley, who promptly rolled belly up, wiggling around so she could rub him just the way he liked. Had she been avoiding reality while she was with Jane? Had she endangered the store? She'd chased every real estate lead Marcia had found for her, but was she being too picky in her search?

"Only in the sense that it's time to adjust our expectations and start looking at storage facilities," Lia said, giving Brinkley a quick scratch under his chin. He let out a contented groan, tail swishing frantically from side to side. "And I thought this afternoon might be a good time to do it, while we're at home and can have a conversation without being interrupted."

"Okay," Rosie agreed. "So what's our next step, then?"

"Let's look at my spreadsheet, if you're ready," Lia said. "We need to finalize a budget we're both comfortable with, but when it comes down to it, this is your store, and you get the final say."

"Bust out the spreadsheet," Rosie told her. "Let's do this."

Lia slid her laptop off the coffee table and opened it. "I've narrowed it down to two storage facilities. One's here in our neighborhood. We could walk over, which would be convenient for processing orders, but as you might expect, it's also more expensive."

"Okay," Rosie said.

Lia opened her spreadsheet and took Rosie through the sample budget she'd developed for the storage facility here on the Upper East Side. "As you can see, I've estimated we could stay at this facility for two months at comfortable profit margins."

"Got it," Rosie said.

"Our other option is a facility in the Bronx that costs about half as much. It would be a pain to get there, obviously, but it's a bigger unit that would give us more space to work as we box up orders, and there's a post office right across the street, which would be convenient for shipping. If we had a schedule like, say, we ship orders on Monday, Wednesday, and Friday, I think the commute would feel more manageable, and here's the real perk—we could afford to stay there for up to six months."

"That sounds like a winner," Rosie said. "But where are you getting these numbers?"

"Ah, let me show you." Lia tabbed over to a different section of the spreadsheet, reminding Rosie why she'd hired her in the first place. Rosie was the one with the vision and the passion, and Lia ran the numbers and put Rosie's plans into action. "I've estimated our online sales to be about half of what we make in the store, based on what I'm seeing with the online store so far, and the income from our subscription boxes will remain unchanged or perhaps even increase."

"I hope you're right," Rosie said.

"We're going to have to lay off our part-time employees," Lia said. "I'm sorry, but there's just no other way. We can always offer to hire them back if we're able once we're in a new space."

"Oh, Lia, no." Rosie didn't notice she'd stopped rubbing Brinkley until he let out a little whine, giving her an upside-down side-eye.

"It's time to face facts," Lia said. "We can either close our doors permanently, or we can cut unnecessary costs and try to rebound in a few months."

"Dammit." Rosie rubbed Brinkley as her stomach pitched. "Betty's been with us almost since the store opened."

"And she talks constantly of retiring," Lia said. "The only reason she's still working for us is that she enjoys talking about books and her husband is convinced she'll get bored once she retires."

"But . . ." Rosie didn't even know how to finish her thought.

"Betty will be fine. And who knows? If she does get bored at home, maybe she'll rejoin us in our new location. And Emma just graduated college. She's working several part-time jobs while she looks for something permanent. She can find something else, Rosie. You have to look out for yourself here."

"I know you're right," Rosie muttered. "But for the record, I hate everything about this."

"I know you do, and so do I. I've already spoken to both of them to let them know this might be coming. Emma is looking for new work, and Betty says it's the universe nudging her toward retirement."

Rosie sighed. "So you and me and a warehouse in the Bronx. We can really survive that way for six months?"

"We likely won't turn a profit, but we should be able to cover the cost of the unit, our rent here, and other essentials. It'll be tight, but ideally, we only have to do it for a few months."

"All right," Rosie agreed reluctantly.

Lia nodded, closing her laptop. "Feel like taking a field trip to the Bronx?"

Rosie blew out a breath. This wasn't how she'd planned to spend her day off, but as Lia had pointed out, it was time to stop burying her head in the sand. "Let's do it."

On Wednesday evening, Jane rode the subway to her parents' brownstone after work. Her mom had invited her for dinner, and Jane could only hope this was a good idea. At the office this week, her dad had been 100 percent focused on work—no mention of anything they'd discussed in Colorado. If she let him, he'd probably never say the word "author" again.

But her mom wanted to know more about Jane's work, so here she was. She'd even tucked a copy of *On the Flip Side* in her bag, just in case. Part of her was mortified at the thought of her mom reading one of her books—especially the sexy parts—but she was trying to push past her insecurities, and this seemed like the logical next step.

She texted Rosie as she walked, needing the adrenaline boost she got every time they talked. Jane had always treasured their digital communications, maybe because their relationship had begun online.

Jane Breslin:

I have a meeting near your shop tomorrow, want to grab lunch?

Rosie Taft:

Sure!

Oh and look, we put up our tree in the store today.

Two images followed. The first one was a panoramic shot of the store, showing a colorful tree in the front corner. The second was a close-up of the ornament Jane had given her. The stack of books glittered on a branch, surrounded by other ornaments.

Jane Breslin:

It looks great!

Wish I could stop by and see it (and you) in person, but I'm headed to dinner at my parents'.

Rosie Taft:

Oh, that's right! Good luck!

Call me after?

Jane Breslin:

Definitely, thanks. xx.

She put her phone away, her spirits successfully boosted from her conversation with Rosie, but as she climbed the front steps and knocked, her nerves resurrected themselves in anticipation of the potentially awkward evening ahead.

Her mom opened the front door with a smile, waving Jane inside. "Right on time. Your father was in the mood for sushi, so I ordered from Wasabi. I hope that's okay."

"Sounds perfect," Jane told her. "You didn't happen to get miso, too, by chance, did you?" Because she was chilled from her walk and craving soup.

Her mom gave her a fond look. "As if I'd order Japanese and not get you a bowl of miso."

"Thanks, Mom." Jane followed her down the hall to the kitchen, where her mother had already put the food on serving dishes, including a hot bowl of soup in front of Jane's seat.

"Jane's here," her mom called, and the murmur of the evening news coming from the living room silenced as her dad shut off the TV.

He walked into the kitchen still wearing his work clothes. So was she, but she'd come straight from the office while he'd left early for a meeting. "Hi, Jane."

"Hi, Dad."

They sat at the table, sharing polite conversation as they filled their plates. As usual when she and her dad shared a meal, he talked mostly about BPD, while her mother occasionally interjected with questions about the projects he and Jane were currently working on. The last thing Jane wanted to talk about tonight was property development, but it had always been the one topic she and her dad had in common.

She focused on her food while her brain worked triple time as she tried to find an opening to steer the conversation away from BPD and onto the topic she'd come here to discuss. The problem was that her dad tended to monopolize a conversation, and Jane wasn't very good at interrupting him.

"You've always been a conflict avoider."

She remembered Amy's words, and she couldn't disagree with them. She definitely took after their mom, while Amy was more assertive like their dad. By the time her plate was empty, she was tired and deflated, wishing she hadn't come. She could be writing right now—or, better yet, having dinner with Rosie—instead of listening to her dad's advice on how to improve her leadership style, which she apparently needed to do if she hoped to move into management.

The problem was that she didn't want that, not next year or ever.

As soon as he'd finished eating, her dad excused himself and went back to the news. Jane lingered to help her mom clean up, loading their dirty dishes into the dishwasher. Once the kitchen was clean, she reached for her bag.

"I should get home," she said, hoping she didn't sound as disappointed as she felt.

"Could you stay for a cup of tea?" her mom asked. "I was really hoping to hear about your books."

"Oh, um, sure," Jane said, forcing a smile. She'd walked through the door an hour ago, ready to share her life as Brie with her parents, but she'd gotten frustrated during dinner, and now she just wanted to go home and have a quiet glass of wine by herself.

This was how their family dynamic seemed to work, everyone trying to pacify everyone else. Her mother was fixing tea, having placated Jane's father during dinner by not mentioning her books, and now she wanted to smooth things over with Jane before she left. Why had she thought it would be any different? Why had she even come?

She swallowed over the ache in her throat as she sat, resting her elbows on the table. She was so tired of toeing this line, trying to make everyone happy. Her mom placed tea bags into two mugs and wiped down the counters while she waited for the kettle to boil.

Jane stared at her hands, remembering the night Rosie had made her tea after Jane confessed to being Brie. The funny thing was that she almost never drank tea, and now it was starting to be synonymous with the difficult conversations in her life.

"Here you go," her mom said as she set two steaming cups on the table.

"Thank you."

Her mom sat across from her in the chair her dad had vacated. "You didn't tell us your pseudonym. I realized that after we left Colorado."

"I know." Jane reached for her tea, even though it was still too hot to drink. Once she told her mom her pen name, there would be no taking it back. Was she ready for that?

"Will you share it with me?" her mom asked, leaning forward in her chair.

"I write as Brie," she said, fidgeting with her cup, watching as amber color spread through the water. She lifted the string draped over the side of the mug and swirled it.

"Just Brie?" her mom asked. "No last name?"

"No last name," Jane confirmed.

"And how did that photo you sent me come about?" her mom asked. "Was that taken at an event?"

"I was signing books to be included in a subscription box," Jane told her. "You know Rosie, the woman I'm seeing?"

Her mom nodded. "And she owns a bookstore. This was for her?"

"She does subscription boxes for her customers, featuring a different book each month. And this month, she's featuring one of mine."

"That's very sweet of her," her mom said. "Does she read your books?"

"Yeah." Jane ducked her head, again staring into her tea. "That's kind of how we met. She's a big fan."

"Oh." Her mom's voice rose. "You have fans. Jane, I feel so out of the loop. Will you show me how I can find your books?"

Jane lifted her eyes, summoning her courage. "I brought you one . . . if you'd like to have it."

"Please," her mom said. "I'd like that very much."

Jane stood, walked over to the counter where she'd left her bag, and pulled out the book. Her hand trembled slightly as she handed it to her mother.

"Wow, this is so official." Her mom turned it over in her hands to read the back cover, and when she looked up, the expression on her face made Jane sit a bit taller in her chair. Her mom's eyes glistened with unshed tears, and she looked . . . proud. "Can I read it?"

"Yes, but . . ." Jane swallowed, giving her head a shake. "You don't have to. I know romance isn't your thing, and . . . well, it's R rated."

Her mom reached over to give Jane's hand a gentle slap. "Jane Elizabeth Breslin, you think I've never read an R-rated book before?"

"Um, you have?" Jane had no idea what to do with this information . . . or her hands. She reached for her mug and took a cautious sip of her tea.

"I admit I prefer mysteries, but I've read romance," she said. "I usually read those on my Kindle so I don't have to explain the covers to your father."

Jane blinked. "Oh my God."

"What kind of romance is this?" her mom asked. "I know it's about two women, and from the cover I'm guessing it's set in present day. I mostly read historical books when I do read romance, so I'm excited to try something new."

"It's an enemies-to-lovers story set here in the city," Jane told her.

"I can't wait to read it," her mom said. "Are all your books set here in the city?"

"Yes," Jane told her.

"And all with women?"

"Yes."

"Do you have book signings?"

"I haven't yet," Jane said, taking another sip of tea. She couldn't quite read her mom's tone. Was she disappointed that she'd been left out? Jane hadn't imagined inviting anyone but Amy to a hypothetical future signing, but perhaps she'd underestimated her mom's support. "I've kept my identity private. Maybe too private."

"But you've been invited to events?"

"I have," Jane told her. "And there's an annual conference for romance authors I might like to attend."

"Oh, you should," her mom said as she set down Jane's book and lifted her tea. "You might make friends there. You need more friends."

"Yeah, I guess I do."

"I'd like to be there when you have your first book signing," her mom said. "I'm so sorry you felt like you had to hide this from us."

Jane blew out a breath. "I know Dad's not thrilled."

"He'll come around."

Jane wasn't sure that he would. Maybe the best she could hope for was that he would quietly ignore her work as Brie. It would certainly be better than his being vocally unsupportive. She hadn't expected this much interest from her mother, though, and that was a happy surprise.

When she left a half hour later, she felt lighter in her boots. The night had gone as well as she could have hoped for. If only the sting of her dad's rejection wasn't still there, bringing her back down.

CHAPTER TWENTY

"Has she started reading it yet?" Rosie sat across from Jane and reached for her sandwich on the tray between them. "Do you think she'll call and let you know?"

"I don't know," Jane said, predictably uncomfortable when it came to the topic of her mother reading *On the Flip Side*. "Part of me hopes she never mentions it again."

"No, you don't," Rosie said, before taking a sip of her soda. Around them, the sub shop bustled with the lunchtime rush, enveloping them in the buzz of conversation. "You hope she loves it and calls you to tell you it's the best book she's ever read."

"That's a bit much to hope for, don't you think?" Jane asked, and the harshness in her voice was a reminder of how difficult this was for her. She'd taken a big step giving her mom one of her books to read, and now she was nervous.

"No, I don't," Rosie said, "because if I had a daughter, I would automatically think her books were the best, even if they sucked. And your books don't suck. They're amazing. I wish I could see her face when she realizes it."

"I wish I had your confidence in me," Jane said, staring glumly at her sandwich.

"Lucky for you, I have enough for both of us, at least where your books are concerned." Rosie picked up her sandwich again and took a big bite. She really loved the chicken-club hoagies here. They got the bacon nice and crispy.

"So you rented a storage unit?" Jane asked, flipping the conversation. "That was a smart decision."

"Yep. Lia's spreadsheet says we can pull it off, and she's usually right, so fingers crossed."

Jane chewed and swallowed a bite of her Reuben. "It will buy you the time you need to find a permanent space, and I have full confidence that you'll be able to do enough online business to stay afloat. Your customers love you, Rosie. They'll support you through this."

"I sure hope so," she said. "It's scary."

Jane looked up, brushing a crumb from her cheek. "I know it is, but this city is full of beautiful spaces. We just have to find the right one for you."

"We?" Rosie still wasn't sure how she felt about Jane's involvement in the process. It was sweet, of course, but Rosie feared she was only helping because she felt guilty about her role in Between the Pages' impending homelessness, and Rosie didn't want her guilt.

"I'm still looking for any leads on my end," Jane said. "I have connections, and I might as well use them, right?"

"If you're sure you're using them for the right reasons."

Jane gave her a sharp look. "I don't know what that means, but in case you didn't notice, I'm not loving my day job these days. I'd rather be home writing books, but helping you find a new space at least lets me feel like I'm doing something useful. Is that the right reason?"

"Maybe," Rosie said. "It's not that I don't appreciate your help. I just . . . I don't want you to feel like you have to do this to make up for evicting me."

"Nothing I do now will make up for evicting you," Jane said, her expression pained, and tension snapped in the air between them, a tension that wouldn't ease until Rosie had found a new location for her store. Sometimes she forgot it was there, but it only took a single comment to bring it back to the forefront.

"What I'm trying to say is that I don't need you to make anything up to me," she said stubbornly. "We're fine, okay?"

Jane nodded, but her smile looked forced. "New topic. What are you doing for Christmas?"

"I usually go to Paige's parents' house for dinner," Rosie said. "You?"

"My parents'," Jane said. "Also just for dinner."

"Speaking of Christmas," Rosie said, "we're throwing a party at the store, a combination holiday party and farewell to Lexington Ave. I'm inviting all our customers and all the authors I know. Will you come?"

"Is that my official invitation?" Jane asked.

"Your official invitation will arrive in the mail this week."

Her eyebrows lifted. "Really?"

"Yep. Only authors get mailed invitations, though. Everyone else will get one in their bag when they shop at the store."

"Of course I'll come," Jane said, picking at her sandwich. "But I might attend as your girlfriend instead of Brie."

"I figured as much."

"Is that okay?" Jane asked, glancing at her cautiously.

"Of course," Rosie said. "I would never pressure you to do something you're not ready for."

"I'm getting there in baby steps." Jane took a pickle chip off her plate and popped it into her mouth.

"Yes, you are," Rosie agreed. "I do have one somewhat selfish request, though."

"What's that?"

"If and when you decide to have your first author event, will you have it at my store?"

"Claiming girlfriend privileges?" Jane asked, eyes sparkling playfully.

"Actually, I'm claiming 'I've waited the longest to have you sign in my store' privileges," Rosie told her.

"It's true," Jane said, her expression softening. "You were the first to invite me to sign, and even if you hadn't been, there's nowhere else I'd rather have my first signing."

Rosie and Marcia looked at several more available shopfronts over the next week, but nothing felt right. Either they were too expensive, lacked the space she needed, were a total dump, or some combination of the above. She got more demoralized about it every day and was almost ready to take a space that felt like a downgrade just to have *something* . . . except as Lia kept reminding her, they had the storage facility now. They had bought themselves a few more months to find a space they loved, but what if that space didn't exist?

On the second Wednesday in December, Jane texted Rosie another address, this time with the addendum that Rosie should call her when she got there so that Jane could explain. She had no idea what that meant, but she trusted Jane, so she asked Marcia to set it up, no questions asked.

And that was how she found herself standing on the sidewalk outside Vitali Café on East 104th Street. "A café?" she asked Marcia as they stepped inside. "Are you sure this is the right address?"

"I'm sure," Marcia said. "The management company said that although it isn't officially listed yet, the current tenants will be moving out at the end of February."

"Okay, that tracks, at least," Rosie said. "I guess it's time to call Jane and let her explain why she thinks this is a good space for me, because it would be a pain to convert a café into a bookstore. That counter would have to go, and there's probably a kitchen in back that I'd have to get rid of too."

"And it's over your budget, so you wouldn't have any room to pay for renovations," Marcia said.

Rosie was starting to feel like she was on an episode of *House Hunters*, where all the properties she saw required some sort of extreme compromise, except her hunt hadn't wrapped up after a neat thirty-minute dramatization. At this point, she felt like she'd been real estate shopping for years, and honestly, she was so sick of it.

She sat at an empty table in the back corner while Marcia went to the counter for a coffee. The shop was modern and clean, with bright-white walls and big windows. Rosie had been here a few times, as it was only about ten blocks from her store and apartment, and she remembered that it was owned by a mother-daughter team. Maybe that was a sign that she ought to keep her mind open, because she liked the symmetry. She pressed Jane's number and dialed.

"Hi," Jane said when she answered. "Are you at the café?"

"I am," Rosie said. "But I'm kind of at a loss as to why. Restaurant space isn't really the same as retail. I'd have to make so many changes before I could open the store here."

"That might turn out to be true," Jane said. "But hear me out first."

"Always," Rosie said.

"This café doesn't make their food in-house. They outsource, because there's not a kitchen on the premises. What they do have is a coffee bar and all the associated equipment, so I thought . . . what if you expand? Instead of having a weekly tea service downstairs in the basement, what if you hire someone to serve tea—and coffee—full time, right in the store?"

"Whoa," Rosie said, blinking rapidly as she looked around the café with new eyes.

"This property isn't ideal for a café. There's too much seating space, and of course the lack of a kitchen, which is probably why the business is failing, but it might be perfect if you turned most of that open space into a bookstore with a small café on the side."

"You're either crazy or a genius," Rosie said. The seating area around her was pretty big, while only a handful of people sat at the tables. And if there wasn't a kitchen in back, it might be functional for book storage.

"Between the Pages Bookstore and Café," Jane said. "Think about it."

"I will," Rosie said. "And I'll call you later, okay?"

"If you don't, I will," Jane said, and Rosie could hear the smile in her voice.

"Thank you. If this pans out, I'll owe you big time."

"Don't thank me yet," Jane said. "First see if the space will work for you."

"I'm on it. Okay, wish me luck."

"Good luck," Jane said.

Rosie ended the call and looked around. The café was laid out completely differently from her current storefront. If she was going to have a café on one side of the store, she'd have to reenvision the layout of her shelves and possibly invest in more freestanding units to compensate for lost wall space.

It would be a big change, but it might be a good one. The more she thought about it, she kind of loved the idea of adding a café. It would bring in more foot traffic, and this space was big enough to host signings and events right here in the store instead of in the basement. If there was enough storage space in back, it might actually work. And best of all, for the first time since she'd started her search, this felt like an upgrade.

Jane sat in the middle of her bed, typing as fast as her fingers would go. She was on a roll with her new book and had almost finished the sample chapters her agent had requested. Possibly, her infatuation with Rosie was fueling her creativity, because she'd never written this quickly before. Her back ached, and she stretched, rolling her neck from side to side. She really should at least try to start writing in the chair instead of on her bed. Her phone buzzed beside her.

Rosie Taft:

Can I stop by? Say yes!

Jane Breslin:

Yes.

Rosie Taft:

That was easy!

Jane Breslin:

I'm easy where you're concerned. Just ring the buzzer when
you get here.

Rosie Taft:

Will do. Want me to bring dinner?

Jane Breslin:

Sure. Whatever you're in the mood for is fine with me.

Rosie Taft:

K. See you soon!

Jane put her phone down with a smile, happy to set her work aside
for the chance to see Rosie. Briefly, she considered changing out of her
pajamas, but they were past the need to primp for each other. Actually,
they'd moved into the comfort of an established relationship a lot more
quickly than she'd expected.

Often, that was difficult for her. She had a hard time letting go of
her privacy and sharing her space. She and Rosie definitely still had their
rough spots—namely the uncertain future of Rosie's store—but these
day-to-day moments felt easy. She didn't have to hide any part of herself

from Rosie, not even her writing. So she picked up her laptop and kept working until she heard the buzzer a half hour later.

She slid out of bed and walked to the door to buzz Rosie in, not entirely surprised to find both Rosie and Brinkley waiting on her doorstep. Rosie carried a plastic bag of carryout food, and she was practically bouncing with excitement.

Jane gestured her in. "Good news?"

Rosie gave her a quick kiss, lips chilly from the December air. "I just signed a lease on the space on 104th Street."

"Oh my God. That's *great* news." Jane pulled her in for another kiss, feeling light on her feet. She was so happy for Rosie and relieved that her actions wouldn't spell the end of Between the Pages. Tears pricked at her eyes as the tension she'd been holding on to for months now drained from her muscles. She felt Brinkley's front paws on her leg, wanting in on the celebration.

"I brought champagne." Rosie pulled back, opening her bag and taking out a bottle. "And takeout from the pub down the street: grilled-chicken salad for me and that vegetable pasta you like."

"Perfect," Jane said. "Let's pop that champagne, and I want to hear everything while we eat."

"Were you working?" Rosie asked, and Jane loved that she knew her well enough to know that she did most of her writing in her pajamas.

"I was, but I'm happy for the distraction." She took the bottle from Rosie and went into the kitchen for a cloth to wrap around the cork. It released with a satisfying pop. Jane poured two flutes and handed one to Rosie. "To your new location."

"Between the Pages Bookstore and Café," Rosie said as she clinked her glass against Jane's. "I was so afraid I was going to have to settle for a space that wasn't as nice as what I have now, but Lia and I walked through the café together this afternoon before we signed the lease, and I think it's really going to be amazing."

"Should you be celebrating with her tonight instead of me?" Jane asked, sipping her champagne. It was tart and fizzy against her tongue.

"I would have, but she has a date, so I'm all yours."

"Perfect." Jane took another sip and chased it with Rosie's mouth, capturing her lips for a champagne kiss. "Does he need dinner too?" she asked, gesturing to Brinkley. There was a bag of dog food in her pantry now, kept there for impromptu visits like this one.

"Yes, but he can wait a minute, because I'm kissing my girlfriend and toasting some good news first," Rosie said against her lips.

"An agenda I fully support." Jane could kiss her all day. She set their champagne flutes on the table and pulled Rosie into her arms to do just that. They kissed slowly at first, lips and tongues teasing. Jane held her close, sliding her hands down Rosie's back to cup her ass over the long flowy skirt she wore. Jane felt warm all over, and not just from their kiss. She was *happy*.

Dinner was waiting on the table and a hungry dog lay on the floor at their feet, so she resisted the urge to kiss her way beneath Rosie's top. They'd have time for that later, but right now she wanted nothing more than to lose herself in the pleasure of Rosie's mouth.

When they pulled back, they were both breathing hard. Rosie's lips glistened, beckoning Jane back in, but she kissed her cheek instead. Then she released Rosie and got a scoop of dog food out of the pantry so Brinkley could eat at the same time they did. She set down a dish and dumped the food into it, and he dived in enthusiastically.

Meanwhile, Rosie went into Jane's cabinet for plates and silverware, and they sat at the table together to eat. Jane scooped a serving of pasta onto her plate. "Tell me everything."

"My lease starts March first, so we'll only be operating out of the warehouse for two months, which should be totally manageable." Rosie spoke quickly, gesturing with her hands. "There's a small storage room and an office downstairs. And we'll be able to host events and signings right in the café area. Jane, for the first time since that letter arrived, I'm actually excited about this."

"I'm so glad." Jane felt tears welling in her eyes. She'd harbored so much guilt over ending Rosie's lease, had feared that in some way it would always be a dark cloud over their relationship, but maybe she could finally let go of that now.

"I mean, I'm definitely going to cry when I close my doors on Lexington Ave," Rosie said, spearing a forkful of salad. "That space is so sentimental to me, but now we have a new home that will allow us to do something we couldn't do in our current location. I hope the café will really help us grow. I'm counting on it, actually, because I need that income to help cover the increase in rent."

"It should," Jane said. "People are willing to pay exorbitant prices for their coffee, sometimes more than they're willing to spend on a book."

"Isn't that the truth?" Rosie said. "And a book will bring so much more pleasure. Plus, you'll have it forever."

"You don't have to convince me," Jane said. "I'm just so glad this worked out for you, Rosie. Seriously."

"Me too." Rosie sat back in her chair. "I feel like I can breathe freely for the first time in months. I don't think I really realized how stressed I was about this until I signed that lease today. Now Lia and I can start making plans for the new space. We're actually going to pull this off."

Jane lifted her champagne glass. "Yes, you are."

CHAPTER
TWENTY-ONE

The tree in the front window blinked with brightly colored bulbs while the shelf beside it displayed a lit menorah, and festive music played through the speakers Lia's friend had helped them install for the occasion. There were bottles of wine on the counter in back, and Betty was positioned at the front door to card everyone who entered and hand out wristbands to their guests to keep them in compliance with the liquor license they'd obtained for tonight's party.

Rosie had feared this would be a sad night, and she definitely felt a twinge of melancholy because it was the last event she'd host in this space, but it felt more bittersweet than devastating. She and her store were going to be okay. It was December 18, so after tonight, she would spend the next two weeks winding things down and packing up to move out.

She smoothed her hands over the front of her dress and watched as the front door opened to admit the first guests of the evening. Dolores and her husband stepped into the store, and that twinge in Rosie's chest sharpened. Dolores was one of the customers who'd started to feel almost like family over the years, and Rosie was so glad to have her here tonight.

She crossed the store to give Dolores a quick hug. "I'm so glad you made it. And you, too, Fred."

"Oh, we wouldn't miss it for the world," Dolores said. "And the sign on the front door says you've found a new space?"

Rosie nodded. "Only ten blocks from here. I hope you'll still be able to stop by."

"It won't be quite as convenient, but I'll be there," Dolores said. "I'm so happy it worked out for you."

"Me too," Rosie told her. The door opened again, and Nikki and Paige came in, stopping to chat with Betty as they accepted wristbands. Rosie excused herself to greet them, and then the guests kept coming. Soon, the store was filled with the sounds of conversation and laughter.

Lia was behind the counter, serving drinks and ringing up book purchases. She and Rosie would be taking turns there tonight. The next person through the door was Darcy Fine, arguably the most well-known author Rosie had invited. She wrote women's fiction and was one of Rosie's favorites.

By the time Rosie had crossed the store to greet Darcy, the author was already surrounded by several excited readers. "Darcy, I'm so glad you made it."

"Oh, it's a pleasure," Darcy said. "You've been so supportive over the years. I wouldn't have missed this party for anything."

"Would you like a drink?"

"Sure," Darcy said.

Rosie led her to the bar, where Lia poured her a glass of wine and gave her a name tag. She'd printed them out for all the authors attending tonight.

Shanice and Ashley entered next, and Rosie greeted them with hugs. So many of her favorite people would be here in the store tonight, and it felt like the best possible way to wrap up her time here. Bittersweet—not sad—Rosie reminded herself when her eyes grew damp.

"Looks like things are going well."

Rosie spun at the sound of Jane's voice. "When did you get here?"

"I snuck in behind that happy couple over there." Jane gestured to a couple of Rosie's regulars, browsing the shelves with glasses of wine in hand.

"I'm so glad you're here." Rosie took her hands and leaned in for a quick kiss. And then, because she was getting increasingly emotional as the evening progressed, she pulled Jane in for a hug until the tears in her eyes had receded.

"You okay?" Jane asked, one hand resting on Rosie's waist.

"Yep. There's a solid chance I'll cry before the night's over, though, so be forewarned."

"I can handle tears." Jane brushed her fingers against Rosie's cheek.

"Also, there's a name tag for you at the counter with Lia if you want it. And if you don't, no worries."

"Okay," Jane said, but the hesitance in her eyes told Rosie she wasn't going to put on the name tag tonight, and that was fine.

Rosie took in Jane's dress, realizing it was the same one she'd worn on their first date, the sleek black one with the open back, and oh yes, Rosie liked this turn of events. She leaned in to whisper in Jane's ear. "Just out of curiosity, are you braless in this dress again tonight?"

"Wouldn't you like to know?" Jane asked with a sly wink, but then she gave her head a slight shake. "Actually, I knew this party would be crowded and likely chilly, so no."

"Bummer, but probably a wise choice, considering," Rosie said. "You should go grab some wine. And if you see any authors here tonight that you'd like to say hi to, I can vouch for all of them as good people."

"We'll see." Jane touched her arm and headed toward the counter to get a drink.

Rosie made her way around the shop, greeting guests and handing out business cards with their new address, inviting people to shop online in the meantime.

"Oh, hey, Rosie."

She turned to find Tracy standing there with a glass of red wine in hand. "Hi, Tracy. So glad you could make it."

"Of course," she said. "I just wanted to thank you for recommending that book by Brie. It's one of my favorite reads of the year. In fact, I'd like to pick up a few more of her books tonight, if you have them in stock."

"Oh, I'm so glad." Rosie absolutely loved it when she successfully helped someone discover a new book or author to love, and she was especially thrilled to have helped Jane find a new reader. "And yes, I have several of Brie's other books here in the store."

She was suddenly aware of Jane standing beside her—had she been there the whole time? Jane's eyes were wide, wineglass lifted as if she'd been about to take a drink, but Rosie's gaze immediately caught on the name tag in her hand, trapped between her palm and the clear plastic cup. Brie's name was visible through the opaque liquid.

Jane had seen Rosie and Tracy talking and walked over to join them, since they were among the only faces she knew here tonight. But she hadn't expected them to be talking about her books, and now they were both staring at her in a way that was making her slightly uncomfortable. Rosie would never have revealed her identity, but then why was Tracy looking at her like that?

"Hi," Jane said awkwardly.

"Hi, Jane," Tracy said, seeming to stare at Jane's wine. "It's great to see you again."

"You too." And Jane's stomach pitched, because she'd let Lia convince her to take Brie's name tag. Lia had suggested she put it in her purse in case she decided to wear it later, and when faced with the anxiety-inducing task of finding someone she knew in the crowded room, Jane had forgotten she was holding it.

She looked down at the plastic cup in her hand. Brie's name was written in big black letters on a name tag that said "Meet the Author," which was pressed against the side of the cup. Her cheeks burned, and she wondered briefly if she could just duck out through the back door and pretend this never happened. For a moment, no one said anything, and then Tracy gestured toward Jane's hand.

"Is that yours? Are you Brie?" She was smiling, looking absolutely thrilled at the prospect of Jane being an author, and Jane's shell-shocked brain couldn't think of a single viable excuse for why she'd be holding this name tag unless it was hers.

"Yes," she heard herself say through the pounding of her pulse in her ears.

Rosie gaped at her before breaking into a huge smile, clapping her hands together. "Tracy was just telling me that *On the Flip Side* is one of her favorite reads this year."

"Yes," Tracy said. "And I can't believe . . . I had no idea you were an author."

"I'm a very shy author," Jane said, taking a fortifying sip of her wine, "which is why I hadn't put the name tag on yet."

"I can't believe you even took it, to be honest," Rosie teased, keeping the conversation moving the way she always did.

"Lia can be very persuasive," Jane said.

"Oh, tell me about it," Rosie said. "Look, dessert." She gestured toward a table in back laden with festive-looking cookies and snacks.

"You aren't worried about stuff getting spilled on the books?" Jane asked. She still felt uncomfortably flushed, but Rosie seemed to have successfully steered the conversation away from Brie. Jane took the opportunity to slip the name tag into her purse.

"Not tonight," Rosie said. "Tonight, I'm only focused on having fun and celebrating thirty years in this space." She glanced at the photo of herself and her mom that hung behind the counter, and Jane's heart clenched.

"I'm so glad you found a new location," Tracy said. "And it's actually closer to my apartment, so I'll definitely still be stopping by just as often."

"That's exactly what I was hoping to hear," Rosie said. "It's been a rough couple of months, but I'm glad to look ahead to new things." She reached over and gave Jane's hand a subtle squeeze.

"Rosie!" A group of women who'd just entered the store waved to catch her attention, and Rosie excused herself to greet them.

Jane sipped her wine, desperately trying to think of something to say. She was terrible at small talk, particularly when there were topics she was trying to avoid.

"If you'd rather not talk about your books, it's totally fine," Tracy said. "I just think it's really cool that you're an author, and I absolutely loved *On the Flip Side*, but I'll just . . ." She mimed zipping her lips with a friendly smile.

"Sorry," Jane said, fidgeting with her wine. "I don't know why I'm weird about this. When I first started writing, I didn't want it to get out at work, so I chose to stay anonymous. But now I feel like it's gotten out of hand. I was trying to push myself tonight, which is why I took the name tag in the first place, so please, ask me whatever you'd like. And thank you so much for the compliment. I really appreciate that."

"Want to get cookies and talk?" Tracy suggested, gesturing toward the dessert table.

Jane nodded, feeling herself relax. "Sure."

They walked to the back of the store, and Jane put a chocolate truffle on a little napkin while Tracy took a couple of cookies.

"Did you always want to be an author?" Tracy asked, breaking off a bite of one of her cookies.

"Kind of," Jane told her. "But I didn't think it was a realistic career choice, you know? And my dad had strong opinions about me joining the family business."

"Did you?" Tracy asked.

"I did." Jane bit into her truffle, and gooey chocolate exploded in her mouth. It was rich and delicious and probably the worst thing she could have picked to eat in a social setting. Already she feared she had chocolate all over her face.

"I worked with my mom for a few years," Tracy told her. "We're both teachers and used to work at the same school. That was fun. I enjoyed having lunch with her when our schedules matched up, but it's not quite the same as joining a family business."

Jane finally managed to swallow, touching her lips self-consciously to make sure she wasn't a mess. "Yeah, I do enjoy seeing my family at work, my sister in particular."

She and Tracy chatted for a few more minutes, and the conversation circled back to Jane's books, but this time it didn't feel any different from talking with Rosie or Amy. Tracy was curious about all the work that went into writing a book, Jane's process, and what she was working on next. Why had she fought this for so long? It was just like convincing herself to come to this party—the hardest part was getting here.

Jane reached into her purse and pulled out the name tag. "I think I'm going to put this on after all."

"Oh, exciting," Tracy said. "Go for it."

She pressed the sticker onto her dress. "Thanks for the nudge. I'm too antisocial for my own good sometimes."

"You're doing great," Tracy said.

"Hi, Tracy." A tall blonde woman joined them, smiling at Tracy before she turned her gaze on Jane. "Oh, you're an author. What do you write?"

Jane felt herself flush again, but this time she pressed on. "I write romance."

"I read almost anything, but I love romance," the blonde said. "I'm Gloria, by the way."

"Brie," Jane said, introducing herself as an author perhaps for the first time. "It's nice to meet you."

"Tell me more about your books, Brie."

Jane had lost track of time, but the crowd in the store was finally beginning to thin, and the fuzziness in her brain suggested it must be late.
She was exhausted after several hours of conversation, but it was a good
kind of tired, because she'd actually worn her name tag and introduced
herself to people as Brie. It shouldn't have been a big deal, but it felt like
one, and for the first time in a while, she was proud of herself.

"Hey, you." Rosie slid in beside her, bumping her shoulder against
Jane's.

Jane turned her head and pressed a quick kiss on her cheek. "Hi."

"You've had quite a night," Rosie said.

"So have you," Jane deflected. "The party seems like a success."

"Yeah." Rosie had a dreamy expression on her face as she looked
around the store. "The turnout was amazing. Everyone seems really supportive about the move, and I sold a ton of books, so I'll call it a win."

"Definitely a win," Jane said.

"Although the biggest surprise of the night was definitely *you*."

Jane touched her fingertips against the name tag, smiling. "I surprised myself."

"You sure as hell surprised me," Rosie said. "I'm so proud of you,
and you should know that so many customers wanted to buy a book
after meeting you that we're sold out of Brie titles. I actually had to
order four extra copies of *On the Flip Side* to fill all the requests."

"Are you serious?"

"So serious," Rosie said. "You're a hit. They love you."

Jane ducked her head. "Well, I hope they like my book."

"I'm sure they will, and some of these people have never read a
queer romance before," Rosie said. "I *love* widening people's horizons

through books, and it's just a win-win situation when I love the author too."

Jane choked midway through a sip of wine, and it burned her throat, making her eyes water. Rosie's eyes went wide as she realized what she'd said, and then she doubled over in laughter. Because it was late and she was halfway delirious from too much conversation and too much wine, Jane found herself laughing, too, which was a ludicrous reaction to Rosie's inadvertent declaration of love.

"I love a lot of authors," Rosie said when she'd calmed down. "But you know you're my favorite, and I'm getting awfully close to saying those words to you for real."

Jane froze, tears in her eyes from her laughing fit, and now her heart was beating too fast. "Really?"

"Yeah," Rosie said, and Jane saw the truth of her words reflected in Rosie's blue eyes. "It's not too soon for me to admit that, is it?"

"No," Jane whispered. It was the last thing she'd expected to hear Rosie say tonight, but her whole body felt warm and fuzzy in an entirely different way now, like she'd just received the very best news. "I think I might be closer than I realized too."

Rosie beamed at her, blonde curls gleaming every hue of the rainbow as they reflected the Christmas tree in the window. "Well, that's a lucky coincidence, isn't it?"

"Nothing coincidental about it," Jane told her, gripping Rosie's hand and pulling her in for a quick kiss. She wasn't exactly sure whether Rosie wanted her customers to know she was dating one of the authors or not, but they'd gotten progressively handsy with each other throughout the night, and neither of them seemed to care who saw them now.

The feel of Rosie's lips against hers never failed to make her ache in the very best way. She'd written about so many women falling in love, and in her books, they usually had a light bulb moment where they realized they'd fallen, but Jane hadn't seen this coming. Real life was less definitive, and emotions were complicated, but she had a sneaking feeling she'd been falling for Rosie since before they'd even met in person.

She tucked one of Rosie's curls behind her ear. "Come home with me tonight?"

Someone laughed behind them, and Jane turned to find Lia standing there with a smirk and a raised eyebrow. "I was coming over to join the conversation, but it looks like you two are done talking. Also, I'll watch Brinkley tonight." With a wink, she walked away to talk to a couple standing beside the Christmas tree.

"Guess that's a yes," Rosie said.

"I feel like I should be embarrassed that she heard me say that."

"Ha—believe me, Lia's no prude. And as long as you don't mind waiting around while I clean up after the party, I'd love to come over."

"I don't mind," Jane said.

The party seemed to be nearly over at this point, with only a handful of guests remaining. Rosie and Lia made the rounds to greet everyone one last time, and Jane walked to the back of the store for a bottle of water. Now that she'd left the swing of the party, she had no energy left for conversation. She took off her name tag and leaned a hip against the counter, staying out of the way while Rosie and Lia wrapped things up and sent everyone on their way.

When Jane finally looked at her phone, she was surprised to realize it was only a little past eleven. She'd been sure it was well after midnight, but then again, socializing always drained her, as did long hours on her feet in heels. She stepped behind the counter and slipped her shoes off, rubbing the arches of her feet.

"I know the feeling," Betty said with a sympathetic smile as she came to stand beside Jane.

She didn't know Betty well, but she had a friendly, grandmotherly vibe that Jane liked. "Chose the wrong shoes to wear tonight."

"They look great on you, though," Betty said. "And I know Rosie was thrilled to see you wearing your author badge."

"She was," Jane agreed with a smile.

"You're good for her," Betty commented, looking thoughtful.

Jane flinched. "I brought a lot of chaos into her life."

Betty waved a hand dismissively. "That wasn't your fault. It's interesting, though, how both of you followed in the footsteps of one of your parents. This store has always been Rosie's calling, but I don't think you can say the same."

"No," Jane said, wondering how she'd never made the connection before that both she and Rosie had gone into the family business. "My father's company has never been my passion, but luckily, it is my sister's."

"These things always work out the way they're supposed to," Betty said with a nod. "I knew Joy—Rosie's mom—you know. She loved this store, but Rosie was the most important thing in her life. More than anything, she wanted Rosie to be happy, and I know she'd just love seeing the two of you together."

"Thank you," Jane said, blinking back unexpected tears. "I hope you're right."

"Oh, I usually am," Betty said, patting Jane's hand.

Rosie and Lia joined them then, and the four of them started to clean up, discarding plastic cups left on various surfaces around the store and wiping down shelves and tables. Soon enough, they were putting on their coats to go home. Betty and Lia struck out in opposite directions, and Jane and Rosie headed for the subway. They were quiet as they rode.

Even Rosie seemed tired. She leaned her head on Jane's shoulder and closed her eyes. "Still can't believe you wore that name tag tonight. It was amazing."

"I can't believe I did either," Jane said. "You know when you build something up in your mind, and then once you do it, it's no big deal, and you can't remember why you were dreading it in the first place?"

"I do," Rosie said. "But this *was* a big deal, and you should be proud."

"I am," Jane said quietly.

The subway car rattled around them, and if it hadn't been so unnaturally bright and a little bit funky smelling, she might have been tempted to close her eyes, too, but one of them needed to watch for their stop. She wrapped an arm around Rosie, holding her close as the subway carried them across the city.

They exited at Union Square and walked the rest of the way to Jane's building. Now that she'd been off her feet for a little while, they felt even more sore, and her ears rang from the noise of the party. Gratefully, she let them into her apartment, where Rosie shed her coat and went into the kitchen for a glass of water. Jane kicked off her shoes and followed her lead.

Rosie pulled Jane in and kissed her with ice-cold lips. "I hope you're not too tired, because I'm not finished celebrating with you yet."

CHAPTER
TWENTY-TWO

Rosie woke with a jolt, at first not sure what had awakened her. Her phone buzzed on the table beside Jane's bed, reminding her that she'd forgotten to silence it before she fell asleep, distracted by Jane and her slinky black dress. Rosie fumbled the phone and found a text from Grace, responding to the photos Rosie had sent her last night from the party.

She smiled as she put her phone on "do not disturb" and went into the bathroom to freshen up, hoping she could doze off again afterward. It was only eight, and Sundays were her days to sleep in, since the store didn't open until noon.

When she got back in bed, Jane blinked at her through sleepy eyes. "Morning."

"Morning," Rosie whispered. "But I don't have to be up yet, so let's sleep."

"Mm," Jane agreed, eyes drifting shut.

Rosie followed her lead. The next time she woke, one of Jane's arms was resting over her stomach, and there was a strand of chestnut hair in her face. Rosie smiled, snuggling closer, loving the warmth of Jane's body spooned against hers. Jane's hand shifted, stroking back and forth over Rosie's stomach, stirring a warmth inside her that had nothing to do with the coziness of the bed.

"Do you have to work today?" Jane murmured, placing a kiss on the tender skin below Rosie's ear.

She shivered. "Yes, but . . ." Did she? Lia and Betty were both in today.

"But?" Jane asked.

"Lia would probably cover for me."

"We owe her a *lot* of favors at this point," Jane said as her hand dipped lower on Rosie's stomach.

"Not as many as you think," Rosie said, arching into her touch. "I cover for her a lot too. It's the way we've always worked."

"Well, that's good."

"I don't want to miss afternoon tea, though," Rosie told her. "It's the second-to-last time we'll be hosting it on Lexington Ave, and I want to be there."

"Understandable," Jane said. "I thought maybe we could have an adventure day, you know . . . find some of those hidden places in the city you like to look for?"

"Yes," Rosie agreed immediately. "I haven't done that in a while. I'd love to."

Jane's fingers slid inside Rosie's panties, and she gasped in pleasure, her body quickly coming awake beneath Jane's touch. Jane took her time, kissing Rosie's neck and shoulder, pushing aside the T-shirt she'd worn to bed as her fingers kept moving, building a delicious heat that blazed through Rosie's core.

She moved her hips to Jane's rhythm, her ass bumping rhythmically into Jane's lap, and she was breathing hard, too, moving with Rosie as her fingers sent her over the edge. The orgasm rushed through her, and she moaned as her body turned hot and tingly.

"My favorite way to wake up," she said once she'd caught her breath, rolling to face Jane.

Jane's cheeks were flushed, she had mascara smudged beneath her eyes, her hair was a mess, and Rosie loved her this way . . . and every way. She hadn't fully realized it until she'd blurted it out last night, but she loved Jane. Of course she did. She'd never felt this strongly about anyone before, and Jane hadn't seemed to balk at the idea of loving her back either.

Rosie rolled on top of her, hands sliding over Jane's soft-gray T-shirt, cupping her breasts over the fabric. Jane whimpered, arching her back to press herself more firmly into Rosie's touch. Her nipples poked against the shirt, and when Rosie looked up, she found Jane watching her, bottom lip pinched between her teeth.

"You're just unfairly gorgeous right now," Rosie told her.

In response, Jane covered her face with the shirt. Rosie giggled, changing tactics. She feathered her fingers over the warm skin on Jane's stomach, making her gasp. Rosie circled her navel and then moved lower, trailing her fingers up and down Jane's thighs.

"Rosie . . ." She squirmed as Rosie drew tiny hearts on her skin, teasing her until Jane uncovered her face. "Please."

Rosie slid a hand between her thighs, and *oh*, Jane was already so wet for her. She gasped as Rosie's fingers skimmed over her clit. Rosie stretched out beside her, kissing Jane hungrily as her fingers worked her body. Jane clung to her, her kisses becoming sloppier the more worked up she got. Her hips moved rhythmically against Rosie's, a steady stream of whimpers and gasps spilling from her lips.

It made Rosie feel incredibly powerful to watch Jane unravel like this, the way her brows wrinkled and her eyes shut as she grew closer to her release. Jane braced her toes against Rosie's, thrusting herself more firmly against her, and then she cried out, spasming in Rosie's arms. Her body gripped Rosie's fingers, release pulsing through her in waves.

Afterward, Jane buried her face on Rosie's shoulder while she caught her breath, and Rosie played with her hair, feeling content with the world. Eventually, they got up and showered and then ate oatmeal together in bed while they looked at the Twitter account Jane had sent her last month, listing unique places to visit in the city.

They decided to start at Washington Mews, a private street not too far from Jane's apartment that had been preserved since the time of horse-drawn carriages. And then, if they still had time, they might stop at the ice cream museum. Rosie borrowed clean clothes from Jane, grateful they were nearly the same size, and she texted Lia to make sure she didn't mind opening the store.

Ten minutes later, bundled in a borrowed sweater and jeans beneath her coat, she set out with Jane. They passed the thirty-minute walk with casual conversation, holding hands like two people who couldn't get enough of each other. Washington Mews indeed looked like it belonged in a period film, with old-fashioned row houses and a cobblestone street.

"Time for selfies," Rosie proclaimed, and they posed, miming as if they carried old-fashioned parasols. Jane twirled, spinning an imaginary skirt, and Rosie snapped a quick series of photos of Jane with her hair flying everywhere and a carefree smile on her face.

Afterward, they made their way downtown to the Museum of Ice Cream, arriving just as it opened at noon. Festive decor out front advertised Pinkmas, which Rosie decided might be her new favorite holiday. Inside, they took yet more selfies in a roomful of pink Christmas trees and sampled some delicious ice cream.

"I think I need real food soon," Jane said, pressing a hand against her stomach. "I'm starting to feel sick from all the sugar."

"Same."

"Hey, tell me if this is a weird idea, but do you want to stop by Vitali Café? They serve premade sandwiches, I think. I noticed it when I was researching the space for you."

"Oh," Rosie said, considering. Was it weird to have lunch at the café whose demise had provided her with a new space for her store? "I might like to see it again, actually, to visualize where everything's going to go."

"That's exactly what I was thinking. It's a haul from here, but it's near your shop, and we need to be there by two anyway for afternoon tea," Jane said.

"Let's do it."

They put their coats back on and left the ice cream museum, then boarded the subway to head uptown. Forty minutes later, Rosie pulled open the door to Vitali Café, entering somewhat hesitantly. "It's still surreal that this will be my store in a few months," she said quietly to Jane.

"It is," Jane agreed. The café was nearly empty, despite it being lunchtime on a Sunday, a time when business ought to be booming, and Rosie wondered why it wasn't. Hopefully the café's lack of customers had more to do with the current business than the location.

A woman about Rosie's age with curly dark hair and a tanned complexion greeted them at the counter. Rosie remembered her from when she'd been in the café before. She was the daughter in the mother-daughter duo who currently rented the space. Her name tag read "Nicole." "What can I get you?" she asked.

Rosie took a chicken sandwich from the case in front of her. The display of cannoli and other Italian desserts would have been tempting if she hadn't come here straight from the ice cream museum. "I'll have this and a flat white, please."

"You got it," Nicole said. "And for you?" She looked at Jane.

"A sandwich and a cappuccino," Jane said, choosing a turkey wrap.

Rosie watched as Nicole rang them up, debating whether to mention who she was and why she was here, but she'd never really been one to hold things back, and she believed in making connections wherever she could. Maybe there was a way she could help Nicole and her mom with their next endeavor.

"I hope you don't mind," she started, feeling somewhat apologetic, "but I also wanted to introduce myself. I'm Rosie Taft, and I own Between the Pages Bookstore on Lexington Ave. We lost our space, and so we're going to be moving here in March after you leave."

Nicole's eyes went as round as the coffee cup in her hand. "Oh."

"Anyway, I hope you and your mom have success wherever you go next," Rosie said. "I just wanted to offer, if anyone comes in looking for you, I'd be happy to give them a new address or phone number. I used to work with my mom, too, before she passed away, so I guess what I'm trying to say is . . . I relate, and if there's anything I can do to help make this easier, please let me know."

Nicole pressed a hand over her mouth, her eyes glossy. "Wow, thanks. Um, let me introduce you to my mom."

"Sure," Rosie said.

"Ma!" Nicole called. "Come out here a minute."

A few moments later, an older woman came out from the back, a worried look on her face. "Everything okay?"

"Yeah," Nicole said. "This is Rosie. She owns the bookstore that's moving into this space after we leave."

"Oh," the woman said, giving Rosie a wary look. "I'm Francesca Vitali."

"It's nice to meet you," Rosie told her. "I hope you don't mind me coming in, but I like knowing the people behind all the paperwork, you know? And like I told Nicole, from one small business owner to another, if there's anything I can do to help, just let me know."

"Well, thanks, but we're going out of business, so I don't see how you can help," Francesca told her bluntly.

"Ma," Nicole said, sounding embarrassed. "Rosie's just trying to be friendly."

"Thanks for the gesture," Francesca said. "I know you're not the one I'm angry with, but it's hard, you know?"

"I do," Rosie said. "It would have been hard for me to meet someone who was moving into my space, too, but they're actually demolishing my building."

"That's shitty," Francesca said. "I wish we'd met under better circumstances."

"So do I," Rosie told her. "Truly."

Francesca excused herself and headed for the back. Jane hadn't said a word since Rosie had introduced herself to Nicole, and when she glanced at her, Jane had a vaguely embarrassed look on her face.

"Sorry about that," Nicole said. "We've had a rough time lately, but I'm glad to know someone nice is taking over our space."

"I totally understand," Rosie said. "And my offer is sincere. If there's anything I can do . . ."

"I appreciate it, but like my mom said, we're going out of business. Anyway, I'll be right over with your coffees."

"Thanks," Rosie told her. She and Jane took their sandwiches and sat at a table along the back wall.

"I didn't know you were going to do that," Jane said as she unwrapped her sandwich.

"I didn't, either, but it felt like the right thing to do," Rosie said. "You disagree?"

Jane shrugged. "I wouldn't have done it, but you're better at these things than I am, so you're probably right."

"I just feel a sort of kinship with them, you know? A mother-daughter duo, and they're losing their business. I'm really sorry they weren't able to relocate like I was."

"Well, your circumstances are different," Jane said. "You're running a successful business that needed a new space. Their business failed for whatever reason, but it had nothing to do with their lease."

"You don't know why it failed?" Rosie asked, suddenly curious how much Jane knew about Vitali Café. How had she found this place for Rosie?

Jane shook her head. "I just put out feelers for commercial space and heard this one was coming available."

"Ah." Rosie's excitement about visiting her future storefront had been dampened a little bit by meeting Nicole and Francesca. If she'd known them sooner, she would have tried to help them succeed. She always rooted for the underdog, especially when it was a local, family-owned business.

Nicole brought over their coffees, and Rosie stirred a packet of sugar into hers.

Jane did the same, lifting the cup for a cautious sip. "I hate to say it," she said quietly, "but the coffee isn't great, and neither is the sandwich, so it might be as simple as that."

Rosie wrinkled her nose. "Yeah, you might be right."

"Have you started to envision it?" Jane asked, glancing around the café.

"Yes, but I'd love to hear your thoughts while we're here," Rosie told her.

Jane nodded, setting down her coffee cup. She started telling Rosie about the best ways to maximize light and space, sounding like the businesswoman Rosie had first met. She listened, fascinated, taking notes in her phone as Jane shared her thoughts on the book café. They spoke in hushed tones, not wanting Nicole to overhear so as not to be insensitive.

"And what do you think about book and tea pairings?" Jane asked. "Like peppermint tea with a Christmas book, or something more inventive than that, but you get the idea. You could even work it into your subscription boxes."

"Oh wow," Rosie said. "That's genius."

"Just an idea," Jane said.

"I know you're an author at heart," Rosie said, "but your business skills are pretty sharp too."

Jane smiled as she lifted her sandwich. "I try."

They were fifteen minutes late to afternoon tea and had to drag over two extra chairs to join the conversation. The last thing Jane wanted was tea right after leaving the café, so she took a bottle of water instead. Brinkley ran over and propped his front paws on her leg, staring up at her in that way she'd learned meant he was happy to see her, mouth open and tail wagging.

"Hi, Brinkley," she whispered, reaching down to pet him. She used to think she wasn't a pet person, but she was starting to realize she just wasn't used to being around them, because she liked Brinkley a lot.

While Rosie chatted happily with a customer over by the teapots, Jane left her chair and went down the hall to the restroom. Truthfully, she was feeling a bit antisocial after the party last night. She'd exhausted her social skills and hadn't had a chance to recharge at home, not that she was complaining about her morning with Rosie.

But she was content to sit quietly in back, listening to the book chatter around her. Eventually she tuned out, jotting notes in her phone about the next scene in her book.

The phone vibrated in her hand as a new text message came through.

Pilar Alonso:

> I just read the chapters you sent me, and Jane, this is the best work you've ever done. So good, in fact, that I couldn't wait until Monday to email you and had to interrupt your weekend to tell you how much I loved it.

Jane Breslin:

> Wow. Pilar, I don't know what to say. Thank you!

Pilar Alonso:

Thank *you* for writing such an amazing book. I have a few notes to send, but they're just small line tweaks. We should be ready to have you on submission after the holidays.

Jane Breslin:

That's wonderful news!

Pilar Alonso:

I set the bar high for you with this one, because we want this to be your breakout series, and you have exceeded all expectations. Well done.

I'll have those notes to you tomorrow. Enjoy your Sunday!

Jane set her phone down and blew out a breath to calm her racing heart. *Wow.* Pilar had never gushed over her work so enthusiastically before. She was generally very conservative with her praise, so if she said she loved something, Jane knew she meant it. *The best work she'd ever done.* She pressed her fingers against her lips to hide her smile. Had her relationship with Rosie helped her write romance more authentically?

Someone tapped her on the shoulder, and she looked up to find Tracy standing there. "Oh, hi," Jane said. "Long time, no see."

"You've been here a lot lately," Tracy said. "Are you and Rosie . . . ?"

"Yeah," Jane said as heat crept up her neck. "We are."

"Cool," Tracy said, pulling up an empty chair beside Jane. "I'm happy for you two. Hey, could I ask a little favor?" And if Jane wasn't mistaken, now Tracy was the one who looked slightly embarrassed.

"Sure," Jane said, hoping this wasn't something she was about to regret.

Tracy reached into her bag and pulled out a copy of *On the Flip Side*. "Could you sign this for me? I don't want to impose, but it's just so cool that you're the author, and I really loved the book."

"Oh." Jane pressed a hand against her chest. This was the last thing she'd expected, so far down the list she hadn't even considered it. "Yes, of course."

Tracy smiled as she handed Jane the book. "Thanks."

"I don't have a pen, but I'm sure Rosie does." Jane had used Rosie's Sharpies and "Autographed by the Author" stickers for the subscription boxes. She stood and walked to the cabinet where she and Rosie had put away the supplies that night, finding everything she needed.

Then she stood with the book for a minute, considering what to say. She hadn't signed many books for people she knew personally, aside from the one she'd given Rosie, and it was intimidating to come up with the right words.

To Tracy,

Thank you for your support and friendship.

Brie

Satisfied, she brought the book back to her seat and handed it to Tracy, who beamed when she saw what Jane had written.

"Thank you so much," she said. "I often regift my books after I've read them to share the love, but this one is going on my keeper shelf."

"I'm honored," Jane told her.

They chatted for a few more minutes until the tea service ended, and then Jane went looking for Rosie, who was surrounded by customers all wishing her well and promising to visit once she'd reopened in the new location. Jane waited quietly until the crowd had dispersed, and then she helped Rosie and Lia clean up.

"What are your plans for the rest of the afternoon?" Rosie asked her.

"I need to go home and finish this chapter I'm writing," Jane said. "Want to make plans for tomorrow, maybe dinner?"

"It's a date," Rosie said, leaning in for a kiss.

"Get a room, you two," Lia called from the other side of the room.

Rosie made a face as she flipped off her friend, who laughed as she wiped down teapots. Jane envied their friendship. Maybe she'd make more friends next year. In fact, as she left the store a few minutes later, she hoped she would. She hoped next year would bring lots of good things for her, and for Rosie.

CHAPTER TWENTY-THREE

The next week seemed to pass in a blur of work and deadlines mixed with time spent with Rosie, and almost before Jane even realized it, Christmas was upon them. Rosie had spent the night at Jane's apartment, so they woke on Christmas morning together, wrapped in each other's arms as the day dawned cold and gray outside.

"Merry Christmas," Jane whispered, brushing aside Rosie's curls to kiss her neck.

"Merry Christmas." Rosie rolled to face her.

"Can't remember the last time I woke with someone in my bed on Christmas morning," Jane said as she kissed Rosie's lips. "I like it."

"Me, either, and same," Rosie said. "Sometimes Christmas has been lonely for me since my mom died, and I thought it might be downright sad this year with the store closing in a few days, but it doesn't feel that way now."

"I'm glad." Jane drew her closer. "I can imagine holidays are hard without her."

Rosie nodded with glossy eyes. "I wish you could have known her."

"Me too." Jane slid a hand down Rosie's back, toying with the hem of her T-shirt.

They moved together under the covers, legs entwined and hands roaming, and Jane couldn't possibly think of a better way to start Christmas than with leisurely morning sex. Rosie rolled on top of her, and Jane gripped her waist, holding on as Rosie's fingers swirled and plunged while she rocked her hips against Jane's thigh.

Jane came first, and Rosie followed soon after, both of them gasping their release into the otherwise quiet room, and then they lay together, sweaty and satisfied. Eventually, they got up and went into the living room for coffee and gifts. Rosie buttoned her coat over her pajamas and took Brinkley outside for a quick walk while Jane got the coffeepot going.

They'd picked up a tube of cinnamon rolls yesterday, something Rosie told her was a Christmas tradition from her childhood, and Jane popped it now. She placed the rolls on a pan and put them in the oven to bake. Usually, she spent Christmas morning alone, reading quietly by the tree until it was time to go to her parents' for dinner. This was all new, and she was loving every moment.

Rosie came back in, and they ate cinnamon rolls and drank coffee as Jane's tabletop tree sparkled from the corner. Rosie's phone dinged almost constantly with messages from her friends, all wishing her a Merry Christmas, while Jane's was notably silent. She didn't mind, not today, because she was with the only person she needed, but next year, she vowed to put herself out there and bring more people into her life.

"This feels like a scene from a movie," Rosie said with a soft smile as they sat on the couch to open presents.

"It does." Jane toyed with the bow on the red-wrapped package Rosie had given her. "Although I'm curious how a woman raised by a single mom became such a hopeless romantic."

"Books, maybe?" Rosie said. "Romance novels showed me what I wanted in a partner, but my mom taught me that it wasn't the worst thing to be single either. She showed me that it was okay to wait for the right person. I guess that's part of the reason I've been so picky about who I date."

"Well, I'm awfully glad you took a chance on me," Jane said as she carefully unwrapped her gift.

Rosie leaned in for a kiss. "Me too."

Jane opened the box to reveal a photo ornament with the cover of her first book on it and a framed print of Between the Pages' window display featuring *On the Flip Side*. "To help you embrace your life as an author next year," Rosie said with a smile.

"I love it," Jane said, feeling warm and fuzzy inside. "Thank you."

She had gotten Rosie a set of wooden bookends that said "Between the Pages" and a scarf covered in quotes from famous books. After they'd opened gifts, they snuggled up to watch Christmas movies together, and all too soon, it was time for Rosie to leave.

She was headed to Paige's parents' house, and Jane had to get ready to go to her own parents'. They'd mutually agreed not to change their usual Christmas dinner plans. It hadn't felt like the right time to play "meet the family," and Rosie would be meeting Jane's family next week at the New Year's Eve party.

So, Jane headed uptown on her own, where she spent a somewhat uncomfortable dinner listening to her father talk endlessly about how Jane needed to push herself next year so she could take on more responsibility at BPD to advance her career. He didn't make a single mention of her books or the fact that maybe she didn't *want* a career at BPD.

Thank goodness for Alyssa interjecting with commentary about her favorite gifts. After dinner, Jane's mother took her aside to quietly tell her how much she'd enjoyed *On the Flip Side*, and while Jane appreciated the sentiment, she disliked the delivery, huddled in the kitchen like it was some kind of dirty secret, one they couldn't let her father overhear.

"I have some news," he said once they'd finished opening gifts. "As you know, I'm not getting any younger, and your mother and I would like a chance to do some traveling before we're too old to enjoy it, so I've decided that this coming year will be my last at BPD."

"You're retiring?" Jane blurted.

"In a year," he said. "You've both known this was coming, and it's why I've worked so hard to prepare you. As we've discussed, I'd like Amy to take the reins after I'm gone."

Amy nodded. "I'm ready."

"And Jane, I know you don't have your sister's drive, but that's why I've been pushing you so hard, so that you can take on a more significant role within the company. I've always envisioned you two running BPD together."

"As much as I love working with Jane, I'm not sure that's what *she* wants," Amy said. Her gaze held Jane's.

Jane straightened in her seat, because no matter how badly she wanted to focus on her author career, she couldn't let her sister down during this transition, and she wouldn't disappoint her father on the day he announced his retirement either. "It is, at least for now."

Rosie locked the door and leaned against it as tears slid silently over her cheeks. Her fingers shook as she took the YES, WE'RE OPEN sign out of the window and replaced it with one that said PERMANENTLY CLOSED. It was two days after Christmas, and Between the Pages had just closed for the last time here on Lexington Avenue.

"Aw, come here," Lia said from behind her, and a moment later, she pulled Rosie into a tight hug. "It's all right. I think we both need a good cry tonight."

Rosie nodded against her sweater. "God, this is so hard."

"I know." Lia's hand rubbed up and down her back. "Quite frankly, I would have been concerned if you *didn't* cry. This is a big deal. It's the end of an era. Yes, we have good things on the horizon, but you still have to acknowledge this ending."

"I can still picture her here, you know?" Rosie said as she pulled back, wiping her eyes. "We made so many memories in this room. I feel close to her here, and I'm so scared to lose that."

"She'll always be in your memories, whether you inhabit this space or not."

"I hope so." Rosie held on to her friend as she looked around the store, wanting to memorize everything, but at the same time, she knew she didn't need to. This space was already etched into her brain in high definition. She'd never forget it, not a single detail.

Her gaze settled on the red chair in the corner, the one where she'd spent so many hours as a child sitting on her mom's lap while she read Rosie all her favorite children's books. Hopefully, familiar things like that chair would help the new space feel like home.

"Come on. Let's go home," Lia said. "We'll start packing tomorrow."

Rosie nodded. They'd given themselves four days to move out, but they'd been packing what they could all week. Rosie's office was already boxed up, and so was the storage room. There wasn't much left except the bookshelves here in the store, and even those were seriously depleted, since they'd quit restocking earlier in the month to cut down on inventory that would need to be moved into storage.

She and Lia went home and shared a somewhat somber meal with Nikki and Paige, where Rosie tried not to cry and failed. After dinner, she closed herself in her room and spent the evening poring over photo albums of herself and her mom, lost in her memories and the almost desperate sadness that sometimes overtook her when she realized how much she still missed her, how much she wished she were here with Rosie for this transition.

Jane called a little past eight. "I just wanted to see how you were doing."

"I'm okay," Rosie told her, eyes growing wet again at the sound of Jane's voice. "I'd be lying if I said I didn't cry buckets when I locked up for the last time, but I'll be okay."

"I'm sorry I couldn't be there with you," Jane said.

"It's fine, really. All I did was lock the door and take the open sign down."

They talked for a few more minutes, rehashing their days the way they often did when they didn't get a chance to see each other in person. Jane's dad was preparing to retire and putting more pressure on her at work as a result.

"I may stay longer than I'd thought," Jane said quietly. "Amy's going to need me, you know?"

"Stay at BPD?" Rosie asked, sitting up in surprise.

"Yeah. It might not be so bad without my dad breathing down my neck, but mostly I don't want to leave Amy in the lurch."

Rosie blinked. "What about your books? I thought you were hoping this next contract might be enough for you to quit."

"Well, I can hope," Jane said. "But I need to be here for Amy too. We'll see what happens."

Over the next three days, Rosie and Lia packed up the store and drove their rented truck back and forth to the Bronx to get moved into their new storage unit. It was going to be an uncomfortable couple of months, but hopefully they'd come out stronger on the other side. She spent the morning of New Year's Eve giving the space a final cleaning. Jane met her there midafternoon to help her finish before they headed to the hotel to get ready for the party that night.

"Okay, here's a weird thing," Rosie said as they stood in the empty room. "I guess I'll just give my keys to you when we leave."

Jane winced. "Yeah, that's weird. I'm sorry."

"It's fine." But it *did* feel weird, now that she'd realized it. It was a tangible reminder of Jane's role in all of this. And now that she was considering staying at BPD to help her sister, Rosie wasn't sure what to think. Deep down, she'd hoped Jane would quit sooner rather than later so that Rosie wouldn't have to think about it anymore, although that was a totally selfish thing for her to wish for.

"This is harder than I thought it was going to be," she said as she handed the keys to Jane.

"Of course it's hard," Jane said.

"Let's just get it over with, okay?" Rosie led the way toward the back door, grabbing her bag on the way.

"Hey." Jane took her hand, slowing her down. "Don't rush out of here. You'll regret it later if you do. Take a minute and say goodbye to the building, whatever you need to do."

"I think I've already done that." Rosie's eyes burned with unshed tears. "I just need to go."

"Are you sure?"

She nodded, averting her eyes from the empty space. "I don't want to remember it this way."

"Okay."

Rosie led the way out the back door. Her chest felt like a kettle ready to boil, hot and tight, and she feared she would scream if she dared to open her mouth. Jane locked the door behind them and put the keys in her purse. Rosie should have insisted on mailing her keys to BPD's office, because this felt wrong. She felt like she'd just given Jane her beloved store. Jane owned it now, and in a few weeks, she was going to tear it down.

Rosie stomped down the street without looking back, not even when she heard Jane calling for her. She made it all the way to the corner before she broke down in big, racking sobs.

Jane's arms wrapped around her. "I'm sorry," she murmured, and it only made Rosie cry harder. "Are you sure you don't want to go back in and try to leave on a happier note?"

"I'm sure," Rosie gasped through her tears. "I just want to put it behind me."

Jane sighed, sounding almost as sad as Rosie felt. This sucked. Rosie hated everything about it, and the last thing she wanted to do right now was go to a fancy party, let alone a party full of the very people who'd ripped this building out from under her. She just wanted to go home and cry.

They stood there until Rosie's tears dried and she started to shiver. She buried her face against Jane's coat as she pulled herself together. It was time to suck it up and go to the party. This wasn't about Between the Pages anymore. It was about meeting Jane's family for the first time and ringing in the new year, a year that was going to contain a lot of good things. She lifted her head, staring at the building that had been hers.

"Okay, you're right," she said, stepping out of Jane's embrace. "I should go back in and try to leave with a smile. And let me lock the door this time?"

Wordlessly, Jane handed her the keys before shoving her hands into her pockets. Rosie set off down the alley toward the back door of the building. She let them inside, greeted by the echoing sense of emptiness that had made her twitchy and uncomfortable ever since they'd moved the furniture out the day before yesterday.

"Okay." She blew out a breath and twirled in the middle of what used to be the romance section. To her surprise, there was a smile on her face when she came to a stop, slightly dizzy from her spin.

Jane watched with a hesitant smile. "That's more like it."

"It is," Rosie agreed. She walked to the front window, peering out at Lexington Avenue for the last time from this vantage point. "Let's take a selfie to remember the place where we met."

"Sure." Jane stepped in and wrapped an arm around Rosie.

They posed for a couple of silly selfies, and Rosie didn't even care that her eyes were red and puffy from her recent sobfest. It captured the emotion of the day, and someday she would want to remember this. She would want to remember all of it.

"Goodbye," she said to the empty room. This time, she went out the front door with Jane at her side. She locked it herself before handing Jane the keys. "All right, let's go get ready to party."

"Are you sure you're up for it?" Jane asked.

"Honestly? Right now, I just want to go home and cry, but I'll enjoy the party once I get there, and I'll be so glad I rang in the new year with you instead of moping around at home."

Jane nodded. "I think you're right, but if you want to leave at any point, just let me know. No hard feelings."

"Are you sure you aren't making an excuse for yourself?" Rosie teased. "Because you're the homebody here. I'll have fun once I get there. I promise."

Jane nudged her shoulder against Rosie's. "Thank goodness at least one of us is social. Come on, then. Let's go."

They walked to the subway station, each of them carrying an overnight bag since they'd be spending the night at the Belvedere Hotel. Rosie could count on one hand the number of times she'd stayed at a fancy hotel here in her own city, let alone on New Year's Eve.

"We're going to have fun tonight," she pronounced as they stepped onto the train.

"Glad that's settled," Jane said lightly.

"Come on. I had you worried for a minute there."

Jane sobered, shaking her head. "I wasn't worried for me. I was worried for *you*."

"I know, and that's why I—" Rosie cut herself off before she said *love you*, because this wasn't how she wanted to say those words for the first time, not under the shadow of leaving the building that had been her second home or with the keys to her business in Jane's purse. "It's why you're the sweetest," she finished somewhat lamely.

Jane leaned in to give her a quick kiss. They chatted about mundane things on the way to the hotel, both of them obviously trying to keep the mood light. Rosie was still somewhat heartbroken. Every time she closed her eyes, she saw the empty store, but she was determined to power through the night. She was looking forward to meeting Jane's family, Amy in particular.

The hotel was glossy and modern, just as Rosie had expected. That seemed to be BPD's style, after all, and for tonight, shiny and new felt like a good way to celebrate the year to come. They checked into their room, which had a king-size bed and a nice view of the city.

"Fancy," Rosie whispered as she stood at the window, looking out.

"And it's almost time to *get* fancy," Jane said behind her.

But first, they stood in front of the window, kissing, while Rosie's sadness and frustration melted into heat and longing for the woman in her arms. She almost pushed Jane onto the bed to have her way with her right now, but it really was time for them to get ready for the party. They'd have all the time in the world to enjoy that bed when they got back up here at the end of the night.

Neither of them had anywhere to be tomorrow, and Rosie intended to stay in bed with Jane until it was time to check out. Since she'd spent most of the day cleaning, though, her first stop was the shower. Jane joined her, and they rinsed off while fooling around under its hot spray. An hour later, she was putting the final touches on her makeup in front of the mirror in the bathroom.

Her dress was shimmery and red, and she'd added a dusting of gold glitter to her hair for a festive effect. She was going to have fun tonight, dammit. Jane wore a demure black dress, her hair pulled back in a twist, classic and glamorous and sexy as hell.

She came up behind Rosie, running her hands over Rosie's hips. "You look amazing."

"And festive?" Rosie asked.

"Definitely festive," Jane confirmed. "I can't wait to introduce you to everyone."

"Me either," Rosie said. "I feel like we've been mostly in my orbit so far, hanging out at my store and with my friends. I'm excited to meet yours."

Jane nodded. "Ready?"

But as they stepped into the hallway, Rosie realized suddenly that she wasn't. Despite what she'd told Jane earlier, her heart was heavy, and she wasn't entirely sure she could fake her way through an evening with the various faces behind Breslin Property Development. It was too much, too soon. For Jane's sake, though, she was going to try her very best.

CHAPTER TWENTY-FOUR

Rosie followed Jane down the hall from their hotel room toward the bank of elevators, determined to pull out of her emotional funk and enjoy this party.

"Jane!" someone called behind them, and Rosie turned to see a couple walking toward them. The woman was about forty, with dark hair and eyes like Jane's.

"Amy," Jane said with a warm smile.

"And you must be the infamous Rosie," Amy said, extending a hand. "I'm Jane's overbearing big sister."

"That's not quite the way she describes you," Rosie said as she shook Amy's hand. "But I'm glad to be infamous."

"I like you already," Amy said. "And this is my husband, Garrett."

As Rosie greeted Amy and her husband, she decided the feeling was mutual. Amy had an infectious energy about her. She was bolder than her sister, easily taking charge of the conversation as they waited for the elevator, but not in an obnoxious way.

"Will you have a grand opening at the new location?" she asked Rosie. "Because I'd love to come. You know, Alyssa still talks about you and the books you helped her pick out. She loved the one you sent with Jane at Thanksgiving too."

Rosie smiled. "Yes, probably somewhere around the end of March, and I'll be scheduling book signings too."

"I bet I know which author you're hoping to land first," Amy said with a sly wink, prompting Jane to roll her eyes.

"She's been my first choice for years now, but she did agree that I would be her first, whenever she decides to have an in-person signing," Rosie said.

"Oh, did she?" Amy asked, giving her sister a look. "Well, that's something."

The four of them entered the party together, and Rosie gripped Jane's hand as she looked around the ballroom. It was large and elegant, with black marble floors and lots of gold and silver party decorations. Already, it was filled with people in fancy clothes, black dresses and tuxedos everywhere. Jane fit right in, while Rosie was a bit of an outlier in red.

They made their way to the bar for drinks. Amy, Jane, and Rosie started the night with champagne, while Garrett got seltzer, explaining that he didn't drink. He was a quiet man, but Rosie got a good vibe from him. He seemed at ease as the only man in their group, joining in as they got to know each other. Jane and Amy pointed out various party guests to Rosie, including George Cass, who apparently owned the building she'd be moving into in March.

"Oh, here we go," Jane muttered as a well-dressed older couple approached them. She stood a little taller as she wrapped an arm around Rosie's waist. "Mom, Dad, I'd like to introduce you to my girlfriend, Rosie Taft."

Jane's mother smiled, extending a hand to Rosie. "It's such a pleasure to meet you."

"You too, Mrs. Breslin," Rosie said.

"Oh, please, call me Carol."

"David Breslin," Jane's dad said briskly, sticking out his hand. His handshake was quick and firm.

"Nice to meet you," she said politely, determined not to let his profession affect her first impression of him. He was her girlfriend's father, and that was the only thing that mattered tonight.

"I hear you're moving into the café space in George's building on 104th?" he said, immediately jumping into the one topic Rosie would rather not discuss.

She nodded. "I am."

"That's a nice spot," he said with a nod of approval. "I oversaw the renovation of that building myself. Definitely an improvement from the space you're moving out of."

She held her smile in place despite the way her stomach swooped. Had she somehow moved into another building owned by BPD and not realized it? Their name hadn't been anywhere on the lease, and Jane hadn't mentioned anything. "I was pretty fond of my old space, actually, but I'm glad to have found someplace new."

He proceeded to spend the next ten minutes telling her every detail that had gone into the renovation, down to the reflective properties of the glass, designed to keep cooling costs down in the summer, while Rosie's emotions boiled dangerously close to the surface, because how had this happened? "It's a magnificent building. You'll be very happy there," he finished before excusing himself to greet another guest, Carol trailing quietly in his wake.

"Jane, can I speak to you for a minute?" Rosie asked, not waiting for her response before she set off toward the nearest exit, leading the way into a hallway behind the ballroom. "What the hell was that about?"

Jane's lips twisted to one side. "I know my dad is a lot to take in, but—"

"You didn't tell me that my new building had ties to your company," Rosie said.

"Oh," Jane said. "Well, BPD did renovate it, but that was over ten years ago, and we don't own the building anymore. I didn't have anything to do with your lease, Rosie, other than scouting the location for you." She twirled the champagne glass in her fingers, a nervous habit Rosie had noticed.

"But why didn't you tell me?" Rosie was dangerously close to crying again.

Jane flinched. "I didn't keep it from you on purpose. I just . . . my industry contacts are all connected to projects and people we've worked with in the past. I figured you knew that, but I should have spelled it out. I'm sorry."

Rosie pressed her lips together, trying not to get irrationally upset. Jane's explanation made sense. She'd known about this space because she knew the owner of the building, and she knew him because her company had sold it to him. BPD wasn't directly involved with her new lease, but somehow the past connection still put a bad taste in her mouth.

"It's fine," she said, because this wasn't the time for her to get upset. She'd process it tomorrow, when the memory of walking out of her old shop wasn't so fresh and she wasn't at a party full of people who seemed to have a hand in every aspect of her business.

"It's obviously not," Jane said, taking a hesitant step closer. "I truly didn't mean to keep anything from you. We haven't owned that building in over a decade. It's no more connected to me than any other building in the city, except that my dad knows the man who currently owns it, which is how I found it for you."

"Okay," Rosie said, blowing out a breath. "I just need to decompress. Today's been a lot, and I'm emotional. We'll talk about it tomorrow, okay?"

Jane nodded, pulling Rosie against her for a kiss. "I'm sorry."

"I know, but you don't need to be. It's just awkward, that's all."

"Seems to be the theme of our relationship," Jane said with a pained look.

"Not anymore," Rosie insisted. "All of this lease stuff is almost behind us."

They made their way back to the party, but Amy and Garrett had disappeared into the crowd. Jane led Rosie through the room, introducing her to various coworkers and colleagues, and Rosie's cheeks hurt from smiling. Was it almost midnight yet? She loved a good party, but apparently not tonight.

"Let's leave," Jane said, obviously having read her mood. "We can go back to your place and watch the ball drop with your roommates. You know that's more my style than this party anyway."

"No," Rosie said. "We're here, and we're going to have a good time, and besides, we've got that hotel room waiting for us upstairs."

Jane stepped closer, kissing her cheek. "We could always watch the ball drop from the comfort of our hotel room. In fact, that sounds pretty amazing right now."

"Okay, it actually does," Rosie admitted with a grin. She and Jane could ring in the new year naked together in a fancy hotel room. Really, what could be better? "Would your parents mind if we disappeared?"

"Honestly, I doubt they'd even notice," Jane said. "They've said hello. We probably won't see them again even if we stay. Amy, on the other hand, will definitely notice, but she'll approve, so . . ."

"Let's do it," Rosie said, her mood immediately rebounding. "How do you feel about overpriced room service?"

"I love it," Jane said, hooking an arm through Rosie's as they made their way toward the exit.

A tall man with gray hair and a mustache stepped in front of them. "Jane," he said enthusiastically. "Great party, as always."

Jane gave him a polite smile. "George, glad you could make it. And this is Rosie Taft. She just rented the café space on 104th Street. Rosie, this is George Cass."

Rosie froze as she realized she was meeting her new landlord. This was something she hadn't planned on tonight and definitely wasn't in the mood for. There was something arrogant in his demeanor that immediately put her off. She forced a smile. "Nice to meet you."

"Likewise," he said. "My God, I'm just so glad to have someone new in that space. The Vitalis were nothing but trouble. I'd been trying to get rid of that café for years."

"Oh." Rosie swallowed hard. This man sounded like an asshole, and she would have probably been better off not putting a face to a name.

"Mr. Vitali died a few years ago," he continued, "and everything went downhill after his wife took over the business. It's why I generally prefer not to rent to women . . . too unreliable. Jane assures me you'll be a dependable tenant, though, Rosie. I'm going to hold you to that." He pointed a finger at her as if they were in this together.

She just blinked at him, too stunned to speak. Beside her, Jane had gone similarly silent, and when Rosie darted a glance in her direction, Jane looked as horrified as Rosie felt.

"Happy New Year," he said amiably before strolling away.

"Oh my God," Rosie muttered as she strode toward the exit. Her vision had taken on a rosy tint, which might've been caused by the tears in her eyes reflecting off her dress, or she might've literally been seeing red, because she was furious. And hurt. And questioning every life decision that had led her to this moment.

"I don't know what to say," Jane said as she followed Rosie into the hall.

"That's a common theme with you, isn't it?" Rosie snapped.

Jane's lips parted slightly, and she blinked.

"I can't rent from that man, Jane. I can't believe you thought I would. You know what he's like, and you still sent me to his building? What the fuck?"

"He's an asshole," Jane said, cheeks flushed and hands planted on her hips. "A lot of powerful men are, and I . . . tolerate it where I have to. But I've never heard him say anything as misogynistic as that before, Rosie, I swear."

"Well, this is a shitty time to find out." Rosie paced toward the end of the hall away from the other party guests.

"I'll call him on Monday," Jane said from behind her. "He probably thought he was being funny, but it's not, and we don't condone that kind of talk at BPD. We're about to be a female-owned business, for crying out loud."

"You know, there was a time after my mom died when I was late on our rent." Rosie's voice shook. "Luckily, my landlord at the time was understanding. He gave me a chance to get back on my feet instead of throwing me out the way George Cass did to Francesca and Nicole Vitali."

"It's . . ." Jane closed her mouth, looking at her feet.

"Don't you dare tell me it's just business," Rosie said as her tears broke free, searing her cheeks. "It was personal for me, and it's personal for the Vitalis. Would you have cut me a break on my rent when I needed it, Jane? Would your father?"

Jane wrapped her arms around herself. "I . . ."

"Yeah, that's what I thought," Rosie said bitterly. The café space she'd been so excited about was tainted now. All she wanted was to go back to her old building, but it wasn't hers anymore. The keys were in Jane's purse, and that felt so fucking symbolic right now that her heart hurt. She pressed a hand against it.

"Rosie, don't let him ruin this for you."

"Oh, it's ruined, all right," Rosie said. Her throat burned, and she couldn't hold back the tears still streaming over her cheeks. "I think . . . I think it's all ruined."

"What? No." Jane's voice sounded rough, like she was holding back tears of her own. "I'm so sorry. Just let me fix this."

"No," she said quietly. "I'm so tired of your apologies, Jane, and not because I think you don't mean them, but you can't just fix this like it's a plot twist in one of your books. This is my life we're talking about." She swiped at her cheeks, breathing hard. "We just seem to go around in circles, and every time I think the worst is behind us . . . it's not."

Jane's chin trembled, and when she blinked, tears spilled over her eyelids.

It was all more than Rosie could take. "I can't do this with you. I thought I could, but I can't be part of this world that flattens beautiful old buildings to put up shiny skyscrapers in their place, that turns people out of their homes for the sake of profit. And I can't rent from a man like George Cass. I'll call Marcia tomorrow and ask her to get me out of that lease."

"What are you saying?" Jane's voice was a broken whisper, mascara pooling beneath her eyes.

And God dammit, Rosie loved her so much, even though this just couldn't work. Hysteria rose in her chest, constricting her lungs. "I have to get out of here, and I think . . . I think this is goodbye."

She turned and ran for the front door, her vision blurred by her tears, but Jane didn't try to stop her. She didn't say anything at all, at least not that Rosie heard. Her coat and her overnight bag were upstairs in their room, but if she went there now, Jane might follow, and Rosie couldn't handle seeing her again tonight.

Instead, she stormed through the revolving door of this stupid shiny hotel and into the frigid night. She walked blindly down the block, powered by hurt and anger. Every step seemed to further fracture her heart, until the ache in her chest made it hard to breathe. After a while, she realized she had no idea where she was. She was shivering uncontrollably, and her lungs ached from sucking in too much cold air. She pulled up a map on her phone to find the nearest subway station, and then she headed home.

CHAPTER
TWENTY-FIVE

Jane lay on the bed in their hotel room, staring at the ceiling. The room was spinning, and she wasn't even drunk. She'd had one flute of champagne before Rosie walked out the door, causing the world to shift beneath her feet, and now she couldn't seem to find her balance. She'd come upstairs, hoping to find Rosie in their room, hoping . . .

But Rosie had run into the night without even stopping for her coat, and she hadn't come back. Jane's phone started to ring, and she lurched upright so quickly she almost rolled right off the bed, but it wasn't Rosie's name on her screen. Amy was calling, but Jane wasn't in any shape for conversation. She sent Amy to voice mail, noticing that it was 12:05 a.m.

Happy fucking New Year.

Tears rose in her eyes, and she blinked them back. She couldn't stay in this hotel room another minute, but going out in the city just after midnight was an impossibility. She'd never get a cab or a Lyft, and the subway would be a nightmare. All she wanted was the comfort of her apartment, her coziest pajamas, and her bed.

Since she couldn't have them, she got up and changed into the only comfortable thing she'd packed, a T-shirt she'd brought to wear under her sweater tomorrow. She went into the bathroom to scrub off her makeup and fell into bed, bone tired but too distraught to sleep. She lay there, dozing fitfully, until dawn began to brighten the sky outside. Then she packed up her things—and Rosie's, since she obviously wasn't coming back—and went home.

Jane stepped into her apartment, feeling hollow inside. Were she and Rosie over? Could they possibly recover from the things that had happened last night? Would Rosie always resent her for losing her store if they tried? Did Jane even deserve a second chance?

That last question was the one that stuck with her. It lingered in the pit of her stomach as she burned off restless energy on her stationary bike and even when she finally collapsed into bed and managed a few hours of sleep. She hadn't heard from Rosie since she stormed out of the party, which wasn't good, but maybe Jane was the one who needed to make the first move here. She picked up her phone, swiping away three missed calls and a voice mail from Amy.

Jane Breslin:

I'm so sorry about last night.

Can we talk?

I have your bag from the hotel.

I know you're tired of hearing me say it, but I'm truly sorry.
Please call?

She sent the texts over the course of a half hour, giving Rosie a chance to reply to each one, but none came. Jane had half a mind to go over to her apartment and apologize in person, but maybe Rosie needed a day or two to cool off. And maybe Jane needed to do a little soul-searching before she groveled.

She needed to quit her job. That knowledge had been rising to the surface of her thoughts ever since Rosie had placed the keys to her shop in Jane's hand yesterday. It hadn't felt right, not to either of them, and deep down, she knew it would *never* be right until BPD was in her past.

Her gaze fell to the strip of photos on her nightstand, the photos she and Rosie had taken on her birthday. God, they looked so happy. So silly. So carefree. Jane didn't have a lot of experience with silly and carefree, things Rosie seemed to bring out in her so easily. And now, she might have ruined everything.

Would quitting her job make this right, or were they doomed to go around in circles, like Rosie said? Unlike in her books, she couldn't just write a way through the obstacles that stood between herself and Rosie. Short of going back in time and choosing a different location for the new high-rise, Jane didn't see a way to fix this.

The buzzer rang, and her heart lurched into her throat as she dashed to the door. "Hello?" she said, breathless.

"Hey, it's me. Sorry to drop by unannounced, but I was worried." Amy's voice came through the speaker.

Jane slumped, because of course Rosie hadn't come. "It's fine. Come on in." She buzzed her in and opened the door as Amy's footsteps echoed down the hall.

"You look like shit," Amy said, giving her a critical look. "Garrett said he saw you and Rosie fighting in the hall last night. When you both disappeared, I hoped you were patching things up in your room, but from the looks of it, that didn't happen, did it?"

Jane shook her head, leading the way to the couch. "I think she dumped me last night."

"You *think*?" Amy asked, eyebrows raised.

"We were both pretty upset, and I don't even remember everything we said, but 'I can't do this with you' was definitely in there, and then she ran out the door, and now she's not answering my texts."

"Okay, you'd better start at the beginning," Amy said.

"I think it started before we even met." Jane scrubbed her hands over her face. "When I sent her that lease-termination letter. It just keeps coming back to haunt us, like when she had to give me the keys to her store yesterday, and then Dad talked her ear off about how modern and fancy her new building is, like he'd done her a favor by kicking her out of her old building, and *then* . . ." She sucked in a breath. "George Cass was an absolute asshole to both of us. He told us he'd basically kicked the current occupants of her new space out because they couldn't pay their rent when the owner's husband died. Amy, he said something like, 'That's why I don't rent to women, because they're unreliable tenants,' and . . . well, that was the last straw. Rosie said she was going to back out of her lease and she was done with me, and she left."

"Well, holy shit," Amy said. "That's a lot."

"Yep." Jane rubbed her eyes. There was a buzzing in her head that had been building all morning, and she still felt slightly off balance.

"And you haven't talked to her this morning?"

Jane shook her head. "I texted her. Should I call?"

"Maybe not yet. Have you eaten?" Amy asked.

"Hmm? No."

"Yeah, you look like you're about to keel over. What do you have here?"

"I don't know." Jane rubbed her eyes again, wishing she could rewind the last twenty-four hours and do everything differently. She wished Rosie's keys weren't in her purse and that they'd never gone to that party.

"You stay there, and I'll find some food," Amy said. "And coffee. You definitely look like you need coffee."

"Coffee," Jane repeated. How had she forgotten about coffee? "Please."

A few minutes later, Amy was back with a steaming cup of coffee and a bowl of oatmeal. "About the only thing I could find in your pantry," she said.

"Thank you." Jane took a grateful sip before she set down the cup and took a bite of oatmeal. She hadn't had anything but a glass of champagne last night, and no wonder she felt like shit this morning. Well, that and a broken heart. Methodically, she finished her breakfast, and then, feeling much more clearheaded, she looked at her sister. "Would you be upset if I quit?"

Amy's lips curved. "Are you actually asking me that question? How many times have I tried to get you to quit so you can focus on writing?"

"But Dad's retiring," Jane said. "I don't want to leave you in the lurch. It would be fun to run the company together the way he wanted, wouldn't it?"

"In another universe, yeah, that would have been fun," Amy said. "And don't take this the wrong way, Jane, but you are replaceable at BPD. Your head hasn't been in the game for years. In fact, I can probably hire someone better qualified for the job—again, no offense—who'll truly help me run the company."

"Ouch," Jane said.

"I want you to be happy. I don't care if we work together or not."

"Okay," she said, giving Amy a shaky smile.

"But I also think you need to make sure you're doing this for the right reason, because you've had a specific plan in place for years, where you stay at BPD until you're able to support yourself as an author, and unless I'm mistaken, you aren't there yet."

"I'm not," Jane admitted.

"Then take your time before you do anything rash, and if you quit, make sure you're quitting for *you* and not for Rosie. If she truly loves you, your day job shouldn't matter."

"I never said—"

Amy waved her hand. "Yeah, but obviously you love each other. So you have to be willing to fight for it, because Jesus Christ, it's not like you defend rapists or something. We renovate buildings. If Rosie can't be okay with that, then I might actually be offended, considering it's about to be my company."

"It's more complicated than that," Jane said.

"I know it is, and George Cass is a misogynistic asshole who's going to get an earful from me on Monday," Amy said. "Dad's on vacation for the next week, so take that time to cool off and think things through before you quit."

"Okay," Jane said, nodding.

"But, Jane, quitting your job isn't going to magically solve all your problems. You're going to have to look deeper than that if you want to win Rosie back."

"If you don't open the door in the next five minutes, I'm coming in," Lia called.

Rosie pulled the covers over her head, sniffling. Brinkley's warm weight rested over her ankles, where he'd been all morning. "Can't you be a good roommate and let me pout in peace?"

"Nope, sorry," Lia said from the other side of the door. "You've pouted long enough. It's time to get up and figure out what to do now that you've backed out of our lease. Plus, Paige made pancakes."

"They're really good ones," Paige said, and *Jesus*, were all her room-mates standing outside her door? "Buttermilk with chocolate chips. Your favorite."

"And I made tea," Lia added.

"Fine," Rosie grumbled. She pulled the blankets down, blinking against the light in her bedroom. Brinkley promptly launched himself at her face, kissing away her tears. "You're the best boy in the world, you know that?"

He wagged his tail, gazing at her adoringly.

She picked him up, cradling him like a baby as she opened her bedroom door and stepped out to find Lia and Paige standing there with matching worried looks on their faces.

"I'm sorry," Rosie said, looking down at her dog. "I should have talked to you before I backed out of our lease."

"It's your store," Lia said, "although it would have been nice to talk things through together instead of you making an impulsive, middle-of-the-night decision by yourself. But for the record, I'm with you. We wouldn't want that man as our landlord. You made the right call."

"Come eat pancakes," Paige said, wrapping an arm around Rosie's shoulders. "They'll make you feel better, I promise."

"I don't deserve you ladies," Rosie said, fresh tears welling in her eyes just when she hoped she'd cried herself out.

"Of course you do," Paige said, giving her a squeeze. "You're heartbroken, and your store is homeless, and it's perfectly okay for you to feel whatever you're feeling right now. Lia and I are just going to make sure you eat and take care of yourself in the meantime."

"And remember what I showed you on the spreadsheet," Lia said. "We can run our online store out of the warehouse for six months. We're going to find a new home for Between the Pages before then. I'm sure of it."

"I wish I was," Rosie said, burying her face in Brinkley's fur to hide her tears. "It feels like things just aren't meant to work out for the store, and I'm so jaded toward all those corporate assholes. I just . . . if you could have seen that man last night . . ."

"I know." Lia guided Rosie into a chair and took Brinkley from her, while Paige went into the kitchen, returning with a plate of pancakes and a mug of tea, which she set in front of Rosie. "We dodged a bullet with him."

Rosie began to eat, surprised to realize how hungry she was. What was Jane doing this morning? Was she anywhere near as heartbroken as Rosie right now? The truly sad thing was that Rosie knew the answer was yes. None of this was Jane's fault, and yet, Rosie just didn't know how to move past it. She didn't know how to move forward with a relationship that was rooted in one of the darkest moments of her life.

She didn't regret the time they'd spent together. They'd had the kind of romance Rosie had always dreamed about, but her mom had picked herself up after heartbreak and had gone on to live a happy and fulfilling life. So could Rosie, if that's what it came to, even though the thought of never seeing Jane again made her want to pull the covers back over her head and sob.

"I'm mad at the universe this morning," she announced dramatically as she finished her breakfast. "It really fucked me over this past year."

"It did, and you have every right to be pissed," Paige agreed, coming to sit beside her with her own plate of pancakes.

"But there are lessons to be learned from what you've been through," Lia said. "I have thoughts, when you're ready to hear them."

"Just tell me," Rosie said, knowing her friend wouldn't let it drop. "Although I really would have appreciated it if you'd let me mope for a full day before you started being all logical."

"There's no time to mope, my dear," Lia said, giving her a stern look. "We've got a store to save . . . as well as a relationship."

"Okay, I'm listening," Rosie said, swiping at her cheeks.

"Well, first of all, Jane's idea about the book café was a stroke of genius, and I think we should run with it, but we need to do it on our own terms this time," Lia said. "We have to find a space by ourselves, with no connection to Jane or BPD. It has to be that way for any of this to work."

"Any of what?" Rosie asked.

"To find a space that suits us, and to save your relationship. The café she found was perfect in theory, but the building was glossy and modern and owned by a corporate asshole."

"I hate to break it to you, but most buildings in this city are probably owned by corporate assholes," Rosie said glumly.

"Well, at least we can find a corporate asshole who doesn't know your girlfriend, and *maybe* we can find a building that's not owned by an asshole. Jane did another smart thing that you and I didn't think of."

"What's that?" Rosie asked.

"She used her connections," Lia told her. "She called everyone she knew and asked them if they'd heard about a space coming available. We can do that, too, Rosie. We know so many people, and your mom knew even more. She knew every small business owner within a ten-block radius. Not all of them are still here, but some are. We can visit them, and if they don't have a lead for us, we'll ask them to ask the people *they* know. Jane put feelers through corporate networks, and we'll put feelers through locally owned small businesses and see what we turn up."

"Shit," Rosie whispered, staring at her friend. "Now you're the genius, Lia. I mean it. This is brilliant."

Lia beamed at her. "I'll take that compliment. Thank you."

"But how does it save my relationship?"

"Because you're going to find a new space that you love and that has nothing to do with Jane. Then you two can figure things out without the fate of the store hanging over your heads."

"It's a tall order." Deep down, Rosie feared the space Lia had described didn't exist, and Jane . . . well, Rosie didn't know how to fix that either.

"I'm up to the challenge," Lia said. "Ready to get to work?"

Rosie forced a smile, because she was an optimist, after all, even if she didn't feel like one at the moment. "I'm ready."

As it turned out, though, she wasn't ready. Rosie spent the weekend in a funk, rarely leaving her bedroom. Unable to bear Jane's apologetic texts, Rosie finally replied to tell her that she needed to take some time to sort herself out and find a new home for the store. They needed a clean slate on that front if they were ever going to make things work.

And Rosie still wasn't sure that they could. She'd tried so hard to get past her hurt feelings about her lease, and it had blown up in her face. Maybe she would always resent Jane for what had happened, even though she knew in her heart that it wasn't Jane's fault. This was Rosie's problem, and she had to be the one to fix it. And that meant focusing on the store for now.

On Monday, Lia forced her to leave the apartment. They rode the train to the Bronx to get set up in their warehouse space and then spent the afternoon processing the orders that had come in over the weekend.

"There are more orders than I'd budgeted for," Lia said as she sealed a box. "That's a good thing."

Rosie nodded as tears pricked her eyes. "This one's from Dolores."

"See? Our regulars are still with us. Tomorrow, we'll start knocking on doors, and we won't stop until we've found a new home."

And for the next two weeks, they did just that. Rosie and Lia rode the bus to the Bronx three days a week to process orders out of the warehouse, which was exhausting and boring compared to being in the store, but work was work. They spent the rest of their time calling everyone they knew and visiting the local stores Rosie and her mom had built relationships with over the years.

"Ever feel like we're just walking in circles?" Rosie asked as she and Lia walked home after yet another afternoon of knocking on doors. They'd put out what felt like hundreds of feelers and had even generated a few leads, but so far, nothing had panned out.

"I feel like there's a saying in that, like sometimes if you walk in enough circles, you'll find a straight line," Lia said. "You can't say we haven't tried."

"We've tried damn hard," Rosie agreed.

"We should go out tonight," Lia suggested. "You, me, Paige, Nikki, Shanice, Ashley . . . whoever's around. We haven't gone out in ages."

"Yeah," Rosie said with a somewhat limp smile. She hadn't felt like going out since she left Jane. "But not tonight, okay? I'm exhausted."

"All right, but you know I'm going to keep asking," Lia said.

"I know."

Instead, Rosie went home and lost herself in a book, which seemed to be her only happy place these days. When she read, she could escape reality: long days packing boxes in a warehouse, the frustrating search for a new storefront, and her endless longing for Jane. She yearned to call her—to *see* her—but she couldn't, not yet.

The next morning—exactly three weeks after Between the Pages closed its doors on Lexington Avenue—Rosie boarded a bus with Lia, headed for the Bronx, her new Monday tradition. She was so engrossed in her book that she almost didn't hear her phone ringing. When she checked, the number was an unknown local exchange. "Hello?"

"Is this Rosie Taft?" a woman's voice asked.

"It is." Rosie was annoyed to feel hope rising inside her, that this call would be the one that changed things, when she'd already fielded dozens of calls that hadn't panned out.

"My name is Kathleen Clarkson," the woman said. "I knew your mom a long time ago, and I knew you when you were a little girl, but I'm not sure if you remember me."

"Your name is vaguely familiar, I think," Rosie told her, crossing her fingers and holding them in Lia's direction. Her friend set down her book and crossed her fingers back.

"You and my daughter Eliza went to preschool together," Kathleen said.

"Oh, okay."

"I heard through the grapevine that you're looking for a new home for your bookstore, and as it happens, I've been looking for an excuse to close up shop for a while now. You see, my husband and I own a building on East Eightieth. I run a craft store in the retail space on the first floor, and we live upstairs. I've been hesitant to close the store, because I wasn't crazy about the idea of renting that space and having to be someone's landlord, but if you're anything like your mother, I think this might work out well for both of us."

Rosie wiped her eyes, which were flooded with yet more tears. The connection to her mom felt like coming full circle, like maybe this was where she'd been meant to land. Could she dare to hope that her search was finally over? "Yeah," she managed. "I have a feeling it might."

CHAPTER TWENTY-SIX

Jane straightened her spine, smoothed back her hair, and lifted her hand to knock on the door to her father's office. She'd done as Amy suggested and had bided her time through much of January while she made sure she had her priorities in order. Rosie was taking time to sort herself out, so it only seemed fair that Jane should do the same.

And what she'd discovered was that she felt nothing but a vague sense of dread about coming to work every morning. She was finished here at BPD, whether she got back together with Rosie or not. For her own sake, she needed to move on, even if it meant taking a part-time job somewhere else until she could fully support herself on the royalties from her books. She'd still have more time to write than she did now, and ultimately that was what she needed.

"Come in!" her dad bellowed.

She opened the door and stepped through. "Hi, Dad."

"Hello, Jane. What can I do for you?"

Her palms felt damp against the envelope clutched in her hands. "I came to give you my letter of resignation."

He went very still. "What?"

"My heart isn't here at BPD. It hasn't been for a while," she said, bowing her head as she set the envelope on his desk.

"This isn't about your heart," he barked. "Your sister is counting on you to help her run this company after I'm gone."

"I've already talked this through with Amy, and she supports me. In fact . . ." A smile touched her lips. "She said she could hire someone better suited to my job."

He made a dismissive gesture with his hand. "Of course she would try to appease you."

"She's not appeasing me, Dad. She just wants me to be happy."

He sighed then, rubbing the bridge of his nose. "Are you truly that unhappy here?"

"No, but I think we both know I never would have gone into property development if you hadn't been so adamant about it. It's just not for me. I have another career that I love, and that's what I want to focus on."

"And how are you planning to support yourself?"

"That's for me to figure out," she said. "I'll stay until you hire my replacement, but then I'm out."

"You're making a mistake," he said.

"Well, it's my mistake to make."

"Don't expect to have your old job back when you change your mind."

She slid the letter toward him. "I won't."

As she turned to leave his office, she felt like an enormous weight had been lifted from her chest. She ducked straight into Amy's office and pulled the door shut behind her. "I did it," she gasped. "I quit."

Amy's lips curved. "Good for you, Jane. Go spread your wings and be happy."

"Thank you," Jane told her, still jittery with adrenaline. "I'll be here as long as you need me, okay?"

"I know that," Amy said. "But I've already got a job description ready to post, so I don't think it will be long."

Jane nodded, turning to go. Since she'd timed her announcement for the end of the workday, she stopped by her office to get her coat and her briefcase, and then she left the building, giddy with relief. She'd planned to go home and write, but her heart was dragging her in a different direction. She needed to see Rosie. Even if Rosie wasn't ready to talk about their relationship, Jane needed to share this with her. Hell, she just needed to see her face. She missed Rosie so much she could hardly stand it.

So she boarded the subway headed uptown and exited at East Ninety-Sixth Street, the way she had during those magical months in the fall. When she reached Rosie's building, she stopped and pulled out her phone. She couldn't exactly ring the buzzer unannounced after all this time. That felt presumptuous, maybe even rude. Instead, she dialed Rosie's number for the first time in almost a month, halfway expecting it to go to voice mail.

"Hi," Rosie answered quietly.

Jane's ribs seemed to shrink until her heart pounded painfully against them. "Hi."

"It's been a while," Rosie said.

"I know. So long. *Too* long," Jane said, dangerously close to babbling, because now that she was talking to Rosie, she was desperate to see her, to kiss her, to beg forgiveness and profess her love. "Tell me if this is too soon, but can I see you?"

"When?" Rosie asked, and Jane heard muffled voices behind her.

"Now?" she asked, crossing her fingers against her side.

"Oh geez," Rosie said with a soft laugh. "Where are you?"

"Outside your building."

"Oh my God," Rosie said, and Jane couldn't tell if she was surprised or upset.

"I just need to tell you something, and then I promise I'll go."

"Okay, stay there. I'll be right down."

Jane put her phone in her bag and tried not to fidget, wishing she wasn't in this damn suit if she was going to stay outside. She probably should have gone home to change, but when her impulsiveness got the better of her, she leaped before she looked and hoped for the best.

A few minutes later, Rosie came out the front door with Brinkley at her side. She wore her blue coat over jeans, her blonde curls just as irresistibly adorable as Jane remembered them. She stepped forward, clasping her hands in front of herself to keep from reaching for her, because the warm, tingly feeling in the pit of her stomach that she hadn't felt in too many weeks had just returned, her body reacting instinctively to Rosie's the way it always had. "Hi."

"Hi yourself," Rosie said, lips quirking as she took in Jane's outfit. "Not playing fair, coming here dressed like that."

"I came straight from work," Jane said, hoping Rosie's smile was a good sign. "I needed to share some news, and I . . . well, I miss you like crazy, so I just hopped on a train and hoped for the best."

"That's worked out well for you in the past," Rosie said. "Let's walk."

Brinkley planted his front paws on Jane's leg, yipping to catch her attention, and she crouched to greet him, surprised to realize she'd missed him too. He wore a little blue coat that matched Rosie's, and it was the cutest damn thing. The day was bitterly cold, and the sun was already dipping behind the skyline to the west, which meant it was about to get even colder. She wasn't dressed for it, but if Rosie wanted to walk, she'd walk, because she was just so glad to be with her.

They started down the street, Rosie and Brinkley leading the way. For a few minutes, they walked in silence. Jane's tongue seemed to have tied itself in knots now that she was here. She shivered, her breath crystalizing in the air before her.

"I was going to call you soon," Rosie said finally. "I have something to tell you too."

"I quit my job today," Jane blurted, flexing her fingers inside her gloves.

"Whoa." Rosie stopped, turning toward her. "You did?"

Jane nodded. "I told my dad I'd stay until he found my replacement, and then I'm out."

"Oh my God. Was he mad?"

"Yeah, but Amy supports me, and she's the one I didn't want to disappoint."

"So you're going to write full time?" Rosie asked, starting to walk again.

"Yes, but I might need a part-time job at first to cover the rent." She gave her head a slight shake. "I just needed to get out of there and start living for myself."

"Wow," Rosie said. "That's huge, Jane."

"I know. It'll be a month or so before they replace me, and maybe I'll have sold my new series by then, or else . . . I don't know, you'll find me waiting tables or something."

Rosie snorted with laughter, resting a hand on Jane's shoulder. "No offense, but you'd be terrible at that."

Jane scrunched her nose. "I would, wouldn't I?"

"You're way too shy to deal with customers. You need a behind-the-scenes job."

"I don't know about that," Jane said. "I did pretty well that time I manned your register."

Rosie's expression softened, a nostalgic look on her face. "You did. Maybe I'd hire you if I had a register for you to work."

Jane desperately wanted to know what was going on with Between the Pages—if Rosie's online store had worked out and if she'd been able to find a new space—but it seemed like a dangerous subject, one for Rosie to broach herself if she had anything she wanted to share.

"I'm proud of you," Rosie said instead. "I think this will be a good thing for you."

"I hope so," Jane said. "I'll probably need to move too."

"What? Why?"

"Well, for one thing, I'll never afford that apartment on an author's income, but also . . . I think it's time to fully separate myself from BPD and let my family just be family."

"Wow," Rosie said. "Where will you go?"

She shook her head. "I don't know. I've got time to decide."

"Big changes," Rosie said. She'd been walking purposefully this whole time, although Jane had no idea where they were going. At least she hoped they were going somewhere, because she was starting to lose feeling in her feet. And she was having a hard time reading Rosie. Was this just a "catching up" conversation, or was it the first step toward their reconnecting?

Jane knew what she wanted, but she wasn't sure if Rosie was on the same page. Maybe a month apart had shown her that her life was simpler without Jane in it. The very thought made her chest ache. "Rosie . . ." She put a hand on her shoulder, stopping her. "I didn't do these things for you, but I didn't *not* do them for you either. I miss you so much." The tears in her lashes felt like icicles.

"I miss you too," Rosie whispered, and she leaned forward, brushing her lips against Jane's.

The frigid air around them seemed to melt away as she kissed Rosie, heat radiating from her heart, which was filled to bursting to have Rosie back in her arms. "I—"

Rosie pressed a gloved finger against her lips. "Save that thought for one minute until we get inside, okay?"

Jane nodded, shivering again. "Going inside sounds like an amazing idea."

Rosie smiled. "I have something to show you."

"Okay." She slipped her hand into Rosie's as they started walking again.

Rosie turned the corner, leading Jane onto a street lined with quaint little shops and residential buildings, and Jane dearly hoped that whichever one they went into would be quiet . . . and warm. A short way down the block, Rosie pulled open the front door of a shop that sold handmade wares. Its front window had a display of brightly colored jewelry and painted plates.

"Can he come in here?" Jane asked, gesturing to Brinkley.

Rosie nodded. "Come on in."

Jane followed her into the shop, which was currently empty and wonderfully warm. An older woman came out from the back room when the bell tinkled over the door. She smiled when she saw Rosie.

"Hi, Kathleen," Rosie said. "This is Jane. I brought her here to see the shop."

"Oh, sure," Kathleen said. "Hi, Jane. I'm just painting in back, so feel free to have a look around together."

"Thank you," Rosie told her.

Jane had no idea what was going on as Kathleen left them alone in the store. She turned to Rosie, waiting for her to explain.

"Welcome to the future home of Between the Pages Bookstore and Café," Rosie told her with a radiant smile as she raised her arms, gesturing around her. "Isn't it perfect?"

"Oh." Jane looked around with new eyes. The store was located in an older building with lots of charm and a well-kept air about it, and it was surprisingly spacious. It *was* perfect. So perfect Jane felt tears brimming in her eyes. "Rosie, this is incredible. You did it."

"We're going to add a café counter over there with a few tables for seating—and thank you for that idea, by the way, because it's my favorite." Rosie waved toward the left side of the store. "And there's a room downstairs pretty similar to what I used to have, where we'll have afternoon tea and book signings. Kathleen and her husband own the building, and they live upstairs. They'll be my landlords. Kathleen and my mom knew each other when I was a little girl."

"Oh, Rosie." She could hardly speak past the lump in her throat. "This is where you were meant to be. It's so much better than the café I found for you."

"That one was pretty great except for the landlord," Rosie said. "But this building is more *me*, and there's nothing to feel guilty about . . . for either of us."

"It would be awfully nice not to have guilt where you're concerned," Jane said, tugging off her gloves so she could wipe away the tears that streaked her cheeks.

"Well, you can stop," Rosie said. "For real this time. The store should flourish here, and we'll have the café that you envisioned for us, plus one of my mom's friends as a landlord. It's an upgrade, Jane."

"And I don't work for the devil anymore?" Jane offered with a wry smile.

"You never did," Rosie said quietly. "I almost wish you hadn't quit yet, because I wanted to have this conversation with you first. I need you to know that this was always my problem, not yours. I'm the one who should be apologizing."

"That's not true," Jane whispered, wiping away more tears.

"It is," Rosie said. "You were only doing your job, but the store is so personal to me that I just couldn't get past my hurt feelings. It's why I had to take this time to myself. I needed to save the store in a way that was completely unconnected to you, so that whatever happens to Between the Pages in the future, it's on me. It's all on me."

"Oh." Jane's heart beat faster, hope blooming in place of fear.

Rosie stepped closer, taking Jane's hands. "I missed you every day."

"Me too," she whispered. "So much."

"I'm so sorry for running out on you on New Year's Eve." Rosie's eyes were glossy, and her lip trembled. "And for making you feel guilty all these months, when you're the most amazing and generous woman I've ever met. Can you please forgive me?"

"There's nothing to forgive," Jane said, squeezing her hands. "You were doing the best you could, and so was I."

"Do you think we can give this another try?" Rosie asked.

"Yes," she whispered, finally giving in to the urge to wrap her arms around Rosie. "God, yes."

For several long minutes, they just held on to each other, both of them breathing hard and gasping with happy tears. When they parted, Jane unbuttoned her coat, having gone from cold to hot since entering the store, possibly with a little help from Rosie.

She touched a finger against Jane's collar. "You know, I think this is the same suit you were wearing the day you first walked into my store with Alyssa."

"Is it?" Jane didn't have the faintest idea what she'd been wearing that day, but the warmth of Rosie's fingers against her blouse might've been the best thing she'd ever felt.

"Pretty sure," Rosie confirmed, toying with one of the buttons on Jane's jacket before leaning in for another kiss. "There's one more thing I need to tell you."

Something in her voice made Jane's heart pound. "There is?"

"I love you," Rosie said, tears glistening in her eyes.

"Oh," Jane gasped as her skin flushed hot and her knees shook. "I love you too. I'm so crazy in love with you. I feel like one of the characters in my books, and honestly, I used to think I was just making that stuff up, because it seemed too good to be true."

Rosie blinked, releasing two tears that slid down her cheeks. "That might be the most romantic thing anyone's ever said to me, especially coming from my favorite author."

Jane quit holding back then, kissing Rosie with weeks of pent-up emotion. She tasted the salt of Rosie's tears and felt the way her lips trembled against Jane's. "I'm so happy right now I can hardly stand it."

"Me too." Rosie clutched at her jacket as she pulled Jane closer. "And now we've written our very own happy ending."

Jane shook her head. "No, because this is just the beginning."

EPILOGUE

Three Months Later

Rosie removed the poster announcing Brie's upcoming book signing from the display window at the front of the store. She crumpled it and tossed it over her shoulder, hearing the scuffle of Brinkley's paws over the hardwood floors as he chased it across the store. Smiling, she pressed a new poster into the window, this one announcing, "TODAY AT 2 PM: IN-STORE EVENT! BESTSELLING ROMANCE AUTHOR BRIE SIGNS HER LATEST RELEASE, *YOURS FOR THE TAKING*."

Rosie carefully taped the corners of the poster, and then she stepped outside to survey the display from the street. Jane's face smiled at her from the poster in her first professional headshot as Brie, and today she would give her first in-person signing. Rosie was so excited she could hardly stand it. She wished she could be with Jane as she got ready at home, but she knew Paige was fussing over her since Rosie couldn't.

The door opened, and Lia stepped out wearing a flowy white skirt with a floral-patterned top, appropriately dressed for the balmy spring weather. "I've got the chairs set up downstairs."

"I think we're ready," Rosie said with a nod. Between the Pages had been open in its new location on East Eightieth Street for two weeks now, and so far, things were going as well as she could have possibly hoped. Many of their regulars had already stopped in, and they'd met plenty of new faces too. Plus, they were still pulling in a lot of online orders from customers who'd gotten used to ordering that way and decided to stick with the website.

She took a picture of the window and texted it to Jane.

Rosie Taft:

Good luck today! It's going to be amazing!

Jane Breslin:

Is it too late to change my mind?

Just kidding. Paige is distracting me.

Rosie Taft:

Glad to hear it! Love you!

Jane Breslin:

Love you too and see you soon 😘

Rosie exhaled in relief. After Jane quit her job at BPD, she'd moved into Rosie's apartment, sharing her room the way Paige and Nikki did, which had allowed Jane to focus on her writing and gave herself and Rosie both a needed break on rent while they got their feet back underneath themselves. She knew living with four other women was an adjustment for Jane, but so far it seemed to be going well.

Jane's celebrity series had sold last month, earning her largest advance yet. Between that and Rosie's increased income now that the store had reopened, they hoped to be able to afford a place of their own soon.

Rosie went back inside. Brinkley trotted up to her with the crumpled poster in his mouth, and she patted his head as she took it from him and tossed it in the trash. A table had been set up to her left, between the display case and the café counter, where Jane would sign.

They would use the basement as a waiting room of sorts, to keep the line out of the store itself.

A handful of customers were seated at the café tables, reading while they enjoyed coffee and tea, while several more people browsed the shelves. Rosie had taken the red chair that used to occupy the back corner of the store and placed it in the new café area, and it had become a sought-after spot for her regulars. Currently, Betty sat in it, sipping coffee while reading a book. She'd decided to stay retired after all but came in a few times a week for refreshments and conversation.

As Rosie walked to the counter, her gaze caught on the photo of herself and her mom, the one that had been there since she was a little girl, first on Lexington Avenue and now here on East Eightieth Street. She'd been so worried she would lose that connection with her mom when she moved, but she felt her here just as strongly. Her memory lived in Rosie's heart, not in a building. And she'd be so proud of what Rosie had created with her new book café.

Over the next several hours, the store filled with excited customers who flocked to the counter to buy copies of Brie's book for her to sign. Everyone was given a number and sent downstairs, where Lia had set up complimentary teapots and trays of pastries while they waited.

Rosie was so busy at the register that she lost track of the time, and the next thing she knew, Jane was walking toward her, wearing a royal-blue sheath dress. Her hair was long and loose over her shoulders, her smile nervous but sure, and Rosie felt like the luckiest woman in the world.

"I heard a rumor that an author's about to give her very first signing in this store," Jane said as she rested an elbow on the counter in front of Rosie. "Can you confirm?"

"Well, it depends," Rosie said. "Have you ever heard of the author named Brie?"

Jane's smile widened. "As a matter of fact, I have."

Jane's fingers shook as she sat at the table Rosie had set up for her. Two Sharpies and a roll of "Autographed by the Author" stickers were at her left elbow, while several neat stacks of books were displayed in front of her, along with bookmarks and a little bowl of candy that Rosie had assured her was always a hit with the customers. She blew out a breath, looking at Rosie.

"Ready?" she asked.

"Ready," Jane said.

Rosie blew her a kiss, and then she opened the door. People began to file into the room, all of them clutching copies of Jane's book and smiling expectantly at her as they lined up in front of her table.

Here goes nothing.

Jane fixed her gaze on the first woman in line, extending her hand to take the book the woman held. "Hi."

"Hi," the woman said, smiling at her shyly. "I'm Layla, and I've been a huge fan of your books for years. It's so exciting to meet you."

"Wow, that's really nice of you to say." The tight knot in Jane's stomach loosened as she signed Layla's book and handed it back.

The next half hour or so was a blur of faces as Jane signed books for more fans and just as many readers who were new to her work. Apparently, Rosie had a loyal group of customers who came to every signing she held, eager to discover new authors, and really . . . of course she did. Why was Jane surprised?

Pilar stopped by to congratulate Jane on her first signing and to meet Rosie. Even Betty and Dolores came to her table, both of them having just bought their first queer romance to support Jane. Eventually the line died down, and she had time to catch her breath while she waited for more customers to come into the store. Lia brought her a cup of tea, and Rosie snuck away from the counter to give her a quick kiss.

"Because you look so friggin' sexy behind that table," Rosie said with a grin before she returned to the counter.

The front door opened, and Jane smiled as she saw Paige, Nikki, and Shanice entering the store. The women all waved enthusiastically at Jane before heading to the counter to buy books for the signing. Over the last few months, they'd become Jane's friends too. She used to think she was a loner, but she'd discovered that she enjoyed having other faces around the dinner table. And it definitely helped that she had the apartment to herself during the day while the other women were at work.

She'd also joined a group of local romance authors, and she was starting to form some friendships there too. It was all new and exciting, and she'd never been happier. For the first time, she truly felt like this was what she was meant to be doing with her life.

"Well, hello there, Ms. Fancy-Pants Author," Paige said with a big smile as she stepped up to the table, holding out a book. "Would you please sign this for me?"

"I would love to," Jane told her.

The women laughed and joked with her while she signed, making plans to go to dinner together later to celebrate. When another group of readers came into the store, they dispersed to let Jane get on with her signing. The bell over the door chimed again, and this time Jane looked over to see her family coming through the door. Amy, Garrett, and Alyssa led the way with her parents behind them, and Jane's heart was beating too fast. She'd known Amy was going to come and probably her mom, too, but this . . .

"Surprise," Amy said as she led the way to Jane's table. "We all wanted to come celebrate our favorite author."

"I've been waiting to buy this one so I could have you sign it for me today," her mom enthused with a smile.

"And Mom promised me that Rosie would help me pick out some new books since I'm not old enough to read yours yet, Auntie Jane," Alyssa said. "But I want a picture with you at your table anyway, okay?"

"Oh, that's more than okay," Jane said. "Get over here, you." She pulled her niece in for a hug. "Thank you so much for coming."

"I'm just here to show my support," Garrett said with a shrug.

"Thank you," Jane told him as she picked up her phone and took a selfie with Alyssa.

Her dad cleared his throat. "I'd like to show my support, too, and I'm sorry that I didn't give it to you sooner. You look happy, Jane."

She sat a little straighter in her chair. "Thank you, Dad. I really appreciate that."

"Your mother and sister tell me your books are very good. I hope you'll forgive me if I don't read them myself." He cracked a slightly stiff smile.

"Yeah, please don't. That would be weird, but thank you." She stood, and he gave her a hug, and before she knew it, she was blinking back tears.

"Oh my gosh, I'm so glad you all could make it," Rosie said, sliding seamlessly into the group. "We're going to need family photos."

Rosie greeted everyone while Jane signed books, and then they posed for photos. Jane held back her tears, because she couldn't quite believe her family was here at her first book signing, or even that she was *having* a book signing. This was several "dreams come true" all rolled into one.

After they left, she signed for another half hour or so until the store was again empty and it was time to pack up. The signing had been a success, and Rosie said she'd sold more books than she'd anticipated, which sounded amazing to Jane.

"Pinch me," she said, looking at the mostly empty table in front of her.

In response, Rosie gave her biceps a quick pinch. "It's real, Jane. You did it. *We* did it."

"You know, there's only one person who didn't show up today," Lia said, joining them at Jane's table. "The elusive Grace."

"She got held up at the last minute," Rosie said, "but she sends her apologies and asked me to have you sign a book for her, Jane. She'll pick it up the next time she's in town."

"The next time," Lia scoffed, and Jane laughed. It *was* funny that Grace never seemed to materialize when she was supposed to, and now Jane was curious to meet her too.

"She's hoping to visit this summer," Rosie said as she began packing up Jane's table. Together, the three of them carried the leftover books and supplies to the storage room in back, and then Rosie folded up the table.

"I'll close today," Lia said, making a shooing motion with her hands. "You two get out of here and go celebrate."

"Thank you," Rosie told her.

Hand in hand, she and Jane headed out with Brinkley trotting ahead of them. He struck out down the sidewalk, and they followed, enjoying the warm spring day. It was hardly a surprise when a few minutes later he led them through the gate into Central Park.

"He's predictable, isn't he?" Rosie said with a laugh.

"He is, but I'm not complaining."

They walked until they came to an empty bench to sit and people-watch while Brinkley barked at pigeons. The sun warmed Jane's face as she relaxed onto the seat, exhausted in the best way after her signing.

"I saved this one for you," she said, reaching into her bag and pulling out a copy of *Yours for the Taking*.

"You're sweet, but you already signed that one for me, remember?" Rosie said.

"Of course I remember, but I signed this one differently. Besides, the other one was an advance copy. This one is the final version."

Rosie's expression turned serious as she took the book from Jane and opened it to the title page.

To Rosie, thank you for showing me that real-life romance can be as perfect as it is in my books. Jane.

"I mean it," Jane said, resting a hand over Rosie's. "You're the one for me, Rosie."

Rosie blinked at her out of tear-filled eyes. "You know, almost from the time I started messaging you—Brie—on Twitter, I wanted it to be real. I wanted some sort of fairy tale where we fell in love in real life, although I never really thought it would happen."

"Same." Jane leaned in, meeting Rosie for a kiss. "I never could have written anything as complicated as the way we met, but in the end, I wouldn't change a thing."

ACKNOWLEDGMENTS

This book had been in the back of my mind for years: the idea of two people who're flirty online friends but enemies in real life (and if you think it was inspired by a certain nineties movie, you'd be right). I imagined several different scenarios before Jane and Rosie's story finally solidified for me, and I absolutely adored writing it.

Thank you so much to my editor, Lauren Plude, for your endless enthusiasm for this book and for giving me the opportunity to write it. I am thrilled to be working with you!

Thank you to Caroline Teagle Johnson for a cover that so perfectly captures the book that it still gives me heart eyes every time I look at it. And to the rest of the team at Montlake, thank you for your help every step of the way.

To my agent, Sarah Younger, thank you for making this possible. We've been a team for a long time, and I'm so glad to have you on my side.

A special shout-out to my #girlswritenight crew: Annie Rains, Tif Marcelo, April Hunt, and Jeanette Escudero. We've been cheering each other on and holding each other up for close to ten years now, and I'm so incredibly thankful for you.

An extra-special thank-you to Annie Rains, critique partner extraordinaire, for reading and critiquing this book (and every book I've ever written). I honestly don't know how I would do this without you.

Last but certainly not least, thank you to all the readers, bloggers, reviewers, and friends who have supported me along the way. I appreciate it so much!

ABOUT THE AUTHOR

Photo © 2013 Kristi Kruse Photography

Rachel Lacey is an award-winning contemporary romance author and semireformed travel junkie. She's been climbed by a monkey on a mountain in Japan, gone scuba diving on the Great Barrier Reef, and camped out overnight in New York City for a chance to be an extra in a movie. These days, the majority of her adventures take place on the pages of the books she writes. She lives in warm and sunny North Carolina with her family and a variety of rescue pets.

Rachel loves to keep in touch with her readers, who can subscribe to her e-newsletter for exclusive news and giveaways (http://subscribepage.com/rachellaceyauthor). Visit her at www.RachelLacey.com or on Facebook at www.Facebook.com/RachelLaceyAuthor, and don't forget to follow her on Twitter (@rachelslacey).